BASTIAL ENERGY
Book 1

Cover and map by Beatriz Garrido: @beatrize_garrido

Acknowledgements

Since the fourth grade, it had been my dream to write a novel. I finished my first one during college, and naturally I thought it was a masterpiece. During the following weeks after its completion, I forced my friends to read it, expecting great praise.

The criticism started slow at first, one friend telling me he couldn't distinguish my characters from each other, another confused about the plot. But some of them actually finished it. Looking back, they must've had the patience of a spider to go through three hundred pages of, "this happened, and then this happened." As you would imagine, they weren't as enthusiastic as me about its quality.

So I edited it as I continued to read other fantasy novels, taking what I was learning from them and my creative writing classes. I went through my story over and over, each time finding room for improvement on every page. Finally, I started to regain my confidence—hubris, I should say. I emailed my English teacher from middle school, Rick Riordan, who had recently had success with his Percy Jackson novel, and asked him to read my story—expecting great praise once again, of course.

I had already been in contact with Rick while I was writing, and he had agreed to take a look. I say this because we should never expect other authors to stop what they're doing and read our work. Rick was extremely generous to do so. He was also generous with his method of critiquing, which some of my friends went about a bit differently. Rick focused on the good, letting me know what was working, though he didn't ignore the bad either, even though the majority of it was bad...very bad. Eventually I let it go and moved on to my next story, taking what worked from the first.

Without readers, authors can only raise their craft to a certain level. For this reason, I would like to thank everyone who has read my stories. Without them, I would still be writing novels that only I was capable of enjoying...though I'm sure my mother would find some way to like them. She always does.

To everyone who reads Bastial Energy, thank you. I'm so grateful to have an audience. Sharing my stories with others has always been my reason for writing. I greatly appreciate all your feedback and support.

And to A.B., an amazing critic and an even better friend. This book wouldn't have been completed without your help.

Dvira
Merejie
The Tail
Nor
Devit
Slepja
Kilmar
Tenred
River's End
Satjen
Academy
Oakshen
Sendock
Trentyre
Sumar

Chapter 1: Experiment
CLEVE

Cleve's hands were steady as he drew the string of his longbow. His eyes didn't see the rest of the forest, only his target. Ready to let the arrow soar, he held his breath, but a noise froze him before he released. He strained his neck toward it.

Footsteps causing leaves to crackle were coming up the hill behind him. Panic pinched his heart, forcing his held breath out through his teeth. By the time his next breath began, his arrow was back in his quiver and his head had swung in each direction, looking for somewhere to throw his five-foot-tall longbow.

The sun was low, striping the forest in shadows from lanky trees too thin to conceal his illegal weapon. The grass of the forest floor was too sparse for it, and the only bushes thick enough were down the hill, past where the footsteps were coming from.

He cursed himself for allowing someone to surprise him. After years of training in the secluded forest, not once had someone sneaked up on him. How could he have let this happen? He took another breath. Figuring that out would have to wait. Right now he needed a plan.

A voice spoke out, just close enough to be understood. "Look at this, Fred." The young man's tone was utterly defeated, as if he were witnessing a calamity. "This goldbellow is mangled. What a waste of a rare ingredient."

Cleve heard no reply, just a scraping sound like a knife rubbing against steel.

The same voice spoke again. "Fred, I thought we had an agreement about chewing on your cage."

With his new plan to flee, Cleve was too busy running to make sense of the strange dialogue he'd overheard. He knew if he hurried, there was a chance he could be out of sight before they came up the hill.

But something stopped him, a different sound from the same direction as the stranger's voice—a loud gasp followed by the unmistakable roar of a bear. On reflex, Cleve tossed his longbow behind the nearest tree, his arrow-filled quiver next, and sprinted back the other way.

He reached the slope of the hill just as the young man came from its other side with wide eyes that stuck to Cleve the moment they found him.

"Please help me save Fred!" The young man pointed behind him as he shouted.

Cleve looked down the hill. He spotted the bear first, brown and thick with lines of drool locked to the sides of its mouth. They wobbled with each step the beast took toward some small cage on the forest floor.

"I don't see anyone else." Cleve spoke with relief, believing Fred had already escaped.

The young man's eyes doubled in size. "The enormous rat in the cage, that's Fred!" His voice was wild with urgency, as if Cleve's calm reply had convinced him he needed to panic for the both of them now.

Cleve found Fred when he looked closer at the cage...enormous rat indeed. Fred's gray fur gave him the shape of a rotund dust ball, while his teeth protruded to twist his mouth into a wide grin that didn't seem to belong on any creature, especially not a rat.

Unamused by the concept of saving him, Cleve made it quite clear in his tone. "I'm not going to risk my life for...that thing."

The bear was sniffing around the cage, trying to find a way into it. Fred was following the bear's nose, nipping at it from behind the steel bars. The little monster sure had courage, at least.

"Come on," Cleve said, putting his hand on the young man's back. "Let's go before the bear gives up on the cage."

"No, I need him!" The stranger twisted free. "Fred's a very important test subject for a potion still in its preliminary test phase."

A chemist, Cleve realized. *That explains a lot.* Cleve decided to give him a question in hopes of calming him. "What's your name?"

"Steffen!" he replied with the same incessant panic.

"I'm sure it's not worth our lives, right Steffen?" Cleve asked.

His rhetorical question seemed to pass through the air without ever reaching Steffen's ears. "Wait, I know you! You're Cleve Polken!"

Steffen grabbed a nearby rock, hurling it at the bear.

"What are you doing? Don't anger the bear!" Cleve reached behind him to draw the other weapon he'd brought that day, his long, and completely legal, quarterstaff.

Cleve was preparing himself for the bear. But now with the weapon in hand, the idea of hitting this crazy chemist was becoming tempting. *Who throws rocks at bears? Someone who needs to be smacked, that's who.*

Steffen shuffled closer to the bear to pick up another rock to toss. Neither one hit, but the bear did give them a curious glance when they fell into the lush bushes behind it.

"Of the rumors I've heard about you, Cleve, I know at least one is true." Steffen clumsily snatched up a third rock that was half-buried. "You win the weapons demonstration every year." Steffen threw it, and this one hit the bear's side, bouncing off without a sound. "If you won't save Fred, I know you'll save us."

The bear eased toward Steffen, stopping to stand on its hind legs and roar. Its steaming breath wafted after the young man while he backed behind Cleve.

Out of options, Cleve gathered Bastial Energy into his legs and ran to meet the bear. He flipped and spun through the air with his quarterstaff extended, slamming it on the ground just in front of the bear as he landed. There was a booming crack, akin to the sound of a tree limb snapping. To an untrained ear, it might have sounded like Cleve's weapon broke, but he knew the ironbark of his quarterstaff to be as strong as steel. He couldn't break it if he tried.

The bear lumbered away, crashing through bushes as if they were paper.

"Look how easy that was." Steffen smiled with pride, as if to show that he'd been right all along. Fred let out a squeak as Steffen picked up his cage. "Fred and I thank you."

With the threat of the bear gone, Cleve's focus turned to the anger pulsing through him. His most menacing tone came out as he spoke.

"I don't like being used."

He turned and started back up the hill before the idea of using his quarterstaff on the chemist became more tempting.

"If you don't like being used, you're not going to be a happy warrior when you're done at the Academy, then!" Steffen shouted to stop him. "All warriors are just used by the King."

Shocked, Cleve turned with a cold stare. He noticed Steffen cowering back a step, so he followed with a step of his own, waiting for the chemist to finish what he had to say. But Steffen finally seemed content remaining silent, or perhaps he only now noticed the anger in Cleve's eyes.

"How did you know that?" Cleve asked.

"That all warriors are used by the King?" Steffen asked sheepishly.

"No, that I was to attend the Academy."

"Oh." Steffen let out a breath of relief. "I met Headmaster Terren on my way to complete housing registration yesterday. I didn't know he was your uncle. It makes sense, though. You're both exceptional warriors." Steffen took a step forward, looking as if he expected Cleve to know what he was going to say next.

Cleve didn't and was in no mood to guess. "He told you what about me?"

"Not too much about you specifically, but he did say that you don't have anyone to room with." Steffen tilted his head. "Surely he mentioned our conversation to you?"

Cleve could feel his brow furrowing cautiously. *What did my uncle do now?* He shook his head. "No."

"Then I guess I get to be the one to tell you." Steffen cleared his throat, leaning forward on his front foot with a wry grin. "Your uncle and I spoke briefly about my living predicament—two friends and I were hoping to live together on campus, but there are no houses for three students. Terren mentioned you, and he signed you up to live with us in a house that accommodates four students." Steffen grew a smile wider than Fred's in the cage beside him. "What do you think?"

Cleve hoped this was just Steffen's terrible sense of humor. "You're joking, right?"

"I thought you'd share my enthusiasm." Steffen's grin soured. "I suppose this living experiment is still in its preliminary phase. We have lots of time to find the right ingredients to make this a success." He had a quick laugh. "Get the metaphor? We'll be just like Fred, here." He lifted the cage up to his shoulder. "It'll work out, Cleve. I'm excited to have a warrior in our household. I have some potions you can help me test."

And here I thought getting caught with a bow and being dragged to the dungeons would be the worst way to spend the next three years. "Fred is a disaster, just like this will be," Cleve muttered. There was no point in staying any longer. He needed to speak to his uncle.

"Where are you going? We should get to know each other!"

He ignored Steffen's shouts, hoping they were the last words he'd ever hear him speak, wishing this was just the delirious ranting of a mad chemist.

Chapter 2: Others
CLEVE

Cleve actually had been excited about his admission to the Academy, until meeting Steffen. He'd lived the last seven years on campus, but only as his uncle's adopted son, never as a student. He hadn't been able to apply until this year, when he'd reached seventeen.

Living with Terren was never ideal, but being his only remaining family member, Cleve figured there were worse places he could've ended up. His uncle was generally considerate and tended to give a good reason when he couldn't be. But to sign up Cleve to live with three strangers without even mentioning it? Cleve didn't even want to hear the reason behind that.

When Cleve arrived home, he threw open the door so that it banged against the wall, yet his uncle didn't even look up from the documents he was reading. To Cleve it was an obvious display of stubbornness in the impending argument.

"You need to undo this housing agreement of me living with three other people," Cleve said firmly, readying himself for the verbal duel. "You do have the power to do that, don't you?" He set down the leather bag that held his bow and quiver, then unhitched the quarterstaff from his back and brought it to the weapons cabinet.

"I have the power, but I won't." Terren let down his pen, giving one eye to Cleve. "This is good for you and necessary. Put the quarterstaff behind the swords."

"I was going to live alone on campus." Cleve rearranged his quarterstaff as instructed.

"There are no student houses that accommodate one person, only two or four. When the King financed the construction of the Academy, he still tried to save some money where he could. It's cheaper to have students living together than on their own." Terren picked up his pen and inspected another document.

"Then I should live with only one person, not three."

"Three will be better for you. You don't know anyone, Cleve. The more people you can meet the better."

Cleve leaned against the weapons cabinet with folded arms. "When does the contract end so I can move somewhere else?"

Terren let out a discouraged breath and set down his papers. "You have to start giving people a chance. Don't go into the situation impatient for it to end."

"Just tell me," Cleve demanded. He couldn't stand to hear any more social advice from his friendless uncle.

"The contract is set for the year."

"The entire year?" Cleve repeated with disbelief. "There must be some way out of it."

"There are certain scenarios when a student can move before the contract is over. But leave it for now. We can revisit this in a couple months." Terren's eyes lowered back to his desk. His voice became quiet. "...If needed."

Cleve grunted, defeated. Never had he won an argument with Terren, and he knew he wasn't about to start now. He turned toward his room but stopped when Terren pushed out his chair to stand.

"One more thing, Cleve. This is going to sound a lot worse than it really is." Terren paused for a slow breath. "One of the students in your house is a psychic."

Cleve felt hot fear winding tightly in his stomach. "No, no, no," he muttered to himself.

"It's going to be fine." Terren pushed out his palms. "Her name is Reela, and I'm sure she's just like every other psychic in the school—nothing like Rek."

Run, just go, into Raywhite Forest, get out of here. Cleve's heart was beating so hard it felt like the skin around his chest was being stretched. He put his hands on his head for some alleviation and strode quickly to the front door.

Outside, he paced in a circle, sucking the cool air into his burning lungs. It took all his energy to keep himself from fleeing.

Soon Terren had joined him, putting a hand on his back. "I know this frightens you, but you'll find out as soon as you meet her that there's absolutely nothing to be worried about."

It took years after Cleve's parents were killed for him to start feeling somewhat stable again. The thought of a psychic plumbing the depths of his mind was worse than any bear. Like a massive dam being destroyed, his memories could pour out like an unstoppable river if she were to fish around.

Cleve made a conscious effort to slow his breathing. Finding the strength to speak again, he asked, "When you say she's just like other psychics, what do you mean by that?"

"I mean she's useless. Most psychics can pick up on a bit of Bastial Energy and it makes them feel special, so they start training as a psychic. But in actuality, even chemists can do more with Bastial Energy than people who think they're psychics." Terren let out a regretful sigh. "Rek is one-of-a-kind. A true master of psyche, and there will be no other psychics like him. He's the only one who could pick up on thoughts, make people tell the truth, or really anything useful, or dangerous, or scary, or whatever it is you're thinking other psychics can do. But none of them can. If Rek was still teaching, the chances of another powerful psychic emerging in the school would actually be possible, but our psychic teacher is no better than a glorified babysitter."

Cleve wanted to believe his uncle but couldn't. If one psychic could become as powerful as Rek, then why couldn't others? "Why aren't there other psychics like Rek?" Cleve asked. "Was it because he was trained in the castle by the King's staff?"

"No, that couldn't be it. He was the King's lab rat, adopted to be studied by the King's team of scientists and nothing more. He's the only Elf I know of to set foot in Kyrro, brought here tied to the back of a wolf like the hero from the children's story *Prince from the Woods*, except the King embraced him not with love but out of curiosity. He was just a baby, so he knew nothing more than we did about his past."

"You never told me this," Cleve said. "I didn't even know he was an Elf."

"That's because when I told you what Rek could do, you didn't wish to hear about anything else." Terren spoke with the same tone as when they'd last talked about Cleve's father.

"You were good friends?"

"That we were." Terren sighed, shaking the frustration out of his face. "Still are, I just don't get to see him very often. At least it's nice to know he's out there in case we need him for anything." Terren looked to the northern mountains with absent eyes. "The Elf is quite extraordinary."

Cleve was exhausted and couldn't listen to anything else about psychics. What may be extraordinary to his uncle was simply scary to most others...and terrifying to him. Cleve started back into the house. "I'm going to lie down."

"Are you still mad?" Terren asked with a hopeful gleam in his eyes.

He was, but there was no point in showing it. Cleve thought to ask, *"Why didn't you tell me about this living arrangement earlier?"* But he knew what the answer would be, *"Because I figured you would react this way."*

Instead, Cleve decided to show some mercy. "It depends on whether you make my favorite breakfast tomorrow."

"You know eggs and toast are all I know how to make," Terren replied predictably.

"You're lucky it's my favorite, then."

Chapter 3: Side Effects
STEFFEN

Steffen had moved his belongings into the student house and organized his potions, empty beakers, and plants in his bedroom, transforming it into the sanctuary he was used to back home in Oakshen.

Today was the first day that students were allowed in their cozy campus houses. Steffen was hoping Cleve would be there as well but wasn't surprised when Cleve didn't show up that day. Judging by their first meeting, he didn't expect Cleve to be eager to move in.

Steffen had spent the last two days analyzing what had happened in the woods with Cleve, convincing himself that he'd come off as disrespectful. He was looking forward to apologizing.

Steffen made sure his plants were in the areas that would get the most light, that Fred was comfortable in his new cage neatly positioned at the base of his closet, and that his potions were separated into the appropriate groups with emergency potions in an accessible area.

His favorite potion he simply called "fire" and considered it to be the most important in his collection, which was common with any new potion he discovered, he realized. However, this one was different from most new potions—the effects were dangerously powerful. It was made from the red petals of queensblood flowers he'd found in Raywhite Forest, yellow petals of goldbellows he'd had to purchase from the market in Oakshen before he left, and enough of his own Bastial Energy for dizziness to overcome him for every few drops of the mixture he produced.

Steffen found himself having difficulty keeping his eyes off the fire potion. It beckoned to him from the shelf. Its golden-red liquid was so beautiful, and the power it bestowed called to be used. He already could taste the bittersweet flavor of it on his tongue as both hands drew toward it.

All new potions should be tested to see if they can be absorbed through the skin, and I haven't done so with "fire" yet. Before allowing himself to further analyze the pros and cons of his idea, Steffen grabbed the potion, snatched Fred's cage, and marched outside to make sure he didn't set the house ablaze.

He looked around for something he could destroy that no one would miss but soon realized he was in a terrible place to be testing. Student houses made of wood were packed all around him.

Without a trek off campus, I'm unlikely to find anything incombustible, he realized with disappointment. *If it can be absorbed through the skin, I'll have to discharge the energy into the dirt to be safe*. He set Fred's cage down.

"Watch this, Fred. If I were a betting man, I'd wager all my money that this works." Fred sniffed at him and squeaked.

Steffen spread the thick liquid onto his forearm. His skin jumped as the potion slowly disappeared into him. Once it escaped his view, he carefully placed the beaker behind him.

"Now we wait, Fred. If it can indeed be absorbed through the skin, it could be anywhere from a couple seconds to thirty minutes until it takes effect depending on the strength of the substance. Based on the amount of Bastial Energy needed to create this potion, we can make an educated guess that it should take effect rather quickly."

Steffen glanced at Fred to find the rat more interested in the round bars of his cage than in what Steffen was telling him.

"Hi, Steffen!" Reela shouted from the distance.

Steffen let out a dismayed grunt. "Reela couldn't have come at a worse time," he whispered to Fred.

He began to feel some heat bubbling in his stomach and chest—the familiar early effects of the potion. He couldn't shout back to Reela without risking an expulsion of the energy.

Reela, please stop there, he thought as strongly as he could. *Don't come any closer. Please hear this, Reela. Stop there.*

The heat was trying to escape his body. If he didn't let it out now, he might burp it out. Or worse, it might come out his other end. He checked and found Reela hadn't come closer and then concentrated on propelling the energy from his hands toward the ground.

From the time of one rapid heartbeat to another, all the energy from the effects of the potion gathered up into his palms, formed a fireball, and shot into the dirt with such force there was an explosion. An eruption of sand was blown back into Steffen's face. He lost his footing and fell backward.

"Testing out a new potion?" Reela asked, now standing above him.

"Yes, it works wonderfully." Feeling the crunch of sand between his teeth when he spoke, he spat three times. He glanced over to find that Fred's cage was filled with dirt. The rat was buried to his eyes but didn't seem to mind as he feasted on as much as he could swallow.

"Don't eat the dirt!" Steffen shouted, scrambling to his feet and rushing over to the cage.

"When did you get a pet rat? He's monstrous." Reela's tone was on the verge of disgusted.

"If he eats all that dirt his stomach will burst!" Steffen reached a finger into the cage to begin scooping it out, but Fred turned and snapped at him, taking off the tip of his fingernail. "Don't bite me, Fred! I'm trying to save you. Reela, please stop him from eating the dirt."

Reela sighed as she slouched over the cage. "You always have the strangest issues, and I don't like this rat. He's aggressive."

"I know, but please help him."

"Let me concentrate a moment." She closed her eyes and took in a deep breath. When she was ready, she aimed her palm at Fred.

"There, he's calm for now. Hurry up and get the dirt out of there. He won't bite you."

Trusting her, Steffen took the cage and slowly turned it on its side, squeezing two fingers inside to lift up the rat. He poured a small river of dirt out as he held the rat above it.

"Fred, you've gotten heavy. I can barely lift you with two fingers." Steffen put the cage back down and took the rare opportunity to pet the rat with one finger, forming a sad smile. "I wish Fred could always be like this."

"Most rats don't eat dirt, nor do they have a creepy grin like that. What did you do to this guy?" Reela asked. "And why is he so big?"

"I developed a—"

"Let me guess," Reela interrupted, "a new potion?"

"Yes, a growth potion, still in experimental phases. Potions like these that drastically change one's physical nature tend to have adverse side effects. It seems that aggression and an increased appetite are the side effects in this case."

"Well, don't pet him anymore. I'm not wasting any more energy keeping this failed experiment tame."

"Reela! Fred is more than just some experiment. You should be more respectful to animals."

"You're the one that turned a happy rat into an angry abomination. If anyone is being disrespectful, it's you. You should let me put him to sleep right now and end his miserable life."

Steffen sighed. He'd had a feeling Reela would prove him wrong as soon as he'd accused her of being disrespectful. "I hate when we disagree. In the end I always feel wrong, and I can't tell if it's because you're actually right or you're just using psyche to make me feel wrong."

"I'm always right."

If it was anyone else, Steffen would have defended Fred. He would have found facts he could twist into logic to prove Fred was worth keeping. But he knew all too well that there was no point in arguing against Reela. The potion he used on Fred wasn't working as it should—too many side effects. He would need to modify it and try again. Whether it was psyche or not, Reela really was always right.

Reela patted Steffen on the shoulder. "Now let's put Fred to sleep, shall we?"

"I suppose it's for the best." Often when Reela would touch him, he would feel chills running down his back. He couldn't remember exactly when both she and Effie, his childhood friends, had become so attractive, but it had to have been in the last two or three years. He remembered it seeming so sudden after it started, almost like their bodies were competing to see who could bloom and shape into a woman faster.

There was something dangerous about each of them, though, which made it easier for his affection to remain that of a friend. It often reminded him of a saying he'd heard many years before it made sense: "While many potions can trick or mislead, none compare to the beguiling touch from a beautiful woman."

More than anything, it made a statement about chemists' relationships with women, one that Steffen easily identified with.

"When did you become powerful enough to kill small animals? Honestly, that's a little scary, Reela."

Reela squeezed his hand, showing a warm smile. Steffen felt his shoulders relax.

"I found out this summer," she said. "And I'm not killing him...not directly. I'm just putting him to sleep. He'll die of starvation while he's unconscious. He won't feel anything."

"Let me say a few words first." Steffen cleared his throat and put his hand on his chest. When he glanced at Reela and saw her eyes rolling with her arms still at her side, he cleared his throat again, this time louder.

"I'm not going to stand like that for a rat," she said.

"Fine."

Knowing he couldn't convince Reela to do anything she didn't want to, he began. "This is a sad day. Not only has an experiment failed, but I'm losing a friend. Fred was the bravest rat with the most hilarious smile. While I'm sure there will be many more rats like Fred as I perfect this potion, Fred was the first and will always have a place in my heart. I'll miss him dearly."

Just then, he remembered what Cleve had said: *"Fred is a disaster, just like this will be."* Steffen shook his head. *No,* he said to himself. *There's no actual relation between Cleve and Fred. This doesn't mean it will end the same with Cleve...at least I hope not.*

Reela closed her eyes and breathed in deeply to concentrate. After opening them again, she pointed her palm toward Fred. He staggered before falling over sideways, still as death. His overgrown teeth kept his mouth grinning.

"Promise me you won't use any powerful psyche on me." Steffen could hear his voice waver.

"If you promise me that I'll never be a test subject for you."

"I can agree to those terms."

Chapter 4: Breathe
EFFIE

It was Effie's last night in her beloved hometown, Oakshen, and nothing would stop her from making it memorable, not even that she lacked money to spend. She just had to make it past her father, who stood in front of the door with folded arms.

"Effie, are you going out? It's late."

"Just a bit of practice with the new wand." She used her most obedient voice. "The metal dummies at Criers' Square need a quick beating before bed." She found it easier to tell half-truths rather than lies. She expected to use her wand, but not on training dummies.

"We're all having breakfast tomorrow before you leave, and then you have a busy day transporting your belongings and moving into your campus house. You need to be home early enough to get plenty of rest."

"I will. Thank you, Father." Effie took a step toward the door, but he didn't budge.

"I know you said you don't want anyone coming with you tomorrow, but your sister really wants to help you move. Please just let her help, and I promise your mom and I won't even ask to come."

"Gabby just wants to come so she can see Steffen. She's obsessed with him, you are aware of that?" Effie noticed her tone had hardened.

Her father's voice became a whisper. "So she likes him a little bit. Steffen is smart and a nice boy. I'm sure he'd never take advantage of her."

"If she just liked him a little bit, she wouldn't be the only chemist in our family while everyone else is a mage."

"Whether or not that's true, Steffen isn't the only reason she wants to go tomorrow. She loves you. Please let her help." He stepped aside to let Effie through.

"Fine." She opened the door to leave.

"Effie," her father called out. "Be careful with your magic. Only on dummies, right?"

"Always." *Yes, dummies,* she repeated to herself, walking toward Criers' Square to give her father the impression she was on her way there.

Summer was ending, yet the nights were still warm in Oakshen. Effie decided to wear a black and gray tunic. The cloth of it was light, comfortable against her skin. It was open at the top and bottom so that she could feel the night breeze against her collar and below her knees as she walked.

The first bar she stopped in was the Gold Hanky, about a ten-minute walk from home. It was loud and lively, but there was still one stool open at the counter near the bartender.

"Effie, going to buy your own beer tonight?" he asked when she sat down.

She smiled at him apologetically. "Sorry, no money with me. I'll bring you some business, though."

"I'm sure you will," he said with some disdain. He'd made it clear numerous times that he thought she should be more careful. "One day you might find yourself in a situation you can't escape from so easily," he warned her.

The man to her left was telling someone about his donkey getting bullied by his rooster, and the man to her right was arm wrestling the person beside him. She swung her stool around to face the rest of the Gold Hanky.

Effie saw a man who must have been close to her age talking with what had to be a prostitute, given her revealing outfit and leaning interest in his conversation. As he noticed Effie's glance, he looked over and met her eyes.

Their stares locked for a moment before he turned back to the prostitute, said something brief, and then approached Effie.

"Brady," he said, extending his hand.

Effie shook his hand and looked at him sideways. "Why are you talking to a prostie? Can't get a woman that you don't have to pay for?" She was genuinely curious, as he was young and handsome.

He grew a smile that seemed to belong on his face, like it was harder for him to relax his mouth than to let it curl. "Yeah? So how many beers do I have to buy you before I can figure out if I even have a chance? At least with her it's guaranteed."

I like this one. He's clever. "Just one," she replied.

Brady studied her eyes for a moment, acting like he could discern if she was telling the truth. Then he nodded and ordered her a beer.

Effie took a small sip and licked her lips.

"So what are my chances?" he asked.

"You'll find out once I'm done." Effie placed the mug on the bar and turned to him. She liked his blue eyes. Even in the dim bar, they seemed bright.

"Are you a class?" she asked. His hands were coarse like a warrior's, but she'd known chemists with palms just as rough, like Steffen.

"Yes, I'm a psychic." He facetiously touched the top of Effie's head with a finger and squinted his eyes. "You want to finish your drink faster...did it work?"

Effie turned to the counter behind her, slowly placed her hand on her beer, picked it up, turned back to face Brady, took a small sip, turned back to the counter, and slowly put the drink back down. "You're not very good at psyche," she said.

Brady snorted. "Then I'm just like the rest of the psychics."

"So by that attitude I'm guessing you're a warrior?" Effie decided not to bring up Reela. That conversation was not worth having with this stranger. She'd convinced Reela to come out with her once and then never again. Reela didn't seem to care for men in bars, or really anywhere else, for that matter. She was always too straightforward with them.

"Actually, a chemist," he answered, using the first sincere tone she'd heard from him.

Effie forced a gag. "A chemist is even worse, especially a horny one."

"We're all horny," he answered quickly, shifting his smile slightly so it sat a little crooked. "While some may give you the idea they want to help the world, really they just want to sell their discovery to the King so they can make money and buy a pretty girl a drink at a bar for a chance to take her to bed."

"I bet the smart ones just pay for the prostie."

"That they do."

Effie let her smile show for a breath. Then she picked up her beer, turned back to Brady, and began to gulp it. She had a skill for drinking quickly, sometimes relying on it to win bets.

She didn't stop until the glass was empty, slamming it down on the bar.

"I'm leaving," she said, holding in a belch. "I may be back later. Thanks for the beer."

"I won't be here much longer," he called after her.

"Leave if you wish," she told him as she went.

Mixing with the beer in her belly was a drop of guilt, but there were other places she had to visit before leaving Oakshen for the Academy tomorrow morning.

She visited two other bars that night, Steels and Fervor, only to be disappointed by the company she found there.

She had a few more free drinks bought by generous older men and got harassed on the street once, but it was nothing she couldn't handle.

It had been a couple hours since she'd left the Gold Hanky, and she decided to hurry back. She still had a longing for excitement, and she didn't know how she would fulfill it.

When she entered the Gold Hanky again, the sight of Brady drinking alone felt like fate. She sat next to him and looked into his bright blue eyes. It was then that she knew what she wanted to do.

"Gulpy, you're back," he said.

She leaned forward and kissed him on his lips. *I bet he's going to thrust his tongue into my mouth*, she thought. But he didn't. In fact, he barely kissed her back.

"Gulpy?" Effie inquired when the kiss finished.

"You never told me your name, and the way you gulped down that beer I thought it was appropriate."

"Gulpy's a good name."

"How drunk are you?" he asked.

She was surprised by his question. He was the first one to ever ask her. "Why would you say that?"

He scratched his head. "I'm not quite sure."

"You're worried about taking advantage of me. That's what this is," she joked. "What kind of man are you to consider my feelings when I'm just some girl in a bar?"

"No, that's not it. I'm trying to take advantage of you, I promise."

She laughed and decided to kiss him again. She'd been with one man before, someone she'd met at a bar—no surprise to Reela when Effie told her the story. At the time it seemed like a fun idea, but it felt like she was just going through the motions.

When it was over, he'd fallen asleep immediately and she'd left. As if the stigma wasn't bad enough, it was neither fulfilling nor exciting, making her decide she wouldn't lie with anyone else until she found someone she actually wanted to see the next morning.

Brady reciprocated more in their second kiss, but it still felt as if he might have been taken by surprise. Both kisses were quick with mostly closed lips, like testing the water with a toe before stepping into a bath. Still, she found the temperature to be just right.

She readied herself for a third and longer kiss, one that was sure to have more passion and playful lip dancing, but she wanted to warn him of something first.

"I'm not coming home with you," she said, "and don't think this is going to turn into some sort of relationship, because I'm leaving for the Academy tomorrow."

Normally she wouldn't divulge her personal information with someone she'd just met, but she felt compelled to do so with Brady. There was something about him that made her feel comfortable, perhaps his irrepressible smile.

"Oh," Brady said, and with that his smile finally faded. "This is a bit awkward."

"No, it's not. Did you think we would see each other again?"

"Actually, it looks like we are going to see each other again. I'm leaving for the Academy tomorrow as well. I've just been here for the summer. I'm a third-year," he said. "I share a student house." A quick breath seemed to cut off his words, then his voice softened. "With my girlfriend."

Effie balled her fist and was about to smack him when she restrained herself. *Why am I upset? Did I expect anything more to happen between us?*

Still, she wanted to hit him, but she controlled the urge, got up, and left without saying anything.

Alone in her quiet bedroom, her lungs grew tight. She knew it was the beginning sign of her terrifying breathing problem that had grown worse over the last two years. With it came the usual panic that started in her stomach and crept through the rest of her body.

The tightness became fierce this time, even reaching the base of her throat. It felt like someone was squeezing their hands around her ribs while another pushed on her collar. She knew no feeling worse than not being able to breathe and not knowing why.

Effie pounded her fist on her mattress until hot pain surged through her knuckles, forcing her to stop. She collapsed on the bed with frustration still twisting through her.

The more she focused on breathing, the harder it was to lose the feeling of breathlessness, so she forced herself toward other thoughts—a trick she'd learned early on.

Brady was next on her mind. She still didn't understand why she was upset with him, and that just frustrated her more. *He's just another man in a bar,* she tried to tell herself. *A man who just so happens to be attending the Academy, with his girlfriend. And you kissed him.* Her hands came over her face, and she moaned into them despairingly.

This is his fault, argued a different voice. *He flirted back with me. He never said he had a girlfriend. He was talking to a prostie.*

That, at least, gave her enough comfort to take her hands off her face.

Reela and Steffen were next in her thoughts.

Knowing she would see them tomorrow eventually calmed her enough to pass into sleep.

Chapter 5: Keep Back
Cleve

Cleve had delayed moving in as long as possible, and now classes were beginning the next morning. Even though he had to face the psychic and see the awkward chemist again, he was at least somewhat relieved to distance himself from Terren's messy kitchen.

Cleve's uncle didn't care for variety in his meals. He had eggs and toast in the morning, meat and rice in the evening with a beer to wash it down. If Terren ate lunch, it usually was cold soup while seated on the grass of Warrior's Field.

It was the system Terren developed and it worked for him, so Cleve never interfered or complained. He didn't like to cook, so he ate what Terren made, but he didn't consider soup to be a meal, so he just skipped lunch. While everyone else was eating midday, Cleve was deep in Raywhite Forest where he could hone his skills without the chance of being seen.

He had to be especially cautious when he wanted to train with his bow, and he still couldn't figure out how he'd let a chemist sneak up on him.

His mother and father were killed eight years ago, and bows were outlawed shortly after. His solitary visits to train in Raywhite Forest began then. Cleve's bow had belonged to his father, Dex, before being presented to Cleve on his eighth birthday.

During their lessons as a child, Cleve's father had made it clear that the bow was more than just a weapon. It was a dedication. Respect for the weapon was just as important to learn as skill. Even after Dex died, Cleve still could hear his father's voice giving tips when he missed his mark or laughing with excitement when he made a difficult shot. It was Cleve's only way of thinking about his father without pain.

Terren cautioned Cleve to leave the bow behind when he moved. No one would search the headmaster's house, and it was dangerous to transport the outlawed weapon.

Cleve agreed with Terren's reasoning and would have been

concerned if his uncle had mentioned nothing of it, but he was taking the bow with him regardless. To leave it would be leaving a piece of himself behind.

Cleve packed it in his leather bag big enough to fit a small man. With the outlawed longbow, a quiver, a one-handed sword, and five throwing knives, the bag could barely close. Cleve wasn't exceptional with throwing knives and would always prefer the bow in a ranged fight, but he had to keep up appearances. Throwing knives were the new bow, and it was expected of any decent warrior to be at least somewhat skilled with them. His quarterstaff couldn't fit with all else, but he needed to make two trips for the rest of his stuff, so he would carry the quarterstaff in the open during his second trip. He liked the feeling of the weapon in his hands anyway.

When he first entered his new house, he readied a fake smile and told himself to be as nice as he knew how, expecting Steffen and the others to be there.

Instead, he found no one home. He let out a sigh of relief and took a quick look around. It was similar to Terren's house, except the kitchen was larger, and there were four bedrooms instead of two.

Terren's house was positioned at the corner of campus and behind it was a private outdoor shower and outhouse. However, students didn't have the same luxury as the head of the school. Instead, there was one bathhouse for every five student houses. It had one entrance for men and another for women. A wall within the building segregated the two genders. Cleve couldn't complain, though, and neither would any other students. Having access to the aqueduct and sewage system was a treat that most people had never experienced.

Cleve had expected to be the last one moving in, so he was surprised to find not one but two empty rooms to choose from. He put down his bag in the room closest to the front door and left to retrieve the rest of his belongings.

When he arrived back at Terren's, he took more time preparing for his second trip, making sure he had all the clothes, toiletries, utensils, and books he would need.

He wasn't surprised to find this bag was lighter than the first. *My weapons outweigh all my other belongings combined,* he realized.

Not more than an hour could've passed from the time of his first visit to his second, yet a King's guardsman was standing outside the student house.

"What's going on here?" Cleve asked.

"Back yourself two steps," the guard said. He blocked the doorway and pointed a sword toward Cleve's stomach. "The house is being searched for a bow."

Cleve was bewildered. *I just brought it here. How could they have known?* He looked inside and found another guard searching the kitchen. *There isn't much to search. They must've just gotten here if they haven't found it yet.* He had no doubt they would find it if he let them continue. He had to do something.

"You have no reason to search this place. Let me inside."

"Step back." The guard looked sternly into Cleve's eyes.

He's looking for a sign of what I'm going to do, Cleve realized. Terren had taught him the same skill. Cleve looked back into the guard's eyes and found apprehension, just what he wanted to see. *Once he believes killing me is the only way to stop me, he'll let me by.* Disobeying the King's guards might give him some time in the dungeons, but it still was better than being caught with a bow.

Cleve readied his quarterstaff. "I'm going to walk inside. Let me through."

"I will cut you if you come closer."

Cleve took a confident step forward, the guard responding by thrusting his sword at Cleve's chest. Cleve turned sideways and pushed the pointed end away from him with his quarterstaff.

The sword slipped in between two buttons on Cleve's shirt, ripping its way out.

They took a step away from each other to assess the damage. A third of Cleve's shirt hung awkwardly, attached by a thread.

"You think the King would appreciate if you killed a student during this ridiculous search for a bow?"

The guard held his sword ready in silence.

"Are you Cleve?" a girl asked from behind, interrupting his plan.

Cleve swung around. At the sight of her, his anger and fear turned into a moment of lust. She had light hair, just between brown and blonde. It had an almost unnatural shine to it, giving it a glimmer as it hung down wavy and thick, falling a little past her shoulders. Her skin was creamy and soft. Her eyes were brilliantly green and pinched at the sides. Her mouth was slightly pressed, giving it a dangerously clever look. She seemed tall for a woman and with full breasts that pushed out her red dress on either side of the buttons that ran down its center.

"I'm Reela Worender," she told him. "Steffen told me about you." Her eyes switched to the guard, bright with curiosity. "What's happening here?"

Cleve's breath was taken from him. For a moment, the guard, the search for his bow, his impending arrest, his ripped shirt, everything was forgotten. Then Cleve remembered that she was a psychic. *Is my reaction because of some psychic spell?*

He'd seen beauty before, and this was far more than that. The way she'd stopped his heart upon first glance was unnatural, crippling. It had to be psyche.

"We're conducting a search for a bow," the guard responded.

"A bow? Now that seems a bit absurd, doesn't it?" Reela replied, offended. "Let me inside and we'll get this all sorted." Reela patted the guard on the shoulder, and he stepped aside.

Soon Cleve could hear Reela's conversation with the other guard inside. "Think about how strange it would be for us to keep a bow here. Look at me. Does it look like I know how to use a bow?"

"No," the guard replied.

"Haven't you searched this place well enough to determine there's no bow here? In fact, it seems to me like a waste of your time to stay here any longer."

"You don't need to tell me that," the guard replied. "I was just leaving."

The guard exited the house and eyed the other one. "Nothing there," he said.

They left without another word.

Terren lied to me, Cleve thought after witnessing the psychic in action. *There are other psychics like the Elf.* He stood outside for a moment, contemplating returning to his uncle's. But he ran through the conversation that would take place and realized he would be forced out before the night was over.

Before Cleve could come up with something else, Reela approached him with a strangely calm smile. "Did you bring a bow here?" Her tone was hinting, as if she already knew but still would be surprised to hear him admit it.

Cleve took the opportunity to see what else she could do. "No, I don't own a bow."

Her face scrunched with intrigue. "I know you're lying," she said slowly, studying his eyes.

"I wanted to see if you would use it on me as well." Cleve jabbed a finger at her face. "Don't ever use psyche on me. If this is going to work, you'll stay out of my head. Got it?"

Reela nodded. "I got it," she said indifferently. Her smile reformed and it stole his breath again. "But I didn't use psyche on you. You're just not a very good liar."

Cleve was puzzled by the lack of anger in her reply. She seemed...entertained, even?

"Oh," he replied apologetically. He'd expected quite the argument between them.

Reela shrugged. "Are you going to tell me why you have a bow, or would you rather I guess?"

Cleve took a breath, or maybe just tried to recover the one that had slipped from his lungs after she'd curled her lips at him. "The bow is more important to me than I can describe. I would rather risk the rest of my life in the dungeons than get rid of it."

"Be aware that the dungeons are almost where you ended up. Luckily, they didn't have more reason to believe there was actually a bow here. I could only persuade them to leave because I'm sure neither was expecting to find one. It's been years since anyone has seen one, so why would there be one here? I just helped them come to that realization sooner."

"So you didn't control their thoughts?"

"No."

"Could you read their thoughts, though?"

She giggled, shaking her head.

I guess that means no. Only then did Cleve notice himself gawking. He relaxed his face.

"What psyche can you use on me, then?" Cleve realized he was being blunt. "If you don't mind me asking."

She looked him up and down, her radiant green eyes stopping for a heartbeat at the flesh under his torn shirt, then rising again and locking back onto his face.

"You're different than most warriors." She tilted her head as if seeing something in his eyes. "Very different," she said softly.

He felt a chill start down his back. It scared him, but he didn't know why.

"I'll tell you," Reela continued. "But I trust you not to share this with others. You wouldn't imagine how scared some people can become when they hear about psyche."

She produced a wicked smile that made his heart race.

"I really can't do that much to the mind of any intelligent or strong-willed being. I can sense some ideas and heavy emotions when they're overwhelming the person's mind, like fear." Reela tilted her head to the other side. "But I'm only able to alter a person's mood or thoughts if what I'm trying to alter is rational to them."

"What about memories?" Cleve asked. It was the only question he really cared about at the time.

Reela's smile became wry as she shook her head. "I don't have access to your mind."

It might have been stupid to assume my memories were at risk, Cleve thought. He felt a calm crawling over him until another thought brought back the feeling of danger. *Or is that just what she wants me to think? Could she be using psyche right now to make me more at ease?*

"I understand the bow is important to you," Reela said. "You don't need to explain, but you have to realize I'm now at risk by it being here. The other roommates can pretend they didn't know, but I'm a psychic who convinced guards to stop searching. If the King's men figure that out, it can't be good for me."

"It won't be a problem. I'm not sure what the process is for switching houses, but if you or the other roommates want me gone, I would go through whatever steps are necessary to live somewhere else." *I never wanted to live here anyway.*

Reela shook her head urgently. "That's not necessary. You seem conscientious for a warrior." Her eyes wandered down to his exposed stomach. "And you're ready to stand up for what you believe in, which may include us one day. I like that, but we're going to have to figure out something with the bow."

"I was going to create a storage space beneath the floorboards in my room, completely concealed. I just need to retrieve some tools from Terren's."

It was Cleve's plan all along. He was going to keep the bow in his bag, learn his roommates' schedules, and dig up the floor when they weren't around, but there was no need to keep it from them now.

"Steffen told me the headmaster is your uncle," she said curiously. "You were living with him, and he knew about the bow?"

Can I trust her? Better yet, can I even lie to her? "Yes. My father, Dex Polken, was Terren's brother. Terren knows how important this bow was to my father and is to me, so he never made me get rid of it."

"Dex Polken? I've heard of him. He was your father?"

"Yes."

"Interesting. I never knew he was brothers with the headmaster of the Academy. I'm sorry for your loss. He was a great bowman."

Cleve felt raw emotions beginning to surface and his barriers breaking down.

"One more rule," he said sternly. "Don't talk to me about my father, and don't let me hear you talk to anyone else about him."

Reela nodded with apparent understanding. Her eyes didn't register the subordination he'd expected to see after delivering his warning. Instead, they looked as if they held pity, the last thing he wanted.

Fearful his emotions would escalate, he told Reela he would be back later with the tools to install the storage space and quickly left.

Chapter 6: Guess
CLEVE

While everyone else spent the day unpacking, Cleve worked tirelessly on a new hidden home for his bow under the floorboards beneath his bed. Ripping up the wooden floor was a loud task, but he took pains to keep as quiet as possible so as not to arouse suspicion from nearby houses.

When the dusty air and his aching back eventually made the idea of a break sound too good to pass up, he found himself stepping out of his room but unsure of where to go.

Unwilling to attempt a conversation with his roommates, he stood at his doorway and peered down the short hall, wondering if he'd ever think of this place as home. He listened to the bumping and shifting of his roommates arranging their belongings. It was pleasant noise, for it meant they were occupied. It was in the brief moments of silence when he became skittish, for only once the busy sounds stopped was there a chance of someone walking into the hall.

He learned that these were the moments when conversations were more likely to occur—when someone had finished putting something away and wanted to chat as a reward.

It was during one of these silences when Steffen popped out to tell Cleve that he and Reela would tour the campus sometime after Effie and her sister showed up, and that Cleve should come with them.

But he declined. It wasn't like him to start something without finishing it. He'd almost lost the bow once when the guards had come to investigate. He wasn't about to let that happen again.

When Gabby first arrived with Effie, she followed her older sister past Cleve's room and into the last empty bedroom, dropped Effie's bags, and looked for Steffen.

She gasped when she found him sitting on his bed reading.

"Your room is incredible!" Gabby exclaimed in what sounded to be genuine excitement to Cleve, who couldn't help but listen and watch from his room across from Steffen's.

"It's the same as my room," Effie called to her, "which you said you would help me set up."

Gabby ignored her. She gasped again and took a vial from a nearby shelf. "Another new potion! It's so pretty."

Cleve thought Gabby looked older than she sounded. In fact, if Effie hadn't said something about her room, Cleve might have figured Gabby was the one moving in.

"Careful with that one." Steffen spoke with grave concern as he reached for it.

Gabby faced him and hid the vial behind her back. "Did you finally create something useful?" she teased. "Wait, is this the fire potion we've been talking about?"

"Yes, and the ingredients are difficult to come by." Steffen reached for it again, and she backed away, giggling.

"You did it? Impressive. You've always had such a thirst for destruction." Her voice had a playful cadence. "Can I try it?"

"There's wood all around us," Steffen said.

"That didn't stop you," Reela exclaimed from her room.

Gabby squeaked, letting her mouth drop. "You tried it here?"

"Outside I did, but I shouldn't have," Steffen muttered.

"Let's go." She took his hand and dragged him toward the door.

Effie yelled from her room, "Gabby! Stop flirting with Steffen and help me unpack."

"I'm not!" Gabby yelled back. "I'm just excited about a new potion. You wouldn't understand because you're not a chemist." Gabby released her grip on Steffen's hand and gave him back the vial. "We'll do it later," she said with gloom, stiffly walking into Effie's room and shutting the door hard behind her.

Cleve could hear them arguing as he continued prying at the floorboards.

Reela checked on Cleve a few times throughout the day. She asked questions about his progress but tended to hover in silence after her queries were answered. It made him feel as if she was waiting for him to speak or possibly ask her something in return, but he was more comfortable with silence than with trying to keep the conversation going.

Though, even with his project keeping his eyes busy, Cleve had trouble stopping himself from glancing at Reela. His gaze seemed to stick to her each time he looked, needing to be ripped away with great effort.

Reela eventually brought in Effie and Gabby to introduce them. After brief handshakes, they were out of his room as quickly as they'd entered, but not before Gabby could say, "He's huge" with a tone like he was some animal.

Cleve felt better when he heard Effie smack her sister after they left his room.

Steffen had stepped in on his own accord earlier in the day. "I'm sorry about what happened in the woods," he led with, reaching out his hand. "Very glad you're here."

Cleve gave the chemist's hand a firm shake, possibly a bit harder than he'd meant. *I may be a little angry still,* he realized.

"How is Fred?" Cleve asked with as much feigned interest as he could muster.

"He's dead. Reela put him out of his misery."

"Dead?" Cleve felt his grip tightening. "After what you made me do to save him?"

Steffen yelped softly. "You're strong! Reela helped me see that he was more of an, um, abomination than a successful experiment." He whimpered softly. "I'd like my hand back?"

"So that other rat in your room?" Cleve released the chemist's hand.

"Leonard. Test subject number two. I'm using a modified formula that should produce the results I want—size and strength without incessant aggression." Steffen gave Cleve a lingering look, as if he might be talking about more than just the rat.

"Hope so," Cleve said, deciding to ignore the insinuation and get back to work. *If he wants me to be nicer, that better have been the last time he makes me risk my life for a rat.*

"Want to know what the formula is?" Steffen asked, nearly bursting with excitement.

Cleve didn't respond, hoping that would be a clear enough sign of his answer.

"There are three ingredients, but one is quite interesting—hair. Human hair! My own Human hair!"

"As opposed to your non-Human hair?" Cleve muttered, hoping it might stop the conversation even for just a moment so he could focus on his floorboards.

Steffen didn't seem to hear. "I've never known a potion that required Human hair. This creates so many fascinating variables to work with because hair itself is different depending on whose body it grows and even where on that body it grows. I tried hair from my head first, but guess where the hair is coming from in this new version?"

"That's disgusting," Cleve replied.

"No, not *there.*" Steffen guffawed. "I'm talking about my arm." He displayed his forearm for Cleve.

Cleve politely looked while letting his disinterest show. There was a patch of hair missing.

Steffen was smiling. "It started to fall out after I poured my fire potion on it."

Chapter 7: Rules
CLEVE

Throughout the day, Cleve's thoughts danced around Reela. Effie was eye-catching, but there was something about Reela that was different from other women who drew his gaze. It felt as if she knew things about him that he didn't know himself and his heart ached to know what they were.

She's dangerous. I can't tell if any emotions I have for her are genuine. It's good to keep my distance.

After his roommates left to explore the campus, he had an urge to look through their rooms. He knew he shouldn't, but he also knew it was a good way to find out more about the people he might be stuck with for a year.

When his project was completed and the bow tucked away, the urge became more difficult to resist. He began unpacking the rest of his clothes and weapons.

Finishing that rather quickly, he brought his mug, bowl, and other kitchenware into the shared eating space in the front of the house.

He was officially done unpacking. He couldn't fathom how it took others so long. All that was left was his workout routine and weapons training, but he decided to take a rare day off.

Dust and sweat had caked together on his forehead, so he wiped it with his shirt. He shuffled toward Steffen's room, stopping in the doorway.

There were dozens of plants fighting for space and more potions and books than Cleve had ever seen in one place, all organized neatly. Cleve liked to keep his room tidy as well but never had to deal with sorting more than his clothes and a few weapons.

He couldn't have possibly read half of those books. Cleve walked into the room to investigate Steffen's reading material.

Most of these aren't even recipe books for potions. History, math...and books about languages I've never heard of. Could he really like this stuff? Cleve tried, and failed, to find a book he recognized.

Soon he found himself just looking for a storybook, anything fictional, yet again he couldn't find one. *What kind of person has this many books but doesn't read any fiction?*

He sneaked into Effie's room next.

Her black staff rested on her bed beside a pile of clothes. Among the pile, a garish blue cloth stood out. It looked soft and inviting but disgustingly showy. Expecting it to be an extravagant mage's robe, he pulled it from the other clothes, curious about how it looked in its entirety. Shocked, he found himself holding the lower half of Effie's undergarments, so petite they were seemingly inadequate. He dropped them onto the other clothes, poking at them until the pile appeared as he'd found it and leaving as soon as the job was done.

Reela's room was similar to Cleve's—neat without a lot to see. There were no clothes in sight. *They're all folded neatly or hung in her wardrobe, I imagine.*

Instead of weapons, as in his room, Cleve found a number of books: fiction, history, biography, and many about psyche as well. One looked more like a journal. The cover was worn and without a title. Although tempted, he resisted opening it.

The room had a fragrance unlike any other he'd experienced. It reminded him of Raywhite Forest after a downpour, when the sun pierced through the wet trees. It was mixed with something sweet, though, maybe honey. He sniffed around the room, curious about its origin. There were no plants or candles in sight. *Could she have left this scent?*

Cleve opened her wardrobe and breathed in deeply. The fragrance was found, and it permeated through him. He let out a soft sigh.

She likes light colors. He thumbed through the dresses in front of him. *I hope I get to see her wear some of these.* His heart jumped. *What am I doing?* He closed the wooden door to her wardrobe and returned to his room.

His earlier decision to skip his workout suddenly was overturned. It was time to get out of the house. Cleve wanted his bow but settled on his sword. He sheathed the blade securely into the leather casing attached to his belt and made his way to Warrior's Field—a stretch of lush grass half a mile long and wide. Terren had explained to him years ago that if he was to attend a class as a warrior, it would be on that field, not sitting in a classroom.

His routine started with stretches, followed by technique and form, and ended with muscle strengthening. Later, he would meditate to regain some of the lost Bastial Energy. He wasn't surprised to find a few other warriors scattered across the field, training as well.

By the time Cleve got to push-ups, the sun had almost set. He heard his name being called in the distance. It appeared to be Reela and the others.

At the sight of her, he felt his heart nervously rattle around in his chest as if she somehow knew he'd looked through her room. She and the others stood on the edge of the field, just before the grass began, like touching Warrior's Field would send them to the dungeons. Steffen motioned for him to meet them where they stood, and Cleve jogged over reluctantly.

"Show them that flip you did in the forest," Steffen said.

"What flip?" Cleve pretended not to know while he thought of some way out of the request without being rude.

"That flip! You spun and flipped at the same time. Then you slammed down your quarterstaff in front of the bear to scare him off." Steffen gestured with his hands to demonstrate. "I was just telling them about it."

"I think that was you," Cleve joked, keeping his tone serious.

There was something about Steffen that made Cleve want to tease him. He hadn't figured out what yet. There was nothing particularly jarring about Steffen's appearance. He was like many other chemists, generally smaller in stature. His nose was neither small nor large, his lips were thin, and his eyes were wide. His hair was brown, lighter than Effie's but still far darker than Reela's. It was short and always appeared kempt, like his clothes.

Cleve assumed the urge to make fun had to do with Steffen's personality. He seemed unreasonably stubborn yet overly nice, if that combination was even possible.

"Me? I can't do that." Steffen looked to be authentically concerned that Cleve wouldn't remember correctly.

"Cleve," Reela interrupted, her puffy lips curving into her usual smile. "We met someone who's hosting a party. We're stopping at our house briefly, then we're going there. Come with us."

"It's a good chance for us to get to know you better," Effie added. "Or you can watch my sister, who'll be staying at our place and going to sleep early so she can leave for Oakshen at sunrise."

"I told you," Gabby squeaked, "I'm coming to this party, and I'm leaving *sometime* tomorrow, not in the morning."

Effie sighed. "I'll let you come if you promise to leave early tomorrow."

"Fine."

"And you can't tell Father about the party."

"Fine."

"Or Mom."

"Stop."

The sisters looked at each other and appeared to carry on the conversation through silent expressions that were lost on Cleve. He couldn't help but notice the two of them looked alike, although they sounded completely different.

"I'll go," Cleve concluded, unable to invent an excuse of why he couldn't.

They talked of their pasts and childhoods on the walk back to their house. Being the only one with an unknown history to the rest, Cleve was the subject of each question.

He wouldn't speak of the first half of his life before his parents died because then he would be forced to remember it. The last half was a boring tale, destitute of anything remarkable besides winning the weapon demonstrations he entered, but Steffen knew of that and probably already had told the others.

Cleve was tempted to make up a story or two, if he was able, but knew he didn't have the ability. Instead, his answers were dull, putting a lid on any excitement in the questions that led to them.

When Steffen asked what he did for fun, his answer was, "Train."

The rest of them followed with, "That's it?" and, "You can't train all day."

Effie made a joke. "I guess after five thousand push-ups, there isn't time for much more before the sun sets." She referred to his big frame, Cleve knew.

Many women, usually older, liked to make comments about him being big and strong. He enjoyed a compliment as much as anyone else would, but usually it wasn't phrased as such. Instead, it was the kind of tone someone would use to tell a little girl how pretty she looked if she wore an extravagant dress.

He didn't have much practice speaking about himself and it showed, but eventually Reela asked him a question that actually felt good to answer.

"What do you like about training, Cleve?"

"Honing your skills is both simple and complicated," he said confidently, "but the good kind of complicated, the fun kind, like learning a new spell." He motioned to Effie. "Or a new potion." He looked at Steffen. But when his eyes fell on Reela, no words came to mind. It served to remind him how little he knew of psychics.

"Don't worry," Effie said, saving him. "Nobody knows what Reela does to practice. She won't tell me, probably because it's cruelty to animals."

One corner of Reela's smile faded, leaving her mouth twisted. "It's not nearly as cruel as what I'd do to you if you spread that nasty rumor."

Steffen added, "I understand the sense of triumph in learning something new or perfecting something old, but what about the physical toll? If I woke each morning knowing I had to work my body until sweat dripped down my brow, I would stay in bed."

"When my body is at work, my mind is at rest," Cleve answered. *I don't need to think of the past*, he almost said aloud. "All my flaws are reduced to numbers—inches and feet, and those can be corrected." His eyes darted to Reela as he spoke. He had trouble keeping them off her and felt like the only reason to look anywhere else was to prevent her from realizing it.

"Steffen," Effie said, "I'm surprised you get out of bed at all when you can break a sweat turning the page of a book."

"He doesn't," Reela added. "Usually he reads lying down."

Gabby's mouth gaped. "That's right, he does!"

"I read a lot. It gets tiring!"

"Luck is on your side that you'll never have to carry a sword," Cleve told him. "It's far heavier than a book."

Later in their house, Cleve was staring at his wardrobe and regretting his decision to attend the party. *Why don't I own any nice shirts?* The answer came quickly: *because I don't do "nice" things*. The best choice he found was a casual, short-sleeved shirt that was too dark to see how dirty it was.

He tested it against his body. It felt strange to think of wearing it to any social event because it was just an everyday shirt, like all the other clothes in his wardrobe.

He sighed as he let it drape over his wrist. *Do people usually worry about what they're going to wear?* He couldn't even answer that.

"Need help?" It was Reela from his doorway. She wore a light gray dress that brightened her green eyes yet mostly hid her womanly figure. It was buttoned up to her collar and fell to her shins. For just a breath, her face was forgetfully calming.

"No, I'll be ready soon," he lied.

"Effie!" Reela called. "Help Cleve pick a shirt."

Effie stomped in wearing a thin flannel jacket atop a matching skirt. The jacket seemed strange to Cleve, like it might have been a men's jacket. *If it was before, it's not now,* he thought. The sleeves had been shortened and the top buttons removed so that a tease of cleavage was visible.

"That one is fine." Effie pointed to the black shirt hanging in front of him after no more than a quick glance. "But change your pants, something darker to hide the grass stains."

These pants have grass stains? There were none on the front. He poked his head around his shoulder and found a brown stain covering his right butt cheek. "How long has that been there?" He didn't mean to ask it aloud.

Only Reela remained when he turned back. She looked as if she was holding in a laugh.

"It looks as old as those pants. We'll be waiting in the kitchen."

Cleve changed into the cleanest, darkest pants he could find and then joined his roommates, who were standing around the table.

"Grab a glass," Steffen said.

Confused, Cleve removed his metal mug from a nearby shelf and took a spot between Steffen and Reela. He'd found nothing to drink in the kitchen earlier, so he couldn't imagine what they were having unless someone had brought back water from the faucet outside the bathhouse. His tall mug was met with sadistic smiles that made him even more uneasy.

He investigated the mug closer. "Is it dirty?" He found a few particles of dirt on the outside that he brushed off.

"Are you sure you want to use that?" Steffen asked.

"It seems fine." *They really care about a little dirt?*

"I think you should use one of these." Steffen handed him one of the small glasses he held.

"I'll just use my mug." Each of their glasses was unmarked and identical. They were large enough only for a single gulp and Cleve was thirsty. "What are we having?"

Effie placed a jug of dark liquid on the table and danced her hands around as if she was selling it.

"All the way from the fine streets of Oakshen and with the coin from my own pocket, I have brought this here, to the Academy, for us to enjoy. With an exquisite beverage like this, the table rules are applied. Whatever is poured into your glass...or giant mug," Effie extended a hand gracefully toward Cleve, "must be consumed by the holder of that glass...or giant mug." Again her hand extended to Cleve. "Respect the pour. Respect the drink. I'm sure we're all aware of the rest of the table rules, so let the pouring begin!"

They all banged their glasses against the table twice, except for Cleve.

This is an Oakshen custom, I guess. He wondered whether he should express his confusion but decided the jug of juice looked too harmless and refreshing to cause any concern.

Effie tiptoed around the table filling the tiny glass in front of each person. When their glass was full, they shushed Effie with one finger held in front of their mouth.

Not a word was spoken, not even a breath could be heard, just the soothing sound of the juice falling into each glass, followed by a soft shushing sound.

When it was Cleve's turn, Effie gracefully poured the juice into his mug, slowly yet carefully. It made a deep and messy noise as the liquid crashed against the metal interior. The contrast between his mug and the other glasses was amusing at first, but the novelty immediately wore off when her pouring speed did not quicken from a painfully slow stream. She eyed him nervously as she went, her face growing more and more incredulous.

Cleve became impatient and held up a hand when his mug was filled halfway. She stopped at his command, and he shushed her as the others had done. It was met with tightly pressed grins from Reela and the others. Gabby stopped a giggle with a hand over her mouth.

Did I shush wrong? He wasn't an experienced shusher, if such a thing existed, but he thought it sounded just like the others.

Finally Effie filled her own glass and then held it in front of her, waiting for everyone to join her before speaking.

"Bastial to us: the strongest psychic, smartest chemist, biggest warrior, most talented mage, and my fourteen-year-old sister who may be something worth mentioning one day and who's leaving in the morning. Bastial."

"Bastial," they all repeated, except for Cleve. They each began to drink.

Finally, what a ridiculous ceremony. Cleve raised his mug to his face as he heard the sound of others slamming their empty glass on the table. The liquid poured from his mug into his dry mouth, his throat encouraging it with loud gulps. Only...after the first gulp, he realized something was wrong.

This is not juice! It was too late for the second gulp, though; it was already in his stomach. Half of the third squeezed down his throat, and the other half spurted back the way it came, causing him to spit out the remaining liquid from his mouth onto the table.

He coughed and wheezed wildly, his chest burning. They were all laughing hysterically. The burning spread to his cheeks as hot shame came over him.

"What is that?" he managed to force out between coughs.

Gabby pointed at the mess he'd made. "Rule foul!" she shouted, still laughing.

"What did you think it was?" Reela asked, covering her face to hide her smile.

Unsure what else he could say, he gave the truth. "It looked like juice..." Cleve's voice trailed off.

"It's sakal," Effie replied. "Expensive sakal! And you're going to finish it."

"I will not. It's disgusting."

Effie and her sister gasped dramatically. "Rule foul!" they shouted in unison.

Steffen quickly explained, "You have to follow the table rules. You can't speak ill of the drink that was offered, you can't spill or spit it out, and you absolutely have to finish what was poured for you." He pulled a rag from the counter to wipe up the mixture of spit and sakal on the table.

"I've never played this before." *"Played" doesn't feel like the right word, but I don't know what else to call it.* He pointed at his mug as he held down a painful belch. "Never had alcohol."

"Never? This is your first time?" Gabby shouted. "How is that possible?"

Reela held up her hands. "Finish what's in your mug, and we won't punish you for the rules you broke."

"Agreed," Effie said, standing beside Reela and hooking her arm around her.

Cleve sighed deeply, clearing his throat as he exhaled. *Far easier just to do it than to argue*, he thought.

He felt their burning gazes as they waited for him, then he couldn't help but think of this as a test. *But for what? Is this to see if I can fit in with them, or is it to prove that I can't?*

A thought came that he should refuse—not only the drink, but the party as well. He didn't need to get along with his roommates. It might even be easier if they just avoided him.

But then he glanced at Reela and noticed the concerned scrunch of her nose as she and the others waited for him. Effie's head tilted to rest against Reela's shoulder as they each stared.

You can't give up that easily, he told himself, hearing some of Terren's voice in it. Without another thought, Cleve lifted the mug, said "Bastial," closed his eyes, and tried his best to imagine he was drinking sweet juice, which he still craved. He emptied his mug into his mouth and slammed it on the table. Hot pain gripped his throat and burned within his chest, but at least he was done.

They cheered, albeit somewhat sarcastically.

Chapter 8: The Party
EFFIE

Effie was eager to get inside when they found the right house. Darkness had come over the Academy, but the noise from the party seemed to illuminate the atmosphere even more so than the mages behind the house who were blasting light into the sky.

"Cleve." Effie pointed at the bursts of light ahead. "Don't be a DDW."

"DDW?" he asked. She noticed his pronunciation was slightly slurred.

"A dumb, drunk warrior. See those lights? Those are from DDMs: dumb drunk mages. But they aren't nearly as bad as DDWs."

Cleve frowned. "How do I know if I'm being a DDW?"

Effie didn't trust herself to explain it as well as Steffen, so she tugged him away from Gabby. "Tell Cleve the list for identifying a DDW."

Steffen straightened his shirt with one hand and used the other to start a list. "Number one, the use of energy or force as an attempt to show off. Two, if you have a weapon with you at a social gathering. Three, if you pretend something is a sword. Four, if you start chanting about warriors, men, or anything related to the previous items on the list."

"Cleve is still standing, a good sign so far that he can handle his liquor," Reela said, continuing to surprise Effie with her kindness to Cleve.

Usually Reela wasn't so nice, especially not to warriors. Effie assumed the change was because they would be living together. It was for that same reason that Effie felt the urge to hold back a couple clever teases until she got to know Cleve better, something she wasn't used to doing for anyone. It felt like holding in a sneeze. She found herself whispering what she wanted to say to the wind, just for some sense of relief.

Effie was first to the door, opening it without a knock. She was met with quick glances by those within eyeshot. The young warrior she'd met earlier, who'd invited them, pushed through a group of three people to greet her.

"Welcome! Glad you made it. This is my amazing house."

"I'm sure it's far more amazing than mine," Effie replied sarcastically, as each of the houses was nearly identical.

"If you count the thirty drunk people within it, then indeed it is."

"How do you know thirty drunk people aren't in my house also?"

"Because you would have to be crazy to allow thirty people in your house with classes the next day, and you don't seem the crazy type."

No she wasn't, but she gave a smile that implied she could be. "You remember Reela, Steffen, my sister..."

"Gabby," she insisted.

"My fourteen-year-old sister," Effie continued, "who will not be touched by anyone. And this is Cleve, a warrior like yourself."

"Alarex Baom," he said, taking Cleve's hand. "Call me Alex."

Effie often tried to find a unique feature about people she met to remember them more easily. For Alex it was his thick black hair, yet short, reddish-brown beard that caught her eye. As well as that, he was nearly as tall as Cleve.

Someone was shouting in their direction. "Rex, Rex! Come meet this girl. She says she's a psychic."

"Rex?" Effie inquired.

"Ignore him," Alex whispered. "That's just some idiot. If I meet a DDW, I tell them to call me Rex so I can keep track of them easier. So Cleve, what's your drink and weapon of choice?"

"The quarterstaff." Cleve looked past Alex for a glimpse at the so-called DDW.

"And drink? We have a whole variety here. My brother, Hem Baom, is the commander of the King's Guard, so he gets a lot of gifts, but he doesn't even drink. Lucky for him he's got a brother who does."

"Sakal," Cleve replied. "The expensive kind." Obviously, he knew no other drink. Effie still didn't know how to label Cleve. Unlike other professions like bakers, masons, merchants, shoemakers, and so on, warriors tended to be so alike to each other in personality that Effie knew all about a man the moment he called himself a warrior.

But not Cleve. Although he looked like a warrior, his behavior didn't seem to match. He was quiet and didn't like to talk about himself. *He didn't even know alcohol until it touched his tongue,* Effie thought. *What kind of warrior is that?*

"We don't have sakal," Alex replied, "but something close. Everyone, come have a drink, except for the fourteen-year-old."

"Gabby!" she exclaimed.

"Gabby, sorry. I just wanted Effie to know that her sister will be monitored closely. No touching and no alcohol."

"She can drink," Effie replied. "She is lawfully a *woman* now, although you wouldn't know it by talking with her. Also she's sharing my bed tonight, so it might make her less squirmy."

Effie followed Alex as he pushed through to the kitchen where a colorful arrangement of bottles and jugs awaited. Lately, beer only reminded her of the embarrassing kiss with Brady, so liquor was what she wanted.

"What's the gold one?" she asked.

"I don't think you can handle that. It's a wine, very bitter, very strong." Alex filled half a glass. "Like my last girlfriend."

"She was bitter for what reason? Did you cheat?" Effie asked, quickly realizing she'd only thought of it because Brady was on her mind.

Alex's grin faded. "No, but if that's what people think when they hear that joke, I should stop using it."

Cleve grabbed for the glass. "Give it here." He brought it above his mouth, leaned back, and let gravity take over. After just a taste, he ran to a nearby window and spewed out the liquid.

"Again?" Effie asked incredulously. She took the glass from him and drank. Bitter was an understatement. It tasted of spoiled lime and fire, but Cleve needed to be taught a lesson.

She finished it quickly, held in a cough, and asked sarcastically with a burning throat, "What did your brother do to receive a gift as kingly as this?"

Alex smiled at first, but then Effie caught him turning his head to sigh.

"Could that have possibly offended you?" she asked.

He shook his head. "No, it takes far more than that to upset me. Your talk of kingly reminded me of something solemn I've been trying to forget."

Effie glanced at Reela, who was leaning her head forward, her eyes focused on Alex. In the rare instances when Effie couldn't decipher whether a man's words were genuine, Reela could.

"What's so troubling?" Reela asked with one eyebrow bent, as if trying to solve a puzzle.

Alex waved his hand in a dismissive gesture. "I would hate to bring up serious matters after inviting you into my home for a night of entertainment."

Normally when a man suddenly changed to a serious topic, Effie assumed it to be a ploy, a cheap attempt at making her more interested in the conversation. But with Reela there, these quick mood changes tended to happen frequently, too frequently, in fact. Truth seemed to be magnetized to her, perhaps the reason she'd never done well with men.

"I'm sure satisfying our curiosity is more important at this point," Reela answered for them.

Alex nodded. "I understand that, but keep in mind that I warned you." He leaned in and lowered his voice. "Do you know of the turmoil between Kyrro and Tenred?"

"Peace was reached with the Tenred kingdom long ago, I thought," Effie said.

"Yes," Alex agreed. "There has been peace since long before the Academy was constructed twenty-two years ago, which is why none of us paid any mind to the service contract we signed upon admission to the school. But the peace between Kyrro and Tenred has been like a torn belt. As time progressed, the belt became more likely to rip. I hear now that the belt has finally come apart."

Is that right? Effie wondered. *Steffen would know. Where did he and Gabby go?*

"Are you shaying wull haf to go to battle?" Cleve asked, now with a heavy slur.

Alex took a sip from his glass. "I'm only telling you what I've heard from my brother. I think people should be prepared, for they may have to fight if it's correct."

"I could use a drink," Reela said, "and not that terrible wine. Cleve, let's get something." She shoved him away from the group.

Effie peered at them. Neither reached for a bottle. Instead, they seemed to talk intensely.

Alex broke her gaze before she could give it more thought.

"I shouldn't have mentioned it," he said. "Would you like something else as well? I know how hard it will be to find a drink more suitable than the last, but I wager we can make that happen."

She could tell his comment was sarcastic, but his tone was still regretful.

"I would like you to tell me more about this war." She was in no mood for anything but information.

He took a long sip as he peered at her over the top of his glass. "We can't be sure of anything yet—let me correct that, *I* can't be sure of anything yet. For all I know, King Welson and his council already know whether or not there will be war. I have no other specifics except that my brother believes there will be war. He isn't allowed to divulge the classified information that has led him to that belief, nor would he."

"Could he have made it up to mess with your thoughts?" She and her sister had shared similar pranks, although never as dark as war.

"It's unlike him to joke, especially about matters such as this. The man doesn't even drink. I think he was dropped as a baby and his sense of fun never developed."

Effie couldn't ignore how strange it seemed for Alex to be sharing this supposed secret information with her when they'd just met. Men had all sorts of so-called secrets to tell her, especially after they'd been drinking, but none like this. Reela would've said something if he were lying, though. She always did.

"Do others know, or are we the first you've told?" Effie asked.

"I've known for weeks, so it's been difficult not to bring it up, but I try to refrain. It's not my place to create panic." With that, he finished all that remained in his glass.

For weeks? "You knew before signing the service agreement to fight and *still* did so?" Effie asked incredulously.

"You wouldn't?" Alex took the golden wine and filled his glass to the brim.

That froze her in thought for a breath. "Give me more of that strong wine and I may have an answer before the night is over."

Their conversation took a pleasant turn to their expectation of the upcoming evaluation week and then eventually to their families. She found that he had a lot to share of himself. Although it was done humorously, it was also mostly negative.

She was not familiar with self-deprecating warriors and told this to him when their discussion of their siblings was put on hold for a refill.

"I have to make up for all the teasing I should have received from my brother while growing up," he answered. "You're the eldest sibling. Don't you tease your sister?"

"Only when she deserves it."

"How often is that?"

"All the time," Effie said truthfully. "But she's a chemist, so that's half the reason behind it."

"I say Bastial to that." Alex held his glass in front of her. A man approached and placed a hand on his shoulder.

She clanked her cup against his. "Bastial. Speaking of my sister, I should at least find where she's run off to." *Finding her should mean I'll find Steffen as well. I want to see what he thinks of this talk of war.*

Alex gave her an agreeing smile and greeted his friend with a nod.

Before looking for Gabby, Effie glanced at Cleve and Reela. They were still in each other's company but now with drinks in their hands and grins on their faces. *She hasn't scared him off yet, must be playing nice.*

Chapter 9: Rumors
EFFIE

After a brief search, Effie recognized Gabby's childlike giggle from outside when she neared the front door.

Effie prepared her eyes for the dark night as she opened it, but instead a bright green light stormed into the house, grabbing the attention of those standing around her, who winced and wondered aloud what it was. Without an answer to give them, Effie stepped outside to find out for herself.

She managed to make out Gabby's silhouette laughing hysterically while she stood beside something so bright Effie couldn't look right at it. When Gabby noticed Effie, the strength of her laughter appeared to knock her over.

Drunk already, Effie thought, shielding her eyes as she waited for the laughter to stop so she could speak.

The brightness slowly dimmed before her sister's manic laughs subsided, fading enough to reveal that somehow Steffen was the source of the glow.

"What was that?" Effie asked.

"A glow potion," Gabby answered between laughs. "Your face...was...hilarious." Her giggle slowly perished.

"It's more of a novelty potion as it doesn't last long, and it's unpleasantly bright," Steffen added.

Chemists. Effie held in a disapproving look. "Steffen, what do you know about war between Kyrro and Tenred?"

His head tilted. "Would you like to be more specific? The rivalry between us goes all the way back to the creation of Tenred."

"Alex says there is to be a war *soon*."

"It wouldn't surprise me," Steffen answered with startling speed. "The only thing preventing one territory from attacking another is that neither has enough power to win a siege. For battles to begin, all that's needed is for one side to gain confidence that its army is powerful enough to overcome the great advantage each territory has in its defensive position."

Effie found it difficult to find the meaning in Steffen's barrage of words. She might've thought it was a sign of too much to drink if it didn't happen regularly while she was sober as well. "Can you try that again?"

Steffen nodded. "Once *either* Kyrro or Tenred has an army big enough to attack and win, one of them will attack. It has always been this way, but the defensive advantage of each territory has been too great."

"So which army has grown powerful enough? Are they attacking us or are we attacking them?"

"That...I don't know, but you shouldn't worry."

Effie hadn't decided yet if she should worry or not, but there was something about someone advising her not to worry that always had the opposite effect. "This doesn't worry you?" she retorted.

Gabby's hands shot up. "Wait," she uttered as if she was just now hearing what had been said. "Father said there would be no more battles. We're really at war? Don't all students need to sign a contract that obligates them to fight in any battles?" She gasped at her own words, her eyes darting between Steffen and Effie. "You'll be sent to battle?"

Steffen raised his hands to relax her. "Psychics and chemists aren't required to fight unless we're under attack. However, all mages and warriors are forced to join any battle if the King demands their assistance. This even includes those who've graduated as a recognized warrior or mage years ago." He turned to Effie. "To answer your question, I'm not worried because we're first-year students, so it's unlikely for us to be needed unless a massive army stormed into Kyrro."

"Does Father know about this?" Gabby asked.

"Obviously not," Effie answered. "You just mentioned how Father said there would be no more battles." *He would've stopped me from signing the contract as well.*

"Your father may still be right," Steffen said. "If war had really started, I'm sure we'd hear of it from the King or someone on his council. We shouldn't assume anything yet."

"You talk as if you knew of the possibility of war before signing the contract," Effie observed.

"The possibility of war has existed for as long as the peace treaty has. It's been nearly seventy years, and I knew of nothing recent that would spark a battle, so there was no reason for me to even consider it. However, even if I did know we'd be at war, I'd still sign the contract so I could come here, wouldn't you?"

"I haven't figured that out yet," she responded sullenly. *Why is everyone so confident about that except me?*

Steffen had never shown signs of bravery before. Of course, the first time would be in response to something that frightened her.

This contract I signed is even scarier than a marriage contract.

"Who better to protect our families than those trained to do so?" Steffen asked rhetorically, speaking of course about students of the Academy.

"The King's Guard," Effie answered tight-lipped, refusing to give him the answer he wanted.

"Most of whom graduated from the Academy. They're required to fight as well."

"And if someone refuses?" Gabby asked.

"That would be treason." Steffen's voice grew quiet. "Punishable by death."

Gabby's mouth dropped open. She stared wide-eyed at Effie. "And this contract is for the rest of your life?"

"Yes," Effie grunted. Her sister's dramatic mannerisms suddenly made her aware of the anger pumping in her heart. She tried to ask Steffen a question but it came out more like she was demanding to know. "Why hasn't there been more talk of the possibility of war?"

"We aren't privy to the internal and external affairs of the King. The only reason we're even discussing this now is because of what you heard from Alex. Did he tell you where this information came from?"

"From his brother, the commander of the King's Guard."

"So, that's why." Steffen rubbed his chin. "For all we know, the threat of war could've come and gone many times, and the only reason we hear of it now is because we know someone who's connected to the information passed around the council. I don't think we should speculate without any facts."

Effie heard the door to the party open behind her. She turned and brushed some hair out of her face to find Reela approaching them.

"This is where you all went. Steffen, what do you know of Slugari?"

"What's going on at that party?" Steffen asked with enthusiastic curiosity. "First Effie comes out here asking about war and now you with Slugari?"

"It's all first-years in there," Reela said. "They like to talk of news from their hometowns, rumors and such. I met a chemist who told me that he heard the Slugari have been discovered, wondered if I heard the same. He seemed strange, though. I only spoke to him for a moment, but I am curious what the Slugari are. I figured you'd know."

"You and Effie should borrow some of my books," Steffen said indifferently, clearly not meaning it as an insult.

"The Slugari are green creatures roughly half our size," Gabby answered, delighted with herself.

My sister knows something that I don't. The world is coming to an end! Under different circumstances, Effie would've thought of a joke. "How is it you know that?" she asked instead.

"You haven't heard of them?" her sister asked in return. "Steffen's right, you should read more." Gabby had to take her victories whenever she could, Effie understood that, but she still wanted to smack the smug grin off her sister's face.

Reela spoke before the thought became more tempting. "That doesn't tell me why they're important."

"Most chemists have heard of the Slugari because of their connection to the caregelow flower," Steffen explained. "It's a remarkable form of nature that's rumored to be a necessary ingredient for a few treasured potions. Evidence suggests that Slugari colonies exist in Ovira. However, they're hidden underground. If that's true, then the only way they could possibly survive is with caregelow plants. Find the Slugari and you find the caregelow plants."

Steffen jerked up his head. "I just thought of something. Effie asks of war, you ask of Slugari. It's possible they're related! Oh, but I said we shouldn't speculate on it any further."

Effie rolled her eyes and found Reela doing the same. "Why don't you finish your thought, at least?" Effie asked. "Then we can be done with these topics."

He nodded submissively. "Someone told Reela that he'd heard we've discovered the underground colony of Slugari. If we really did, this information would be invaluable to the Krepps, worth going to war for even."

Unlike Slugari, everyone knew of the Krepps. Effie had seen drawings, even read about them. She thought of them as reptilian men because of their lizard-like heads and their scaly skin. The Krepps had been scattered along northern Ovira long before Humans arrived, and that's where they'd remained.

"Why would the Krepps care about a bunch of small Slugari hiding somewhere?" she wondered aloud. "The Krepps are taller and stronger than Humans. They can't possibly be threatened by something half our size."

"Krepps aren't threatened by Slugari. Krepps eat Slugari," Steffen said. "They hunt many animals, but nothing compares to their hunger for Slugari. It's an urge incomparable to anything Human, from what I've read—some instinctual craving. The Krepps' sole purpose of living is to eat Slugari, which is why the Slugari have resorted to hiding deep underground. If we know the Slugari's location, the Krepps would surely fight with us in exchange for it, but..."

Concern made his mouth go flat. He took a breath before continuing. "But by revealing the hidden Slugari colony to the Krepps, we'd be assisting in the extinction of an entire species of intelligent beings. The Slugari aren't just some brainless animal. They talk, read and write, and they live and die by rules within their community. I'd even argue they're more civilized than the Krepps that hunt them."

Effie shared a solemn glance with Reela.

"Talk of war and massacring a species to extinction—this party certainly has been fun," Reela quipped, sounding a bit annoyed.

"It's merely a theory," Steffen muttered, lowering his head. "I don't wish to upset you. This is why we shouldn't speculate."

"The encyclopedia is right," Effie concluded, hooking her arm around Reela's to comfort her friend. Reela placed her free hand on Effie's wrist, giving it a light squeeze that sent a wave of relaxation through Effie.

This wasn't the subject matter Effie was used to on a night out. It reminded her of the history lessons her father had subjected her to as a child.

Nothing was more sobering than hearing about Kyrro's past, which was basically just a cycle of battles for kingship: *First this guy was king, but everyone hated him, so this guy formed an army and took over, but he was hated even more, so someone else formed his own army and took over.* She could never remember the specifics or the names of the kings a week later, so she found no point in it.

"Where is Cleve?" she asked in an attempt to change the subject. "That was a lot of sakal. We should keep watch on him."

"He nearly got in a fight with Alex," Reela answered.

It was Effie's turn to joke. "This just keeps getting better." *At least he's finally acting like a warrior.* It wasn't that she wanted him to, though. It was more that it was strange to expect something of someone, only to find he acted completely different.

"It may have had to do with what I told him," Reela continued, "but in the end he and Alex appeared to resolve whatever it was. They hugged like you would expect two drunken men to hug."

Rough and sloppy, came to Effie's mind, which regrettably reminded her of the night she'd lost her virginity.

"What could you have told him to cause a fight?" Effie asked. Usually Reela caused men to get upset with her, not each other.

"I got the sense that Alex desperately wanted to tell Cleve something when they first met, and that desperation never faded. So I pulled Cleve away to let him know about it. Later, I watched him confront Alex while that chemist spoke to me of Slugari and other chemist-like subjects that I didn't care for. Whatever Alex said, it must've shocked Cleve because he became quite aggressive, at least until they talked more and resolved whatever it was."

"That's stranger than a chemist with a sword," Steffen said.

Gabby smacked him in the stomach with the back of her hand. He gasped and wheezed as a result.

"I told you not to use that stupid line," Gabby told him.

"It's funny," he replied defensively, regaining his posture and fixing his shirt.

"But you're a chemist. It's insulting. You should say something like, 'That's stranger than a warrior making a potion.' "

"That's terrible," Steffen said.

"It truly is," Reela agreed.

Effie unhooked herself from Reela. She decided to check on Cleve, catching some of Steffen's explanation to Gabby as she walked back toward the house. "There are many problems with it," he argued. "Some chemists actually do try using a sword, only to look awkward and strange. Warriors don't care for making potions..."

Once inside, Effie found Cleve asleep in a chair. She shook his shoulder, yet he didn't awaken. It felt like trying to shake a tree loose from the ground. She faced him to grab each shoulder and shook hard enough so that his head fell to his chest then bounced back to life.

He groaned. "I feel dizzy."

"Too much to drink. I'll help you get back home. You need to get up, though. You must be twice my weight at least."

He pushed himself upright. She put an arm around his torso to help him balance, but he must have misjudged how much weight she could support because he leaned on her with what felt like more than a hundred pounds.

She screamed as the floor came at her. But in the blink of an eye, a disorienting yank on her arm pulled her upright.

It took a few frantic breaths while she stumbled to realize that somehow Cleve had managed to stop his own fall and catch her as well. She glared at him in disbelief, for he looked to be having difficulty staying afoot.

"Sorry, I didn't mean to make you fall," he mumbled. "I won't put that much weight on you."

Reela came to his other side with an excited smile. "I saw that. In a moment he was more sober than anyone here. Yet look at him." She laughed and put an arm tightly around his torso. "Can't even stand straight."

Now Reela's touching him? Effie couldn't remember the last time her friend had thrown an arm around a man, especially a warrior. Sure, she would give a friendly touch to Steffen every so often, but the way Reela looked to be holding Cleve as close to her as possible made Effie wonder.

Cleve mumbled with a wide grin. "Let's go home."

Outside, Steffen and Gabby joined them. They directed a few questions at Cleve, only to be answered with, "Let's talk tomorrow" in the same mumbled voice.

Effie tried asking, "What happened between you and Alex?" With that, Cleve's grin faded and there was no reply.

By the time they'd arrived at their door, Cleve had pushed himself away from Reela and was at least stumbling on his own.

"No more sakal," Effie heard him whisper as she watched him flop face first onto his bed.

Something caught her eye before she passed his room. Even in the darkness she could see that it was the floorboards under his bed—

they had been removed. She used Bastial Energy to create white light from her hand for a look.

There's no bow, she realized.

"Cleve, your bow is gone. Did you move it?"

The only response was the sound of his breathing flowing in and out. He was already in a deep slumber.

Tomorrow is going to be a bad day, Effie thought.

Chapter 10: The Army of Krepps
ZOKE

It had been two years since Zoke was given the task of overseeing discipline against all Krepps. In that time, he'd grown no more than an inch, coming up only to the shoulders of other adult Krepps around his age of *pra durren*—four, which meant it had been four years since the shedding of his birth skin, the painful transition into adulthood.

Besides Zoke's height, however, he looked like any other Krepp. His face was longer than it was tall. His nose consisted of two holes above a lipless mouth that wrapped nearly around his entire head. His scaly skin was dark gray and tougher than the old leather that the Krepps wore to cover their bodies. The claws on the ends of his ten fingers and toes were short and sharp. He walked with two legs on bare feet, and his body was thick with muscles, even at each bend of bone.

The Krepps had lived in Ovira longer than their limited history books had to tell. The Humans had appeared nearly two hundred years ago, Zoke had read. In that short time, the Humans had built cities and grand castles behind the mountains to the south. It was written that some could even cast magic.

But history had no tales of battles between Humans and Krepps, and for good reason. Krepps towered over most Humans and weighed almost twice as much.

Luckily for Humans, the Krepps had no reason to travel as far south as Kyrro.

To Zoke's understanding, Krepps hadn't changed much throughout the years. Though never skilled builders, their ability to hunt and kill remained unparalleled. Even Zoke, at his lesser height, possessed enough power and skill with his treasured sword to easily slay any other creature known to him.

The major difference for present-day Krepps was that all tribes had merged only recently into one army under the leadership of Doe and Haemon—two monstrous Slugari driven by revenge who shared the Krepps' near fanatical drive to find the hidden underground Slugari colony.

The week was nearly over, so it was time for Zoke to gather the Krepps who'd failed to fulfill their duties to the tribe and bring them to the judgment chambers for punishment.

To make his presence known, Zoke clawed loudly at the cloth shielding that hung in the doorway of the first hut.

"Leave us," a female Krepp snorted in reply from within.

As much as Zoke wanted to, he couldn't leave them. His task wouldn't allow it. So Zoke pushed through the hanging door and drew his sword. He found doing so made the process easier.

A quick look around the small hut was all he needed to see that no male Krepp was inside.

"Where is husband to you?" Zoke asked in their language of Kreppen.

The mother Krepp was stitching a tear in leather pants not unlike those that Zoke wore. It had a long gash from the thigh to the shin. Her daughter was seated next to her, soaking a leg in a barrel of warm water. Neither would look in Zoke's direction.

"What do you want with him?" the mother asked, keeping her eyes as low as her tone.

Zoke sheathed his sword. "Your family didn't complete your weekly tasks. Now the oldest male needs to visit Vithos for judgment."

The mother lifted her gaze for a long examination of Zoke, clearly thinking of an excuse. "Daughter was cut deeply. She couldn't pick her share of kupota yesterday. I couldn't either because I needed to care for her wound. Husband is in the field now, doing what he can." She spat toward Zoke, then looked back to the pants strewn across her lap. "Not that you care, *gurradu*."

There was no reason to stay, so Zoke left, but not before turning his head to say, "Endure." He waited a breath for a reply but received none.

Zoke was used to being addressed as *gurradu* by now. The real *gurradu* were nose plugs made from oily rags. They were used to punish misbehaving child Krepps. With *gurradu* in, even the most delicious meat would lose its taste.

Zoke was born with the rare inability to smell, and the inescapable nickname came soon after.

As instructed, Zoke did find his quarry at the kupota field, and the husband spat at the sight of him. "I'm getting your plants now," the husband said, lifting a claw to point at the bucket next to him.

Zoke investigated the bucket of hacked and peeled kupota plants and frowned, knowing what could come next after he delivered the bad news. "They should have been delivered last night, and you don't have enough here. Bring what you have to Vithos. Explain the situation with wife to you. The rest is up to the Elf." Zoke had never met this Krepp before so he kept his hand ready on the hilt of his sword. He gave the same warning as he did to all first-timers: "Remember not to lie to him. He'll know."

"Fine, small *gurradu*." The Krepp threw down his shovel and, thankfully for Zoke, followed him to the judgment chambers without a fight.

It was the most fortified building in the encampment, a strong wooden structure that put the huts for each Krepp family to shame. It housed Vithos, an Elf who passed judgment on every deserving Krepp.

On the way there, Zoke received many condescending looks, some from Krepps who knew he would visit them shortly, the rest from others who knew nothing about Zoke except his reputation.

When they reached the judgment chambers, Zoke scratched on the wooden door to make his presence known. It opened from within, and Zoke stepped aside to let the accompanying Krepp through.

"Endure," Zoke told him.

"Endure," the Krepp replied with more fear than disdain. The door was shut behind him.

The day was young and Zoke would be escorting many others, so he tightened the lace on his official disciplinary cloak and made his way to the house of the next family on the list. It would have been easier to gather them all at once, but there was too much danger in that. It wasn't uncommon for Krepps to react aggressively when he tried to bring them to the judgment chambers. If there were more than he could handle, they easily could take control—a dangerous thing to lose.

Eventually, the rumblings of his stomach notified him that lunch should be soon. By then, there was only one more family who didn't meet their quota. But on his way to their hut, someone tugged on his cloak from behind to stop him.

"Zeti needs your help," a soft voice said.

Zoke turned to find Grayol, a friend of his sister. Zoke knew him as a boy Krepp who still had several years before the shedding of his birth skin.

"What's wrong?" Zoke asked earnestly, leaning down to match his eye level with Grayol's. It was unlike Zeti to need anything from Zoke, so it wouldn't be wise to ignore the summons.

"She can barely stand. She says her whole body aches." Grayol was careful to speak quietly, as if he was afraid to hear himself say the words.

The beginning signs of her shedding, Zoke thought, straightening his back. *Nothing to worry about.* "She is twelve—*pra durren.*" Zoke kept his voice calm to help ease Grayol's worry. "Twelve years she's been alive without shedding. The time fits. Tell sister to me she'll finally be a woman soon. It's a slow process that's very painful, but I'll come by soon and prepare janjin plants for the pain."

Grayol's face remained pinched with panic. "She says it really hurts, and she's much stronger than I am."

"It will hurt even more later, but she needs her new skin to continue getting stronger as an adult." Zoke thought that would be it, so he continued forward, but Grayol kept pace with him.

"Will the same happen to me?" the young Krepp asked with a wince of fear in his bright yellow eyes. His long mouth was curled down at the edges.

"How old are you, nine—*pra durren*?" Zoke guessed.

Grayol nodded.

"Then you have two or three years before the shedding of your birth skin, but don't be frightened of it because you're not a man until your *pra durren* is completed. Krepps don't show fear, we endure."

Grayol stood up straight and pushed out his chest. "Endure," he squeaked out.

Zoke heard the sound of another Krepp spitting toward him and felt hot saliva land on the top of his bare foot. "Grayol, don't listen to this *gurradu.* He's small and weak."

Zoke lowered his shoulders in disappointment when he saw it was Dentar, an associate of his father.

"Father to Zoke tells me his weak son is *pra durren*—four, but look at him." Dentar lazily waved a claw at Zoke. "He's still the size of a boy because he doesn't enjoy meat like a true Krepp."

"I don't have time for you," Zoke said. "Grayol, you shouldn't waste your time with him either. Go to sister to me."

Grayol ran off without a look back.

"Always busy with the work of the Elf. No time for your own race," Dentar said with a false smile, letting his sharp teeth catch the sunlight.

"We all serve Doe and Haemon, and the Elf serves them. If you don't agree with their rules, then you can leave the tribe. Leave me no matter, though." Zoke drew his sword and pointed it at Dentar.

"You kill a couple Krepps with that thing and think no one will stand up to you?"

"Yes." Zoke held his weapon still, hoping Dentar would draw his. His father's associate was a head taller, but Zoke knew Dentar's skill did not match his own.

Dentar checked to see if other Krepps were watching and found no audience. He forced a wider smile and grunted as he left.

I hope I find your name on this list someday, Zoke thought, sheathing his weapon. Delivering Dentar to the judgment chambers to watch him try to talk his way out of a burning would be like finally scratching an itch that had been impossible to reach.

By the time Zoke delivered the last Krepp to Vithos for judgment, he was ready for his usual meal of starchy, bland kupota. He picked up enough for him and his sister, Zeti, from the resource center, along with some janjin plants to help with her *pra durren*. Normally he liked to watch the proceedings of judgment day, but first he would see to Zeti in the hut they shared.

Chapter 11: Must Endure
ZOKE

Zoke's sister was lying in bed but tried to get up when he entered.

"Lie down," he told her. A quick glance was all he needed to see that the young Krepp who looked up to Zeti wasn't around. "Where is Grayol?" Zoke asked, sitting at their wooden table to begin grinding janjin leaves. As always, the table squeaked with each shift of his weight.

"I made him leave because he was annoying me." Zeti grunted in pain and rested her head once again.

"He's concerned."

"About himself," Zeti retorted.

"He knows how tough you are, yet he sees you like this, so he gets scared," Zoke explained.

Zeti moaned and turned on her side to see what Zoke was doing. "How is it you have answers to everything, but you never know where Father is?"

Zoke grunted. "Only those with him know the answer to that." He poured water into a wooden bowl and sprinkled the ground-up janjin leaves across the top. "Here, for the pain." He handed her the bowl.

She sat up with a groan but didn't take it. "All Krepps say this hurts, but I thought they were just weak."

Zoke moved the bowl closer to her claws. "It's the worst pain most Krepps ever feel, but you haven't gotten to the peeling yet."

"When does that start?" Zeti's lemon colored eyes lowered to the bowl for a blink, then shifted back to Zoke. Her pride was palpable.

Zoke held the bowl steady. "It will be sometime tomorrow, probably at night. It's bad. But once it begins, it's over quickly."

Zeti moaned, slumping in defeat. "I won't even sleep tonight."

Zoke nodded regretfully. "No one does."

She looked at the janjin leaves drifting across the top of the water, really looked at them for the first time. Her straight mouth relaxed to match the rest of her body. She reached out to accept the bowl. "Should I save this for the peeling?"

"It won't help. You might as well take it now. I'll make more before the night is over."

Zeti took a breath then started gulping. Zoke waited patiently for her to finish every last drop, taking the bowl once she was done and setting it on the table.

"I'll be back later, sister. Endure."

"Endure." Zeti slid back down to lie flat.

When Zoke returned to the judgment chambers, most of the Krepps he'd delivered had already received their verdicts. Just one still waited to make his case, along with one other Krepp who Zoke hadn't brought in and didn't recognize.

Zoke figured it would be a strange scene to any Human, but the conversation between a monstrous Slugari, an Elf, and a scared Krepp was common in Doe and Haemon's encampment. In fact, Zoke often was the scared Krepp, although he never did anything deserving of punishment. Fear was just a natural part of his task to the tribe.

The judgment quarters was stripped of all the wood that possibly could be removed without compromising the structural integrity of the building. Cold dirt was the floor, large rocks were used as seats, and thin sheets of black metal covered the wooden walls so they couldn't catch fire. Vithos the Elf always sat to discuss the case against each Krepp and stood when it was time to pass judgment. He was seated when Zoke entered.

"What is your age?" Vithos was asking the nervous Krepp before him.

"*Pra durren*—one."

"So you're an adult at least, but only by one year. Are you really the oldest male in your family?"

Zoke's heart jumped at hearing the question. If the Krepp wasn't the oldest male, then he'd brought the wrong one.

"Yes, I am the only member of my family," the Krepp answered to Zoke's relief.

"Are the rest dead?"

It was a cold question, but Zoke had heard Vithos ask it so many times it no longer affected him.

"I believe Mother died when I was very young. Father left the tribe two years ago."

Vithos nodded. "You tell the truth so far. Now for the tougher questions." He glanced at a scroll in his pale Elven hands. "I see your task is to assist a team of Krepps in searching for the hiding Slugari. Your designated search was to take place in northern Satjen, but your team never made it through Kilmar. The leading Krepp reported that you were to blame. I've heard his reasons. Now I wish to hear yours."

The Krepp shifted uncomfortably, scratching his cheek with a claw. "I ate too much of the meat, and we were unable to find enough through hunting, so we had to return early. My portion was smaller than the rest, and I was hungry."

"Did you steal from the meat locker while everyone was sleeping?"

"Yes." The Krepp answered with feigned indifference, as if it was an acceptable act.

"Did you know what you were doing was wrong?" Vithos asked—another question Zoke had heard countless times before. Zoke knew this was often the beginning of the end of the trial.

"I didn't think it was wrong." The Krepp held the same indifference in his tone as before.

A few spectators grunted. "That's a lie," Vithos replied calmly. "Don't lie again. Did you know what you were doing was wrong?"

The Krepp's elongated mouth twisted in anger. "It was their fault. If I'd had the same portions as they had, I wouldn't have needed to do it."

Vithos folded his arms. "Did you also need to eat all the remaining food while everyone was sleeping?"

The Krepp's eyes lowered to the dirt between him and Vithos. "No."

"Was it their fault you did that?" Zoke knew the question was rhetorical, though Vithos didn't make it clear in his tone.

"Yes. If I wasn't so hungry..."

Vithos waved his hand and stood. "You're lying again, and I've reached my decision. Your portion was smaller because you're smaller. You're also younger and new to the search group. You're to blame here, and you know it's true, yet you chose to lie. Because you lied, and because you're at fault, you will receive double punishments—a burning and an appropriate psychological punishment that I will think of. Stand and Haemon will begin the burning.

The Krepp stood and puffed out his chest. Haemon slithered next to Vithos to face the Krepp.

Haemon was a legless, bulbous mass the shape of a slug, with short claws on the ends of two diminutive arms. Being the same height as an adult male Krepp, Haemon was so large and discolored that most wouldn't guess he was a Slugari.

Generally, Slugari were a third the size of Haemon, and their green, translucent bodies shimmered. However, Haemon's skin was mud brown, and light did nothing to him except brighten his ugliness. His claws had become jagged and black over the years. His pointed tail had rounded to a bulbous nob. He still had two antennae atop his head like other Slugari, but they'd shrunk while the rest of him had grown, and now they doubled over impotently. His nose hung limply in the same way on top of his head. It came from a long stem between the two antennae and had a fish hook shape.

Many Krepps couldn't tell the difference between Haemon and Doe, another Slugari just as massive and feared, but all Krepps knew that these Slugari wanted revenge on their own kind. Zoke had heard the tale of their exile from their underground home twenty times at least but never what had caused them to grow so massive.

Haemon motioned for the Krepp to come closer, and he obeyed, moving cautiously forward. The Krepp said nothing—probably the best idea he'd had so far.

"Hold out your arm." Haemon spoke Kreppen with a hint of an accent, his voice as rough as stone.

The Krepp raised an arm and looked at Zoke with uncertainty.

Endure, Zoke thought, nodding to him. The Krepp had said it was his first judgment when Zoke had escorted him earlier.

Haemon's claws glowed until a light exploded from them, brightening the yellow eyes of each watching Krepp in the judgment quarters. After the flash, all that remained was a thin ray so white Zoke could see the reflection of the black metal sheets on the walls as he stared at it. Haemon steered his hands down to navigate the light over the Krepp's wrist. As it passed, the Krepp's skin was singed. He quivered and grunted, but his arm remained steady.

Smoke rose from the fresh scar on his wrist and an unsettling silence followed. Each Krepp was waiting to see if he would whimper, Zoke included.

He didn't, just clenched his sharp teeth and breathed heavily.

"The burning is complete," Haemon announced.

"I have decided on the appropriate psychological punishment."

Vithos spoke nonchalantly while the wound still sizzled. "The problem was your inability to control your hunger. So for one day you'll feel so hungry even your own kind will appear edible. You'll still receive the same amount of food from the tribe, and you won't steal any other food or eat anything inedible, otherwise we'll see you here again tomorrow. Endure."

"Endure," the Krepp repeated, staring at his wrist.

Vithos approached and placed his pale hand firmly on the Krepp's head. The Elf shut his eyes and sucked in air for several breaths. The Krepp's eyes closed next while the rest of his face grimaced.

Vithos opened his eyes and dropped his hand. "Your judgment has passed. You may leave."

The Krepp doubled over and held his stomach for a moment. He quickly rose, trying to walk out with his head high, but he was hunched again by the time he exited.

"There is one more Krepp awaiting judgment," Vithos said, glancing at a scroll. "Loggur, have a seat." Vithos pointed toward the rock in the middle of the room.

Loggur sat down proudly and the murmuring of the room died down.

"It says here that you left the tribe, and now you wish to return. Is this true?" Vithos asked.

"Yes." This Krepp was either far more prepared than the last, or perhaps just better at making it seem that way. He sat straight, keeping his mouth from quivering and his nose from twitching.

"Why did you leave?" Vithos glanced at the scroll as he spoke.

"I thought I could hunt for more meat on my own, and if I found a Slugari in the wild I wouldn't have to share it." Loggur kept his eyes ahead on Vithos, making his best effort to ignore the stares of the audience.

"Did you find any signs of wild Slugari?" Vithos asked pessimistically.

"No," Loggur answered, taking a quick glance at the watching Krepps.

Haemon interrupted, "Because they're all hidden underground."

"When did you leave?" Vithos asked, ignoring Haemon.

"Almost a year ago."

"What other reasons do you have for returning?"

"If the tribe does find the underground Slugari colony, I need to be part of it. I need Slugari meat." Loggur clenched his claws at his sides.

"We'll find it in time," Vithos responded as if reading from a script. "You knew you would be punished upon returning?"

Loggur's yellow eyes fell to the dirt. "Yes."

Vithos nodded to Haemon to show the truth had been told.

"We accept your return," Haemon announced loudly for the audience. "The punishment for deserting the tribe is the same for all Krepps. You will be marked with an 'X' on the back of one claw. If anyone asks about the mark, you'll tell them what happened and make sure they know why you returned."

Loggur stood, keeping his eyes ahead to avoid looking directly at the enormous Slugari slithering toward him. Haemon was wheezing loudly as he often did before casting magic. Laces of emerald green smoke rose from his small claws and danced toward the ceiling.

He squeezed his claws together with a grunt. Upon releasing them, a cloud emerged of the same emerald color and quickly dissipated. All that remained in his claws was a thin X-shaped object that shone like two blades of grass in the sun.

"Hold out your arm and look away," the Slugari commanded. Krepps in the audience stood and shifted to get a better view around Haemon's enormous body.

Loggur did as he was told, keeping his eyes away from his arm and squinting.

With meticulous precision, Haemon grasped the marking stone, aligned it over the back of Loggur's hand, and dropped it. There was a yellow explosion when it reached the Krepp's skin, engulfing Loggur completely for a blink. Then it was gone.

Loggur moaned, shaking his claw in agony.

"Your judgment has passed," Haemon said. "Endure."

"Endure," Loggur replied, staggering toward the exit. The spectators stood and conversed with each other. Two ran after Loggur.

They want to see his new marking, Zoke knew.

While charred skin still smoking after a fresh punishment was a sight to behold, Zoke had seen it before, and his presence was usually requested by Vithos the Elf or one of the Slugari. This time it was Haemon. "Zoke, come." The Slugari motioned to him. "We need to discuss something with Doe."

Chapter 12: Chosen
ZOKE

Zoke followed Haemon into Vithos' quarters, where Doe, the other Slugari leader, awaited. The room contained no more than a bed, a wardrobe, a wooden table with two chairs, and a sullied mirror hanging loosely on the wall.

Doe had the same grimace as usual. It had taken Zoke months before he figured out that he wasn't the cause of the disdain always found on Doe's fat Slugari face.

"We have a task, and we believe you'll be the best fit for it." Doe's voice was even deeper and coarser than Haemon's. "To be sure, we need you to answer the following questions honestly." Doe glanced at Vithos, who then took a step toward Zoke.

Zoke still hadn't gotten used to the way Vithos looked at him as he posed questions. Although the Elf was shorter than most male Krepps, he was still taller than Zoke, and would dip his chin toward his throat to stare through the tops of his eyes.

Vithos had wide eyes that came to a point on both ends. As he stared, the only whites of his eyes that could be seen were under and around his dark brown irises, forming two troubling grins within each socket. His mouth always remained flat.

"Do you wish to harm me?" Vithos asked.

Zoke jumped back, wondering what he'd done recently that might have given Vithos this impression. "No," he answered honestly. He almost asked the reason for the question but knew that explanation would come soon enough.

"Do I pose a threat to you?" Vithos' tone didn't change. There was no pitch to it, nothing to let Zoke know what he was thinking.

"No," Zoke said and gladly let his confusion show.

"If your task was to search for Slugari and you found one in the wild, would you kill it and eat it without notifying anyone?"

"No, I would capture or kill it and bring it back. I have no significant interest in Slugari meat." He knew that Doe, Haemon, and Vithos were aware of his inability to smell, but he'd never been asked about it in a situation like this. Vithos nodded at Doe to let him know Zoke had been truthful.

Doe spoke next. "As you know, we've been searching for the hidden Slugari colony for many years now. While there are several teams of Krepps involved in the search, Vithos and I have been leaving our encampment whenever time allowed to contribute to the search as well. Vithos' ability to sense the presence of the Slugari may be the only way of finding them. However, we can't use Vithos to search as much as we would like because we don't have enough time to constantly leave the encampment."

Zoke noticed that Vithos' eyes had wandered to the ground, not that he knew what it meant. The Elf looked something between bored and upset. Doe didn't seem to notice it or just didn't care. His beady Slugari eyes were focused on Zoke, glaring.

"You and Vithos will spend six days traveling north to Nor. There, you will search for the Slugari. The southwest corner of Nor is where you should look. Vithos hasn't searched that area yet. We expect the entire trip to take no more than fifteen days. If you find this task to be more enjoyable than your current task, these trips can become more frequent. Do you understand what we're asking?"

More enjoyable? It was strange for Doe to even feign interest in another's enjoyment. "Yes," Zoke answered. Though he wondered what he could do to help protect Vithos that the Elf couldn't already do with his psychic power.

"Good. If you have questions, direct them to Vithos. You'll be leaving tomorrow morning." Doe started to turn his rotund body, an arduous process it seemed.

Tomorrow...that's too early. Zoke knew he shouldn't say anything, but he blurted it before he could stop himself. "Zeti has started the shedding of her birth skin, and I wish to prepare food, water, and medicine for her during this time. I would like to wait one more day before we leave if time allows." The confidence in his voice startled him, especially as it was the first time he didn't silently follow an order.

"No," Doe grunted. "All the preparations are set for you both to leave tomorrow."

"May another Krepp be selected for this? It's an honor to be chosen. However, I fear for Zeti." Again he surprised himself, though Zoke noticed dread creeping into his voice.

Doe growled. “No! Vithos chose you, and Zeti can endure on her own as many other Krepps have done.” His black claws began to glow.

Not another word, Zoke told himself. He turned and found Vithos looking at him with the same dangerous smile in his eyes. Suddenly, everything he’d just heard felt fallacious. *Something’s wrong about this...or is Vithos making me feel this way?* Doe’s mind was set, though, so there was no point in disagreeing.

“I understand,” Zoke replied.

Should I try to find Father to let him know about Zeti? I may as well after another visit myself. At least I know Grayol will help look after her...not that she’s going to let him be much help.

A small pack of food was thrown to his feet. “This is all you’ll need,” Doe said. “Don’t bring anything else. It’s fashioned to be worn on your back. Meet Vithos here at first light. Haemon and I will then escort you to the edge of the encampment. Endure.”

“Endure,” Zoke replied subordinately. He skirted any further looks from the Slugari or Vithos and left quickly.

Chapter 13: Family
ZOKE

Soon, Zoke was back at his hut and found Zeti with an unexpected visitor. Their father, Ruskir, sat in the corner of the room, sharpening his claws with a rusty hunting knife.

"You here for more food to wager?" Zoke asked, letting his contempt come out in his tone.

"That depends. What's in the bag?" Ruskir answered, keeping one eye on his knife.

"Nothing for you. I'm leaving with Vithos tomorrow, and this is needed for the trip. We're looking for the hidden Slugari."

"Good. Maybe you'll actually do well for the tribe and find them."

Zoke ignored that. "Will you be here with Zeti tomorrow? I can't, and she needs someone."

Zeti grunted to sit up. "I don't need anyone." She carefully placed her feet on the ground and shifted her weight from the bed. She teetered and winced but bent her knees to keep her balance. Like most female Krepps, she wore tough leather pants as well as a short leather shirt that came around her shoulders and cut off at her stomach.

"Look at that, she stands!" Ruskir pointed with his knife. "Zeti is much tougher than you, *gurradu*. She will be an adult soon and already has many strong suitors."

Zeti spat. "Your friends have a better chance of stealing an eppil plant from Doe and Haemon's garden than being my *seshar*."

Ruskir put down his knife to admire his newly sharpened claws. "You should reconsider how you feel about these suitors. You don't know what could happen if you ignore them."

"I do know," Zeti replied. "They'll fight and bring me gifts until I choose one. But I am not going to choose any of them. They're all too much like you."

Ruskir pounded his fist on the table and stood. "They have power among this tribe, Dentar especially."

Zoke shuddered at the thought of Dentar and his sister. It was already irritating enough that the Krepp harassed him on a daily basis, but to come between him and Zeti? Zoke shook his head, rage swelling in his stomach. Luckily, he knew Zeti felt the same way.

"He's worse than the rest!" Zeti yelled with a slight wobble. She grabbed on to the bed. "And I don't care that he's a weapons trader. I have my bow. That's all I need."

Ruskir stood and pointed a claw. "You think you're better without a *seshar*? You're not."

"I'll wait three years for my friend Grayol to have his *pra durren*. He'll be my *seshar*."

If Father knew her at all, he would realize she was joking, Zoke said to himself. However, at the rate Ruskir was breathing, it was clear their father didn't.

"Did you take a blow to the head? He's young, he's weaker than Zoke, and he has no family. His duty to the tribe is worse than Zoke's. He'll never have power!"

"He cares for me, and that's all that matters," Zeti replied sternly. Zoke was impressed by her ability to lie so convincingly. It even made him wonder if there was some truth to what she said.

"I expect this kind of weakness from son to me but not from daughter to me." Ruskir shoved Zoke out of the way to leave the hut, and Zoke gladly let him go.

Outside, Zoke heard his father stop and speak to someone. "You! You were listening? Next time show yourself. Don't be a coward."

Zoke pushed aside the cloth barrier to peer outside and found Grayol staring down the end of Ruskir's hunting knife.

"I should help her make the correct decision by getting rid of you right now," Ruskir said.

"Leave him, Father." Zoke had a claw on the hilt of his sword.

Ruskir's chest heaved as his glare turned to Zoke. "I have no hope for you or Zeti, and especially not for this pathetic Krepp." Ruskir put away the dagger. "I thought wife to me was stupid to mess with Doe and Haemon's eppil plants, but now I see she got herself killed because she couldn't stand this family. She knew what kind of Krepps you and Zeti were when you were still on the teat and didn't want to wait to see how much worse you would get. Now I have to live alone with the shame that you both bring our family." Ruskir retreated back to wherever he'd come from.

"Bring Grayol in here," Zeti grunted from within. Zoke motioned with his head for Grayol to follow him and stepped back inside.

Zeti was lying down again. "I was joking, Grayol," she said. "You'll never be my *seshar*. I just wanted to upset Father."

"I know," Grayol replied, seemingly insulted she had to explain it. "It will be someone much stronger than me."

"Why are you here again?" she asked.

"To see if you need help. Does it still hurt as much?"

"Worse. But I don't need anything. You can come back tomorrow, though."

"Can I stay here for a while?" Grayol asked in a pleading voice.

"I need to discuss a few things with Zeti," Zoke interrupted. "Come back later."

"Tomorrow," Zeti corrected.

"Endure." Grayol ran out, leaving Zoke feeling guilty.

Zoke grabbed their only chair, brought it beside Zeti's bed, and sat. "I'm going to be leaving for a while with the Elf. But I know you'll be fine."

"Of course I will. But what about you? Will you be alone with Vithos for long?"

"Fifteen days. I feel uneasy about it."

"I do, too. If it were me, I would much rather go on my own than with that creepy Elf."

"They need him to start searching for the Slugari more often. The Slugari are most likely hidden underground, so the only hope of finding them is with Vithos wandering through Ovira until he's above their underground colony and close enough to sense them. I still don't know why they need me, though."

"I'm in too much pain to figure that out." Zeti held up a claw to probe her cracking skin. "I hope you find them. I can't wait to try the delicious Slugari meat. Every time I see Doe or Haemon I can think about nothing other than biting into them and ripping off a chunk. They smell wonderful, and those who've eaten Slugari say Doe and Haemon don't even smell good compared to normal Slugari." Drool glistened on Zeti's scaly chin.

Zoke carefully ran a finger down Zeti's arm, testing the looseness of her skin while making sure his claw didn't catch her accidentally. It still clung tightly. She had far worse to endure. He sighed and tried to think of something to take her mind from the pain.

"You've never had Slugari meat. Maybe you wouldn't like it," Zoke said.

Zeti giggled and then winced and moaned. "Don't make me laugh, brother. I am more certain about that than I am about the sun rising tomorrow. There's nothing I want more than to eat it." She opened her mouth and licked her teeth.

"Nothing more?" Zoke asked incredulously. He'd never understood this urge to feed on Slugari, especially when most Krepps hadn't even tasted it before.

"Nothing more," she confirmed.

Zoke thought of a question he hoped wouldn't be tough to answer. "If both a Slugari and I were about to fall off a tall cliff, who would you save?"

Her light yellow eyes squinted. They always reminded Zoke of a golden frog Grayol found outside the encampment one day. He killed it and brought it back to show Zeti. She scolded him for killing something for no reason, but he argued that it was the only way to catch it and show it to her. She scolded him again after that.

"What are you doing on the edge of a cliff?" Zeti asked with pure wonder.

Zoke shrugged, not thinking that far into it. "Why does that matter?"

"Were you playing around like a fool or doing something better, like chasing after the Slugari so that you could deliver it to me?" Zeti restrained a chuckle.

"You don't know why I was up there. You just see me about to fall."

"The Slugari." She pushed herself upright to enjoy his reaction. "Your dying wish has always been for me to eat one, right?"

He spat.

She smiled before lying back down. "Be cautious out there with the Elf. Keep that sword with you always."

Zoke noticed some of her black hair had gotten caught in her mouth. He carefully pulled it out. "That's another thing." He took a breath before continuing. "They won't let me take my sword or anything else besides the food in this sack. I need you to keep it here, but in secret. Don't let Father find it. He would just barter it." He didn't need to explain to his sister how much his weapon meant to him.

"Bury it under your bed. I'll make sure no one finds it."

Zoke nodded and rose to do as she suggested.

When he was done, he felt destitute without his weapon, almost as if he'd buried his only pair of pants.

Zoke spent the rest of the night making sure Zeti was fed and as comfortable as possible. They joked about all the wonderful suitors who kept their father company and how it was going to be difficult for Zeti to choose just one. They discussed what life would be like with Dentar as her *seshar* until Zeti forced Zoke to stop, claiming the thought of it hurt more than her shedding.

Soon, Zoke found himself dozing off, waking only once during the night from a vivid dream of Vithos reaching into Zoke's ears and pulling out pieces of his brain.

Chapter 14: Trust
ZOKE

He and Vithos spent half the day walking north without a single conversation. Zoke followed behind the Elf, the same questions circling in his mind as he tried to gather the courage to ask them. *Why me? What am I doing here?*

Vithos finally spoke when the sun was overhead. "We'll stop here. Take out the food."

Zoke released the knot of string on their bag of food and delivered it. Vithos peered inside with disinterest and removed precooked kupota. "Ask whatever it is you need to ask," he said, handing back the bag.

It didn't surprise Zoke that the Elf knew he had questions. Even without psyche, it should have been obvious. Zoke seized the opportunity. "What am I supposed to do to help?"

"Carry food and guard as I sleep. We'll take shifts," Vithos answered with surprising speed, as if he knew Zoke would ask that very question.

Zoke spat. "Anyone can do that."

Vithos bit into the round kupota, his eyes avoiding the spit on the dirt near his leather shoes. "I needed someone I could trust."

Can I trust you, though? Zoke thought but quickly stopped himself from wondering further. He wasn't sure what Vithos could sense with psyche. Instead, Zoke dug a hand into the dirt and squeezed his claws together. He concentrated on the feeling of the grass coming loose with the dirt crumbling against his palm.

"I know you must have many more questions," Vithos continued with half his mouth full. "By tomorrow night we may reach Lake Lensa if we can keep this pace. I'll tell you everything then. For now, eat."

Their quick pace was no easy task to maintain, at least not for Zoke. Most fully grown Krepps stood a head taller than Vithos, but Zoke was shorter than him. Without long legs, and no experience walking long distances, he already felt a dull ache in the soles of his feet. *Longer strides, less steps,* he told himself.

They walked, again in silence, until the low sun began to walk with them on the western horizon. By then, Zoke's calves had become as tight as the string on a bow. He knew that the Krepps who left for weeks at a time to search for the Slugari easily could walk twenty miles a day on the flat lands of Slepja, but his body couldn't endure that distance.

"How far have we gone?" he asked, making an effort to hide the exhaustion in his voice.

Vithos stopped and turned back with what seemed to be a scowl before Zoke realized that the Elf was actually looking over Zoke's shoulder. It looked as though he was checking for something...or maybe even someone? Zoke couldn't understand why that would be, so he figured he probably read the Elf's expression wrong.

"We've gone ten or fifteen miles, nearly halfway there," Vithos said. "You need a break?"

"A long one. My body has endured as much as it can for now without risking injury." It hurt Zoke's pride to admit, but it needed to be said.

With a hand over his eyes, Vithos looked to the sun in the golden sky. "Then we'll eat and sleep."

They found a huddle of smooth rocks. Vithos sat on one with his ankles crossed around their bag of kupota. Zoke sat across from him against a tall stone that he used as a backrest while stretching his legs on the cool grass. He saw that his feet were swollen. *Whatever aches I feel cannot compare to the pain Zeti is enduring right now,* he thought.

Vithos tossed him a fist-sized ball of kupota. Even though they were given the plainest food for their trip, Zoke was at least thankful the kupota had been cooked. The first bite always reminded him of stale bread, hard to chew and tasteless, but the crisp texture after he was through the exterior felt satisfying being mashed between his sharp teeth.

He followed the kupota with a long swig from his water pouch and began to feel sleep taking him. He let himself go, falling into a dreamless slumber.

When he woke, he found Vithos still seated on the same rock, but night had come. He wrestled to sit up, noticing the Elf's dark eyes on him. They looked black in the moonlight.

"How long have I been asleep?" Zoke asked.

"Three hours, maybe four. You can continue to rest if you would like." Vithos was slouched with his wrists dangling between his legs, clearly exhausted.

"You're not going to?" Zoke's body was tugging him back down, but curiosity kept him up.

Vithos sighed, then straightened his back. "I still have much to think about. I'll keep guard for a while longer."

Zoke was too tired to wonder what they needed guarding from and let his head fall against the grass.

The rock had left a dull ache in his back, but the pain dissolved when he shifted to lie flat. Falling asleep the second time was just as easy as the first.

It was morning when his eyes opened again. Beige light from the sun twisted into the gray sky from behind a cluster of clouds. In the stretch of land ahead, Zoke saw only two lonely trees, waves of hills, and nothing else.

Vithos was lying on his side, wrapped in a thin blanket. Zoke didn't know whether he should wake him.

He decided to create some distance between himself and Vithos, squatted behind a large rock, and lowered his pants to make waste. The soreness in his feet and legs reminded him of the toll yesterday had taken.

By the time Zoke returned, his task leader had awoken, twisting to stretch his back while glancing at the flat terrain surrounding them.

"I thought you might have left," Vithos said with what sounded like a hint of fear in his voice. Zoke had never known the Elf to be afraid. *I probably misheard,* he thought.

Figuring out what Vithos was thinking was like listening to Grayol tell a joke incorrectly. There were clues about what the young Krepp meant, but usually not enough to understand the punch line.

"I needed to make waste," Zoke explained.

Vithos nodded and dug around in their food bag, passing Zoke's breakfast to him.

"We can refill our water pouches when we reach Lake Lensa," Vithos said, taking a swig and swishing it loudly. He took another swig, leaned back to gargle, and then swished some more.

"I don't think it would be wise for me to walk another ten or fifteen miles today. I may not be able to walk at all tomorrow if I do."

That stopped Vithos from taking another sip. "Most Krepps are accustomed to walking that much each day."

"Then you should have brought one of them," Zoke said as plainly as he could.

Vithos shook his head, his shoulder-length hair shimmering in the morning light. "No, time is not a priority. I brought the right Krepp. If you can't walk to Lake Lensa today, then we'll slow our pace and reach it tomorrow."

Zoke finished the rest of his inadequate breakfast in silence. Already, he was wishing for something besides kupota and it had only been one day of it. When he stood, Vithos did as well.

"We'll walk straight north," Vithos told Zoke. "You lead and I'll follow. Walk as slow as you like, and we'll stop when you wish." His tone was friendlier than Zoke was used to, leaving him with an uneasy feeling. There was nothing that made Zoke more uncomfortable than someone being nice for reasons he didn't understand, especially given his task within the tribe.

The faster we finish this, the faster I return to the camp. He set off, reaching for a comforting touch to the hilt of his sword. However, it wasn't on his belt. *Waiting for me back with Zeti,* he reminded his hand.

Their route was flat for now, as most hills were miles ahead. There was more moisture in the dirt by then. He could feel it on the bottoms of his toes as his claws dug into the ground with each step.

It reminded him how different the dirt felt beneath his feet after his shedding, when he could feel each grain of sand compressing together under the weight of his sensitive skin. *Zeti's pra durren should be over by now. I'm sure Grayol helped her with whatever she needed, if she allowed it.*

Zoke's stomach ached before his feet. "Let's stop for lunch now." Zoke unstrapped the bag of food from his shoulder.

Vithos took a long breath. "I can't wait for more delicious kupota." He spoke with a sarcastic tone, reaching out his hand.

Zoke stopped himself before handing over one. "It sounded like you just made a joke," he observed incredulously.

Vithos was put off. "Is it easier to believe I find kupota to be delicious?"

Zoke plopped the round plant into Vithos' hand. "I've seen you eat kupota. I've never heard you make a joke."

"I enjoy jokes." Vithos took a small bite and made a sour face.

"Perhaps another will lighten our mood." He gestured with the kupota and started talking even though Zoke gave no indication he wanted to hear it. "They sound and look the same, but one act between two Krepps leads to regret a year later, while the other does not. What are the acts I describe?"

"I haven't heard this riddle," Zoke said, slightly interested now. "I don't know."

"Fighting and mating." Vithos grinned in anticipation.

Zoke pondered it for a breath. "The child from mating is the regret?"

Vithos grew disappointed. "Of course."

Zoke didn't hide his distaste. He'd never mated, but his understanding was that the act looked little like the fights he'd been in. "Are Doe and Haemon telling you jokes of Krepps?"

Vithos was visibly irritated now. Zoke could see it on his face, and that just made Zoke more annoyed. *Why is he the one getting upset?*

"Humor is lost on them," Vithos said with some disdain. "Paramar and I share a joke or a riddle sometimes. Vithos took another breath, lightening his tone. "You know Paramar?"

"Tough-looking Krepp, chief of the Slugari search effort? I wouldn't have expected him to tell jokes, and neither did I expect that of you."

"Then you don't know me," Vithos said, his voice ice cold.

Zoke spat. "No, I don't."

An awkward silence came over them that continued throughout lunch and the rest of the day.

Chapter 15: Disquieting Questions
ZOKE

Zoke and Vithos reached the mountainside they'd been walking to just in time for them to still find it. The black of night had become so thick by then that Zoke couldn't see farther than he could spit.

"Carry food and guard as I sleep. We'll take shifts." Vithos had said that about Zoke's tasks, but curiously there had been no further talk of sleep shifts. Zoke had become deathly bored walking to the mountainside in silence and wanted nothing less than three or four more hours of boredom, so he didn't mention sleep shifts. He couldn't determine what threats there were to watch for anyway. There had been no animals. In fact, there was really nothing else besides the two of them, at least that he'd seen.

They lay under the cover of a steep cliff. The wind was chilling. Luckily, most of it was blocked by the mountain. Vithos was five steps away, curled in his blanket.

Even though they hadn't spoken, in Zoke's mind they'd already reached an understanding that his new task of searching for the Slugari wasn't a good fit. There was nothing more to say after that. His previous questions seemed silly now. If it wasn't necessary for him to continue on these hunts after this one, then that's all he needed to know.

He woke several times from a guilty feeling in his stomach. Each time, he checked on Vithos, who never moved an inch or made a sound. Zoke turned to try and get more comfortable against the bare dirt. He knew the guilt was from the unresolved discord between them, so he decided he would offer a simple greeting when they both awoke. Even if they weren't a good match for this task, there was no reason to make it worse by not talking.

The following morning his mouth was dry. At first he figured his body was without sufficient water, but after peeling his face from the ground it became clear that dirt had found its way into his mouth while he slept. He spat to clear any remaining grains and wiped his face with his coarse hands. Vithos was seated with his eyes closed until Zoke spat. The Elf opened them to gaze silently with indifference.

"Ektol," Zoke said.

The corners of Vithos' mouth turned up slightly. "*Ek tolbaru ren,*" Vithos said, using the non-abbreviated form, and then stood. Zoke couldn't remember the last time he'd used or heard the phrase told to him. Roughly translated from Kreppen, it meant "May we be rewarded appropriately for our efforts," a greeting or a goodbye spoken among Krepps working together—usually he worked alone.

Zoke bent his legs one by one, shaking them to measure the pain. "You say Lake Lensa is ten miles from here?" he asked.

"That is correct," Vithos answered, standing.

"Then we can make it there before sunset." Zoke's legs felt up to the task, but more so he just wanted to get there. Lake Lensa was only halfway to their destination in the southwest corner of Nor. *And then we still have to walk all the way back,* he reminded himself, wanting to spit.

They ate little and spoke less as they walked. Even he, a *gurradu*, was craving something with more flavor than kupota.

"I realize this may be dull compared to the tasks you normally do for me," Vithos said to break the silence, taking a bite of kupota. "But excitement awaits us farther north. The land changes drastically, and you'll see inspiring sights."

Zoke held in a judgmental snort. "How far north have you gone?" he asked. It was an attempt to redirect their attention away from his discouraging thoughts that Vithos might have been able to sense.

"Deep into Nor, but far east, not toward western Nor where we're headed. I've always wished to travel through western Nor." Vithos suddenly seemed nervous, like he'd said something he hadn't meant to.

Zoke was surprised by this reaction because the Elf usually spoke very carefully. "Why haven't you gone before?"

At that, Vithos chewed in silence until his kupota was finished. "I have information I need to share with you. As much as I'd like to do so now, it's best that I wait one more day. You'll understand after you hear it."

That stirred up serious thoughts, but he knew Vithos to hold to his word. If the Elf wouldn't speak of it until tomorrow, there was no point in prying.

Miles later, Lake Lensa finally crept into view from behind small hills. The sun hidden below the horizon colored the lake magma as it reflected the sky above. Mountains guarded the lake's northern end, while a line of trees stood along its eastern side.

By the time Zoke was close enough to feel the humidity from the water against his dry skin, there was no longer a trace of the sun. The lake had grown black, merged into the surrounding darkness.

"It's too dark for any more walking tonight," Vithos said, stopping. "Any farther and we may stumble into the water before we know it's there. I'll take the first watch while you rest." With that, the Elf took two steps and disappeared into the black of the night without even waiting for an answer. As Zoke could hear him pacing away, he decided not to wonder where he might be going. As usual, there was no way to know what Vithos was thinking.

Sleep wouldn't take him. Zoke's mind raced in curiosity about what Vithos had to say, while the dry sand he laid on sounded like it was screaming with each shift of his weight. He tried to focus on the physical relief he felt pulsing from his back to his feet, and soon the sounds of the sand stopped completely and he drifted away.

Deeper he went, floating on a small island into the middle of the lake. He could hear the sound of water growing louder as he drifted. His name was called, but he couldn't lift his heavy head to find the caller.

Zoke, Zoke, she continued to shout until it came to him; it was Zeti, but he was too tired to shout back.

"Zoke, time to wake."

Reality had returned in such a rush his head spun. Vithos was shaking his shoulder. "Do you need help waking?"

"Help?" he asked with confusion. "No, I'm awake." Zoke sat up. Everything was still masked in black.

"Need help staying awake, I mean? I could use psyche." Vithos had a hesitant tone, well aware Zoke probably would refuse.

Even with the Elf's tone, Zoke was annoyed that Vithos would ask. "No," he answered, refraining from spitting. Zoke had never known a Krepp to wish for a psychic spell, and he was no different.

"I'm going to sleep now," Vithos said.

Zoke grumbled, still getting used to being awake in the middle of the night. "What am I watching for while you rest?"

"Anything that moves. There's nothing near us at the moment, but it's rare for this lake to be left undisturbed for an entire night. And some animals are hungry enough to let their curiosity overcome their sense of danger. Don't wake me for an animal, though, unless you can't handle it. Do wake me if you hear or see another Krepp. Understand?"

"Yes." Zoke stood to patrol the area and shake off the drowsiness.

He began to wonder why Vithos seemed concerned about other Krepps. He thought every tribe had joined with Doe and Haemon.

Could there still be wild Krepps willing to attack an Elf? That battle ended before I was born. The Elves are no longer a threat, I thought.

When his internal discussions began repeating without answers, his thoughts turned to Zeti. *She's certainly a woman by now. If she grows tall, she may pass my height in the next few years.* His hand reached for his absent sword.

When the light from the sun began to peek over the hills, Zoke was looking for a stick with the same weight as his beloved sword. He found one that nearly matched. It was just long enough to reach the ground from his grip, making it useful for walking.

He squatted to wake the Elf. "Vithos, the sun is rising."

Vithos sat up and rubbed his eyes with a grumble. "I would like to rinse my face," he muttered. His long hair was matted against his cheek. "I can fetch water for us as well. I know how Krepps hate the water." He reached out a hand. Zoke dug out the leather water pouches from their bag and passed them.

"Come with me," Vithos said, now on his feet and making adjustments to his groin. "If there are any fish near the shore, I'll catch one."

Zoke followed him to the edge of the azure water and watched as Vithos filled the pouches from the sandy shoreline, left them there for Zoke to retrieve, and then slowly walked into the lake. He splashed his face and drank from cupped hands.

"There are fish. Do you know how to clean one?" Vithos held a hand beneath the surface.

"Not without a knife..." Zoke let his voice trail off.

"You already know I have a knife on my belt," Vithos replied plainly, keeping his back to Zoke.

That was true. It had caught Zoke's eye during the first few hours of their trip.

Vithos lifted his hand from the water and calmly turned toward the shore, holding what appeared to be a dead fish. Vithos extended the handle of the knife to him, but Zoke didn't accept it. He couldn't take his eyes off the fish in Vithos' other hand. He waited for it to move, but it didn't.

"Did you kill it with psyche?" Zoke asked, finally taking the dagger.

"No, it's unconscious but still living," Vithos said, slapping the fish against his hand twice as if to show off and then handing it to Zoke. "Show me how to clean it."

Zoke stared at the live creature within his claws. Its steady eye looked right through him. There was no difference between it and a dead fish.

"Can you do this to Krepps?" Zoke asked hesitantly.

"You have trouble sleeping?" Vithos asked.

"No, that's not...I mean can you do *this* to a Krepp." Zoke lifted the fish and shook it. "This fish won't wake even though it's suffocating."

Vithos smiled in a way that made Zoke regret his question. "I'm unaware of my full abilities because they've never been tested. If you're asking if I could put you in such a deep slumber that even submerged underwater you wouldn't wake, then the answer is"—Vithos stared into Zoke's eyes and then toward the tranquil waters of Lake Lensa—"maybe."

He'd hoped for a different answer.

"Want to help me test it?" Vithos asked with a frightening smile.

"No."

If this was Vithos' sense of humor, the trip would feel even longer than he'd first thought.

Zoke began to cut into the fish, explaining the process of removing the entrails as he went. They ate the meat raw, following it with kupota to fill the emptiness in their bellies.

After they finished eating, Vithos' mood grew serious again. Zoke could tell he was finally going to hear what he'd been waiting for. He could see it in the Elf's eyes, and it made his full stomach clench, causing him to feel nauseous.

"I'll now tell you what I've been regretting to say." Vithos puffed in air and then exhaled loudly. "First, you should know we're going northwest to Merejic, and we're not looking for the Slugari colony."

Chapter 16: Wrong Answer
ZOKE

Merejic...

It took a moment before Zoke could place it on the map of Ovira in his mind. "The great forest west of Nor? What'll we be doing there, and why aren't we looking for the Slugari colony?"

"We're ignoring Doe's order—it was delusive anyway. Let me explain." Vithos tensed his shoulders. "I believe Doe and Haemon want me dead and have for some time. But like you, they don't know what I'm fully capable of, so they haven't made an attempt on my life in fear it would fail and I would retaliate. Sending me off to Nor was just a way to get rid of me safely. For all I know, they may have sent Krepps after me—after us, I mean. Even if not, I'm confident they've already moved the encampment."

He's gone mad with paranoia! Zoke tried to hold back a judgmental look, but he realized there was no point. The Elf probably could sense his cynicism anyway. Zoke figured he might as well ask exactly what he was thinking.

"How can you possibly believe that?" He decided to leave off the part about Vithos being insane...for now.

"It's true. They want me dead." Vithos stated it with such seriousness that Zoke was afraid to argue back. The Elf's tone remained that way as he continued, staring deep into Zoke's eyes. "I've been sensing their ill-harbored emotions toward me in recent years, and the responses I've received from them to certain questions about my past have tipped me off. I don't expect you to understand yet, but you should trust that I'm confident they wish to get rid of me." Vithos' glance shifted south toward the land they'd already traveled. He held his hand over eyes for a better view and took a long breath before turning back to Zoke.

"Now that you're out here with me, this involves you as well," Vithos said. "It's best we start working together more." He started north, keeping one eye on Zoke as he went. "First, we're going to Merejic so I can look for answers about what really happened to my family."

Zoke didn't move. "Stop!" he ordered. His chest tightened with fear, for he'd never disobeyed Vithos before. But he couldn't let this madness continue. "Even if you're right, I don't want to be a part of this." He turned south. "I'm going back."

"As I said, the camp has been moved, and even if you somehow find them, you'll be killed as soon as you're seen." Vithos raised his voice as he continued to shout after Zoke. "That's why I needed to wait to share this with you! I didn't want you to return before they moved or you would be given a traitor's death!"

Traitor's death? That stopped Zoke. "Why would I be considered a traitor? I've followed every order. My loyalty is with Doe and Haemon and the tribe. You truly are insane."

Vithos tilted his head and squinted. The insult had clearly offended him, but he kept his voice low and strong. "Think about this through their perspective. They want me dead, and they must assume that I know that because of my psychic ability. To protect themselves, they've sent me off and moved the camp. That was the whole point of this fake mission—to get rid of me. Even if you returned without me, they would still assume you were on my side, so they must have given orders to kill you. They don't care about your life. As long as there's a small chance of you leading me to them, they would eliminate you."

Zoke couldn't believe it. Vithos didn't sound like he was lying...but still. *Me—a traitor?* It couldn't be right. He wouldn't be cast out from the tribe simply for following an order. And what about his sister? His head was spinning.

"Zeti wouldn't leave with them," Zoke stated firmly. "She would wait for me. Other Krepps may not have left as well." He thought of Grayol next. Neither of them would think he was a traitor. But then he thought of Dentar. *He always considered me a traitor just for following orders...could others as well?*

"Why would Doe and Haemon give her, or any of them, the choice?" Vithos opened his palms. "Any Krepps remaining in the camp have the chance of communicating with me later if I returned. That makes them a threat. Zeti either left with them or they killed her." Vithos knelt to clean his hands with lake water. "I'm curious what they discovered that could be used to find the Slugari now that they no longer need me."

"I don't care about that! I don't care about Merejic or what happened there! You don't need me for this!" Zoke threw the bag of food at Vithos. "You should've told me this before we left! You could've given me the option to stay."

"Unfortunately that's not true." Vithos sighed and slowly rose. "Your fate was determined as soon as I chose you as my companion. If you'd stayed after that, they would have considered you a possible traitor and killed you." Vithos walked over and scooped up their bag to check on the rope keeping it closed. "I thought you would want to come. You've always seemed to enjoy your work with me, and the other Krepps treat you no better than they do a weed." Now Vithos was firm, glaring even. "You've even admitted you have no interest in eating Slugari. So what reason did you have to stay?"

Zoke was so frustrated he couldn't contain it any longer. He screamed as loud as he could, "I wouldn't have left Zeti!" He wanted to draw his sword, but all he had was the stick. Nonetheless, he aimed it at Vithos, unsure why.

Vithos frowned, and a silence followed that was so thick Zoke thought he could hear his shout echoing over the land. Vithos turned back to the water and lowered his head.

"I didn't realize that." He spoke with the softness that only comes from deep regret. "Most of you Krepps regard family with such indifference. I didn't consider you might be unlike them, but I should have." Vithos sighed. "You've always been different, and without that I would've never been able to trust you. Any other Krepp would kill me while I sleep and bring my head to Doe after hearing what I just told you."

"How do you know I won't?" Zoke asked, anger still pulsing with each beat of his thundering heart.

Vithos turned. A bored look came across his face. "Because I know you, even if you don't know me. To prove it to you, I'll even ask and tell you if you lie. Do you have any intention of killing me?"

Although Zoke was still upset, he knew the thought of severing the Elf's head was no task he would ever choose. "No, but I'd like to hit you with this stick right now." He gestured with it. "I'm sure you're aware I'm very angry."

Vithos smiled. "Yes." He approached Zoke with an arm extended. "Go ahead. Pass judgment on me."

Zoke lifted the stick but didn't strike. *Is this some sort of trick?*

"I know you want to," Vithos encouraged. "One hard whack. I

deserve it."

Still, Zoke refused to move. There was much to consider first. *Does hitting him demonstrate I think he's right about all this? Because I don't. There's no way they moved the entire camp just because of Vithos. There's no way. But if I don't believe him, why am I so mad? Maybe some part of me does believe him...thinks it could be true.* "How sure are you about all this?" he decided to ask.

"I'm certain. Have you ever known me to be wrong about Doe or Haemon?"

No. But he couldn't say it aloud. It would be too close to admitting defeat. "There must be some way out of this, some way to see Zeti again."

Vithos was nodding. His arm remained steady, waiting to be struck. "I'm sure we can find a way."

Zoke tried to remain angry but couldn't. There was still too much he didn't know. There was still a chance the camp hadn't been moved, and he was nowhere near accepting that he would never see Zeti again. It would take far more than one conversation to extinguish that hope. Vithos needed some punishment, though. The Elf had deceived him, dragged him into something that could change the course of his entire life.

"For your actions, you'll receive a physical punishment." He imitated Vithos as best he could, raising his pitch and lowering his head to stare from the tops of his eyes.

He raised the stick over his head with a mix of anger, hesitation, and excitement. It was a privilege to be the first Krepp to pass judgment on Vithos—a fantasy shared by all Krepps. He'd heard many stories about what others would do to Vithos if the roles were reversed.

Not as good as hitting Doe or Haemon, but still good.

"Don't break it," Vithos said.

Zoke inspected the stick. While somewhat thin, the wood was sturdy. "I wouldn't worry about it."

"No, don't break my arm. I'm going to need it."

"Endure," he said, promising nothing.

"Endure."

With half his strength, he brought down the stick onto the smooth, pale skin of the Elf. The force of the blow caused Vithos to wince through his teeth.

"Judgment has passed." Zoke spoke with ample satisfaction, watching as Vithos hopped in circles and nursed his arm.

"I feel a little better," Zoke said truthfully. "But don't think you've swayed me completely." He pointed his stick again. "I'm still considering returning to camp."

"We can return together so that you can see everyone has left, but first come with me to Merejic. I need your help, and we've already gone this far."

My help with what? Though curious, Zoke couldn't decide if he wished to follow the Elf farther north or turn back.

Vithos must have seen it in his yellow eyes, for he spoke up again. "I realize it's difficult to trust me, but going back now would prove to be useless unless you're planning to live in the wild alone for the rest of your life. Stay with me, and we'll devise a plan for you and Zeti to be together again. I believe it'll coincide with my current strategy for Doe and Haemon."

"Which is what?"

"*Vantikar*," the Elf uttered.

Zoke felt chills from the word and the hard glare that followed.

The word itself meant revenge through killing whoever wronged you. Perhaps because of some psychic spell, Zoke grew too afraid to ask any more of the Elf. That didn't stop him from wondering, though. *What did Doe and Haemon do to you?* Zoke found no scars on Vithos like on others who'd disobeyed the leaders of the tribe.

"I'll continue with you for now." Zoke didn't believe any other choice was better. "But I might change my mind later." *Especially if I find out there's more you should've told me.*

Chapter 17: Death and Secrets
ZOKE

By midday, the western coastline came into view as they walked northwest. Now three days from the camp, the breeze felt fresher against Zoke's face, the grass greener, even the water in the ocean looked clearer. Zoke had never been this far north. They were still in Slepja, home of their encampment—unless it really had been moved like Vithos said—but it was beginning to feel like a different territory. Zoke soon wondered if this was what all of Slepja used to be like before the tens of thousands of Krepps came to live on its southern end.

Each hour presented a new hill to climb and then descend. The more hills they traversed, the more bushes, shrubs, and even trees could be seen. Eventually, Zoke saw the first animal since they'd left: a bluebird perched on a tree. It took off north just as Zoke glanced at it, as if startled by the sight of him.

When the last light of the sun was gone, they found a thick stretch of grass to spend the night. They hadn't spoken since Vithos revealed that he wanted to kill Doe and Haemon. Zoke was still too nervous to ask about the reasoning. Each time he considered bringing it up, tightness welled up in his throat, choking down his words.

Just after their twists and turns to find comfort on the ground ceased, and silence started to blanket Zoke in a calming embrace, Vithos disrupted it with his voice. "I've always wished I had a sibling, someone who has some idea what it's like to be me."

Zoke's eyes popped open from the surprising statement. *Why is he telling me this? What does he want me to say?*

There was the distinct sound of Vithos sitting up. "Is it like that with Zeti? Does she know what it's like to be you?" There was open curiosity in Vithos' voice, reminding Zoke of Grayol. Never did Zoke think he would find any connection between the two of them. Grayol was still at the young age of being incautiously curious about everything, while Vithos was wise, finding truth in situations when no one else could. But his tone in this question was just like that of

Grayol's: childlike.

"I suppose she does. Not entirely, though, she's no *gurradu*, nor is she too short. But if anyone knows what my life is like besides me, it's her."

Vithos slowly reclined again. "Yes, I think I'd like that."

Zoke's cavernous mouth stretched open for a yawn. For just that brief moment, he wondered what it was like to be Vithos, to be raised by Doe and Haemon, to serve them, to be the only Elf, and now to want to kill them. It was too much to consider for longer than a yawn, at least right then. Instead, he let his heavy eyes close once again.

The next day, there were even more hills. Zoke was beginning to hate them even worse than the barren flatlands. By sundown, they'd come far enough to the coast that the sound of the waves crashing could be heard if Zoke and Vithos were completely silent. However, Zoke's focus was drawn instead to Vithos as the Elf finally spoke, and with heavy disdain, about the Slugari who'd raised him.

"Doe and Haemon must know of my interest to visit Merejic, so we can't stay there long, just long enough for me to search for clues about what really happened before I was taken by them. When I was a child, Doe and Haemon told me that they and the Krepps found me abandoned in the woods, left for dead by my family." Zoke had heard this story before from other Krepps, and it had ended there. Vithos continued, though.

"When I got older and my psyche was stronger, I discovered that specifics related to the story were being kept from me, like what happened to the other Elves? Asking Doe or Haemon would only lead to physical punishments. If I asked a Krepp who was old enough to know, the Krepp would tell the same story as any other and notify Doe or Haemon that I'd asked about it. Again, I would be punished."

Vithos rubbed his arm as if reliving an old punishment. "My own concept of what really happened started forming in my adolescence and continued to take shape as I picked up more clues. I'm fairly certain now that my parents didn't leave me in the woods to die. Even Krepps wouldn't do that to their children."

Zoke spat. "I'm not so sure that's true about father to me," he muttered.

If Vithos heard him, he ignored the comment. He kept his eyes forward, focusing on the hill approaching. "Though I don't remember my parents, I somehow know they cared for me deeply. Perhaps I was old enough to know of their affection when we were separated. I *was* old enough to know my name, so it's a possibility. Understanding the mentality of Doe and Haemon, it makes more sense that they attacked the Elves and took me, not that the Elves left me to die."

For the first time, Zoke felt that Vithos might be looking for compassion. "If I were old enough to know, I'd tell you what happened," he said, not knowing what else the Elf wanted to hear.

"Then you'd be dead," Vithos replied, utterly deadpan.

It was true, he realized. He'd seen Krepps killed for less, which reminded him of something he'd wanted to ask since they'd left. "Do you know what Doe and Haemon do with the eppil plants? Why are we killed just for entering the garden that contains them?"

"They melt them between their claws like some sort of potion and drink it. It's how they are so large and their magic is that powerful. Without the eppil plants, Doe and Haemon are nothing. When I was younger, they allowed me a taste after months of begging, but my body rejected it, causing me to throw up continuously until nothing remained in my stomach."

Zoke wasn't shocked by this, somewhat relieved even. He'd expected the plants to be extremely valuable to his leaders, hoped for it even, as his mother was killed because of them. If she'd died for absolutely nothing, it would have only frustrated him more. It was strange to feel relief when considering his mother's death, Zoke realized, but it was what he felt nonetheless and was impossible to take back now that it had happened.

A new question formed in his mind. "What happens if a Krepp drinks the eppil plant potion?"

"We can't know. Any Krepp to have even touched one has been incinerated by Doe publicly to show everyone what happens to those who try."

Like mother to me, Zoke almost said aloud. But he held back. There was no point in bringing her up.

He'd been too young when she'd died to mourn her now. Instead, curiosity about why she'd entered the eppil garden was what had stuck with him these many years. He refused to believe his father's theory—that she'd wished to die. He'd hoped Vithos had information about the eppil plants that would give him insight about what she was doing there, but unfortunately that wasn't the case.

The sky had become crimson in the last hour. They ventured a hill, and the thick forest of Merejic came into view. A line of trees stood side-by-side like sentinels, as if to guard the entrance. He'd never seen trees clustered so closely. Each one was touching at least two others.

"It's..." Zoke couldn't describe how the forest made him feel. In Kreppen, there weren't many words for beauty or grandeur. He almost said *majestic* in common tongue but knew Vithos didn't speak the language.

"It's something," Vithos said, sounding more eager than anything else.

"Imposing and peaceful at the same time," Zoke concluded.

"We won't reach it by nightfall. Let's find a place to sleep."

They descended the hillside and found a cove on the beach where the wind wouldn't disturb them. A wide stretch of sand separated them from the dark blue sea, and a slab of mountainside from Merejic hooked into view from the north. "Is that where we're headed?" Zoke asked, pointing to the mountainside.

"Not quite. The Elven city lies in the center of Merejic, so we don't have to travel as far as the edge. Does this mean you've decided with certainty you're coming with me?"

Zoke was reluctant to reply. No words came to mind that accurately described how he felt. He could feel the Elf's pain when he spoke of Doe and Haemon, but Zoke was still angry with him at the same time. Finally, he just said, "Not with certainty."

Chapter 18: Let's Play
ZOKE

They both agreed the cove provided adequate safety for each to sleep the entire night. There was only one way in from land, and even with the ocean waves nearby, it was quiet enough for them to wake under the rare circumstance they were found.

Sleep came easy to Zoke. He didn't dream that night, not that he could remember. When he awoke, Vithos was standing in the sea with his leather pants rolled up, peering out over the water. The sun brightened the clear sky, but half of the beach was still shrouded in shadow. Zoke's back and bottom were damp, and he was a bit chilled. His empty stomach called to him, so he approached Vithos.

"Are there fish?" he asked.

"Yes, and there is a large creature looking for fish as well."

Zoke took a step back. "Where?"

"Close, around thirty yards in front of us." Vithos pointed toward the waves ahead. "It's smarter than a fish, yet well below the intelligence of a Krepp. I'm curious as to what it is. Want to find out?"

"How big is it?" Zoke asked, taking another step back from the dark blue water.

"Can't be sure," Vithos said happily. "But because of the way it carries itself confidently, I'd assume large."

"Could it be a *gektar*?" Just saying the word made the memory of the beast clear as the sky above.

Six years ago, when Zoke was ten—*pra durren,* a dead *gektar* had washed up on the beach where the Krepps fished. It was too large for anyone to move, so those who wished to see it needed to complete their weekly tasks to the tribe. Then they were allowed to join an escorted group that walked the two-day trek to the beach. The sight of the monster from the sea showed up in Zoke's dreams for months after.

It was the first *gektar* any living Krepp within the tribe had seen. Each of its many tentacles was as long as a massive tree and as wide as a full-grown Krepp. Those who saw it the first day it was beached said the suction cups on the tentacles still attached to anyone who touched them—Zoke was glad he didn't see that. The body and head of the beast appeared to be the same part, the middle, where each tentacle was connected. That's where its eyes were, two massive spheres stuck open and half buried in the sand. But worst of all was its mouth, which was large enough to easily fit a full-grown Krepp.

Those with Zoke's group wanted to see its teeth and Zeti, at just six—*pra durren,* volunteered to hold down its lower jaw. Zoke stood at a safe distance, petrified, as his minuscule sister climbed onto the monster's face. When she pried open its mouth, he saw that each tooth was at least her size. She even reached a claw inside to feel the sharpness of one. Vithos had visited the beach that day to see the *gektar* as well. Zoke remembered seeing him there.

Now Vithos found the knife on his belt and drew it. "Could be." His voice was playful, like he was somehow enthusiastic about finding a *gektar*. "I have no way to be sure without seeing it."

Vithos placed his free hand in the water and pulled out a fish after a few quick breaths. "Here," he said, handing their breakfast to Zoke along with the knife. "Take this back to the cove. I want to see what creature is in front of us. I love playing with confident animals."

Zoke gladly returned to the mountainside to watch from a safe distance, removing the head of the fish along the way.

Vithos cautiously backed into shallower water while pointing his palm out to sea. Zoke watched, a nervous feeling taking the place of what used to be hunger in his stomach.

It happened so quickly, Zoke found himself bumping into the mountainside when he tried to move back even farther. A dorsal fin cut through the water, and Vithos began retreating. The speed of the fin increased as it headed toward the shore where Vithos now stood. The fin submerged, and for a heartbeat Zoke couldn't find it, but then the next wave broke. The fearsome face of a great white shark came at Vithos with its teeth bared. Vithos' other hand shot forward, and the shark twisted and spun in the shallow water.

Vithos created more distance, retreating farther from the water as the shark turned left, right, back, and then forward.

Vithos let his hands rest and sprinted. The shark chased after him, even onto the sand, until it couldn't use its momentum to move any farther.

Giving up, the shark shimmied back into the sea, and Vithos cackled with excitement.

Zoke was disgusted by what he'd just seen. *How is he amused by this? He must have a death wish.* "You play with sharks, you're bound to be bit."

But Vithos just continued to laugh.

Zoke sighed, slowly feeling the nervousness seep out of him. "What did you do to stop it?" He was curious, figuring it had to be some sort of psychic spell that caused the shark to twirl in the shallow water. He'd never seen anything like that in the judgment chambers.

With a big smile, Vithos said, "I won't be able to explain it, so I'll show you."

"No, don't..." But it was too late. Vithos reached his hand toward Zoke. Spots of bright colors began flashing in front of all else. It was like looking directly at the sun through a thousand rainbows. He closed his eyes to escape it, yet colorful dots continued to flash under his eyelids.

He screamed for it to stop, and then it did, as abruptly as it began.

"I'm not sure what to call it, but in my mind I label it 'mesmerize,' " Vithos said proudly.

Zoke spat. Anger surged through his veins, and he was barely able to keep himself from screaming. "That makes it sound more tolerable than it really is! It should be called 'torture.' "

"No, I already have something by that name, want to—"

"If you do, I'll beat you with my stick." Zoke pointed it at Vithos and spat again. "You were almost killed by a shark, yet you laugh. You waste energy entertaining yourself at my expense with the offer of doing it again right after. You're acting like a child!" Zoke felt a wave of dizziness come and then pass. He held his head and took a breath, remembering his hunger.

"No," Vithos answered sternly. "My childhood was nothing like this, and that's the problem." A solemn silence fell over them, and Vithos breathed in slowly. "Don't you see? For the first time I'm free to do what I want, and you as well."

Zoke would have spit again, but he'd run out of saliva for the moment. "Except for return to the tribe." Zoke spoke as contemptuously as he could.

Vithos scrunched his face. "If you really wish to return, I won't stop you, but you have a better chance of swimming past the shark to Grendor Isle than finding the tribe and joining them again." Vithos pointed across fifty miles of ocean at the mountainous island and waited for the impossibility of the task to sink in. "After searching the Elven town in Merejic for clues, we'll return to the camp so that you can see I was right about everything." Vithos' shoulders relaxed and his head turned back to Zoke. "Let's work together to get what we want."

Zoke approached Vithos, giving the Elf a hard look to show how serious he was. "No more psyche on me. Don't even ask to use it."

Vithos nodded slowly, regretfully.

They ate quickly and quietly, listening only to the sounds of the tide. Zoke was a slow eater, as Zeti repeatedly told him. It gave Zoke time to think. He stared at Vithos, feeling like it was the first time he was really seeing the Elf for who he was. After all the years they'd worked together, Zoke had never seen Vithos smile or laugh. He was always reserved to a point of predictability, even. But Vithos had surprised him so many times in the last five days, Zoke no longer had any idea what the Elf would do next. It was like traveling with a wild animal—one with immeasurable power. The thought sent a chill through his reptilian body.

When Vithos was done eating, he simply closed his eyes and waited quietly, completely at peace, or so it seemed.

"I'm ready," Zoke said when his meal was consumed, eager to break the silence. As he stood, the top of the sun burst over the hill, hitting his skin with a tingle of satisfaction.

Vithos opened his eyes and glanced around cautiously, like he expected to find someone spying on them. "We should be able to reach Merejic before lunch if we hurry."

They climbed the steep hills on the edge of the sand to return to where they were the evening before. Even in its second viewing, the mystery and beauty of the forest touched somewhere deep within Zoke, but that didn't take away the sense of danger it gave him. *What will we find in there?* He'd heard nothing of Merejic, and he'd never been in a forest before.

A dark thought came to him. *Or what will find us?*

Chapter 19: Evaluation Week Begins
CLEVE

"Practice, patience, and progress. You may have heard it before, but not many know it came from here, from this very field, where students like yourselves have learned to become true warriors for twenty-two years."

Cleve stood alongside forty-nine other students, thankful for the booming tone of the teacher addressing them. It helped him focus—a task he'd found nearly impossible since the terror that had gripped him that morning when he'd realized his bow was missing.

The teacher was a thick man, a mass of fat and muscle, and must have been older than forty. From the look of the man's hardened face, leathered from years in the sun, Cleve figured many of those years had been spent on Warrior's Field, where he himself would be much of the next three years, unless his missing bow wound up putting him in the dungeons.

"Evaluation week starts now," his teacher bellowed. "For those who don't know, that means every warrior and every mage will be judged during this time. When the week is over, each of you will be placed in the appropriate group that matches your skill level. Luckily for us, the mages are judged separately from the warriors and kept far from this field, where they can cast fire without risk of injuring the class that makes up two-thirds of the King's Guard: the warriors. Unluckily for you thick-skulled men, you're going to have to listen to some math in this next part.

"First of all, when I say warriors, I mean student warriors. No matter who you think you are, you're not officially a warrior of Kyrro until your three years here are completed. Now listen closely. Three thousand students attend the Academy. They're split evenly into three grades: first-year, second-year, and third-year. That means there are how many per grade? You." The instructor pointed at someone far down the line.

"One thousand," he answered somewhat sheepishly.

"One thousand," the instructor repeated loudly. "Out of those one thousand per grade, five hundred are warriors, three hundred are mages, one hundred and fifty are chemists, and fifty are psychics, or claim to be psychics at least, and were convincing enough to the recruiter." The instructor clapped his hands once loudly. "Pay attention. I know that's a lot of numbers, especially for a group of half-wit young men, but the important part is still to come. Five hundred warriors per grade, that makes how many in the school? You." He pointed at another student warrior Cleve couldn't see from where he stood.

"Fifteen hundred." The answer sounded like a whisper.

"Five hundred multiplied by three is fifteen hundred," the instructor repeated, even louder than before. "The Champion title, how many have heard of it?" He waited for every warrior to raise his hand. "As I expected. Each year, only three—*only three*—of those one thousand five hundred warriors will receive this very prestigious title, just one warrior from each grade. This title comes with a certificate. It's an indication of tenacity, overall ability, and dedication to the warrior class. So not surprisingly, the most questions I get are about the title, which is why we discuss it on the first day now. There is only *one way* to receive it, and it has nothing to do with evaluation week." The instructor held a single finger and met each student's eyes one by one. He repeated it three times as he looked down the line, "One way...one way...one way. And that is to win Redfield."

None of this was new information to Cleve, but he heard whispers and hums of understanding from others that suggested they hadn't known.

"Some of you may believe that the only way to be selected to compete in Redfield is by placing well in evaluation week. This...is...not...true." Each of his last four words was yelled in staccato. "Not all Redfield competitors are selected from Group One. Instead, the selection is based purely on every student's independent abilities. So even if you do not place in Group One, that does not mean you should give up. Practice, patience, and progress. Remember these words throughout the year and follow them. Practice what you're told, be patient with yourself, your teacher, and your fellow students, and keep track of how you progress, find out what works for you, and utilize that.

"Lastly, who knows how many student warriors will graduate with a certificate stamped by the King, the certificate that officially recognizes them as warriors? You, what do you think?" He pointed down the line again.

"Most of the third-years?" the nervous student replied, just loud enough for Cleve to hear.

"All of them! Every year, all of our warriors have graduated, and each first-year and second-year warrior has moved up to the next grade. Twenty-two years this has happened, and this year will be no different. Follow our rules to ensure this is the case: Do not do anything to decapitate yourself or anyone else. Do not do anything to break bones or lose limbs—yours or anyone else's. Do not speak ill of the King or of your instructors. Do not drink alcohol during training, and do not show up drunk or hungover. I will repeat that—*do not* drink during training or step on this grass drunk or hungover! You can get silly and stupid on your own time, but when you're on this field, it's time to work. This grass is to remain clear of alcohol, piss, and vomit, three things that go along with drunken warriors.

"Now, jog a lap around our section to warm up your body because we're starting with duels. Let's go." The instructor clapped his hands twice. "Move!"

They hurried off like a herd of sheep, zipping around the square section of field designated for their groups of fifty for evaluation week. Their instructor barked commands at them from the center. "Don't cut corners! Stay together!"

As Cleve jogged, he wondered the same thing that had been bothering him all morning. *Who has my bow, and what will happen to it?* He figured it was unlikely that one of the King's men was involved because he hadn't been arrested yet. That meant that someone had stolen it, but only his roommates and Terren knew of its existence, or so he'd thought until speaking with Alex last night.

While some memories of last night couldn't have been clearer, mostly those with Reela, many were riddled with holes. Reela had told him that Alex knew something about him, something Alex had really wanted to say. Cleve remembered that clearly enough. He also remembered most of his conversation with Reela before talking to Alex.

Something had started Reela on a path of guessing everything she could about Cleve. "You're not ticklish," she'd said and then quickly added, "You don't bruise easily. You've never broken a bone. You can't remember laughing so hard you cried. Am I right so far?"

It was a dangerous path, a psychic starting at his skin, moving deeper through muscle and bone, getting to raw emotions underneath. If she kept at it, she was likely to discover something he didn't want her to find.

"Yes. What about you?" he asked in an attempt to shift focus away from himself.

"What about me?" she asked back with a playful smile.

"Those same things, what are your answers?"

"I don't bruise easily. I've never broken a bone. The last time I laughed so hard I cried was a couple months ago." She didn't let her eyes off him as she sipped from her glass.

"And ticklish?" It felt strange to ask her but still better than the mute stare Cleve found himself slipping into when she stopped talking. He hated how his eyes were always drawn to her.

"I'm only ticklish when I'm not expecting it," she answered. "Surprises can be quite powerful. When we're not prepared for something, it's far easier to become emotional and act in ways we normally wouldn't." The way she raised her eyebrows at him made it seem as if she was referring to something about him.

Is she saying I surprise her? Just the mere idea of having any effect on Reela's emotions caused his breath to catch in his throat. He couldn't even formulate a full thought. The silence had grown too long. He needed to say something. "What do you mean?" was what came out.

"So you're telling me it's *normal* for you to wildly spit out drinks as you've already done twice tonight?" She seemed to be holding back a laugh.

"Oh, that," Cleve chuckled in relief, and she joined him. "No, you're right. I wouldn't have spit if I wasn't so surprised by the taste." His heart calmed.

When their laughing subsided, she said, "It's not often that I find something to be surprising. It seems to be the same for you?"

He nodded. "But that's not because I don't surprise easily. Surprise just doesn't find me. There's no room for it in my day, too much routine." As he reflected on those words now, he was amazed by how much surprise had reached him since then. Just waking up to find his bow missing was enough shock for a lifetime.

"Let's change that." She'd taken his hand and tried to pull him toward Alex. "Come on, let's confront him," she'd said. "Find out what he knows about you." Even though Cleve was half numb from the liquor, her touch gave him chills of pleasure that made it nearly impossible to let go, but somehow he managed to slip free.

"I'd like to speak to him alone," he'd told Reela. He figured Alex knew something of his family and didn't wish for Reela to be there in case he became emotional. As if she'd known it was just a matter of pride, she'd nodded with an understanding smile.

She's always smiling, Cleve thought as he reflected on his memories of last night, *but I hardly know what about.*

Alex hadn't denied knowing something of Cleve, but Cleve remembered being stunned to find out what it was. "My brother told me they're looking for someone proficient with the bow," Alex had said. "And you're being investigated. He said they're looking into the son of Dex Polken, Cleve Polken. That's you, correct?"

Cleve couldn't recall his own answer or anything else of that seemingly important conversation with Alex. He didn't understand why that was, especially when he could remember not only what had been said with Reela, but also what he'd felt during each turn of their conversation.

He'd hoped to find Alex on Warrior's Field to speak about it again but hadn't spotted him yet.

When the lap was finished, Cleve focused to prepare himself for duels. He expected he would be more nervous about them if his missing bow wasn't causing far worse alarm. He'd dueled many times but only against Terren. Cleve worried that he'd learned to fight the man, not the sword, so he was concerned someone who fought differently than his uncle might use techniques to which he wasn't accustomed.

I guess I'll find out soon enough, Cleve thought, taking a slow breath to ready himself.

Chapter 20: Hitting Hard and Clean
CLEVE

"Gather in front of me here," the instructor boomed. He had a sword drawn now and pointed it at the grass ahead of him. "Some of you may have different dueling rules where you came from, but at the Academy they are as follows: All duels must be done on Warrior's Field. All duels must be with wooden dueling swords while you're wearing protective dueling tunics. You will not use your mouth during the duel, which means no spitting or biting, and keep talking to a minimum. These are civilized fights. The first combatant to disarm or strike the other is the victor, so long as the strike is hard and clean. Strikes can be made with the blade or hilt of the sword, or with your fist, elbow, knee, or foot, but not your head. The last thing we need is two imbeciles slamming heads."

The instructor glanced at the papers on his clipboard. "First to duel are Cleve Polken and Fez Betson. Polken..." His eyes lifted curiously to Cleve. "Any relation to Terren Polken, the head of school?"

"He's my uncle," Cleve answered indifferently, hoping his tone would prevent any future discussion of it. If people thought about it more, they would realize that Terren needed a brother or sister for Cleve to exist, and that would only lead to more questions about his family.

"Well then, let's see how well he taught you. Both of you step forward."

His opponent had thick brown hair that came down wildly across his forehead, but the fuzzy splotches of hair across his cheeks and chin were faint, almost blonde, seeming to belong on another man's face. His eyes were hard and glared into Cleve's. His face was nonthreatening, though. It was without edges, long to the chin, which made his expression to show more anxiety than aggression.

"Ready your weapons," the instructor announced.

Pretend he's the one who took your bow, Cleve told himself so he could draw his sword without showing his reluctance to hurt the likely innocent man in front of him.

Cleve could feel everyone's eyes on him. This was when he was most comfortable, with a weapon and an opponent...and an audience only amplified the excitement. He wanted to give them a show but wisely knew to focus instead on winning. He breathed slowly to calm himself, drawing Bastial Energy into his hands, one molded around the hilt of his sword and the other relaxed at his hip, closed and set. Fez held his weapon loosely, swaying back and forth.

"Using one hand to make a point or do you actually fight like that?" Fez teased.

"It's this hand you should watch out for." Cleve wiggled the fingers of his left hand.

"Without the drama, *men*," the instructor said. "Fight."

Fez was as quick as Cleve expected, hopping toward him with feints, but Cleve knew himself to be even faster. He waited for Fez to commit to a strike and then deflected it with his wooden sword, driving his left fist into Fez's stomach. His wiry opponent doubled over in reflex, and Cleve backed away.

"One for Cleve," the instructor announced. "We fight until two strikes are made. Ready your weapons."

If Fez was in pain, he hid it well. "You move quickly for a man built like an ironbark stump, but I'll find a weakness."

"It's that I like to show off," Cleve answered. It's what Terren had always told him and a good intro to what he had planned for the next bout. Leading by a point, he wished to take the opportunity to give his future opponents something to fear.

"Shall I find two toothpicks for you to fight with your mouths? Enough talk!" The instructor cut his hand through the air. "Fight!"

Cleve was now the one moving in and out of range with feints while his opponent positioned himself more cautiously. He needed to understand Fez's defensive tendencies for his next move to work. He let his opponent come at him. After backing away from a quick flurry of swings, Cleve was ready to retaliate. With Bastial Energy bubbling in his legs, he ran toward Fez. It was no more than three steps before he leaped, flipping with a spin. He hadn't practiced solely for scaring off bears, after all.

He brought down the meat of his sword on Fez, who was only quick enough to raise his weapon in defense. Cleve's sword crashed against wood so hard, at first he thought his blunt dueling sword had somehow cut through Fez's weapon. Instead, he saw that the force of his blow had loosened the weapon from Fez's hand and knocked him over in the process. Cleve put a foot on the disarmed weapon, with his own aimed at his opponent's face.

He heard a few whistles from the crowd, but they were interrupted by the unimpressed tone of the instructor. "The duel goes to Cleve. Next time try to get the point without risk of shattering a man's skull. We're all on the same side here."

Cleve extended a hand to Fez, uncertain if he would take it, as his face was filled with shock. Soon, though, Fez's eyes mellowed and his mouth opened slightly in defeat. He accepted Cleve's hand and was smiling by the time he was back on his feet.

"Do you have springs in your shoes?" Fez quipped. "I was so shaken by the sight of a gigantic man flying that I forgot to move."

Cleve won the rest of his duels just as easily and with less flair. Fez and he spoke as they watched the others fight. It turned out Fez was from Trentyre, where Cleve had been born as well. Cleve had lived there until he was ten, which is when Terren was offered the job as headmaster and moved to the Academy, bringing Cleve with him. Cleve didn't mention this, though. Nor did he offer anything else from his past.

Fez won the rest of his duels as well, but he took a strike in many of them, as did most of the other victors. Cleve couldn't have been more pleased with himself, being the only one not to have given up a point. By the end of it hours later, Cleve was one of only six who weren't sitting on the grass, exhausted or nursing a wound.

"We're done for today, *men*. Tomorrow we look at technique and accuracy with the sword and throwing knives. Then the day after is my favorite: the rightly infamous endurance testing. This gives you two days for any wounds to heal before the endurance testing begins. I do not recommend any further duels until then. Think of it like preparing for battle. Bring your real swords tomorrow. We'll supply the throwing knives. You're dismissed."

A soft mumbling among students could be detected through the busy noise of each person picking himself up. Fez came over to walk alongside Cleve. "I've heard Warrior Sneary is a strict judge of form," he said.

Cleve had seen their instructor in the years he'd lived at the Academy but had never known his name or reputation. "Why didn't he introduce himself?" Cleve suddenly wondered aloud after hearing the name for the first time.

"When does a man not give his name? I can think of two reasons," Fez said. "If he doesn't believe it to be important, or he has a reputation he would rather not be known. I could imagine him providing either answer if we were to ask."

"I won't be asking." Terren had told Cleve not to ask teachers personal questions, especially warrior teachers.

"Neither will I."

There were hundreds of students walking from Warrior's Field to their campus houses. Cleve searched for the thick black hair he remembered of Alex. He found some with hair of the same color, but none were of the same height or build.

"You're the only one who beat me," Fez said.

"I noticed."

"I would like a rematch tomorrow after class is finished. Do you accept?"

Warriors don't reject the challenge of a duel, Terren had told him. *To do so is the same as losing.* Cleve thought of Warrior Sneary's recommendation to avoid combat until endurance day was done. It sounded like good advice, but as he glanced at Warrior's Field and saw dozens of students still there dueling each other, it became impossible to follow.

"I accept. Bring your dueling sword and tunic tomorrow."

"Good. I'll be ready for your leaping this time."

"We shall see." Then Cleve spotted Alex, who was still out on the field, dueling. Excitement fluttered up into Cleve's chest from his stomach. He mumbled to Fez, "I need to speak with someone. Until tomorrow." Then he jogged back onto the field.

The duel had ended by the time Cleve reached the combatants, who were breathing heavily. Cleve couldn't tell who'd won, nor did he care. He rounded on Alex and said, "I need to speak with you."

"Cleve!" Alex sounded pleasantly surprised. "So speak. How were your duels?" He positioned himself for another bout with his opponent.

"I need to talk in private."

Alex let down his sword. "I'll give you another chance tomorrow if you like," he said to his opponent and followed Cleve to an open spot on the field. "I hope this is good news. You wish to notify me of your lovely roommate's infatuation with me?"

"What? Effie?" He'd seen them talking for some time but hadn't spoken to her since the party. "No, this is about much more serious matters. What do you know about the investigation we discussed last night?"

Alex nervously checked in each direction. "Did you tell someone? Is that why Javy Rayvender is here? What did you say? I should never have spoken to you about that." He suddenly seemed even more panicked than Cleve.

"I told no one. I'm trying to figure out something, and I can't remember everything you told me."

"It's better if you don't remember. It might help me stay out of the dungeons. I have no idea why I was so compelled to tell you last night. I think the unannounced threat of war has been pushing so hard on my conscience that I may be losing my mind. The war! I can't believe I brought that up either." Alex slapped his palm on his forehead.

He seemed to be in the need of consoling, but Cleve was in no mood. "Do you know that my bow was taken last night? It happened while I was at your house."

"I didn't even know you had a bow!" Alex whispered loudly. He held his face with two hands. "More secrets. A bow, why?"

Cleve maintained his serious tone, suppressing the hot frustration he could feel building within. "I need to know everything you know about this investigation."

Alex's eyes and mouth became rigid. "I told you everything I know last night."

"I *can't* remember what you told me." Some frustration slipped out in his tone.

Alex peered at someone over Cleve's shoulder. "He's back. Are you sure that no one knows I told you about the investigation?"

Cleve began to turn. "Who's back?" But Alex grabbed him.

"Don't look so obvious. You've never had a girl pointed out to you in a bar? I'll tell you when he turns away so you can look. It's Javy Rayvender. He's been nosing around Warrior's Field since class began today. He's a member of the King's Council. I was hoping they were looking for a promising warrior for some mission, but now I fear it may have to do with your bow." Alex's gaze drifted past Cleve once again. "He seems to be focused on writing something. You can take a quick look."

Cleve snapped his head around. Javy was dressed in a long black coat closed by two sets of buttons. Cleve *had* seen him that day, multiple times, in fact, as he was searching for Alex but hadn't known who Javy was. From a distance, the man had no discernible features. A black hat hung low over his eyes. He was neither fat nor thin, tall nor short. He had a way of blending naturally into his background, like a hawk perched atop a cliff.

"If the King's Council knew anything of my bow, wouldn't I have already been arrested?"

"You might think so, but you never know with King Welson. My brother says he's the most clever king that Kyrro has seen yet and also the most insidious, setting complex traps to catch people in illegal acts." Alex's eyes lit up. "Someone should put that into song." He shook his head and looked cautious again. "I don't like this, Cleve. Something is telling me we shouldn't even be talking. Are you certain you told no one about what I said?"

"I don't see how I could've when I don't even remember it."

Alex took two breaths to think. "Whatever is happening, I now feel involved. I can't understand why I told you about being investigated. If my brother knew, it would be the last time he spoke to me."

It was Reela, Cleve realized. *Would Alex even believe me if I told him a psychic persuaded him to speak the truth?* He decided that was a conversation best saved for another day, if ever.

"I still need to know everything you do about this investigation," Cleve stated firmly. "If you don't feel comfortable here with Javy watching, come back with me to my house. Effie may be there," *and Reela as well, in case there's any other information you're not telling me.* Cleve hated psyche, and the thought of using it deceitfully on a friend he'd just begun to trust made him sick with guilt, but finding his bow was far too important to jeopardize with ethics.

"Effie, yes. They say alcohol cures all that ails you, but I say that is truer about a beautiful woman. Although, both are known to cause vicious fighting." Alex made sure his sword was secure in its sheath and ran a hand through his hair. "Yes, let's go, but don't speak of you-know-what until we get there. Talk to me instead of your roommates. Remind me of their names. Who's the other girl, Reela was it?"

"Yes, Reela," *the psychic.*

“She has a sweet look about her. You’re fortunate to live with two attractive women.”

It was refreshing to hear another speak of Reela’s beauty. Steffen hadn’t mentioned how either Effie or Reela looked, so Cleve had concerns he was the only one to see Reela as he did. However, it still didn’t prove whether or not his affection was because of some psychic spell, as Alex could’ve been influenced by it, too.

“It’s not as great as you might think.”

Chapter 21: Chemists
STEFFEN

The day of his first class had finally come, but when Steffen awoke that morning, all his enthusiasm for learning had been drained. His thoughts, instead, were clouded by Gabby sneaking into his room last night as he lay naked and asleep in bed. And if that wasn't enough, he heard from Reela right after waking that Cleve's bow had been taken, and no one knew by whom.

The excitement he used to have about sitting in a classroom and listening to a teacher speak of chemistry had been pushed out of him by these recent events. It also didn't help that he was more than familiar with the material his professor said she would be covering that year.

His mother had encouraged his reading and practicing from the time he was old enough to understand words on a page. She'd said that all his effort would lead to a better future, but he wondered now, especially after last night, if he should've devoted at least some time to chasing after girls like the other boys did. He probably would be in the same place he was today, but he would know a little less of the material being covered that year and a little more about women, or girls, or whatever Gabby was to him. He hated being confused. *That's why I try not to think about the opposite sex*, he said to himself as he attempted to organize the thoughts flooding through his mind. *Warriors tend to know what they're doing with women. I wonder how different my relationship with girls would be if my warrior father hadn't died when I was three.*

His father wasn't the biggest warrior, his mother had told him, but he was cunning, strong, and full of surprises. "Like a coconut" she would add, "nearly impossible to open without the right tools, yet sweet on the inside if you can get there."

Steffen thought every warrior he met would be just like his mother's description of his father, but he found most of them to be more like lemons—sour and terribly brash. He hadn't given up on Cleve, though, not yet.

Even with class being a disappointment, Steffen still was excited, at least, to discuss his potions with Jack Rose, the best chemist at the Academy and perhaps even in Ovira. Steffen was planning to save the meeting with the head of chemists for another day, but after class, he needed to reinvigorate his passion for potions and decided the best way was a discussion with his hero. Unsure of the policies regarding students meeting with faculty, he figured he would just meet Master Chemist Jack at his home.

With the cage of his new rat, Leonard, in hand, Steffen examined a directory near the middle of campus. It showed the faculty housing area as being along the northwestern edge with the dining hall to its east. He'd been to the dining hall, so he knew how to find the faculty housing. What the directory didn't show, however, was which house belonged to which teacher.

A female joined Steffen on his left side to look at the directory after flashing a smile. Leonard, on his other side, suddenly produced something that sounded between a cough and a squeak.

The young lady peered around Steffen to see what it was. "What a strange sound," she commented. Her eyes were green, but everything else—her hair, eyebrows, cheeks, and lips—was red. Her hair was the red of a dying ember calling out for a breath of air. It cascaded without waves down to her breasts, where the ends curled playfully together. Her smile was what he noticed first, though. With a slight overbite, her grin cutely came down onto a thinly curled lip.

"Is that a giant rat?" Her eyebrows lifted as she pointed.

"Yes, meet Leonard." He held the cage up to match the rodent to her eye level. Leonard turned away from her to sniff at Steffen, showing her his rat rear.

"Leonard, that's not very nice," she said. nudging closer to Steffen to get a better look at Leonard's front. The soft side of her shoulder pushed against his.

"Can I pet him?" she asked, beginning to stick a finger within the cage.

He quickly closed his hand around her finger. "Unfortunately, Leonard would bite you. He likes to chew on everything, an effect of the growth potion I've been giving him. I've been trying to perfect the formula to achieve the growth without the aggression."

"I thought I saw you in my class earlier, now I'm certain of it. You were sitting in the front, so you probably didn't see me. Our instructor is Chemist Leandra, right?"

"Yes!" Steffen exclaimed with more excitement than he meant. "That's correct. I'm Steffen Duroby." He extended a hand without a clue why he'd given his last name.

She seemed to hold back a laugh. "You can just call me Treece. It is short for Marratrice, a name I would've never chosen if it were up to me." They shared a handshake.

"I love the name Marratrice." *Love? I don't even know what I think of the name. You're sounding strange. Stop it.*

"Really? Someone you know must have carried it well."

"Actually, it's the first time I've met a Marratrice."

Her eyes slid down and found Leonard along the way. "He's a little odd, isn't he, Leonard?" She crouched to push her long, elegant nose against the cage, and Leonard immediately nipped at it. She jumped back with a scream, and two hands rushed to her nose.

"Leonard!" he yelled at his rat. "I'm sorry for that." But then he saw in her eyes that she was smiling.

She gave a laugh and let her hands drop from her face. "You warned me. He didn't bite me anyway, just a fun little startle. Are you taking him somewhere?"

"Yes, to see Jack Rose, but the faculty's individual houses aren't listed here. So I'm unsure how to tell which one is his."

"There's another map on the road to the faculty housing area that'll tell you. I just came from there. I thought it would be a good idea to take a tour around campus. My roommate had already walked around yesterday, so I have no one to explore with." She looked at him with eyes that seemed to beckon for something.

"Thank you, that's helpful." A strange silence came over them. He felt as if she was expecting him to say something, but he didn't know what.

"Goodbye, then!" she chirped with a quick turn. Then she was off.

"Goodbye," he called after her.

He found the sign she'd mentioned. The map had each house listed by number. In the corner, each number was etched with a teacher's name next to it to show where they lived. More than a few teachers shared a number, to his surprise, though they usually also shared a last name. Out of curiosity, he looked to see how many were listed in total. The last number was fifty-six. *I would have expected more,* he thought, which reminded him of last night. *Gabby expected more*. He felt his heart sink into his stomach.

When Steffen found the right house, his knock was answered so fast that Jack Rose had to have been by the door. The head chemist was barefoot and leaning against the doorway to put on his socks. He had on a white shirt with a turned-up collar that seemed to glow immaculately against his charcoal skin. With the streaks of gray in his hair, he looked at least ten years older than Terren, the head of school who Steffen knew to be in his thirties. "You must be a new student chemist." His welcoming eyes squinted as he smiled.

"Yes." Steffen nodded. "I'm very excited to meet you, Chemist Master Jack! I'm Steffen. I was hoping I could discuss a few potions I've been working on. Leonard here is an example of a growth potion."

"A growth potion! And look at the success you've had; he's huge. We should talk, indeed. Unfortunately, I must be leaving shortly." He pulled the school-issued blue coat over his shoulders and began buttoning. "In the future, please only visit during visiting hours." He hooked a finger around the doorway where a paper was pinned. Steffen thought it might have been a note for someone, so he hadn't read it before knocking. He read it now and saw that visiting hours for that day already had passed.

"I apologize. I would be happy to come back tomorrow."

"I look forward to it." Jack sat to slip his feet into a pair of shoes. "I have a few tasks to do before I leave, if you could shut the door."

"Of course."

"One last thing, Steffen!" he shouted as the door was nearly shut.

"Yes, Chemist Master Jack. What is it?"

"Actually, make that two things. Just call me Jack or Chemist Jack if you prefer. More importantly, be careful with the growth potion. Make sure you don't drink it or give it to others. Don't tell anyone of it either. Potions can be far more dangerous than weapons, remember that. We chemists have to be very careful. Some mixtures could change the world forever."

"I'll be very careful."

"Good. We'll talk more tomorrow."

Steffen closed the door and suddenly realized what he'd just heard. *Some mixtures could change the world forever*. It's something he'd thought of many times, but never negatively as Chemist Master Jack had implied. He wanted to create potions that cured sickness and diseases. He wanted to find mixtures that could protect Humans from bears and women from rape. He figured the right potion existed for every problem. Although he looked up to the master chemist, Steffen still wouldn't believe one mixture could cause so much harm. He trusted history, and never had he read of such an event.

With his last plan for distraction foiled, his mind brought him back to last night. He realized showing up at the wrong time was not unlike what Gabby had done. However, he was only off by hours, while another year or two might have made all the difference for him and Gabby.

Chapter 22: A Visitor in the Night
STEFFEN

Usually, experiences under the influence of alcohol had a haze about them when Steffen reminisced, but not this time. Gabby's scent, her words, his response, her touch—he remembered all of it, every detail:

He awoke to the sound of his door opening, someone stepping into his room, and then the door closing.

"Who's there?" he asked, only able to make out her silhouette.

"Steffen, it's me," she whispered.

"Me, who?"

"Gabby," she said, just before kicking a book he'd left on the floor. "Bastial hell! That hurt."

"I'm naked," he blurted, not sure what she would make of it.

He could hear her suck in air. No words followed. He waited, looking closely at Gabby but still unable to see more than the shape of her.

"I didn't know you slept naked," she finally said.

"Why does it matter?"

It was silent for what may have been a second or a minute, he couldn't tell, not from memory at least.

"It doesn't," she finally said.

"What are you doing in here?"

Again, she wouldn't speak.

"Are you still there?" he asked, confident she was but unsure what else to say to get her to answer him.

"Yes," she whispered regrettably, like he'd said something to upset her.

"Is something wrong?"

"No. I thought..." A breath interrupted her. "I was thinking we should lie together."

That's when his suspicion was confirmed. Suddenly he was hard, the sheets pushing heavily against him. "I don't think that's a good idea," he managed to get out. His heart was beating so loudly he wondered if she could hear it.

"We're not going to see each other for a long time. Don't you want to spend a little more time together?"

"I do." He did. "But I don't think we should."

"Why?" she whispered, clearly hurt.

Gabby truly was her sister's sister. She had Effie's face and body, but years younger. Seeing them next to each other, it became clear that Effie was older, but there was nothing discernible about Gabby that made it obvious she was only fourteen—until she spoke. Her voice, if it ever was to change, seemed to be the last thing about her to do so. It was still high and young. It did not have the crisp texture of a woman's tone—of Effie's tone.

Steffen found it difficult to use the remaining blood in his brain to process the situation and figure out what he could say to have her leave without a broken heart. But before he could think, she was suddenly on his bed straddling him with only a blanket between his naked body and her. He'd never felt so much pain and pleasure at the same time as when Gabby pressed her weight down onto him.

"You're hard. I knew you wanted me."

"I do." He did. She leaned over and pressed her lips against his. Right away he knew she was a good kisser, and he wasn't. His lips felt lost, always in the wrong place. But hers were confident and rhythmic, and soon he fell into her pattern. A wild sensation of excitement and anxiety stormed through his chest as they kissed harder and deeper in each passing moment.

It was too dark for him to tell what she was wearing, just that it was something—unlike him. His hands beneath the sheets found her bent knees and grabbed them in the hope he could somehow physically lift her off him with such subtlety that she wouldn't even know it had happened. But of course, his efforts were futile. If he wanted her to stop, he would have to say so.

"Stop," he whispered so softly even he couldn't hear it. His body was screaming at him to shut up. "Stop," he said louder this time.

She moved her lips to his neck. It felt as if he was being stroked with a brush of pleasure, its bristles dancing from his neck to his feet, giving him goose bumps as it passed. "Stop," he moaned, then said firmly, "I don't want this," even though he did.

That disengaged her lips. She brought her eyes above his. They were dark and deep-set, yet they were the only thing in the room he could see clearly in that moment. Her black hair fell over his face and smelled of her—blackberry pie, sweet and tart at the same time.

"It feels like you do want this." She sat back to push herself against him once again. Even through the blanket and whatever she had on, there was a softness he suspected had to be the entrance to the inside of her. He'd never felt in less control of himself, grabbing onto the edges of the bed, pushing back against her even though it hurt.

When he began wrestling with the idea of removing the barriers between them, he realized that if she kept at it he would succumb, so he made a final stand. He slipped out from under her so that she was left kneeling to his side.

"I'm sorry," he said. "I can't do this."

She let her body plop next to him with a sigh. She fell so close, her nose brushed his cheek.

"I thought this is what you wanted," she whispered painfully. They were sharing a pillow. He could feel her warm breaths blowing against him. First, he noticed that she was panting. Then, he realized that so was he.

"I like you," Steffen said. "But I've known you nearly all my life, and you've always been so much younger than me."

"But now no laws would be broken. I'm fourteen. I thought you were just waiting for me to turn fourteen. I'm a woman now."

"The laws weren't the only reason. You're Effie's sister. She and Reela are my closest friends. My mother is friends with your parents. Your father knows me. He and your mother looked after me many times when I was younger. What would they think if they found out? What would Effie think? Even Reela, what would she say?"

For a while, Gabby was silent. Steffen simply listened to her breathing and waited.

When her breathing finally calmed back to normal, she spoke. "I love you. I always have. I don't care what they think or what they would say."

Then it was his turn to be silent. If he did love her, he didn't know it. He'd never allowed himself to consider it. Suddenly, she flipped over to face the other way. A moment of panic came over him that she was going to leave. Instead, she reached down to the floor.

"Here," Gabby said, tossing his underwear behind her. "Put these on. We'll cuddle."

He followed her instructions, and she slid under the covers. Still facing away from him, she took his arm and put it around her waist.

Suddenly, he was hard again. *Dammit*, he thought as he scooted his lower half away from hers.

"I was so nervous about this night," she said. "But not half as worried as I'll be when I leave you here for nearly a year with so many other girls."

"I've never been good with girls. I don't think that will suddenly change."

"But now you're cute."

"What do you mean?"

"Before you were, *meh*, not bad, but recently you got cute. I've always loved you, though. So it wouldn't be fair for you to end up with someone else."

Steffen was baffled by her declaration of love. She spoke so confidently it seemed as if she was absolutely certain. "I don't understand how you can be so experienced with love. I'm three years older, and I can't even tell if I've ever been in love."

"*Men*." She blew out air loudly. "You may be stronger, but you sure can be dumb. You've loved me for a year now. You just haven't realized it yet."

It didn't sound impossible, but still, he had no idea if it was true. "When did you become so wise?"

She turned to face him so that each could see nothing but the other's eyes. She pressed her nose against his until it slid loose and stopped against his cheek. Then she pressed her soft lips onto his for a long, forceful kiss. There was a loud smack as she pulled away.

"I've always been wise. It's just been hidden under a layer of childhood foolishness." She got to her feet and then turned back for one last kiss, which he gladly gave. "Come visit me in Oakshen," she whispered. "Don't wait until the summer."

"I will," he whispered back.

The next morning, she was gone by the time he rose.

Chapter 23: Did That Just Move?
ZOKE

They stood just before the entrance to Merejic, a sturdy line of thick trees that dared Zoke to enter. Vithos strained his neck to see how far his eyesight could go.

"We'll break for lunch inside, under the shade of the forest." The Elf spoke as if he wished Zoke had a good reason to disagree, but Zoke knew of no reason, so he said nothing.

Stepping into the shaded forest was like entering a different world. The temperature was refreshingly cool, the grass soft and damp beneath his bare feet. The trees made a creaking sound, sometimes so choppy it sounded like they were laughing. Zoke dug the claws on his toes into the soil to feel the wet dirt on the tops of his feet. He noticed Vithos peering around with caution. "There's wildlife everywhere," the Elf said.

Zoke saw only two blood-red birds perched in a tree, chirping to each other. "Anything large?" he asked hesitantly.

Vithos shut his eyes and placed his fingers upon his forehead. "Yes, and small, and in the air, and on the ground, and looking for a mate, and hungry. There's so much happening at once." The Elf opened his eyes and the corners of his mouth pinched. "Let's eat here on the edge before we go deeper in and become completely encircled by unknown animals."

The farther from the edge, the louder the forest became. Squeals of annoying birds, sticks cracking, and rustles from nearby bushes grew common, but the worst were the chilling howls Zoke began to hear later in the day.

Their pace had slowed since entering the forest. Zoke had gone back to following Vithos, for there was not enough room for them to walk side by side without a tree or a bush scratching them. The plants were merciless, even seeming to move on their own at times, leaning into Zoke's path just as he walked by and then snapping back into place before he could turn to confirm that he wasn't imagining it.

"Does it seem to you that the plants are moving to touch us?" he finally asked when something got him on the back of the neck.

"That would help me feel better about all the scratches I'm getting from running into them clumsily, but they have no conscious mind I can detect, so I don't believe so. At this rate I'll bleed to death before we make it there." Vithos held out his arms.

Zoke was surprised to see the Elf was hardly exaggerating. He was covered in cuts, most of which were deep enough for blood to show. Although it had been only four years since Zoke's shedding, it was a clear reminder that his skin was far tougher than the Elf's. Vithos had told Zoke that his skin, and so the skin of all Elves—Vithos assumed—seemed to be as frail as that of a child Krepp. It seemed like a terrible disadvantage, like wearing paper into battle instead of armor.

"How long will we need to travel before we reach the Elven village?" Zoke asked.

"My understanding is that it's near the center of this forest, maybe twenty miles from where we are now. We could easily reach it tomorrow on open terrain, but it's tough to say with all these trees. I have no experience with this land. It could be two days, it could be five, especially if I'm wrong about its location. Finding food will be easy, though, as I can lure any animal to us, so try to keep your spirits up."

Vithos had been right about the north; nature still owned it, so there was much more to see. A few plants in particular caused Zoke to stop for a closer investigation. There was one type he noticed more frequently than others. It stood with a lean, always toward him, reminding him of the way Vithos would lean over him as he listened for lies. Impossibly so, it somehow felt even more otherworldly than when the Elf peered into his mind.

The tall plant had wormlike legs that wrapped around its body. They connected it to the dirt, where the legs trailed off in all directions like a cape twice too long with shredded ends. Its head was always composed of six to ten long leaves that never hung in the exact same shape, but they always created the image of eyes or a mouth, and sometimes even both. Zoke noticed that this particular plant only grew near trees, liking to lean out from behind them, as if to spy.

He poked one with his stick and it seemed to reply with an annoyed shake, moving just a bit too much and too long for his light touch. That's when Zoke decided he didn't like this forest.

"How will we find the village?" Zoke asked. "These trees stretch on forever."

"Signs of intelligent life are easy to spot, even after years have passed since anyone inhabited the area," Vithos answered cheerfully. "Look for trails, markings on trees, or even a river or lake. They couldn't have lived too far from water." Vithos sounded as if he was quoting something he might have read or heard. "I wouldn't expect to find anything today, though, as we couldn't have traveled far from the edge of the forest."

In their time through the forest, Zoke saw more creatures and plants than he had in his whole life. He'd heard or read about some of what he saw, mostly because of the danger they posed, so he recognized a snake when it hung from the limb of a tree and hissed at Vithos.

"Look out!" Zoke warned.

The Elf knelt and shot a hand at the wiry creature. It slipped from the branch like a rope coming loose, falling onto Vithos' shoulders and knees. Instead of pushing it off him, Vithos balanced its weight across his shoulders and continued walking.

"Snakes will bite. Their poison can kill you!" Zoke said, completely shocked the Elf didn't know or didn't seem to care.

Vithos turned and flashed a grin. "This one won't, not while I'm conscious."

Zoke felt his eyes go wide. "Why carry it with us?"

Vithos shrugged. "For fun."

The snake slithered around Vithos' arms and neck as he walked, its forked tongue shooting out to dance at lizards and birds they passed. Sometimes it would wrap around Vithos' body to stare at Zoke, its head nodding back and forth silently with each step the Elf took. He didn't understand the fun it gave Vithos, but it wasn't his place to judge.

The nights were freezing. While Zoke, at least, could sleep through them with some difficulty, the Elf could not, even with his blanket. Zoke was awakened the first night by the frigid wind. He heard Vithos making an odd sound, like his teeth were rattling against each other. It was too dark to see him, but it sounded like he was shaking against the dirt he lay on as well.

"What's wrong with you?" Zoke whispered and sat up. Just as he did, he heard something scamper away from him. It gave him quite a startle, as it appeared to be within spitting range before it ran off. "What was that?" Zoke jumped to his feet and readied his stick, though he saw nothing but black of the thickest kind. His heart went wild with fear.

"What did you say?" Vithos whispered back. When he spoke, the sound of his shaking grew louder. "I think I may have somehow been asleep finally."

Zoke waited for a few breaths, listening, but heard nothing except Vithos. He lowered the stick and felt himself calming. "You're making a strange sound. Are you sick?"

"No, this happens when I'm too cold." The Elf's teeth were chattering very loudly now. "My body and teeth tremble. I don't know why."

"Must be an Elf thing." Zoke thought for a moment of how he could help with the cold but came up with nothing. "In this dark, it would be impossible to gather the supplies to make fire. To make matters worse, I think some creature is waiting for us to sleep. When I spoke, I heard something move that was nearly on top of me."

"There are creatures all around us, but I'm not sensing anything aggressive right now. Maybe it was just curious what could cause such an appalling stink." Vithos gave a shaky laugh that cut off early from the clacking of his teeth. "I don't think I'll be getting much sleep anyway, so I'll keep guard. It may be impossible, but I'm going to try to start a fire. At least it'll get me moving."

"If that suits you." Zoke didn't want to waste his efforts on the impossible when he was able to sleep.

He woke again maybe two or three hours later to the squeak of sticks being rubbed fiercely. He stayed up with Vithos until the fire was lit.

On the fourth day, they finally discovered a trail, but it didn't prove to be as useful as Vithos had implied. It was only visible where the dirt was bare. Otherwise, it wound through piles of leaves, even going under bushes and clusters of plants at times. They lost it more times than Zoke could keep track.

The light within the forest grew dim, and the sound of rustling from behind them became louder. It gave Zoke a growing panic he couldn't shake.

At last Vithos stopped. "Look." He pointed ahead.

There was an open gateway made of wood. On top were letters in a language Zoke didn't recognize.

"Elvish?" Zoke asked. He knew how to read common tongue, so he could tell it wasn't that.

"Must be," Vithos said as he studied it.

Although there didn't appear to be anyone around, Zoke spoke quietly once they passed through the gate. He felt as if he didn't belong here, that he was an intruder. It only made his panic worsen.

"It's late." Zoke could hear his tone was nervous. "We should find somewhere to rest. You can look around in the morning."

"It's fine, Zoke. No one is nearby." Vithos chuckled. "We'll find a good place to rest as we look around." The Elf's eagerness was palpable.

Chapter 24: They Must Die
ZOKE

The path split into three, each leading to clusters of ornate houses in wide areas where trees had been cleared. Every house was touched by streaks of black from fire, some burned so badly they were no more than darkened, incomplete walls.

"Doe and Haemon were here," Vithos said. He touched the scarred wall of a nearby house. "And it looks like they won whatever battle occurred."

As they continued on, Zoke no longer could find the sun piercing through the trees as it had an hour ago. A light mist appeared to be seeping into the forest from the treetops. The sky was colored a deep blue, turning everything below into black silhouettes. Even Vithos, with his pale skin, had grown dark gray like a Krepp.

They checked the inside of each house that still had four walls and a roof, but there were no signs of Elves. "There's a smell," Vithos commented. He sniffed, then grimaced. "It's a terrible stench of rotting flesh."

Zoke had no way of empathizing. Being a *gurradu*, he knew not what rotting flesh smelled like, nor anything else for that matter.

They continued farther northwest through another one or maybe two hundred yards of destroyed houses. Their pace had slowed to a near crawl.

"It's getting worse." Vithos held his nose and coughed. "How I envy you right now."

"I think we should go back. It's becoming difficult to see." A troubled feeling was seeping through Zoke's body. It was heaviest in his stomach, making him feel sick with worry.

Vithos gagged and stopped for a moment to compose himself. "We're close to whatever it is."

Zoke's heart started thumping against his chest. He thought he heard dried leaves crackling underfoot. There were hundreds of places to hide. Someone could be within spitting range without him knowing. "Is anything near us?" he asked.

Vithos extended a palm but quickly shook his head. "I can't tell. The smell is too overpowering."

Fear gripped Zoke. *Something bad is about to happen,* a voice told him, a voice he trusted. "We need to go, now." He wrapped his claws around Vithos' wrist, but Vithos shook free.

"What's wrong?" The Elf finally looked worried.

Two yellow eyes connected to what could only be the body of a Krepp stepped out from behind a house. It appeared to be holding something, lifting it in front of its chest. *A bow!* Zoke could see it now. Zoke pushed Vithos behind a wide tree as an arrow zipped by and scraped the side of his shoulder.

They pushed their backs against their only cover, each panting nervously. "How many did you see?" Vithos asked.

"Only one." The sting of pain surged through his shoulder. With a finger he found a small gash that didn't concern him.

Vithos aimed a hand to his side. A second Krepp dropped a bow and fell to his knees with a groan of pain from the psychic spell.

Zoke and Vithos ran back the way they came, but an arrow cut them off, flying just past Zoke and glancing off the edge of Vithos' hip. The Elf fell with a quick grunt, but Zoke grabbed his arm, popped him up, and pulled him into the nearest house four steps away.

"There's at least three," Zoke whispered, "probably more." The house was like Zoke's hut but bigger. It had two beds, a table, and a dilapidated chair. Everything was charred or covered in soot. Most of the roof was missing, but worst of all there was no door. They stood just behind the wall that connected to the doorway. "Did the arrow pierce you?"

Vithos checked the wound. "It's fine."

"Can you use your psyche on them?"

"Not unless I see them. I can't sense their presence because of the stench. They must have been sent by Doe. He knows about this weakness." Vithos drew his dagger, keeping his eyes on the doorway.

There were two open windows. "We can't stay in here or they'll shoot through one of those." Zoke pointed at the gaping holes in the wall. Vithos checked and grumbled under his breath.

"How good are you with a bow?" Vithos asked.

"Decent. Much better with a sword, though."

"Let's get you one. We need to take them out, all of them. They'll track us wherever we go. Doe wouldn't let them return without proof of killing me."

"Fine," Zoke agreed while monitoring the windows. Surprisingly, he no longer felt afraid. His mind was clear. A plan came to him—possibly the only option they had. "Can you run?"

"I'm not leaving you," Vithos stated firmly.

"No, are you *able* to run? When we dash out of here to fight them it needs to be at full speed."

"Yes," Vithos answered confidently. "I can do that."

"Get ready to follow me. If you see any Krepps, mesmerize them with psyche. I'll engage the closest one I see."

Vithos nodded. "Endure."

"Endure." Zoke dug his claws into his only weapon—the stick from Lake Lensa. *I will not die here,* he vowed, thinking of Zeti. He waved the stick in front of the door and around the edge of the doorway. Arrows zipped past it, some even whizzing into the house and sticking into the back wall with a humming *thump*. "Go!" he shouted and then sprinted out with Vithos behind him.

Two Krepps with bows faced them. Luckily, each needed to reload his arrows. To his side Zoke detected movement—a Krepp stepping out from behind a tree with an arrow already strung. But before the Krepp could pull the string back, he twisted his head in a disorienting lurch and dropped the bow. *Good, Vithos.*

"Look for more behind us and to our other side. I can take care of these two!" Zoke screamed, still running as fast as his legs could carry him.

The two Krepps must have realized they wouldn't load another arrow in time, so each dropped his bow and drew a sword. Zoke's strength had always been underestimated because of his small size, so he knew to use that to his advantage. He leaped into the air and brought down the stick over the head of the Krepp who dared to stand farther forward. The Krepp held up his sword for protection, but it was not enough. Zoke felt the blow connect to more than just steel but couldn't take another second to see if he would rise because the other Krepp was thrusting a sword at him. Zoke swung the stick back around, swatting the sword clean from his attacker's grip. Zoke took a quick glance to the first one—he was lying motionless. The other produced a dagger, so Zoke jabbed him hard in the stomach with his stick. It created enough distance between them for Zoke to trade his stick for the nearby sword from the unconscious Krepp.

He pointed it at his opponent, who took a step back. "You should be scared," Zoke muttered, more confident than ever as only a dagger stood in his way. He used the opportunity to glance behind him. Vithos was not there, yet another Krepp was, dashing at Zoke with a sword in hand. *Better finish this fight quick.*

Turning back, he found the Krepp with the dagger to be running. Zoke chased after him, but Zoke's legs proved to be too short. He was much slower than needed to catch up, so he turned to engage the Krepp behind him instead.

He deflected an overhead swing and retaliated with his own, which was blocked at the last moment. The force must have been a shock to the Krepp because he stumbled backward. Zoke used his momentum to stay on the offensive, delivering constant powerful blows. His enemy blocked or moved out of range of each one, never gaining position to attack back.

Zoke continued to swing, putting more power into every advance. The Krepp soon backed into a belt-high rock and fell onto it, so Zoke shifted his grip to stab the blade into the Krepp's chest, but the Krepp rolled out of the way, and Zoke's weapon was driven into solid rock. His sword snapped in half, and a shooting pain flew from Zoke's palm to his shoulder. *Of course, they were given cheap weapons,* he thought. Doe and Haemon never gave more than they felt was necessary. *Then they too have underestimated me.*

Zoke held the half-sword as confidently as he could and faced his enemy. In the distance behind the Krepp in front of him was Vithos, who held his hand over two debilitated Krepps, each on his knees. With his free hand, Vithos stuck a sword into the chest of one and then the other. Meanwhile, a sword came at Zoke from his attacker, so he dodged sideways just as he'd practiced thousands of times, pushing the weapon away from his body with his broken sword. He then jabbed it toward the Krepp, but it lacked the distance to make contact. He had no training with a weapon so short, so he would have to improvise. The Krepp easily sidestepped Zoke's advance and clawed him across the face, following with a swing of his sword from the hip. Zoke leaped backward, feeling only wind against his stomach. Unfortunately, it was not the same for his face, which burned wet with blood.

Like other Krepps after a small taste of victory, his opponent predictably lunged straight at him. Zoke was ready for it this time. He moved aside and whacked the handle of his broken sword down onto the steel of the advancing weapon, then jabbed the jagged end of his sword into his enemy's chest. He released his grip and his sword remained within his enemy's body. The Krepp staggered back and then fell forward.

Before his attacker's body came to a stop on the dirt, Zoke noticed the sound of another Krepp coming from behind. He turned to find that the one who had the dagger was wielding a sword now.

Unarmed, Zoke was now the one retreating. The Krepp ran for him. The blood-hungry look on his enemy's face made Zoke feel like an ambushed Slugari—there was nowhere to hide, and he already knew he would be unable to outrun his opponent. Just as the Krepp's sword advanced into range, it stopped and fell to the ground with a *clink*. Zoke had never heard such a relieving sound. The disoriented Krepp lost his footing and crashed into the hard dirt near where his sword had fallen.

"This is the last one," Vithos said, approaching with his palm extended. He stopped over the fallen Krepp. "And he's going to tell us what we need to know or he'll feel a pain worse than the shedding of his *pra durren*." The Krepp curled into a ball and screamed loudly. It pained Zoke just hear it. "That's just an example of what's to come unless you answer honestly," Vithos threatened. He glared at the scar around the Krepp's wrist. "You think a burning from Doe is bad? I can make your blood feel like it's on fire."

This was the wicked attitude Zoke had expected from the Elf when they'd first set out, but he hadn't seen it until now. "Stop! Show some mercy!" he blurted without thinking.

"Get away from here!" Vithos screamed. "Leave! If you can't handle it...leave." The last word was a regrettable whisper.

Zoke took another look at the Krepp whimpering at his feet before leaving to search the bodies of the others.

While making his rounds, he periodically heard the Krepp scream and moan. Zoke knew Vithos was trying to get all the information he could before killing him. It hurt to let it happen, but Zoke was unable come up with a better alternative. They couldn't allow the Krepp to live.

Chapter 25: Dark Dreams and Howls
ZOKE

Around the corpses Zoke found bows, swords, and daggers, each lower quality than the rest. He equipped himself the best he could from among the array of worn weapons. Soon, though, he found the extra weight was too much to bear for the long walks he knew lay ahead.

He removed half the arrows from his quiver. *Still quite heavy, but I'll manage.* By then, Vithos had finished with the captive and executed him by piercing his heart with a sword.

The night was cold and dark, as usual. The howls of what Zoke assumed to be wolves began growing louder. He was resting against a smooth tree when Vithos approached.

"Let's go south," Vithos muttered, "away from this stench so I can focus."

Zoke walked next to him, the Elf's order of *"leave"* still fresh in his mind. Zoke tried to ignore it, asking instead, "What did he tell you?"

"Everything he knew." Vithos' tone was without solace, deep with regret. "Doe sent them here. He expected me to come to this village instead of following his orders. I should've realized he would do that. They killed some animals five days ago to produce the rotting smell. They were to take back my head to Lake Lensa, where an escort would meet them and bring them to the new location of the camp. Doe was smart not to reveal it to them before they left." Vithos stopped to lean on a nearby tree. He held his forehead.

"Are you not well?" Zoke asked.

"My head is screaming. I've spent too much energy without enough food or rest. It's nothing sleep can't cure." He continued walking, even slower than before. "I don't like what happened back there. I regret what I said to you, though not what I did to that Krepp."

Zoke glanced up but couldn't see Vithos' face clearly enough to read his expression; night had become too thick. "I understand your actions. There's no need to discuss it further."

"It pained you to watch another suffer. Compassion is important for any good leader, which I see you being one day."

"I'm not in the mood for flattery," Zoke replied. Sycophants were regarded as worse than beggars within the tribe, and it sickened Zoke to think Vithos would resort to fawning when he was out of energy.

"I'm not making this up." The Elf spoke louder now. "I see you as a leader. I always have, but there was no opportunity for you within the tribe. Why else would I make you the lead Krepp of the disciplinary committee? You're compassionate, responsible, yet tough and fair, all rare qualities for a Krepp."

"I've never thought about it, and I see no reason to now." It was the last thing Zoke cared about, and it still seemed like Vithos was just trying to make him feel better with false compliments. He changed the subject. "Did you find out more about what happened in this village from that Krepp?"

"All of the Krepps sent to kill us were too young to have lived during that time, and Doe told them nothing of it." He stopped next to a house, brushing his hand against the charred lines on one wall. "I may never know exactly what happened, but there's enough evidence to demonstrate that Doe and Haemon cared no more for this village than they did for me." He opened the door to the house, and Zoke followed him inside.

There were three bed stands, one smaller than the rest, as if for a child. Everything was burned or looked ready to collapse, so they found space on the wood floor to lie down.

As Zoke was removing his weapons to sleep more comfortably, the loudest howl yet startled him. "Vithos?" he asked. The Elf's eyes did not have a faint yellow glow like a Krepp, so he couldn't tell if they were open. "Are we far enough from the smell that you can use your psyche?"

"Yes. There's a pack of wolves nearby." His voice was grumbly, as if he'd been asleep already somehow. "They're hungry, but the corpses we produced will suffice. They've picked up the scent of blood, I presume. If you're worried, we can sleep in shifts, but I need to rest now. Wake me later if you stay up."

Zoke didn't have it in him to stay awake much longer, either. He noticed the two large windows, though. Their huts back home were built without windows, so it was a strange concept to find them in each house here. *What did the Elves do when the weather was bad?* He had endured colder nights than this one, but the holes in the wall let in an unrelenting breeze that was likely to wake him as the night got colder. There was nothing he could see that could be used to block them.

He ventured outside and found a rock not five steps away. It was heavy and lopsided. He tried to balance it within the window, but the bottom of the window was too thin, so the rock wouldn't stay on its own. While he was fiddling with it, a claw brushed against something above the window. It felt like a hinge for a door, and above it was an extra layer of wood. He set down the rock to investigate it closer with both hands. Atop the extra wood was a sliding lock. Suddenly, he realized what he was looking at. *Those smart Elves,* he thought. *There's a cover for the windows.*

Zoke braced the slab of wood above the window and unhooked the lock atop it. The weight of the wood fell into his hand. He slowly let it come down so that it rested against the wall, completely covering the window. He did the same for the other window, then went back inside with some satisfaction.

His dream proved to be eerie that night. He was back with the tribe, gathered with many others in the judgment chambers. Zeti was there as well. There was lively chatter. Soon, he found his mother, Junni. She was dead, he knew, killed by Doe when he was just six—*pra durren,* but she talked with the others as if she were still alive. He noticed other Krepps suddenly appearing who'd been killed during his lifetime, specifically the two who'd come at him with swords last year when he'd tried to take them in for judgment.

Soon, Zoke and the other Krepps were escorted out of the room by Doe. He found himself on a game board as a piece. He could cast magic—something no Krepp could do. While everyone attacked each other, he aimed his finger along their feet and a trail of fire emerged where he pointed. They burned, but without pain. As their lives came to an end, they faded, disappearing from the game board.

Back in the room from before, everyone was seated on a separate rock. They were singing a rhythmic yet ominous song that sounded familiar. As he looked at each of them, he noticed their skin was sickly pale, there were holes in their faces and chests, and many had bloody wounds across their necks. *They're dead, all of them,* he understood. Then Zoke noticed that he was the only Krepp standing and that he faced them, and they faced him. *They're singing background and expect me to sing the melody,* he realized. But he didn't know the song.

When he awoke, night had ended, yet the backbeat to the song looped continuously in his mind. *How do I know this song?* He tried to remember the melody but couldn't.

Vithos must've left the house where they'd slept and closed the door behind him because he was gone. Light crawled in from underneath the door and around the edges of the windows. Dirt was caked around Zoke's eyes and ears, so he used a claw to scrape it out. The hair on his head was thin and short, like most other male Krepps, yet soot still clung to it. He brushed his hand to and fro to clean off the dark flakes. The coarse skin on his palm scratching against his scalp was refreshing. He opened the door and stepped out.

The sun on his face immediately melted last night's chill. He buried the claws on his feet into the dirt and squatted to dig the claws on his hands underneath as well. He squeezed the dirt between each finger and yawned like a wolf howling.

"You're up," Vithos said. His face and clothes were covered in soot. "This place is breathtaking. It's a waste that no one lives here."

"These houses are far superior to our huts. Why didn't our tribe stay if they took it over?"

"More important than living comfortably is finding the Slugari. Doe and Haemon must've known the underground colony was farther south, especially because the only thing north of here is the ocean."

Zoke nodded. "How much water do you have?"

"Enough to make it back to the stream we found two days back."

"Then are you ready to leave this place?" Zoke was eager to return to the Krepp encampment he'd left. Even with everything that had happened, he still hoped others would be there, especially Zeti. She could be waiting for him, perhaps hiding.

Vithos rubbed dirt from his hand. "Not quite."

Zoke didn't push the Elf to leave before he was ready, so he nodded and followed. Zoke wasn't too enthusiastic about walking back on his own, and they had come all this way.

The deeper they went into the village, the more Zoke was amazed by what they found. There were metal pipes sprouting from the ground with a lever that produced water when pumped. Neat squares of dead gardens were fenced off with sturdy pickets of wood.

While most houses looked the same, a few buildings were built large enough to fit fifty Krepps and stood upon ten feet of solid wood so that steps were needed to reach the entrances. Many of these great buildings used to have a balcony, it appeared, but Zoke and Vithos never found one still completely intact. The damage from fire was extensive.

The most extravagant structure was in the center of the village, where hundreds of stone steps were built next to a river that flowed from hills high above. They climbed the steps to follow the river, and it led them to a small lake. A waterfall brought clear water into the lake from so high above that it seemed to pour straight from the clouds. Encircling half the lake were stone pillars that served as legs for sleek, pointed roofs. But it was just an entrance, Zoke realized, for farther in through the stone legs were walls of solid stone that composed what had to have been the living quarters for the highest members of the village.

"Any memories?" Zoke asked with hope.

"No." Vithos brushed his fingers against the carved stone carefully. "How could I forget something like this?"

They entered the once luxurious building and it became clear immediately that a major struggle had ensued within. The walls were stained with explosions of black. Most of the furniture had been upended and damaged beyond repair.

"Something has been bothering me," Zoke said as he gazed around the room. "It looks as if this village fell to an attack, but then where are the bodies? We've seen no skeletons."

"Displaced by animals, I assume." Vithos had no other answers he wished to share.

They explored room after room, each one different from the last. Vithos admitted to no memories. Eventually, Zoke opened a door to find a room covered in paintings of Elves standing heroically. Something in Elvish was written on the top of one wall.

"It looks as if this room wasn't touched," Vithos said with sheer excitement. He was right. All the paintings were hanging straight, and there were no signs of fire as in many other rooms.

"Krepps wouldn't destroy portraits," Zoke said. There were a few superstitions taught to every Krepp. One was that if you caused pain or suffering to a being and then destroyed their portrait, they would haunt you as a spirit. Only those who were at peace with the deceased could destroy the painted image of them in a ceremonial burning to help their passing.

Vithos examined the paintings meticulously. Most were families headed by a male and female Elf, with multiples of the same family at different ages, showing a history of their lives. Almost every family ended up with a child or two, according to the paintings.

"Look at this," Vithos said. "Does this look like me?" He pointed at a toddler holding onto the leg of his father. If Elves aged like Krepps, then the small boy couldn't have been older than two, Zoke figured. Also in the painting were what appeared to be the young one's mother and another boy of the same age. Zoke looked closely at the face of the young Elf who Vithos pointed toward. Right away the long eyes coming to a point on either end jumped out at him.

"That's you." But then he looked at the other boy in the picture. He had the same eyes. "Or him...one of them for sure." The two boys looked identical.

Vithos stared in silence for a long while. "You're right," he finally whispered. His face held no smile, no cheer. He looked like he did in the judgment chambers. He was serious and nothing else, like all his emotions had left him.

Twenty paintings in the room, Zoke estimated. *About three or four of each family, nowhere near enough to represent all the Elves.* "These are probably royal families," Zoke offered.

Vithos nodded as if he'd already come to that conclusion. "And I had a brother."

Zoke still felt like an intruder and even more so in this room, staring at the paintings of lost Elves. He was eager to go but tried to keep himself calm as he waited for Vithos.

Eventually, he asked, "Are you going to take that painting?"

"No," Vithos replied sullenly. "It belongs here."

Zoke let silence come over them once again. He waited as patiently as he could as Vithos stared at the painting as if trying to memorize it.

Finally, Vithos cleared his throat and looked away.

"Time to go?" Zoke asked quietly.

Vithos sighed. "Yes."

By the time they returned to the entrance of the village, a cool mist was setting in.

"I'd hoped to find another of my kind still alive, but I couldn't bring myself to mention it aloud," Vithos muttered. "Even in my head I knew how ridiculous it sounded."

"There's no shame in hope." Zoke thought of his own hope to see Zeti again.

"They'll pay for what they did," Vithos said, anger burning in his eyes. "But I'll need some support."

Zoke took a nervous breath. "I hope you don't mean me."

Vithos shook his head with a sly grin. "I know you're still unsure what you want to do, and I accept that. Also, I'm not so crazy as to believe that just the two of us could get to Doe and Haemon. There's another way to get the help I need."

Zoke was perplexed. *But who else is there? Who would ever wish to help Vithos take revenge against Doe and Haemon?* "Which is what?" Zoke asked.

"The underground Slugari." Vithos raised an eyebrow at Zoke. "I know where they are."

Chapter 26: Evaluations
EFFIE

Effie pushed her way through the crowd. *People need to find their names and then get out of the way*, she thought. Being too short to see over anyone, she couldn't tell how many more bodies she would have to squeeze through before she could get a glimpse at the evaluation week results.

"Excuse me." She shouldered through a small space between two hanging arms. Some couple was hugging in her path. "Move, please." She nearly tripped over a girl tying her shoe. "Tie it somewhere else."

She felt a hand slap her rear. *The results can wait. Someone is about to be hurt.* She turned with a balled fist.

"Easy, punchy!" There stood Reela with a guilty grin.

"Reela!" Effie felt her teeth unclench and her mouth curve into a smile. "What are you doing here?"

"Congratulations to both you and Cleve." She wrapped her long arms around Effie's shoulders. On reflex, Effie's hands came up to meet around Reela's back. No matter the situation, a surprise embrace from Reela always made her feel better.

"I haven't seen yet," Effie admitted. Someone shoved against her back to get through, disrupting their hug. "I hate this crowd," Effie muttered. "Let's chat at home later."

"Right. I'm off." Reela smiled at her and disappeared among the bodies.

Soon, Effie came to the wall and found the mage listings. She discovered the specific list she needed: the A through E names. With a finger, she located her name toward the bottom. "Effie Elegin: Group One." She took a moment for a breath of relief. Sweet satisfaction filled her lungs. The week had been especially tough, but not because evaluation classes were difficult. In fact, they hadn't been, and that was the problem.

When she'd entered her assigned classroom for the first time at the beginning of the week and had seen the many black streaks of old burns across the walls and chairs, she'd had high hopes of the dangerous challenges ahead. The giant vats of water in each corner to put out fire only helped amplify her excitement. The room looked as if it was designed as a tribunal where arguments for justice were made with fire instead of words. A metal podium stood in the front. It was littered with singe marks that colored its shiny, silver exterior with dozens of small red and blue heat circles.

To her disappointment, though, no fire could be cast within the walls. Her teacher was adamant about that. She was a young woman, younger than twenty-five, Effie guessed, and started the first class of evaluation week by rambling off a list of rules that sucked out all of Effie's passion to learn. All spells were to be performed outside in the designated casting area, which was a depressingly small section behind the classroom with metal training dummies burned black, uneven sand to stand on, and charred brick walls pelted from so many wild fireballs that the only color they had left was a mangled mix of orange and red near their ten-foot tops.

"If no spells are allowed within this room, how can there be so many fire marks?" Effie asked her instructor when class had finished.

"Because each teacher has different rules once evaluation week is over. Rules tend to be more lenient for the students in more competitive groups because those students usually have more control. This room is used by the Group Two students every year. As you can see, many spells have been cast within it. If you'd like more freedom within the classroom, I'd recommend trying your hardest to be placed in a lower group."

"Aren't you the one who decides which group I'm placed into?"

"Why, yes I am," the teacher answered with feigned discovery.

"Any tips for a young lady like yourself?"

"Yes, don't try to flatter me and don't cast within these walls."

Not a good start, Effie thought.

Class each day focused on a different spell to give the teacher a sense of each student's ability. The only day that was different was the third—endurance day. She'd heard it was the same for warriors—a brutal, four-hour test of fortitude, focus, and all-out strength. Her teacher explained it was designed to see how well they would perform in a battle, something Effie had been considering much more since speaking with Alex about war.

They were told when to cast a fireball, how big it should be, where it should strike, when they would get a chance to meditate, when meditation had to end, and when they were allowed water. To conclude the day, the students had to demonstrate how consistently and often they could cast incapacitating fireballs before exhaustion overcame them. If the students barely were able to stand before that, they certainly couldn't after.

As was common of mages in general, there were far more women in her class than men. Magic was seen by most as a way to fight, and men tended to choose swords over wands. Swords were far easier to learn because anyone could swing one, but no one could use a wand without training. When she'd started learning about the different classes as a child, Effie had learned that women could never be recognized warriors, but she didn't mind. She'd rather fight with fire instead of steel anyway.

She excelled in each spell they were asked to perform that week. It made her realize that if she didn't place in Group One or Group Two, she would have to spend the rest of the year as she had during evaluations—bored and without enough excitement or challenge to distract her from all the thoughts that caused her lungs to tighten. It had been especially bad that week. She'd awoken each morning with a cough that manifested from her inability to find relief in each breath. It would get worse throughout the day. Not her cough—that seemed to go away—but her ability to breathe. If there was nothing to distract her after class ended, it would start to feel as if sucking in air was entirely useless. No matter how much she took in, her body told her it wasn't enough. Nothing in her life was more frustrating. It consumed her. Every thought and emotion was based on whether or not she could breathe.

But that tension in her lungs was gone, for now. The panic it brought her was left in the crowd she fought through to find her name with Group One beside it. Her relief was like waking after a full night of rest—something she hoped would finally happen now that she'd finished evaluation week.

In addition to her group, a time was listed next to her name: 5:30. Her young teacher had explained that the head mage, Marie Fyremore, and Wilfre, the Academy's liaison to the King, would meet with every Group One mage for a quick introduction. Effie was usually no enthusiast of pageantry, but she had to admit to herself that she was excited.

To check the time, she peered through a slit between heads at the giant clock atop the tower of Redfield in the center of campus. *It's 5:10, just enough time to see how Cleve ranked before I go.* She migrated to the warriors' listings, pushing through a cluster of sweaty men hovering around the paper with names A through E listed above it.

"Want to see how your boyfriend did?" one of them asked with a teasing cadence.

If my rear gets slapped now, there will be blood. With a finger she found "Cleve Polken: Group One." She wasn't shocked. Even if Reela had said nothing of it, it still wouldn't have been a surprise.

He was born to be a warrior. She knew he would rank well, and she hadn't even seen him use a weapon. It was clear from the way he did everything else—he spoke carefully and concisely, ate meticulously so as not to waste one stroke of his fork, never gestured unless absolutely necessary. He was well aware of his actions in every situation, treating conversations with purpose more than entertainment. Strangest of all was that, even with his size, he was so light on his feet that she couldn't even tell when he was right behind her. This led to some problems, as Effie hated being startled.

She and Cleve shared the same schedule during evaluation week, so they were often in the house at the same time. Cleve liked to wake early, and Effie couldn't sleep much anyway with the unrelenting attacks of her breathing problem, so they started walking to the dining hall together for breakfast. She expected him to be up when she awoke, so it was rare for him to startle her in the morning. It was the evenings that led to the worst scares.

She remembered the first time it happened. She thought no one else was home. Lost in her own thoughts, she moved about the kitchen aimlessly. After a few minutes, she backed into Cleve, who had come behind her to retrieve his mug.

Effie screamed and swore at him—her usual response to being startled. She would always lose control for a breath or two, saying awful things she often would regret a moment later. She couldn't help but feel like her skin was being turned inside out, that there was no longer a filter to her emotions.

After screaming at Cleve and calling him names she didn't want to remember, she punched him in the arm. Only, she didn't curl her fist correctly. Just two of her knuckles struck him and at an awkward angle. Pain stung her, and she swore at him again.

"Sorry if I startled you," he said when she was finally done hitting him. But his tone was unforgiving. She could tell that he thought she was overreacting, and she knew she was.

"You're like a sack of bricks! How can you be so light on your feet?" she yelled, nursing her hand.

"Training, I guess." He shrugged. It was an annoyed shrug, done with a glare.

Because he hardly ever elaborated, it made it far easier to twist his words. Sometimes she just couldn't resist. "I knew they teach you warriors some unnecessary stuff, but sneaking up on women?" She shook her head and tightened her eyes to show harsh judgment. "That's just not right."

"No. That's not what I meant. They don't teach us that." He held up his hands defensively.

"Oh, so you've trained *yourself* to sneak up on women?"

"Of course not!" His face scrunched with frustration.

She smiled to save him and to save herself as well. She didn't want to anger him, after all, and the anger had melted out of her by then. He lowered his head when he realized it. "You're teasing me." He wasn't amused.

"It's called humor. You should try it sometime."

He opened his mouth to speak but looked to the side as if searching for what to say. Finally, he said, "Well, you're the one punching a sack of bricks." Again, he seemed to search for the right words. "You're...not...smart," he said sluggishly. When he heard himself, his shoulders sank in shame.

She applauded slowly in a sarcastic manner. "Maybe you should stick with weapons. Words can be tricky." At that, she got a defeated chuckle from him—a major victory as it was the first time she'd made him laugh...the first of many to follow.

On her way to the faculty housing, she thought of how Marie Fyremore and Liaison Wilfre were going to respond when she asked if Kyrro was at war. She'd never met either of them, hearing little of the King's liaison but much of Marie.

Until seven years ago, Marie had been headmaster of the school, stepping down into the role of head mage by choice. Rumors were that she'd grown too old for the tasks required, as it was common for the headmaster to travel to the King's castle in Kyrro City four miles away. However, while her legs had become too frail for the long walks, her spells still were stronger than any mage in the King's Guard.

Effie loved Marie's last name: Fyremore. It wasn't her birth name but belonged to her late husband, Poast Fyremore. If ever there was a man Effie might consider marrying, it would be someone like him. Even without the glorious name, he was a legendarily handsome and skilled mage who unfortunately died during the coup twenty-something years ago to overthrow some king whose name she couldn't remember—the coup that brought Westin Kimard to power, the father to their current king. It was the only history she accurately could remember—that, and how Westin Kimard was assassinated with a long-range arrow two years before she was born. Now his son, Welson Kimard, was their ruler. She figured she should at least know how the current king came to power, so she quizzed herself on it every day until the quizzing was no longer needed. Spells she could learn in a week, but remembering history seemed more hopeless than performing psyche.

Marie Fyremore and Liaison Wilfre were silent when she entered. Wilfre was standing, while Marie sat behind a desk. The rumors of Marie were true, at least of her age. Her hair and dappled skin had lost color over the years. She had a healthy amount of weight about her, though, masking any physical frailty she might be suffering from. Effie recognized the sky blue coat of mastery over her shoulders, the one issued to the head of each class. Liaison Wilfre had on a blue coat like hers, though he had no training as a mage or any class that Effie was aware of. His coat was uniquely marked with the symbol of Kyrro—a gold crown lined with silver—over his shoulder.

It was difficult to guess Wilfre's age. His face was stiff with tightly stretched skin that gave no sign of an expression. Even when he greeted her, she couldn't tell if he was forcing a smile or trying to pass a fart.

"Welcome, Effie Elegin," Wilfre said formally. "Congratulations, and thank you for being punctual."

"Congratulations, Effie," Marie added with a far more friendly tone. "I'm Marie Fyremore and this is Wilfre, the King's liaison. I'll be teaching you and the other Group One mages starting next week. Liaison Wilfre and the respective class head like to meet with all the Group One students within the first week. Being the most experienced of your classmates comes with harder work and a chance at a few opportunities. The King may require the assistance of students."

"Which is why I'm here," Wilfre stated proudly. His nose turned up as he spoke. "I'm very good with names and faces. If Kyrro needs help from its students, usually I decide who to select. As you can imagine, if the opportunity arises to directly assist the King with anything, it's a high honor to do so. Therefore, I need to select the right person for the job. I receive a copy of the skill chart of each mage and warrior in Group One, but a man or woman's skills for all tasks can't be completely told through numbers, not for some of the highly complicated missions required for the King. Luckily, I'm also a great judge of character."

Effie had difficulty refraining from rolling her eyes. Instead, she adjusted her weight to the other foot and tried to hold her smile. *Does he really give this speech to all Group One students?*

"I see here you have great strength with Bastial Energy." He waved a hand at the paper in front of him. "But you're also highly skilled with Sartious Energy. Can you tell me when you began to study it and why?"

She thought of Horen and wondered what they would say if she told the truth—that when she was fifteen, some man had made her a heart of Sartious Energy because he wished to get her drunk and bring her to his bed. "I was practicing at the training center in Oakshen at fifteen years of age, and I saw someone casting spells that left strands of green SE disappearing into the air. I asked him for tips, and he taught me a lot. After that, I practiced what he told me and learned most else from books."

"You're a fast learner." Wilfre pointed his pen at her before bringing it down to paper. Effie stole a glance at Marie. She had cunning eyes and a light smile to match, like she knew that Effie was hiding something. It created an uneasy flutter in her stomach. Wilfre continued. "What do you know of Slugari?"

"What?" She was so shocked by the question that words somehow tumbled out before thoughts. "Sorry, can you repeat that?" she asked to buy more time.

"Slugari, have you heard of them?" Marie asked with a sweet tone, relieving some of Effie's nervousness.

She had, less than a week ago in fact, but what had Steffen told her again? She could remember what Gabby had said, so she started with that. "I've heard they're green animals, half our size." Suddenly she remembered something else. "And they have some sort of plant, a flower I believe, that is very valuable. And I think they live underground?"

Wilfre let out a high hum as he scribbled some notes. "Where have you heard this?" he asked.

"From one of my roommates, Steffen Duroby. He's a chemist and knows far more about Slugari than I can remember at this time."

"Steffen Duroby," Wilfre said slowly as he wrote. "I would like to speak with him once time allows. I have one more question for you, Effie Elegin. How well do you work with others?"

She almost answered how she might if asked by anyone else: *I work well with others, but they don't work well with me*, but it seemed as if she was being interviewed for some sort of mission, and she didn't want to ruin the opportunity before finding out what it was. She needed all the excitement she could get while the closest bar was miles away.

"I love working with other people," she said with a smile on her face, yet a sour feeling in her stomach. "I work well in teams." *No I don't.* "I'm social, yet I like to stay on task." *There's some truth to that at least*, she figured, but it was difficult to tell for certain. She couldn't remember the last time she'd shared a task with someone other than her sister, and that rarely ended well.

"I can tell when people lie." Liaison Wilfre pointed, making her heart skip a beat. "And you tell the truth."

I'm glad someone believes so. Effie certainly didn't, and Marie had the same knowing look in her eyes as before.

"May I ask a question?" Effie asked politely.

"Of course, dear," Marie said.

"There's been talk of Kyrro being at war with Tenred. Is it true?"

Wilfre guffawed, though it seemed forced. "Who said that?" He blurted when he was done pushing out laughter.

Effie didn't know what to make of his reaction. "I've overheard people speaking about it," she lied.

"Give me their names." Wilfre held a pen steady as he hovered over paper. "Go on, let's hear them." He was clearly angry now, though Effie didn't know why. Whatever the reason, she was reluctant to tell him about Alex.

"I have no names to give. I apologize, but I don't know them," she lied again.

Wilfre scowled at her. "Do you know what would happen if we were at war? Do you realize how you would find out?" He was becoming even more agitated.

"No, I don't." Effie was regretting her question.

"I would tell you. I would tell everyone here at the Academy. All the students would be gathered at Redfield for the announcement. It's part of my job to do so. You're asking if I've chosen not to do my job, do you understand?"

Maybe you just don't know yet, she thought, feeling the child within her lashing out. *It seems like a lot can get by you,* she almost said. However, she held her tongue and pushed guilt onto her face as best she could. "I apologize once again. I wasn't aware."

"I'm sure Liaison Wilfre understands." Marie turned to give him a smile. "He's quite good with people and knows how rumors can be spread. Isn't that right?"

Wilfre coughed to clear his throat, some anger dissipating from his face. "Yes, of course. But Effie, if you hear a student speak of war again, please learn his or her name and come to me with it."

"There may be many who are wrongly convinced that war has begun," Marie said. "Might I suggest an announcement at Redfield to clear everything up and stop the rumors for good? It would be a good way for all the students to learn who you are as well."

"Yes, that idea suits me," Wilfre said. "I'll speak to Terren Polken about setting up a time."

Marie stood. "Thank you, Effie. Unfortunately, others are waiting to meet with us so we must bring this meeting to an end. I'll see you in the Group One classroom when class begins."

Effie was both excited and nervous about Marie being her teacher, as it seemed like the old woman was clever in a somewhat dangerous way.

Effie thanked them and shuffled out, shutting the door behind her. She could hear what sounded to be angry murmurs between Marie and Wilfre as she left.

Chapter 27: Locked on
EFFIE

"What's happened?" Reela asked before Effie even had both feet inside the house.

"What do you mean?" Effie asked.

"You're upset." Reela was seated at the kitchen table but stood to take Effie's hand gently and bring her to a seat. "Come, sit with me and have a drink." Reela ran a finger through Effie's wavy hair, straightening out a snag. The sakal jug was there on the table waiting, along with two liquor glasses. It was strange for Reela to initiate drinking, but Effie didn't complain. A drink or two sounded perfect right then, maybe even three.

Effie filled each glass as Reela sat.

"Bastial," she said.

"Bastial," Reela repeated with a concerned smile.

They drank. Reela blew out air to relieve the burn while Effie merely sighed.

"Talk," Reela said. "I don't know where the boys are, but they aren't here. I expected you to be far more excited. Tell me what's on your mind."

"Too much at once," Effie said. She filled her glass once again and then Reela's as well. She took a breath before throwing it down her throat. Reela ignored the begging glass at her fingertips and stared at Effie instead. She loved the way Reela's radiant green eyes gazed at her as they did during these moments. It reminded her of the emerald green of Sartious Energy. Looking into those eyes was the one time when she truly could speak freely because she knew it was the only time someone truly would listen. There was no ulterior motive to be guessed, no games to be played.

"Start with whatever just happened," Reela said.

"The one person who has the task of informing the Academy when war has begun wouldn't know he was in a duel until his opponent's sword had been run through him."

"Liaison Wilfre," Reela acknowledged. "He sat in on the first class I had to 'observe the new psychics.' You're right. His orders need to be delivered by spoon. This worries you because you now believe we're at war and haven't been told so?"

"I guess I do. You told me Alex spoke the truth when he discussed it earlier."

"Yes, what he *believes* is the truth," Reela made sure to emphasize. "That doesn't mean it's accurate."

Effie nodded to show she understood. "It's the not knowing that I can't stand. I'd rather be told we must prepare for battle than be left to guess. And I think the King is planning some mission for students, but I insulted his liaison." Effie eyed the sakal in Reela's glass, wanting her to catch up so she didn't feel guilty for drinking more.

"I'm saving this for later." Reela pushed it behind her arm and then reached out to squeeze Effie's hand. A tingle swam up through her arm. Then Reela retracted her hand. "I don't think you're as capable of offending men as you believe yourself to be," Reela said playfully. "Even the delicate Liaison Wilfre. I'm sure something else has angered him enough since then for him to have forgotten. Did he tell you he was a good judge of character?"

"He did."

Reela giggled. "He tells that to everyone in hopes that he may be able to convince himself of it. He's good with names and faces, yes, but very forgetful of more important details."

Effie knew not to doubt Reela. It was unlike her to speak without committing to every word.

Relieved to hear this about Wilfre, Effie decided to move on to her next thought. "Steffen's been acting strange ever since classes began. He turns away from my face as if overcome with shyness. But it's not the same as the quiet men in Oakshen who sneak looks at women and then turn away when the women look back. It's as if he's avoiding me completely."

Reela's smile faded. "I've noticed that as well." She leaned over the table. "He has a secret that he can't escape from, and the sight of you seems to cause it to swell, pushing the rest of his feelings aside. I've never known him to hide something from us."

Effie frowned. She'd always loved Steffen as a friend, but she'd definitely never had the same desire for him as her sister, Gabby. "Dare I say he's developed feelings for me?"

"No, it's not that," Reela answered, just as confident as usual. Effie was relieved. She would be flattered, but it would only make their situation tricky. Reela leaned in closer. “But it’s something for sure.”

“Something is better than nothing. I can deal with something.” She noticed the familiar veil of alcohol pressing down on her. She reached for the jug to fill her glass again. “Is there *something* more we know about Cleve’s missing bow, or is that still *nothing*?”

Reela leaned back and pressed her lips together. “Just what I told you from when he brought Alex by and had me help force out the truth. The King’s Guard suspected Cleve had a bow. Alex’s brother had asked to be notified if Alex found out anything, but he hasn’t said anything and has no plans of talking. We still don’t know who took it or what they’re planning.”

“The possibility of war, Steffen keeping secrets, the missing bow, all this uncertainty, yet you don’t seem bothered?”

Reela grinned. It was the sly smile this time—the one that sometimes made Effie feel slightly uneasy. “If I was troubled, then who would everyone come to for help with their problems?”

Effie had to ponder that. Meanwhile, she whipped her glass back up to her mouth. Reela always had been there to talk about her problems, and there had never been a shortage. But when did they speak of Reela’s troubles? She couldn’t remember. “Everyone has issues, why not discuss your own?”

“While I’m helping others, I can’t possibly focus on my own. The more I hear of others’ issues, the more mine seem trivial. I like it this way.” Reela shrugged.

Suddenly Effie had the urge to stand and hug her friend. She did, wrapping her thin arms around Reela’s collar and pressing her head down onto her shoulder. Reela reached up to squeeze Effie’s arms.

“The next time something is bothering you,” Effie said, going back to her seat, “I want you to talk to me about it, no matter how little it might be.”

“You’re in luck,” Reela said as she pulled the glass of sakal back in front of her. “I do have something, and it’s...uncomfortable to speak about. That’s why I brought out the sakal, to help the nerves.”

What could Reela possibly be nervous about telling me? They told each other everything, and Reela was never shy. Effie always figured there was nothing Reela could admit that would surprise her. At least, she used to believe that. She was getting the idea that was about to change. “Please, share it.”

Reela looked...nervous? Effie had to stare at her to tell she was really seeing her friend this way. Reela's almond eyes and puffy lips held nervousness just like any other person, but Effie hadn't seen it before on Reela's face. It took her a few breaths before she concluded that—yes, Reela was indeed nervous. It made Effie nervous in return.

"I've been feeling something in the past week, and it took until today for me to finally realize what it is." Reela blew out air. "I can't believe I'm about to say this out loud." She threw back the drink into her mouth and swallowed with a cringe. As she slammed down the glass, she started coughing uncontrollably.

Effie stood to pat her back. "Are you alright?"

"No, *cough*, something has been, *cough*, very wrong with me, *cough, cough*."

"What can I do?" Effie began to pat harder.

"Nothing, *cough*. I'm locked on someone."

Effie jumped back. A leg got caught on her empty chair, causing her to stumble. Her feet became crossed, and she fell on her rear. She pulled herself up onto the seat so fast she thought for a moment that her friend hadn't even seen her fall until Reela started laughing between coughs.

"You what? You're locked on someone? Are you sure about this?" Effie asked incredulously.

"Yes." Reela looked toward the door, then her head shifted to hang over the table.

Have I ever been locked on a man? Effie nearly wondered aloud. *No, this is Reela's time.* "Do I know him?" she asked instead.

"I think I need another drink before I can answer that." Reela filled their glasses.

"I do know him!" she realized when Reela was too embarrassed to look up from the table. She gasped as she thought of the way she'd seen Reela behaving around him. "Cleve. It's Cleve!"

Reela stood and cupped a hand over Effie's mouth. Reela was as red as the enormous pillar over Redfield—its color could be seen from anywhere on campus. Effie figured it could have been from the coughing, or the sakal, but she liked to think instead that she was seeing her childhood friend humiliated for the first time.

"I don't think the teachers heard in their faculty houses. Perhaps you want to shout it even louder?" Reela quipped, slowly removing her hand.

"I'm sorry, it just came out."

Reela nodded forgivingly. She looked absolutely adorable, nervously fidgeting back into her seat. "What confuses me is that he seems more scared of *me* than of his missing bow. I can't figure out why."

Effie finished the drink Reela had poured for her. "What did you do to him?"

"Nothing!" Reela slapped Effie's arm lightly. "He's terrified. I'm not sure it's even me that he's scared of, but I do seem to be the cause of it. Every time we talk he gets this panic about him. The drinks helped, that first night, but even then everything about him was bottled up inside, guarded with a thick layer of fear. He never talks about himself, have you noticed?"

Ignoring Reela's question, Effie had a far more important one. "What do you think he would do if you kissed him?" She giggled at the thought of it.

Reela gave a soft chuckle of her own. "I haven't the faintest idea, maybe push me away and then run like a little boy. I wouldn't anyway. I think it's best not to act on my feelings. We are living together, after all."

For a moment, Effie wondered what she would do if Brady, who she'd kissed in the bar back home, lived in their house. *Probably ignore him best I could,* she figured. She shook her head before the embarrassment could fully come back to her, focusing instead on Reela, who looked ready to pout. Effie rested her hand on Reela's. "This seems so unlike you."

"It is." Reela took her other hand and put it on top of Effie's. "In fact," Reela continued, "this is the first time I've felt this way, and it took me a lot of thought to figure out what it was. When I first met Cleve, I looked deeply within him—I was skeptical about living with a warrior after your stories from the bar, especially one who brought a bow. I expected to find the qualities of other warriors within him: inflated sense of worth and purpose, twisted visions of reality, no regard for other classes, no interest in the needs of others, especially women. But instead, I found something I'd never seen before in a man, especially a warrior of his size. He was scared, and under that fear was a blank canvas. It was like looking into the mind of an innocent child, yet with a tenacious strength buried so deep I don't think he's even aware of it."

"He seems pretty aware of his strength to me."

Reela politely shook her head, her light-brown hair shimmering as it waved. "This isn't physical strength I'm talking about but mental, like that of a master mage or psychic—something I've never seen in warriors." She sighed as if frustrated.

Effie let her eyes rest on the table. Something seemed off about this conversation. She tried to figure out what it was. Then she realized it was Reela's tone. "You're talking about being locked on to Cleve as if it's a dilemma."

Reela let out a smile that a parent might show to a child who'd misbehaved but hadn't known any better. "That's because it is."

"Well, can't you just stop liking him then?" Effie figured if anyone could fight an attraction successfully, it would be Reela.

Reela stared at her as if waiting for the end of a joke. "Are you serious?"

Effie's hand slipped from between Reela's so she could open her palms and shrug. "I don't know everything you can do. I thought you could control your emotions pretty well. You've always seemed to in the past."

"This isn't just some emotion. It's like he has a grip on my heart so that every time it beats, my blood runs through his fingers like a filter, filling the rest of me with this new life force that's tainted by his touch." Reela grabbed Effie's hands somewhat forcefully. Immediately, Effie felt flushed. "This burning blood brings life to my limbs and mind, but with new purpose, with new desire." Effie could feel what Reela was describing, at least it seemed that way. Her blood was burning hot. "All my old problems cycle through his filter until they dissipate and are forgotten, leaving only this new blood—pure of everything except his touch. All that's left is him."

Effie's heart beat with wild enthusiasm. It was craving something, some kind of relief. The hot feeling swarmed through her body, completely taking over and making her head light. "It feels like I need him," Reela continued softly. "It really does." With her last words, she gave half a whimper, half a laugh, and released Effie's hands.

Effie gasped loudly, her heart still thumping hard. *Did Reela mean to just do that?* Her friend showed no signs of it on her face. Instead she was looking at the door again.

Effie had been told by some men that they needed her, but that was different. She was lost on this subject and had little to offer.

Being compelled to speak, but not knowing what to say, she asked, "So, you must be attracted to him."

"Didn't I say that yet?" Reela laughed to herself. "Absolutely. The way his hair is never the same, molding to every touch it takes, the way his mouth and eyes can give him fifty different expressions just by the difference of a centimeter here and there, how his muscles bulge beneath his skin. You don't think he's sweet on the eyes?"

"If you don't mind being crushed into the bed by twice your weight of man-flesh, then I guess so."

"I don't." Reela had a sneaky grin.

"Reela, I had no idea!" Effie slapped the table in excitement. "That explains why you've never showed interest in guys before—you were waiting for someone who could physically crush you, yet is terrified of you."

"Oh, be quiet."

Effie's laughter was interrupted by the sound of the door being unlatched. Cleve stomped in, stopping abruptly at the sight of them. "Hello," he said with his usual feigned indifference.

"We weren't talking about you," Effie uttered. *I must be drunk*, she thought, realizing she didn't even have to say something. Cleve wouldn't have asked.

Confused, Cleve held out his palms and said, "Good?" His tone was as if he was just hoping to give them the answer they wanted so he could get out of there. Effie couldn't think of what else to say, and soon he marched to his room.

"Why?" Reela mouthed with a shrug.

"It just came out," she whispered.

"Make sure that's the last thing to *just come out*." Reela placed a finger across Effie's lips, which Effie playfully kissed. Reela smiled, and they stood to clear the table.

Effie hadn't even seen Reela kiss a man, so the mention of these deep affections gave her an awkward feeling in her stomach, like she'd swallowed something still squirming. To make it even stranger, she couldn't imagine Cleve with *any* woman. If he had any emotions for women at all, then he hid them well.

She tried thinking of the two housemates being intimate with each other. The first image that came was utterly ridiculous. It was of them standing, facing one another in Reela's bedroom, Cleve gawking with an open mouth at Reela undressing herself. His messy dark hair was strewn across his forehead. His light-brown eyes were wide, pushed open from the spell cast upon him by Reela's large breasts spilling out from her undergarment. She held a hand forward and demanded he disrobe. His tongue dropped from his mouth as he hurried to remove his pants. Effie nearly laughed aloud at the absurdity of it.

She tried to think of a more realistic setting, and to her surprise it came easily. She pictured Cleve and Reela sharing a sheet as they spooned after a fiercely passionate tumble of enjoying the pleasures of each other's body. His arm encircled her like a child tightly holding his blanket in fear of it slipping away. They whispered secrets to each other with their bodies intertwined, and a layer keeping their heart protected was peeled away gently. More layers peeled away the more secrets they shared.

Soon there were no layers left—nothing to hide behind. As they clung tightly to each other, they shared their deepest secrets of all, as if it was the only chance they would ever have. When they finally left the bed to dress, all the layers returned, including a new one—containing the love they shared. It was stronger than all the other layers combined and squeezed so tightly around their hearts it would be impossible to remove without ripping it apart.

I've never been locked on to a man, Effie realized then.

A knock at the door disrupted her image like a stone being dropped into a serene lake. She gave Reela a curious glance.

"Not someone I know well enough to recognize," the psychic answered.

Effie went to the door as Cleve came out of his room and watched with folded arms from the hall.

A man dressed in dark gray with a low-slung hat was standing there patiently. "I'm Javy Rayvender of the King's Council," he said. Three guards stood behind him, each with steel battle armor and swords ready at the hip. Effie saw his eyes go over her shoulder and tighten. "Cleve, come with us please," he said.

"Where are you taking him?" Reela put herself between Cleve and the door, folding her arms to match Cleve behind her.

"It's best we discuss that with Cleve in private," Javy answered with a look that showed he would say no more. His hands rested comfortably in the long pockets of his trench coat. If there was a hurry somewhere, it didn't concern him.

Cleve put a hand on Reela's back as he stepped around her. "It's alright." Reela's arms sank back to her sides.

Effie noticed then that rain had started to fall, bouncing melodically off the steel on the guards behind Javy. Cleve hunched into a long coat and walked outside. He closed the door behind him, but not before a last glance at Reela.

Chapter 28: Walls
CLEVE

Many times Cleve had imagined how he'd be caught. It would most likely be someone who saw him training in Raywhite Forest and then ran off to tell a guard. He would hide the bow and deny the accusation until it went away.

But when hiding the bow failed, he would imagine this moment—being escorted to the castle by armored guards.

In his mind, he would be chained like other prisoners he'd seen. The heavy metal connecting his ankles would clink shamefully with each step. But he was fortunate because Javy Rayvender decided the restraints wouldn't be necessary.

"You should know why we're here," Javy had told him as they left the walls of the Academy. "This is because of your bow."

At least I know who has it, Cleve thought, *although I still don't know why the King's men waited so long to come and get me.*

Except for the sound of raindrops splattering against them and the wind whistling by, the walk from the Academy to Kyrro City was two long hours of silence. It gave Cleve time to ponder his options besides cooperating; there was only one really, and it was quite terrible—to run. The penalty for resisting detainment was death in most circumstances. With that settled, his thoughts went over a conversation with Alex and Reela earlier in the week. He wanted to see if he could remember anything Alex had said that might give him some sort of clue as what to expect when he reached the castle.

Reela had been at the kitchen table when Cleve had stepped inside with Alex. She was writing in the journal he'd seen in her room when he went snooping.

"Have a seat," Cleve had told Alex as he stretched out his hand toward a chair. It felt a little forced, more so than he'd meant it to, anyway.

"You make it sound like I'm on trial," Alex said and forced a smile, but there was some sincerity to his words.

Reela set down her pen. "Hi, Alex, Cleve. Need me to move?"

"No, stay," Cleve replied quickly, again more forced than he intended. "Please," he added. It was his missing bow making him tense, he knew. "You can help us." *You can help me find the truth,* he really meant. He could see she understood by the nod she gave back.

Alex found Effie's sakal as they were settling into their seats. Without asking, he took three glasses from the counter and carried them to the table. "I think some of us could use this," he said, glancing at Cleve.

After each had a drink, Alex began without preamble. "My brother told me to keep an eye out for Dex Polken's son, Cleve Polken." There was a noticeable change as he spoke. His voice was low and serious. His warm friendliness dissolved. "He said they believe you have a bow in your possession."

An uncomfortable silence followed.

"Did you know our house would be empty during your party?" Reela wisely asked. She stared closely at Alex whenever asking a question or listening to him speak, but in between, she stole glances at Cleve. In the fleeting moments when their eyes locked, it gave his heart a squeeze.

"No. I didn't even know Cleve lived with all of you when we met," Alex replied. "If it was the King's Guard that took it, they must've had eyes on the house to know it was empty."

"Cleve, think about who could have known that you had it." Reela spoke with such intent it seemed she cared about finding out who took the bow just as much as he did.

"Terren, you, Alex, Effie, and Steffen, that's it." As Cleve glanced at Alex, he let his judgment show.

"I had no idea you actually had one until you told me," Alex replied with his hands up, as if to block Cleve's stare.

"I believe him," Reela said. Cleve knew that meant, *"I know he's telling the truth."* Even clearer than her words, he remembered the wry smiles she would show when telling him something. Sometimes, the faces she made were so cute it annoyed him to realize he was having trouble looking away.

"I swear on never taking another drink, it is the truth." Alex said. He brought a fist down to the table that pulled Cleve's focus back to the discussion.

They sipped on Effie's sakal while speculating further. Alex drank three times what Cleve and Reela did. A sheen of sweat came over his flushed face the harder they tried to figure out who'd taken the bow and why. Their conversation concluded with no leads, but at least Cleve felt as if there were two more people he could trust. With Terren, that meant three now, triple what he had last week. Reela had tried to convince him that Effie and Steffen had nothing to do with the missing bow, but even she couldn't persuade him to trust them yet. Not that he believed they would've taken it, just that they might be hiding something. Steffen especially had been acting rather devious when Effie was around.

Cleve wondered how little he would've believed of what Alex told him if it weren't for Reela. He was beginning to appreciate the perks of knowing a psychic, even if being in the same room with her still sent terror through his bones.

Reela—her name evoked so much emotion, even in his thoughts. He hated how years of training to focus were instantly undone the moment he thought of her. It was like building a wall brick by brick and watching it stand against all elements until she came along. Now, Reela's path had taken her alongside his wall, her hand reaching out to run her fingers along it. Bricks came loose from her touch, so Cleve ran behind her, repairing the damage by picking up the fallen pieces and putting them back in their places. It was only a matter of time before she'd knock over bricks faster than he could return them and the wall would crumble completely.

By the time he entered Kyrro City, the rain was so loud Javy Rayvender needed to shout to be heard. "The King wishes to speak with you. Will we need to chain you now, or will you continue to cooperate?" The guards with Javy waited for Cleve's answer with their hands on their hilts.

"Chains will not be necessary." He might not have his bow, but at least he had some dignity.

He'd been to Kyrro City once before for his parents' funeral. The King had required their bodies to be buried not in Cleve's hometown of Trentyre, but in the graveyard of Kyrro City. The King even attended the ceremony and made a brief statement about Cleve's father being a great warrior.

In retrospect, their bodies being buried in Kyrro City didn't make sense. Usually, people would be buried in the town where they lived, and only a guard of the King would have a funeral service like that of his mother and father, yet they hadn't worked for the King.

As he walked between Javy and the three guards, Cleve saw nothing familiar about the city. He might have recognized the graveyard, but luckily he never saw it. Even with the cold rain beating down, the path to the castle was filled with street merchants and a beggar farther down who waited for them to pass before reverting back to his pleas. They walked by bars, weapon shops, a brothel, and many homes standing only a foot taller than him. It was all similar to what he recalled of Trentyre, except the warriors walking about here in Kyrro City were all of the King's Guard, usually wearing armor dyed the color of Kyrro—light blue, with a gold crown outlined in silver on their chests. At the sight of Javy, they skirted to the side of the road to let him pass, giving Cleve a hard look as he followed behind the King's Council member. *I would have harsh judgments for a prisoner as well,* he realized.

The massive castle in the center of the city could be seen even from the Academy, so to say it dwarfed the houses around it was an understatement. A small army of guards stood at the entrance, which was a black, ironbark door that looked sturdy enough to deny admission without the men clad in steel in front of it.

How could such a fortress fall to an attack? Cleve wondered. But it had, he knew, many times even. One wouldn't know by looking at it, as each new king had rebuilt it stronger, replacing stone with ironbark in the areas the castle had suffered damage.

A boy servant ran from behind the leg of a guard at the door to deliver an envelope to Javy. Cleve noticed the King's stamp on it as Javy thanked the boy and then ripped it open. He gave the note inside no more than a quick glance before he sighed and met Cleve's eyes with a slow, upward swing of his head.

"This is where I hand you off," Javy said. "Approach the castle guards and answer any questions they put to you." He took a step closer to Cleve so that he could speak softly without the guards overhearing. "It's been too long for many of them since they've seen a battle. Don't give them any chance to use their weapons or they'll take it." With that, he lowered his hat and turned to walk back the way they'd come.

Cleve approached, only to be met with the points of several swords.

"State your name," the lead guard ordered.

"Cleve Polken."

The guard inspected him from head to toe. "We've been expecting you," he said bitterly.

And if you hadn't been, would I have one less arm? Cleve kept his thoughts to himself and nodded.

"Wait here." The guard sheathed his sword and walked to the door.

Ten minutes passed before the door was opened and the guard returned with a smiling gray-haired man. "Hello Cleve," he said, extending a hand. The man's face was in his memory, but Cleve wasn't sure from when or where. "I'm Councilman Kerr."

Councilman is a strange first name, Cleve might have mentioned if his mood was better. Instead, he replied with just a nod as he shook the man's hand.

"A man of few words, like your father."

That's how I know you, he realized. A decade ago, Cleve had seen Kerr and his father meeting several times but had never known why.

"I see Dex didn't speak of me, but he had much to share of you. Please follow me to the King's quarters. I wish we were meeting under different circumstances so I could give you a tour of this magnificent castle."

Guards closed the door behind them. There was a deep thud as it was locked into place by some hidden bolt. *Getting out may be just as hard as getting in.*

Chapter 29: Follow
CLEVE

The ground floor was paved with stone. Doors, hallways, and more doors were in every direction but gave no sense as to what was behind them. Councilman Kerr moved lively for an old man, pacing quickly up the first of many flights of stairs and giving Cleve no time to look around.

"We're going to the top floor. Six flights of stairs, forty stairs each. I make this climb several times a day." Kerr had a cadence of pride in his voice.

The floors of the second level and above were made from black and glossy ironbark wood. Decorative banners were placed along banisters and walls. Cleve glanced at one but had never seen it before. *I bet Steffen has a book about them.*

"Oof," someone blurted as they collided with him. In the two steps Cleve had taken without looking ahead, he'd knocked over a short woman who must've been a server judging by her plain tunic and unwashed hair. He pulled her up from the ground with an apology. She kept her head down and apologized as well.

"Careful," Councilman Kerr said. "We keep ourselves very busy here, so the castle is populated with all sorts of people always on the move. You'd be surprised how much work the upkeep of the castle takes. The ironbark will hold forever, but much of the structure is still stone, and stone doesn't hold up as well against the years. We have fifty masons on staff, most of whom live within these castle walls. I'll explain more as we walk. Use those young legs. The King doesn't have time to wait. He has prepared himself to meet with you."

Cleve kept himself closer to Kerr as they continued up another set of stairs.

"The men and women in long coats of white or gray are chemists," the councilman explained. "We have many who work here, but not just on potions. They serve as medical staff as well." A chemist passed by them holding a beaker that bubbled with some sort of steaming substance. Cleve leaned against the railing of the stairs to ensure it would avoid him.

As they reached the third floor, two warriors in chain mail moved aside to let them through. "I'm sure the warriors of the King's Guard are obvious to you," the councilman said, "but you may not have seen our mages yet." Without slowing his quick pace, he pointed ahead to three mages huddled over a scroll. Each woman wore a blood-red robe. "You can tell their specialty by the color of their robe—red to represent hot Bastial Energy and green to represent heavy Sartious Energy. As you may guess, there are far fewer mages in green. But what many don't know is why we use red to represent Bastial Energy. Do you?"

The answer seemed simple at first. Sartious Energy was green, so green represented it. Cleve figured Bastial Energy must be red to follow suit. But then Cleve realized it wasn't that. When Effie created light from Bastial Energy it was always white, strangely white, white as snow.

"I don't," Cleve replied.

"What I love about this question is that the less people know about magic the higher the chances they'll get it right," Kerr said with a wry smile. "You must know something about magic to answer the way you did. Bastial Energy is red, thus we use red to represent it."

Cleve knew he was being led on, but without any idea where he was headed, he had no choice but to follow. "But Bastial Energy is white."

"Yes, in low doses, which is usually the only time we see Bastial Energy. But like steel being heated by fire, Bastial Energy can change color. Depending on how concentrated and hot it gets, it can become red. If you see a stream of red Bastial Energy, watch out. It's going to be hot enough to take off a limb with just a touch."

"Some mages can cast such a spell?" Cleve asked incredulously.

"Only a few ever have, and that's after hours of meditation for a single blast." Kerr curled his mouth into a sly grin. "Scary stuff, isn't it?"

Then he realized that truthfully it really wasn't. A sword could take off a limb just as easily. The thought of fear just brought his uncle's Elven friend Rek to mind—nothing was scarier than the most powerful psychic in the world.

Next he thought of Reela and realized she was a close second.

The third floor was by far the most crowded, at least from what was visible to Cleve. There were now many more men and women dressed like the server he'd nearly trampled earlier, most of them carrying trays with empty plates and cups. Councilman Kerr stopped Cleve so they could move for one woman wobbling her way through with a pile of sheets stacked up to her nose.

"If you think this is bad, you wouldn't believe the kitchens," Kerr said after she went by.

They walked up two more flights of stairs. On the fifth floor, two prostitutes giggled as they followed a man into a room down one of the hallways. The councilman had no words to share for that. He kept his head straight and pushed off the railing for support every few paces. The old man was a bit winded by then.

The lack of chatter on the sixth floor made it clear how noisy the rest of the castle was. Except for two guards standing as still as statues near the stairs, no one roamed the halls and all the doors were closed. The eeriness of the sudden change produced a dark thought. *Is this where they take people to be executed?*

"No one goes up to the sixth floor without permission from the King or his trusted council. You should hear the ridiculous speculation about what others believe is up here." Kerr laughed between heavy breaths. "Someone once told me they heard we kept a Slugari up here. Isn't that funny?" His laughter grew louder. "It doesn't even make sense. Why would we keep one, let alone in secret?"

What's a Slugari? Cleve wondered but forced a smile instead.

The prune-skinned man had a friendliness to him that lifted Cleve's spirits. *If this guy is leading me to the ax, then he sure hides it well.*

"Here we are," Kerr said, unlocking the heavy door and pushing it open with both hands.

Cleve recognized King Welson immediately, which was easy because of the throne he sat on, but a stick of a man Cleve had never seen before was to the King's right. He stood tall, about Cleve's height. He had curly dark hair atop a high forehead, pointed cheeks, and a sharp chin. His eyes appeared as black as the darkness that had set in outside the castle, and his skin was sickly pale like it had never seen the sun. Between him and the King was Cleve's priceless bow—resting against the throne.

Cleve avoided eye contact with both of them and hoped to hear something else from Kerr as they walked forward together. Instead, the councilman was silent, matching the room.

The King's lips twisted into a smile. "You're grown up, big like your father."

The mention of Dex felt contrived, as if the King wanted Cleve to ask. So he did: "Did you know him?"

"I knew him well enough." Welson spoke regretfully. The way his eyes shifted to the ground made it seem like there was far more to it than that. "You must have some idea why you're here." The King gave a commanding nod to the tall man to his right, who reached beside the throne to lift Cleve's bow. "The man who holds your bow is my top psychic. He can tell if you lie, so you'll tell the truth, correct?"

Of course there's a psychic, Cleve said to himself bitterly. "Yes."

"Unannounced sweeps were done throughout each city to collect the bows, and the manufacture of them has stopped. So where did you get this one?"

Cleve glanced at the psychic. His head was stretched forward, his eyes peering deep into Cleve's. "It was my father's. It was hidden during each sweep."

"Do you know that possessing a bow is a crime, that you could be put in jail for years?"

"I do," Cleve answered.

The King sat back on his throne and let the unsettling silence waft through the room. "And how long have you been using the bow while it was illegal to do so?"

"Since the day after the outlaw was announced. If it wasn't hidden, then it was in my hands."

Cleve expected that to be the last question before he was dragged into a cell, but instead there was a friendly grin on Welson's face. "Good," he replied. The smile didn't befit the King, Cleve thought. It didn't seem to take shape naturally. It didn't help either that his nose was thin, especially for his wide face, or that his cheekbones looked to push out too far. "So you are as skilled with this awful weapon as you are with a sword?"

Cleve squinted curiously, ignoring the comment about the bow. "You know of my skill with the sword?"

"I know you've won each annual weapons demonstration in the three years since you were old enough to compete at fourteen." King Welson spoke proudly. "We've also been watching you since your admission to the Academy. I needed to make sure of your abilities before bringing you here." A frown formed and his tone softened. "Unfortunately, there is still more I need to know about you before I can provide details of what you're doing here on the sixth floor instead of locked in a cell under the castle. So I ask again—your skill with the bow, how is it?" There was a patience in Welson's words that came as a surprise.

"Better than my skill with the sword."

"As I'd hoped." The King's smile reformed. "Your father was the best sharpshooter Kyrro has ever seen. Not only could he shoot far and accurately, but consistently as well. Rain, wind, it didn't matter. He would hit his mark as long as it was still." He raised a finger to prepare Cleve for his next statement. "But even Dex Polken, with his unparalleled focus, couldn't predict where his target would be after he released the arrow, not if the animal—or man—had mind enough to move."

"Like my father," Cleve interjected, "I would never shoot at a man."

"Wouldn't you, though?" King Welson retorted. "If you believed he was an enemy or a threat to the people of Kyrro?" He stopped to let Cleve ponder, then quietly finished with, "Your father did just that."

Cleve could not respond with words, only a baffled look.

"You act as if you didn't know," Welson said with amused shock. "Is this true? You've never heard of Dex Polken shooting at a man?"

"I have not," Cleve answered, holding back his anger at the accusation. There'd been no wars in Ovira during his father's lifetime. Why would he shoot a man? The King gave a glimpse to his right. The ghastly psychic replied with a nod.

"Thank you for your honesty so far." Welson's tone was proud once more. "I've been curious about that for quite some time." He used his forearms to brace his weight so he could lean forward. "But we still need your answer to this, and I'll make the question very easy. Would you shoot a man—shoot to kill—if your King commanded it?" He lifted a finger to stop Cleve from answering right away. "Keep in mind that all citizens of Kyrro must obey a direct order from the King, especially the Academy attendees like you, who've signed the contract to fight."

Cleve looked to Councilman Kerr and discovered an anxious

glance back at him. *The answer to this will determine what happens next,* Cleve thought. Inflicting pain or death was never something he wished. Sure, he'd imagine enemies in place of his targets, but they were faceless attackers who would stop at nothing to kill. Giving a name to them hadn't been something he'd considered.

"I believe I could do that. I've never thought of it before."

The King glanced at his psychic, who continued to stare at Cleve, eyes locked. Suddenly the psychic snapped out of his trance to nod at the King.

"The psychic would say if you lied." Welson Kimard stood to pace in front of his throne. "I'll need more certainty that you can complete the mission, but we can come back to that. First, there's something I need to see." He stopped his pacing. "Councilman Kerr, would you please retrieve the bow and hand it to Cleve?"

Kerr followed the order without a word, giving Cleve his weapon with a nervous grin.

The weight of the fine ironbark in Cleve's hands put his mind at ease for a heartbeat, but then the King spoke again and disrupted his calm. "Come with me." Welson disappeared behind his throne, and the psychic followed.

Cleve didn't wish to move. Wherever they wanted him to go, he felt safer where he was. "Come along, it's fine," the councilman said, walking toward the throne. Cleve reluctantly followed him, finding there to be a hidden walkway that was blocked from view until he was closer.

He was the last one into the tunnel, followed by no one, not even a guard. He had his bow but no arrows. *How far would I get if I ran right now?* Then the solid ironbark door that stood between him and the rain outside jumped into mind. *There's no way through that door, and I don't know how it opens, probably some lever somewhere. That's even if I made it to the first floor.* He decided his odds were better doing as he was told.

Chapter 30: Target
CLEVE

The tunnel was dark, made from brown, flammable wood instead of ironbark, so there were no lamps or torches to light the area. Unlike the rest of the castle Cleve had seen, there were no windows or arrow slits either. The sound of the rain bouncing off the low ceiling echoed within. There was an incline as well, Cleve found out as a surprise when his step came down onto the ground quicker than he anticipated and he stumbled but quickly regained his footing.

"Did you fall?" Kerr asked.

"No, I'm fine."

"Sorry, I should have mentioned the slope. I've lived in this castle for so many years, I forget about small things like that."

"Not a problem." Cleve found himself wondering again why his father would've been meeting with Kerr and what other clues might be in his memory that were buried so deep that some sort of reminder would be needed to dig them out. He felt something else coming loose as he searched through his mind—the image of his mother using her wand to light the wood in the fireplace as a storm was setting in outside. Sorrow came with it, filling his stomach like a gallon of water.

He gave his head one violent shake before his memory could fill in other details about her. *Think about something else*, he commanded himself and pushed that memory away. Suddenly, Reela's burning green eyes appeared. They were the last things he'd seen as he'd shut the door to their house. He could feel his heart beating harder as her face and bosom took shape. *Not that*, he thought, and resorted to multiplication tables to distract himself—a strategy he found to work quite well when his mind became relentless. The sorrow had dissolved, but his focus was lost by then.

The tunnel led them outside to the castle's roof. There was a walkway in between parapets that was designed for archers to use when defending the castle. Not even the King's own staff was allowed bows, so Cleve figured it just wasn't worth the expense to change the design. The walkway was square, wrapping around the entire top of the castle. Pelted by the heavy rain, he remembered where he was again, and his mind cleared of all other thoughts as he prepared himself for whatever would be asked of him.

The King met with a nearby guard, who handed off an arrow. The King took it with two fingers as if its touch might poison him and stretched his arm toward Cleve. After a moment of hesitation, Cleve accepted it. He bobbed his hand up and down to feel its weight. It was definitely one of his arrows.

"You have one chance to hit the target." The King pointed to the other side of the roof.

Cleve found what he believed the King was referring to—a cut of wood maybe as wide as a man's shoulders.

"That?" he asked incredulously as he pointed.

"And the arrow must stick. It's soft wood, so if the arrow doesn't, it wouldn't be a kill shot."

Cleve judged the distance to be around seventy-five yards. Simply shooting an arrow that far wasn't the main problem because his weapon was a longbow, nearly as tall as him. Instead, it was hitting his mark over that far a distance and in the rain.

"What if I miss it?" Cleve asked before he could determine whether or not he wanted to know.

"Then bringing you here was a mistake," Welson replied with a frown. The rain was splattering against his scalp, bouncing off in all directions. The guard nearby offered the King his cloak, but he denied it with a shake of his hand, keeping his eyes on Cleve. "I need to know you're capable of the mission before I tell you its details. If you're incapable, then I'll have to send you to a cell for disobeying the bow law until I decide what to do with you. Make it easier for both of us and hit your target."

Cleve's heart was thumping and a slight shiver ran through his body. *I need to calm myself.* He closed his eyes to meditate, clearing his mind of everything except a tranquil river. Trees began emerging along the banks, filling in all the empty spaces. Soon the sun appeared, bouncing off the water to make it shimmer. The sound of the rain disappeared into that of the river coursing lightly over rocks. Cleve pulled in the hot, red Bastial Energy he imagined he could see floating about, sucking it into his stomach and chest. The more he pulled in, the warmer he became. When he opened his eyes, he was calm and itching to use it.

He secured the arrow onto his bow and began to draw the string. He didn't think of the target, not at first. Instead, his focus was directed within as he transferred hot energy to his arms and back so that he could pull hard without a shake. His heart slowed, and he held his breath. Strong wind blew at him, so he aligned the arrow a few inches straight above his target and released.

The arrow shot through the air with so much speed it hissed. When it pierced the head of the wood there was a faint thud, no louder than a whisper.

"Good!" King Welson shouted. He clasped Cleve's shoulder and turned to walk back. "Come."

Cleve obeyed and walked beside him back into the tunnel.

"Did you learn to shoot from your father?" Welson asked.

"Yes." Cleve held onto his longbow tightly. "What now?"

"You make the same shot tomorrow, but it will be a man you shoot this time."

His nerves were jumpy again. "Who is it?"

"He's the most dangerous man known to us. He can sense your presence and use psyche against you, so you have to take him out from afar, at least fifty yards. If he gets too close, you'll have no chance against him. Bring his head back to show it has been done."

"What did he do?" Cleve needed far more than that to feel comfortable taking another man's life. He wanted to hear that this man had killed women and children, raped them first. He wanted Welson to describe the most sinister man who'd ever drawn breath.

Instead, the King said nothing.

They returned to the secluded room where the King poured a glass of water for himself and offered one to Cleve as well. He accepted it, glad to relieve his dry throat.

"I must explain something first for you to understand why he needs to die," Welson said. "Right now, Javy Rayvender is delivering a message to Liaison Wilfre at the Academy. Tomorrow, Wilfre will make an announcement to all the students. The same announcement will be made by my liaisons in Oakshen and in Trentyre. It will even be announced to the few hundred who live at Gendock by a messenger who I'll send at sunrise. The purpose will be to notify all of Kyrro of that which I'm about to tell you.

"The treaty between Kyrro and Tenred is renewed every year at this time, and each year it has been more difficult to agree to peace." The King took another sip of water, only to make a face as if it were sour. He handed it to his psychic. "Could you have someone fetch me some wine? I won't need you just yet, but hurry back soon."

The psychic moved his long legs quickly, shutting the door behind him as he hustled out. Councilman Kerr stood silently beside the King, and that's when Cleve noticed the similarity in their stares. The gray-haired councilman must have been thirty years older, but both he and the King had the same eyes. They looked battered and swollen from overuse, with long crow's feet wrapping around their temples. It seemed like just keeping them open was a struggle. Welson gave a smile to Kerr and told him, "You should get some rest. We have many busy days ahead."

"Thank you," the councilman replied, nodding graciously. He stopped in front of Cleve on his way out. His head hung low on his shoulders. "We're all doing what we think is right." He took Cleve's hand and whispered quickly as he shook it, "No matter what anyone tells you, make sure you do the same." He grabbed the guard from the room with him as he walked out, leaving just the King with Cleve, now more worried than ever.

"This is where you tell me we're at war and the target is someone from Tenred?" Cleve asked to disrupt the silence.

"Close. It would be more accurate to say Tenred hasn't agreed to renew the treaty, and the target isn't someone *from* Tenred, but he is on their side. What you'll be missing in the announcement tomorrow is a brief history lesson and what we can expect in the near future. All kings should study the history of Kyrro. I wish I had when I became king at just fifteen. Instead, I was determined to find the man who killed my father. His death was not all that different from your parents—killed by an arrow from an unknown shooter—but that is a discussion for another time."

Never is the time for that discussion, Cleve thought.

"History reoccurs, so it's almost like looking into the future to revisit it. The roots of our rivalry with Tenred started earlier than even the creation of their territory. It began with the birth of Lansra Tarcos seventy-nine years ago. Who thought one baby girl could cause so much chaos? Her mother was Doree Rose. Her father was Sid Takary—at least that's what Sid Takary thought."

Cleve knew of the Takary family; most everyone did. They were the original rulers of Kyrro, coming from Goldram across the Starving Ocean, and with great wealth. To his knowledge, they still ruled in Goldram, but their legacy had ended here when King Welson Kimard's father and his army had taken over the kingdom by force. Cleve didn't know much about Sid Takary, though, and certainly nothing about Lansra Tarcos, who the King said had started this rivalry in the first place.

Welson had paused as if expecting Cleve to speak. Perhaps he wondered whether Cleve would say how much of this he already knew, but Cleve knew little and figured it would be faster just to listen, so the King continued.

"Sid Takary was by far the worst king of Kyrro, in case you didn't know. The marriage to his wife, the beautiful and wealthy Doree Rose, was forced upon her. She did get pregnant eventually, but it was by another man, one more famous in history—the Piranha." Welson paused again, but this time he asked, "Have you heard of him?"

"Jenick Tarcos." Cleve knew his real name. "Yes, I've heard of him. No enemy of Kyrro's people stood a chance against him and his army. He was exceptionally skilled at close-range combat."

"So, you must know he led the first rebellion against the Takary family's rule over Kyrro?"

Cleve nodded, still unsure what this had to do with anything.

Welson gestured toward the throne as he continued. "When the Piranha defeated Sid Takary, he became king, with Doree Rose as his wife. Shortly after, Doree Rose announced that the daughter she supposedly had with Sid Takary actually belonged to the Piranha—Jenick Tarcos. From then on, the baby girl was known as Lansra Tarcos instead of Lansra Takary, but later in history she would be nicknamed 'The Catalyst.' For when Sid Takary died, he still had a brother, Jinn Takary, and his ambition for power came from his need for revenge. He took back the throne five years later after the Piranha died from heart failure, the unfortunate curse that most men of the Tarcos family have shared throughout history."

Welson sighed sadly. "Jinn Takary, even with the Piranha dead, would stop at nothing until revenge had been dealt in full. He demanded Lansra Tarcos be executed, an innocent little girl mind you, along with every person of the Tarcos or Rose families for supporting the traitor who killed his brother."

There was a click as the door behind Cleve opened with a quick push. He spun to see the sun-deprived psychic rushing over. A reflex caused Cleve's hand to reach over his back for a quiver that wasn't there. The psychic had a glass of wine in hand and hurried past Cleve with a quick nervous glance.

"Thank you," King Welson said, closing both hands around it and taking a sip. "Obviously, many people did not take kindly to the demands of eliminating two popular and powerful families, nor to the King calling for the execution of an innocent child. Another rebellion had begun to form, but it was discovered before becoming powerful enough to act. Someone on the inside gave up everyone to Jinn Takary, the King at the time. There were a few who escaped the city; ten to be exact. They were chased all the way to where Tenred castle is now, northwest of the Fjallejon Pathway. The rest were killed where they were found."

Cleve nodded as he prepared himself to hear the story of the battle over Tenred. Most knew the details, although the specific numbers seemed to differ depending upon who told it. Even though history portrayed Kyrro as the enemy, it was a story where few had come together to defend themselves against many; a tale everyone could appreciate no matter what side they were on now.

"The ten who escaped couldn't have had better positioning. They were up miles of hills, mountains at every side and the ocean behind them. The one hundred men who Jinn Takary sent after them were defeated in a slow battle of range weapons. The surviving attackers retreated back to Kyrro when they knew they'd lost. Jinn Takary sent five hundred men next." Welson was using both hands to gesture, one holding on to his glass of wine, which threatened to spill over the side.

"By the time those five hundred got to Tenred, many people from Kyrro had brought supplies to the newly formed territory, and some even stayed to join the fight. Three more battles ensued, with Kyrro losing them all, before Jinn Takary finally agreed to speak about terms for a treaty. Part of the treaty was that no members of the Tarcos or Rose families would be harmed." Welson gestured his glass toward Cleve. "The master chemist at the Academy is a Rose, if you didn't know, Jack Rose."

Cleve did know that, but he never would've thought to make the connection. He didn't spend much time thinking about chemists.

Welson paused for more wine, which he sucked down in a quick slurp to hurry back to the story. He seemed to enjoy telling it, holding a faint smile and using a loud voice. Cleve suspected there were many more details in the private history books of the castle that the King wasn't sharing, though.

"That same year, Jinn Takary died mysteriously of heart failure, which was the first case of heart related death to be known within the Takary family. His son took over, believing the death of his father was an assassination through poison by someone within Kyrro who sided with Tenred. Against the advice of his council, he negated the treaty and tried to attack Tenred. He was easily defeated and reluctantly agreed to terms of peace again.

"By then it was clear there would be no hope of overcoming the great advantage Tenred had defensively, and there were far too many more in Kyrro for Tenred to ever take and hold any of our cities. There have been no more battles since then, but peace was never really reached. There have been many more deaths within Kyrro at the hands of Tenred spies, even within these castle walls since my coronation. It's as if both sides have immunity from total annihilation, so there has been no end to the growth of hostility and covert operations to diminish power."

"So why did they wait until now to disagree with the terms of the treaty?" Cleve asked.

"They've gained an extremely powerful army." Welson sipped his wine. "I know," he said the moment his swallow had finished, "how does one simply *gain* an army? It didn't come from Kyrro, that's for sure. These men have lived in Ovira well before we Humans came...I'm not sure if 'men' is even the right word. They're called Krepps, somewhat intelligent creatures with scaly skin who stand taller than us, are stronger than us, and most importantly are thousands more than us. For reasons we haven't yet determined, they've joined forces with Tenred." He had a quick gulp from his cup. "We believe they may attack in the near future."

"I have no problems shooting a Krepp that sides with our enemy." Cleve had heard of Krepps from Terren but knew little of them. If they were to attack Kyrro, that's all he would need to know.

"I'm thankful for your attitude, but remember you are to kill a psychic, and there are no psychics among the Krepps—no mages, chemists, or warriors, either. We have people here who know much about their race, and they have told me that the Krepps have no grasp on Bastial or Sartious Energy. They do fight like warriors, however, possessing great skill with swords and bows, even without the use of Bastial Energy. Your target is no Krepp, though. He has been seen meeting with the King of Tenred, Tegry Hiller, in Corin Forest. That is where you'll go to find him."

Cleve listened closely, knowing full well this was how he was about to be connected to everything. His nerves were on edge, making him feel like he was either about to explode or become overwhelmed with great relief.

"With war coming, the law against bows will have to be rescinded. As much as it's an insult to me and to my father's memory, protecting Kyrro is more important. Training will take some time. Meanwhile, you're the only one with the skill to take him out from the necessary distance. But be aware, if you have any doubts about your ability to shoot him, I'll find a way for him to be taken out through force, and many will die in the process. However, this would still be better than sending you if you cannot do it. A failed attempt would alert him of our plan, and he would retreat to Tenred castle. Surprise is our only advantage right now."

"If it's to protect Kyrro, I can do it. What does he look like?"

Welson had another gulp of wine, swishing it in his glass while his eyes steadied at Cleve's feet. "I hate to command his death, but I have no choice." The King lifted his head to show his sadness. "He's an Elf, one I've known for a long time."

An Elf? A wave of shock stormed through Cleve, tightening his throat so that he gagged. "Do you mean Rek?" he asked when he was capable of forcing out the words.

"So you've heard of him."

Chapter 31: Decision
CLEVE

So much panic was coursing through Cleve, he could barely breathe. *How could a friend of my uncle's wish destruction upon Kyrro and all its people?*

"You're certain Rek has sided with Tenred?" Cleve asked, fighting down the urge to retch.

"I'm certain of my decision, and it's not your place to question it." King Welson stood. "I just need to know whether you're capable of this task. I'm not sure what you've heard about Rek, so tell me, are you having doubts now? If so, keep this in mind: If you don't do this, you'll be disobeying a direct order. I'll charge you with possession of a bow, reneging on your admission contract to the Academy, and disobeying the King. You'll be held in prison. If ever you were to be released, you would never be accepted back to the school and never recognized as a true warrior. While you're in prison, I'll find another way for the mission to be completed. I'll protect Kyrro at all costs. No king before me has given up any land, and I'll be no different, no matter how much more powerful the army of Krepps is. However, with Rek on their side, this war is lost before it begins. We have nothing to stop a force that strong. This elimination needs to happen."

What is Terren going to think of this? Could his friend really be a traitor? "I'll do it," Cleve answered reluctantly, as ten thoughts collided. It was the only answer he could give, so he found no reason in hesitating.

"I can hear the doubt in your voice even without my psychic." King Welson spoke regretfully. "I need to know before you leave that you're certain you can do this. You only need to be a hero for a moment to change the world forever. Be that hero." His voice deepened and he closed his fists. "Give us the opportunity to win this war. Say what you'll do."

"I'll kill Rek and bring you his head," Cleve muttered, still overwhelmed by the flood of emotions he was feeling. Welson glanced at his psychic, who shook his head, *no.*

The King slammed his fist into his cupped hand. “It’s not genuine. You’re having doubts! You need to be certain, otherwise my guards will take you to the dungeons right now. What will you do?”

“I’ll kill him! I’ll kill Rek and bring you his head!” Cleve shouted. He felt anger boiling through his veins, but even with his rage he had no confidence behind his words.

Again, the psychic shook his head, *no.*

“Guards!” the King shouted. Two guards threw open the door and rushed into the room. “Take this young man to prison to grow old while everyone else fights the war for him.” They each grabbed one of his arms and began to pull him toward the door. They were close to his height, but older and less strong, he could feel it.

“Wait, I’ll do it!” Cleve shouted, but of course they didn’t obey him. “Stop, give me more time!” One of them hit him hard in the stomach to stop his resisting. A dull pain surged through him, but at least he still had his breath. His frustration took control. Only one thought was going through his head: *I just need one more try to convince him and without these guards jerking me away.*

He was nearly out of the room when he managed to tug his right arm free. He made a fist and slammed it into the other guard’s temple. The man stumbled and let loose his grip.

Cleve brought his right elbow back to slam into the stomach of the first guard and then used his newly freed left hand to follow with a straight punch to his forehead. The guard went down.

The other guard, still stumbling, drew his sword, but before he could get a firm hold on its handle, Cleve kicked the weapon. It flew across the room, too far to retrieve, so Cleve let it out of his mind. Another kick, this one between the legs, and the guard keeled over. Unsatisfied that the guard was still on his feet, Cleve followed with a fist that crunched into his cheekbone.

Cleve then heard the sound of metal behind him. *The other guard’s sword unsheathed,* he knew. *It worked the first time, so why not again?* He spun to kick his shoe into the steel coming toward him. It connected, protecting him from a stab, but this guard didn’t let the weapon fall from his grip. In a blink, Cleve focused Bastial Energy into his legs and leaped. He spun and extended a leg so that his heel connected with the guard’s cheek. Down the guard went, yet he still managed to hold on to the sword.

With both guards on the ground, Cleve had time to pry a sword from one of their hands. Although the guard nearest to Cleve seemed confused about where he was, he still seemed to know he was in a fight, making it quite difficult to steal his weapon. So Cleve stepped on the man's wrist and tried once more. This time it was easy.

The King must have called for more guards without Cleve noticing because they began flooding into the room, each with a sword in hand.

"Wait!" Cleve shouted once more. "I'll do it! I'll do what you ask!" He held the sword at the lot of them as he backed away.

"Hold!" The King held a hand forward, and the guards stopped. "Tell me what you'll do."

In defeat, Cleve's anger melted. A strong sadness squeezed his heart, for he knew he meant it. "I'll kill Rek. I'll bring you his head." He had a strange feeling, like he was about to weep but couldn't remember how. He didn't even bother to look at the psychic's reaction, knowing there would be a nod.

"Good," the King replied. "Then it's settled. You'll carry the longbow concealed in a bag. A guard will escort you to the Fjallejon Pathway and teach you the code for the Fjallejons. The pathway will take you through the mountains, and then Corin Forest will be to the east. There are hills you can use for cover as you wait for Rek to emerge from his cabin, which is right on the edge of the forest." King Welson shooed away his psychic and the guards. The two on the ground picked themselves up and hobbled out of the room after the rest.

Cleve didn't hear one word of whatever the King had just said. He was someplace else, somewhere deep within himself. Cleve didn't realize he was still holding one of their swords until he noticed the King glaring at it. Cleve lowered it to his side, unsure what to do with it now. "You won't need that tomorrow." Welson pointed as he spoke. "If he gets within melee range, it'll already be too late. It's late in the night, and the trip is likely to take the day, so you'll sleep here and leave with one of my guards at sunrise."

If Cleve slept at all that night, he didn't remember waking.

Chapter 32: Stuck
CLEVE

The next day, Cleve found himself thankful that the Academy was directly between Kyrro City and the Fjallejon Pathway. It was comforting to walk through, bringing it back to his thoughts even if just for brief moments between stubborn despair. The strain of his task was heavy on his shoulders, constantly finding its way into his mind no matter how hard he tried to ignore it. Some part of him wished to see Reela as he walked through, but more of him hoped not. The guard wouldn't allow him to speak to anyone anyway, so the situation would be only awkward and troubling.

Cleve had difficulty grasping the idea that he was to kill someone without giving his target a chance to fight. *This man is a friend of Terren's, and I need to sever his head?* He'd had to be sure he would do it when he'd told the psychic, but the doubts had returned as soon as he'd left the castle.

Could Terren know what was about to happen to his old friend? Cleve couldn't predict how his uncle would react after finding out. He ran through some scenarios in his mind: "*Cleve, you killed Rek, sliced his head from his neck, stuffed it in a bag, and brought it to the King? I understand you had to, and I forgive you." No, Terren would never say that. "You killed Rek and severed his head? You're evil! Your presence in this world serves no other purpose than to bring death and heartache to others! I should sneak poison into your water and rid this world of you!" No, Terren never would resort to poison when a quick swing of the sword would be all he'd need.*

Cleve didn't want to think about it anymore after that terrible thought.

The Fjallejon Pathway was the only non-treacherous way through the mountains. The Academy was positioned so close to the pathway that the school would be the first line of defense if any army invaded from the north.

Standing at the beginning of the pathway now, Cleve saw it wasn't a man-made road but merely a gap that dissected the steep mountains. The ground sank inward like a dried river.

Just before he entered, Welson's guard stopped him. "The Fjallejons control these mountains and watch this one narrow road that passes through. They're allied with Kyrro and report suspicious activity to the King via pigeons."

"It's nice to hear you say something besides a grunt or barking commands," Cleve said facetiously, finding himself craving a conversation with Effie now more than ever to take his mind off the gravity of the situation.

"Pay attention!" The guard spoke with a bitter tone.

Cleve figured the guard was probably not pleased about escorting someone ten years younger than him to carry out a mission with an illegal weapon. He took a breath and waited for the guard to continue.

"The Fjallejons are also required to stop you as they wait for confirmation from the King to let you pass. However, there's a code that will allow you through without waiting. For this week, it's 'like father like son, like brother like none.' Speak it once you're stopped and again when you return. We don't have time for mistakes because your target could move any day now."

"You're not coming with me?"

"The more of us there are, the more likely we'll be sensed or seen. You'll go alone from here. We expect you back before tomorrow evening."

Cleve was relieved. Without the guard at his side, he might think of something yet to get him out of killing Rek.

"Any questions?" the guard asked.

"Does the head of the Academy know of this?"

The guard grimaced as if offended. "Why does it matter?"

Because he's my uncle, and Rek is the only friend he has. Because he wouldn't believe the Elf is a traitor and would do everything in his power to stop this. "I wish for my teachers to know why I'm absent." *That sounded genuine enough.*

"You can speak to the King about issuing a statement when you return with the Elf's head." Without giving Cleve a chance to ask another question, the guard turned and paced back south.

Like father like son, like brother like none. Cleve couldn't help but think the code had something to do with him and his task. He thought about it more as he walked between the mountainsides, yet the magnificence of where he was soon settled in, giving him a pleasant distraction.

Giant slabs of rock shielded him from all elements. It was eerily quiet. Though, he thought he heard the *clank* of metal yet couldn't decipher from where.

As he continued, he saw that in some places the two mountainsides still were connected, turning the pathway into a tunnel for a stretch. Twists and turns were everywhere, causing no part of the road to look exactly the same as any other, but it also prevented Cleve from seeing where it ended.

After what felt like five miles, the mountains dipped and the gap widened. Cleve spotted a tiny man with mud-brown skin, wearing ragged clothes that looked as if they'd never been washed. He was sitting with a spear across his lap but stood when Cleve was close. His head came up no farther than Cleve's chest.

"Speak common tongue?" The deepness in his voice came as a shock. The short man spoke with a thick accent as well.

"Yes."

"Speak the code and we let you pass. Or you wait. Or you have trouble." The Fjallejon used his spear to point up, where dozens more waited atop the mountains, peering over curiously.

"Like father like son, like brother like none."

"You may pass." He shuffled his little feet to stand aside.

"How much farther do these mountains go?"

"You halfway."

The second half was no different from the first—except light was quickly beginning to fade, and Cleve's thoughts of despair were becoming unhinged again.

When he emerged from the canyon, he found Corin Forest to his right just as the King had described for him once again that morning. The sun was setting behind it, painting the tops of the trees with a touch of gold. Rek's wooden cabin was difficult to spot among the surrounding trees, but Cleve found it after climbing a tall hill.

He sat back on his heels and retrieved his bow from the bag, refusing to let himself think about anything. The hill evened out, giving him a comfortable observation point. The cabin was roughly as far as the wooden target was atop the castle. Although this time, he would need to shoot at a forty-five-degree angle. It wasn't something he'd practiced.

Even after the hours he'd walked in silence, not one better idea came to him. One thought was simply knocking on Rek's door to explain the situation, but nothing good could come of that.

Now thoughts swirled into his mind so strongly, he couldn't ignore them any longer. *The King wants his head, so I can either get it here and now or run and never return.* The thought of running was worse than the rest. Cleve knew he'd rather die than live in fear and marked as a traitor for the rest of his life. *No man wants to live in fear.* It suddenly made him more aware of why King Welson Kimard had outlawed bows.

Cleve had a similar dread of the weapon after his father, the strongest man he'd known, was killed by one. It made Cleve realize how fragile life could be, especially his own. It had to have been the same for Welson Kimard. But unlike the King, Cleve discovered that training with the bow was the only way to remember his father without the depression that came with it. He still hadn't found a way to do the same for his mother. That sometimes made him worry he might forget about her completely.

Now the threat of Rek's power is what's terrifying the King—something I understand completely. And with that realization came his answer. *It was a direct order from the King. I hope Terren will understand.* Cleve made himself bury everything else he was feeling deep down. It made him sick with disgust, but it gave him the strength to do what he knew needed to be done.

The sky became black with waves of stars before there were any signs of the Elf. Then a light popped on within the cabin and the Elf—*Rek, his name is Rek; no, don't think about that*—walked by the window.

Another hour passed. The Elf had walked by the cabin window many times, but unless Cleve's target stationed himself within view, Cleve had a better chance of using his words to convince the Elf to take his own life.

After another hour, weariness came over Cleve, making it impossible to keep focused. His nerves had been restless for so long, and his lack of sleep surely wasn't helping. The concern developed that he couldn't make the shot without regaining his energy. He tried to think about how many hours he'd been awake but gave up quickly, realizing it was too much work to figure out. He lay on his back with the bow across his body. Instantly, he was blanketed in bliss and knew he wouldn't rise until his weariness had been relieved with rest.

Cleve awoke with a gasp and his heart racing. Although light had come, there was no sun in the gray sky. The wetness of dawn was cool against his face. He peered down into the cabin. The lamp must have been blown out. It was impossible to tell if the Elf was inside or not.

For reasons he couldn't describe, he suddenly felt soothed, more relaxed than he ever remembered. Suddenly he thought of Reela—of how beautiful she was, and he wanted to tell her that. He stood to stretch his legs and arms. Tingles of pleasure washed over his body.

"Hello," a voice spoke from behind.

He calmly turned to see who it was and found an Elf. "You must be Rek." Cleve smiled and waved.

"Yes, and what's your name?" Rek smiled back. He was tall and thin with ears that came to a point at the top, like Cleve had seen in drawings of Elves. With his clean, long hair and smooth skin, Rek was easy to look at. He had Reela's almond eyes, although they were the color of his dark brown hair, not the radiant green Cleve could picture so easily. The Elf was the friendliest person Cleve had ever met, with a smile that exuded cheer. He felt as if nothing would be more pleasing than helping him.

"Cleve Polken." It was satisfying to answer the question. He wanted more of them.

"What are you doing here, if I may ask?"

Cleve's palms opened. "Of course, you can ask anything. King Welson sent me here to kill you and bring back your head..." Something snapped when Cleve heard himself speak those words. Every muscle tightened, the relaxation squeezed out of him. He drew the knife from his belt.

"Stop." Rek extended an arm at him and pain swarmed through Cleve's body. It was as if every muscle had cramped.

Cleve screamed as he fell, first to his knees and then onto his side. He could feel the knife drop from his hands but could do nothing to reach for it. Pain overwhelmed every muscle on his body.

Rek sighed, walking over to retrieve the knife.

The pain began to leave his body as Rek walked to the bow and slung it over his shoulder.

"Can we talk or will I need to do that again?" Rek looked forlorn.

Cleve sat up, panting. It felt as if even standing would be a monumental task. "Talk."

"You're strong-willed. Not many can fight their way out of a spell. Lucky I found you while you were sleeping."

Cleve sighed. "Not strong enough, apparently."

"Tell me what happened. What did Welson Kimard tell you about me?"

It was clear lying would be impossible, so with surprising relief Cleve revealed the situation to Rek. He told the Elf that he was considered an enemy, that he was found to be joining Tenred and the Krepps to attack Kyrro. Cleve told him everything Welson had said about him, how dangerous he was, how his death was necessary, everything Cleve could remember.

Rek took the news with his emotions put aside, that is, until Cleve was finished. Then Rek closed his fists and pressed his lips against his teeth. "This harassment needs to stop. I'm no enemy of Kyrro. Yes, I talked with Tegry Hiller, King of Tenred, but that's it. Someone must have seen and reported it to Welson Kimard." He sighed. "What a mess this has become. This is the first I've heard of Tenred not renewing the treaty, although it makes sense."

"What were you speaking about with their king?" Cleve asked, still unsure he could trust the Elf.

"I wanted the help of an army, and being exiled from Kyrro I turned to Tenred. I'd heard of the turmoil that existed between the two kingdoms, but I never knew how bad it really was until Tegry agreed to help only if I joined an attack on the Academy. I accepted so he would agree to assist me, knowing I could change his mind later, but I believe he may have figured that out, for he hasn't visited again."

Cleve felt his head whip back in shock by this. "What could you want with an army if you have no interest in attacking Kyrro?" Cleve wanted to trust Rek, but anyone trying to obtain an army seemed dangerous to him. He rose to his feet gingerly, his muscles still aching from the recent spell.

"My reasons are unrelated to both territories," Rek said, turning his mouth up in a warm smile that reminded Cleve of Reela, which then made his heart flutter. "I'm trying to free someone who's being held by the Krepps." Rek's mouth straightened and he held his chin in thought. "Although now that I've heard the Krepps are joining with

Tenred, Tegry Hiller would never help me do any harm to them." Rek shook his head and sighed. "I need to speak with Welson Kimard. If he thinks he can win this war, then he hasn't seen the massive Slugari within the Krepp army or doesn't know what they're capable of like I do."

Cleve realized he was shaking his head back at Rek. "That's going to be difficult, as he's given the order for your head, and mine too as soon as it's clear my mission has failed. He's convinced you're a threat to Kyrro."

Rek scrunched his mouth like he tasted something sour. "Welson Kimard thinks anyone who has power is a threat. His father was the same but far worse." Rek handed the dagger and bow back to Cleve without any sign of worry.

Cleve accepted the weapons, knowing by now they were pretty much useless. It made him quite relieved knowing he wasn't going to have to behead his uncle's only friend. Though, he still had no idea what to do about the order from the King.

As if able to sense Cleve's hostility had dissolved, Rek gave him a friendly nod and continued. "I grew up with Welson Kimard. He was my older brother for five years yet always kept his distance from me. I was seven and he was fifteen when his father, Westin Kimard, was killed. He then became King and happily released me from the custody of the castle, knowing I didn't wish to stay there. We didn't speak for nine years, until he asked me to start teaching at the Academy when its construction was completed. I thought it was his way of telling me the grudge had finally subsided. But as I taught, and my powers continued to grow over the next five years, concerns from students and teachers must have reached him, for he summoned me."

"And he exiled you out here?"

"Yes, but only after we got into an argument and I forced him to answer a few tricky questions. He revealed information I'm sure he meant to keep secret." Rek's gaze locked on Cleve's face. "Did you say your name was Polken? Cleve Polken?"

"Yes."

"Your father was Dex Polken?"

"Did you know him?"

"Not personally, but I've heard the name."

"From King Welson? Did he say something about my father?" Cleve asked before he could consider the question further.

Rek fell silent and his eyes became tense. He held out a palm toward Cleve's forehead. Suddenly it felt as if ten thousand thoughts were all trying to surface at the same time, causing his head to feel like it was being ripped open.

"What are you doing?" he yelled, grabbing hold of his temples.

Soon, the pulsing pain subsided, and Cleve found himself to be panting.

"I apologize for that. I needed to make an assessment. I don't think we should get into this, at least not now."

He knows something. My parents must have been involved with the King, but why wouldn't they tell me? Curiosity pressed at Cleve, but he knew that was a barrel of worms best saved for another day. He nodded. "We need to figure out what we're going to do." He had no doubts anymore that Rek was on Kyrro's side, and the King should be informed. Though, he still didn't like the feeling of being near the powerful psychic. At least Cleve wasn't strangely infatuated with Rek like he was with Reela. That made everything much easier.

"Welson believes I'm a threat..." Rek's voice softened as he looked south toward the Fjallejon Pathway. "If I could just convince him otherwise, I'm sure he would appreciate my help. Then, he would be thankful you didn't kill me and probably would spare your life as well."

"Easy, we'll just march into his castle so you can talk to him," Cleve said sarcastically.

Rek tilted his head, eyes at Cleve's feet. After a moment of thought he said, "Yes. That's what we'll do."

Sudden terror gripped Cleve's heart. "You can't be serious."

"I am." Rek began walking down the hill. "I realize you were joking, but it's a good idea."

The terror spread to his limbs, making him want to jump. "No, it's a terrible idea. It's the worst idea. Any idea would be better than that one." Cleve chased after him. "Are you truly serious?"

"I'll wear my hood." Rek pulled a gray hood over his forehead, concealing his ears. "Anyone close enough to recognize me would be close enough for psyche as well."

"What are you going to do about the hundreds of guards between us and King Welson? They're expecting me to come back with your head. If a hooded figure is with me, they would have to assume it was you!"

Rek was frighteningly calm. “I have plenty of tricks. I just need to be close enough to them. I can start using psyche around fifty yards.” Rek pointed at Cleve with a slight grin. “Your job will be to get me within that distance safely.”

Cleve smacked the Elf's finger away from him. “This is suicide.”

“Then think of something better.”

Silence followed and Cleve took a few breaths to gather himself. He could think only of being impaled by throwing knives or maybe even by the arrows of unskilled bowmen as soon as he and Rek entered the city.

The Elf waited patiently, running a hand through his shoulder-length hair, folding his arms, shifting his weight once or twice.

“This is ridiculous...storming the castle?” Cleve grimaced in defeat when no other ideas came to him. “This can't be the best idea,” he stated grimly.

“It is,” Rek replied with an unnerving smile.

“I hope you have some armor for us in that cabin,” Cleve said with thick optimism.

Rek laughed from his stomach. “Now *that's* ridiculous.”

Chapter 33: New Tasks
ZETI

What happened to brother to me? The question had been rattling around in Zeti's mind for the last week. He'd left with Vithos in the morning, and by sunset Doe had announced the relocation of the encampment. No one seemed to know or care that her brother had been sent away with the Elf.

After days of asking around, Zeti came to the disappointing realization that the only way to find out more would be to ask Doe or Haemon herself.

The Slugari's wooden fort was far too large to transport from the old camp, so construction of their new home began moments after arrival at the new location around the coast of Eastern Kilmar.

She couldn't complain about the spot Doe and Haemon had chosen for the tribe, as a strong river flowed just five miles north, but the reason behind the move was still unclear.

Why did we move just after Zoke was sent away? Does he know where our new camp is? Zeti hated riddles and all games without rules or weapons. She was more inclined to shoot an arrow through the Slugari's grotesque bodies than listen to their lies, but the chance of finding even some truth was better than nothing. So she had to try.

It was a game on its own—to get information from Doe or Haemon without angering them and getting punished. Zeti knew this just as well as any Krepp, even though she'd never spoken to either of her leaders directly.

With no door, Doe and Haemon relied heavily on Krepps acting as guards to maintain privacy until construction was completed.

When she approached, the Krepp on duty flashed his blood-stained teeth, and his thin yellow eyes widened. "A fresh suit for a new woman. Come looking for a *seshar*?" The light gray tone of her skin was a clear indication of her recent shedding and had been even more annoying than she'd imagined it would.

"Let Doe or Haemon know I wish to speak to them." Zeti had to be firm. If there was a hint of interest in anything besides her current business, Krepps took that to mean she could be wooed.

"What business do you have with them?" The guard leaned on a longsword, resting both hands on its hilt.

"Nothing I can share with you." It was easier than the truth, or so she thought until he scowled and came toward her.

"The new woman thinks she can do anything she wants." He grunted and then spat. "Your skin looks weeks old. I bet I could cut it with my tongue." His mouth peeled open so his sharp tongue could dance around his lips.

Not yet a week, she dared not say aloud.

He wrongly took her silence as a cue to keep talking. "You shouldn't be sticking your claws where they don't belong when the smallest scratch can open you up."

He clawed at her shoulder with a quick snap. Zeti's reflexes took over and she ducked under his arm and kicked the sword out from under him. He fell and she sat on his back.

"My skin may be soft, but I'm not." She held a dagger to his throat. "Toss your sword away, get up, and tell Doe or Haemon I need to speak with them."

"Fine." He pushed away his weapon. She stepped off him. He spat as he got up. "Any time you want to straddle me again, let me know. I'll be face up next time." He let his teeth show as he sucked in drool.

"I'd rather sit on a knife," she muttered, unsure he'd heard it as he left his post.

Soon, he was back. His mouth was now without a grin, steady, as if he'd just been scolded. "Doe will see you. Leave your weapons with me."

She handed off her dagger, and the Krepp let her pass. She could feel his eyes on her rear.

The entrance to Doe and Haemon's new home was a mere hallway made of wooden walls with two turns, first left and then right. It opened into a room that shared a wall with a mountainside.

Zeti faced the back of the room, which had no wall yet. She first noticed she could see the ocean, and before it she saw a long beach. In front of the beach was fertile dark dirt that led back into the room. An area on the dirt already had been secluded with a fence, *no doubt for the eppil plants*, she figured, although none were there yet. *They must have planted seeds.*

The room was bare except for a rectangular table as large as her bed. There was plenty more space that she expected would be used later, but she liked the room as it was. If she had a space to herself as big, she would set up targets for archery and practice in private so she didn't have to deal with the harassment she got whenever she visited the shooting range.

Only Doe was inside, looking at what appeared to be a map spread across half the table. She waited patiently for him to speak before taking another step.

"What is it?" he growled without turning his long body to face her.

"Will Zoke return?" She'd never spoken directly to Doe before but had seen conversations between him and others. They tended to erupt disastrously when Doe was asked complicated or continuous questions.

The massive Slugari shifted his head to glare at her. "Who are you and why do you ask?"

"Sister to him, Zeti. We shared a hut before, and I would like to see him again."

Doe's face turned back to the table with the map, dragging the end of his fat body along, which noisily rubbed against the dirt. "Vithos was working against the tribe. When we sent him away, he requested that Zoke join him. So they're both traitors. We can't allow them to return."

Zoke, a traitor? The accusation was such a shock that her disbelief registered on her face in a brief moment of weakness. She saw that Doe noticed her expression. He turned again, moving more of his body with his head this time.

"Do you think I lie?" His stare morphed into a scowl.

"No. It's surprising is all." *No, surprising would be a dagger through your head while you slept.* She wore a mask of indifference. The faintest sign of insubordination would lead to a punishment, she knew.

"Is that it?" Doe's patience was already worn out.

So many questions that she couldn't ask swirled in her mind. *Zoke told me he was sent to Nor to look for Slugari. Did a trap await him? Where is he now? Does he know where we are? He's no traitor. Could Doe really think he is, or is he just saying that for some other reason?*

"Yes," she answered in defeat. She left with more questions than when she'd entered.

Determined to find the answers, she thought of one other place to turn. However, Grayol found her on the way there.

"Zeti!" He ran to her. "Have you found out where Zoke is?"

She put a claw over his mouth to shut him up. "Quiet about that." She looked around. No one seemed to hear. "Like I said before, I'll tell you when I know. For now, don't mention it. If Doe or Haemon hear of you discussing it, they won't be happy."

The young Krepp's face showed fear. "I understand."

"Good. If you want to help me, my bed was torn during transport. I can sew it, but it lost grass that needs to be stuffed back in. Would you collect some for me?"

"I can do that." He nodded eagerly.

"I could use about ten armfuls if you can manage that."

"Definitely!" He smiled.

"Leave it in my hut."

"Endure," he said, running off.

"Wait," she called after him. He stopped so quick he nearly toppled. After regaining his footing, he sprinted back, and Zeti put her hand on his shoulder, leaning down toward his face. "Remember to ask a border guard before leaving the camp, new rules."

"I will." There was a hint of annoyance in his voice. She understood, for the lack of freedom frustrated her as well.

"Endure."

"Endure," he repeated.

When he was gone, she resumed her mission. The camp was both three miles wide and long, and the Krepp she wanted to see was on the edge of the opposing side of Doe and Haemon's home. He was Paramar, head of the Slugari search group and the Krepp who worked closest with Doe and Haemon. He wasn't known for being talkative, but she thought she could get him to tell her what she needed. She was a tempting new woman, after all.

With easily ten thousand-plus Krepps in the encampment, she couldn't count how many men she had to walk by to get from one side to the other. Thankfully, most just looked. That she didn't mind. Someone stopping her wouldn't be so bad, but it attracted others. *The sight of a fresh-skinned woman talking with a man must appear as a challenge*, she guessed. *Or maybe walking by without taking a chance makes them feel less of a man.* It certainly seemed so.

"Zeti," someone called to her. When she turned and saw Dentar—

her father's irritable friend—walking toward her, she felt physically ill for a moment.

"Leave me," she said as she continued on.

She expected him to grab some part of her to make her stop, perhaps her arm or belt, but to her surprise he just sped to catch up, walking alongside as he spoke. "Father to you says you haven't found a *seshar* yet." Dentar's tone was without the normal scorn behind each word.

"How would he know when we barely speak?" Zeti was still upset that her father hadn't offered to help her transport her belongings, even with her shedding occurring during the move.

"Is it true or not?" Dentar's usual annoyance was beginning to come out.

"It shouldn't matter to you either way."

Dentar pulled a dagger from his belt. At the sound of the metal singing, she stepped away and drew her own dagger. However, he held the handle of his weapon toward her with his head lowered, showing it as a gift.

"Being a weapons trader, valuable steel passes through my claws. When this dagger came through, I couldn't let it go. It reminded me too much of you." His sweet tone was that of a child begging for a treat. It caused the sickness to rise higher in her stomach. The dagger he presented was unsullied. Its steel glistened, calling to be dirtied by blood.

"That's quite a pretty blade," she said. "But I don't like pretty. Perhaps if you shoved it up your ass first."

He stood tall and pointed the weapon at her. A slew of raunchy curses flooded from his mouth along with gobs of spit.

"There's the Dentar I know," she said, walking away without a look back.

Paramar's hut looked like everyone else's, except for the red flag dancing atop it. *Red for chief. That's the one.* A small amount of tribal tasks were done by groups instead of individuals, and each group had a chief. Being the head of the Slugari search team, Paramar was the most important chief to Doe and Haemon, therefore the most important Krepp.

He was leaving his hut as Zeti got close. With sword in hand, he either didn't notice her or pretended not to.

"Paramar," she called, but he didn't face her. "Can we talk?"

Instead of her face, he looked at her belt for a breath. Finding only her dagger, he offered his sword. "Here."

Confused, she took it. *If a chief wants you to do something, you do it*, Zoke had told her.

Paramar went back into his hut and came out with another sword. "You can talk, and I may listen, but we spar during it."

"If you wish," she conceded, knowing full well she didn't have a chance against him.

The fence marking the edge of the encampment was five steps away. He banged his sword on it and raised a claw to a guard standing watch. Without waiting for the guard to acknowledge him, Paramar hopped over the fence. Zeti waited for the guard, though. He nodded to her, and she followed Paramar.

He pointed his sword, so she followed suit, readying herself.

"Half speed," he said calmly. He tapped his sword against hers, stepped back, and then rushed forward with a strong overhead swing that surprised her.

Paramar was a large Krepp, both tall and wide. Lacking the strength to block his blow, she needed to retreat a step. He followed with a lunge, which she guided clear with her sword. His *half speed* statement seemed to be a trick, for his attacks came at her fast. "Talk," he said as he continued to search for a way in. "Talk or attack."

"I want to hear what you know about Vithos." She nearly took his blade into her shin as he swiped at her while she spoke.

"You're quick on your feet, especially for a young woman." He swiped again, this time at her sword. She moved it below his advance, but then he kicked it hard. The dull blade flew from her grip, bouncing off her knee.

Her new skin was its own double-edged sword, extremely sensitive. A hot bath or scratching out an itch felt wonderful, but it cut too easily. The coarseness of her bed had never bothered her before, but now she was waking often, her skin hot with irritation and even new wounds sometimes. The sword left a red gash that felt like the sting of a scorpion. Blood trickled down.

Paramar frowned at her. "But you treat your sword as if it's just a weapon when it's so much more."

She picked it up and aimed it at him. "I need more practice. The bow is my primary."

His brow furrowed. "Why the bow?"

"Because I can kill things from afar."

"Scared of getting close," he said with a knowing smile.

"I didn't say that," she replied defensively, not giving herself the time to figure out whether or not it was true.

He grunted, holding his grin. "I have a game for you. Each time you draw blood, I'll answer one question. We'll play until I touch you three times with my claw." He wiggled the fingers of his left hand. "I won't attack with my sword."

She felt her eyes go wide with excitement. "I like it." This was her chance to find out more about Vithos and, in turn, her brother.

They touched swords again and she attacked, swinging wildly side to side, up to down, down to up, trying desperately to remove a slice of flesh. But he was too fast, not so much with his feet but with his sword. It always intercepted her steel. Even when she thrust it at his stomach, he swatted her sword away with his. It flipped through the air, and he grabbed her to pull her close, her shoulder into his chest.

"Does it make you nervous to be this close?" She could feel his breath across the hair atop her head.

She wiggled free. "No," she lied.

"That's one touch." Paramar playfully twitched his claws.

She retrieved her sword and ran at him. She motioned for an overhead attack, but slid on her bottom when close, swiping at his thighs. It must have surprised him because he didn't block her sword. She slipped through his legs, but he managed to spin and claw her shoulder before she was out of range.

"Good move," he said. "But that's two touches."

"Check your leg," she replied smugly while she checked her own stinging wound on her shoulder, finding red when she drew back her hand.

There was a small cut in his leather shorts, but when Paramar lifted them there was no blood, not even a scratch. She looked at the sword in her hands. It looked sharp enough. She slid a finger over it and it bit back, opening her up.

"How did that not cut you?" She felt a gust of wind and then her blood dripping down her back.

He showed her a coy smile. "You'll have to swing harder than that."

She ran toward him again, this time determined to injure or at least cut him once. Behind each swing she put more and more force, grunting and letting the spit fly from her mouth. But just as before, he blocked each one with his sword.

Eventually, she noticed a pattern in the way he moved his sword from one side to the other when she changed directions. She finally tricked him by motioning to use her backhand but then switching back to her right side as he held his sword up for protection. While he couldn't intercept the attack fast enough with his sword, he did manage to get his other arm up, and her blade slammed into his forearm.

As a reflex she stopped, fearful she may have cut his arm deeply. In that moment he swung his hand down to grab hers, which still hung on tightly to her sword. "That's three." He said, changing his grip to a slow pat. Then he checked his arm for wounds, letting her see as well. There was a scratch, but blood did not come.

Zeti was baffled. "How is your skin so tough?"

"Since you got your sword on me, I'll answer that, but no others." He motioned with his claw for her to come closer. She hesitantly took a step toward him, upset with herself she hadn't done better. "If you weren't scared of getting close, you'd notice something about my skin. Look." He held out his arm. She took hold of it and peered closely. It was rough to the touch, nearly hard as wood. She noticed faint lines crossing up and down the arm.

"What are these? They look like scars, but there are too many." She traced her claw along his arm to prove she wasn't afraid of the proximity.

"Scars are correct."

"That can't be. There must be hundreds."

"Yes, on that arm. Thousands if you count my whole body." She looked up at his face. His eyes were a darker yellow than most others. All around his face were more scars but so faded she never would've noticed.

"I've heard of wounds healing stronger, but not like this."

"Jekra juice on open cuts," he replied, "an old family secret."

She openly gawked at him. "But that's poison!"

"Yes, which is why no one can know. If you use the wrong amount, you could die."

Zeti waited to see if he was joking or maybe wanted to correct himself, but no. He stood with arms folded, waiting for her to reply.

She never would've believed that the poisonous, red juice of the jekra vine could make the skin tougher if she hadn't seen Paramar's arm for herself. It was the first time she'd been in awe since seeing the *gektar* on the beach so many years ago. Paramar was clearly full of secrets. She'd come to the right Krepp.

"I wish to join your Slugari search group." It was the original reason she'd come to his hut. Joining the group would allow her to find out how they were hunting for the underground Slugari without Vithos. Any information about the Elf could help her find out what happened to her brother, and she also didn't hate the idea of spending more time with Paramar now that she knew him better.

As he stared in silence, she felt like he was looking through her, searching for secrets. "I hate first impressions," he said. "You're likely to see a side of someone that you'll never see again. That's why I'd rather fight them." His voice was heavy with pride. "You can't fake who you are during a bout."

Paramar was silent again as he scratched his forehead. "I see the real determination you have and also your real weaknesses." Then he nodded once and smiled. "You would be a good fit. Tell the coordinator you're switching tasks."

Later she would wonder what weaknesses he'd found. But at the time, joy overcame her.

The coordinator was old but still tough. Zoke and Grayol had told Zeti of having difficulties with her, but Zeti's experiences didn't fit their stories. She always got along well with Suba.

The coordinator's hut was near the center of the encampment, within earshot of the market that was always loud with activity. Whenever Zeti crossed through the market, she felt as if her identity had been sucked out of her, joining the mass chaos. No longer an individual, she felt liberated and frightened at the same time. If something happened while she was there, she was part of it, no matter what it was. She'd heard of brawls starting in the market involving hundreds of Krepps. Luckily, she was never there when it happened.

Most of the wares being sold were crafted by the sellers behind their booths or by a family member to them. If a bowl or spoon broke, its owner had better have something to trade for a new one because unless he could make his own, the only chance of getting another was from the market.

Years ago, Zeti's father had left with hers and Zoke's last bowl one night. It was during a drunken rage induced by a lack of luck. The next morning, Zoke had traded food for leather and spent the day creating a pouch. He'd then traded it for two bowls that he and Zeti hid when not in use. Zoke was always resourceful and good with crafting. If their situations were reversed, Zeti was certain Zoke would find out what happened to her. He'd figure out a way.

Shedding her skin without his support was difficult, especially because she was forced to suffer through the worst part while walking to the new encampment. It was the hardest thing she'd ever had to endure. The skin under her feet began to tear while crossing the hot desert of Kilmar. She'd never imagined such pain existed. Luckily, Grayol didn't have much to transport, so he'd carried her sheepskin bed, which she'd shared with him each night they'd traveled. Many Krepps were sharing beds during the four-day trek, so it was easy to ignore the implications of it. Her feet became so sensitive, she was forced to trade water for a pair of shedding shoes. Even they didn't completely protect her feet from cuts and blisters. She was thankful that was all behind her now.

The coordinator shot a friendly grin at Zeti when she entered. "Zeti, finally some decent company, and now a woman I see." Suba walked around Zeti to get a full look at her new skin. "You're all cut up. Did a man do this to you?" Suba spat.

"It's nothing." Zeti smiled. "I'm changing tasks, joining a search group."

"No more picking plants. I'll put that on the record. Are you sure this is what you want?"

"More than anything else right now."

"Good, certainty is important, remember that. When you're put in a confusing spot, find something you're sure about." Suba was always eager to give advice.

"I'll remember."

"How is Zoke? Last time he was in here I was hard on him."

He's said to be a traitor and could be dead for all I know. "He's missing."

"Missing? Zoke has always been too smart for his own good. What has he gotten into now?" Suba sounded more annoyed than anything else.

"I don't know yet. If anyone asks you, don't tell them I spoke of him."

At that, Suba's annoyance quickly changed to worry. "Of course, my *jerrendi,* I understand."

I'm not going to be so sweet or innocent much longer, Zeti thought. The nickname Suba used was often a compliment for female Krepps who were friendly, never wishing to induce harm. If anyone else called her that, she would claw them across the face. But Suba actually had known her when the nickname would've applied, so Zeti figured she was still the same Krepp in Suba's mind.

She forced a smile and turned toward the exit.

"Come see me again soon and let me know how you're doing."

Zeti looked back reassuringly. "Endure."

"Endure."

Before Zeti could think of the next step in her plan, a crowd caught her eye, usually the sign of a fight. Crowds quickly pulled in hundreds of Krepps, and the obligation to watch was not lost on her. But this was no fight. She saw right away that it was a much greater spectacle.

Being nearly a foot shorter than most of the Krepps there, she had to push her way to the front, where she just about collided with a creature she'd only seen on paper.

"Stay back!" a Krepp yelled, tugging her back into the crowd.

In front of her was a Human holding some banner that Zoke surely would've recognized because he read everything he could get his claws on. The Human had two other Human escorts and five Krepps acting as guards within the entourage. The Krepps were shouting for the crowd to make way, that these were allies who needed to speak to Doe and Haemon.

Zeti felt her mouth drop open in shock.

Each of the three Humans varied so greatly that it was hard to believe they were all the same race. Their heights and weights were similar, taller than Zeti but shorter than any full-grown male Krepp, except for maybe Zoke. But one had golden hair that hung down to his shoulders, another was as bald as a baby Krepp, and the man with the banner in the front had brown hair full of curls. Their skins were of different colors as well—tan, brown, and almost black—and each was so clean and smooth it screamed to be cut. Then she wondered what they tasted like, although they didn't look particularly appetizing, and there was no smell she could pick up over the musk of the surrounding Krepps. It was more just a curiosity.

She heard members of the crowd wondering her thoughts aloud. *Where are they from? We have allies?*

Someone recognized the banner and was proud to prove it. "Ten red stars on a black flag, that's Tenred's seal."

Zeti waited for answers about why they were there, but only more questions were murmured within the crowd.

Chapter 34: Manipulate
CLEVE

Each step closer to Kyrro City felt like walking toward the edge of a cliff. Even with the most powerful psychic at his side, Cleve felt he had to prepare for their blood to be spilled. Yet, somehow his hands were steady, his heartbeat regular. He couldn't imagine a scenario that didn't involve him dead or imprisoned, so why was he calm?

"Are you using psyche to relax me?" he asked.

Rek's hood was pulled so far forward his face was completely hidden from the side. "I'll need all my energy to get us into the castle, so I wouldn't waste any on you."

Before leaving, Rek had prepared them a small feast, figuring they wouldn't have another chance to rest or eat. His cabin was loaded with various meats. "It's unlikely I'll return. Eat as much as you can," he'd told Cleve, explaining after how hunting as a psychic was easy. With the ability to sense the minds of animals and entice them, finding food was the least of his troubles. But none of that distracted Cleve enough to ignore that Rek had admitted it was unlikely he would return.

Nearly halfway through the Fjallejon Pathway, Rek whispered, "Don't look up. We're being watched with curious eyes. Surely we're to be questioned by the Fjallejons soon, and if they recognize me, they'll send a pigeon to notify King Welson. That would change our chance of success from unlikely to impossible."

More like from impossible to absolutely impossible. The thought made his nerves jumpy. Cleve put his hands on top of his head and forced himself to take a few long breaths.

After another mile, a Fjallejon stood in their path. It looked like the same man who'd questioned Cleve yesterday. Rek squeezed Cleve's shoulder. "Walk in front of me until we're closer," he whispered. "I'll talk."

"Who walks behind you?" the Fjallejon called out when Cleve stepped in front of Rek.

Cleve whispered, "How much farther do you need?"

"Ten, twenty steps," Rek replied, pushing Cleve gently to let him know they needed to hasten their pace.

"A friend," Cleve answered the Fjallejon with a shout and sped his steps.

"Move, so I can see friend." The Fjallejon gestured with his spear.

Cleve felt his stomach tighten. "We can't arouse too much suspicion," he whispered, "or they'll call the guards without needing to see you."

The Fjallejon jabbed his spear at the air. "Move now!"

"Do it," Rek whispered.

Cleve stepped aside and the Fjallejon squinted his beady eyes. "What is your name?" he called out.

"Cleve. I crossed this road yesterday."

"No, the other. Remove hood."

Rek slowly extended his hand and pivoted his elbow to wave. His hood remained. "I'm merely a visitor from Tenred wishing to see Kyrro. I wouldn't harm anyone. You can tell by my friendly face."

The Fjallejon lowered his spear. "Yes, I see that. You may pass."

Rek put his hand back on Cleve's shoulder as they walked by, and Cleve felt relief slowly move through him.

When their path twisted and the Fjallejon was no longer in view behind them, Rek took his hand from Cleve's shoulder and leaned in to whisper, "He still may alert the King if other Fjallejons convince him I was too suspicious. No matter how powerful my psyche, the spell won't last on intelligent minds."

He felt his muscles clench. "Can you stop the pigeon, then?"

"If it flies low enough, I suppose."

Only a sliver of the sky was in their line of sight. Finding a bird would take more than a little luck. "How long until your spell wears off?" Cleve asked.

"I changed the way he observed me. That's done. It's over like any other first impression, and nothing can change how he felt during it. But I have no more control now that we're out of range. He could've been persuaded to send a pigeon already. There's no way to know." It was the first time since they'd met that Rek didn't sound confident.

"I guess we'll find out soon enough," Cleve muttered. "Although it may be an extra few miles, we should go around the Academy instead of through it. I think they may have lookouts watching for me."

Rek's hand found a comfortable spot on his chin. *He doesn't like the idea,* Cleve thought. *He's thinking of a better option, but there is none.*

"Do you have friends or family within the Academy's walls?" Rek asked.

Oh, that's right. He doesn't know Terren is my uncle. Nor will he. No one else needs to get involved in this mess.

"Absolutely not." Cleve was firm in his answer. But the grin he got from Rek made his words feel inadequate. "If you use psyche on me to change my mind, you'll regret it." He spoke sternly.

"You want their help." Rek stated it like a fact. "Whoever they may be."

"I do, but only because their company would be comforting, not valuable. With more people around, we'll stand out like prostitutes in a training center."

Rek took his hand off his chin. "Right, you don't want to risk them being hurt. I understand."

True. Cleve felt silly for trying to hide it from Rek. He nodded to show the Elf he was right.

They walked for half a mile without speaking until the silence began creating questions in Cleve's mind. "You told me earlier that you changed the way the Fjallejon saw you. Does that also mean psychics can make themselves beautiful in others' eyes, even if they're not?" If anyone had answers to the questions that came with Reela, it would be Rek.

"Not even I can cure ugliness." Rek turned to show Cleve a wry smile. "Yes, powerful psychics can slightly alter feelings. We can make people appear friendlier than they would normally. Mind you, the word I use is *alter* not *change*. If a woman already is beautiful in your eyes, I may be able to amplify that beauty, even spin it into lust. However, the best I can do with a woman who you have no interest in would be to make her slightly more attractive. In order to maintain the spell, I would have to use energy for it constantly. As soon as the spell was over, you would see her as your mind naturally would, which wouldn't be much different."

Cleve's heart fluttered. *So Reela is either constantly using psyche on me or the way she makes me feel is naturally happening without psyche? No, neither of those could be true. But would Rek lie to me about this? No, there would be no reason for that. Still, it doesn't make sense.*

Rek turned Cleve's shoulder to get a better look at his face. Most of the Elf's coffee-brown hair was tucked into his hood, but a few strands had come loose, glistening conspicuously. Rek looked concerned.

"You may figure our attractions should be easy to alter because of how quickly they can arise." Rek subtly shook his head. "But that's not the case."

"This morning you made all my muscles convulse." Cleve could hear frustration coming out with each word. "You're telling me you can do that but you can't make someone be attracted to you if they normally wouldn't be?" He realized this was the answer he wanted. If Reela had used psyche on him then everything would make sense. But if that wasn't the case, then it would open the door to new possibilities...possibilities he didn't even want to consider.

"A slight attraction? Yes, I can do that. Staggering beauty or lust, however? No, I cannot, not to intelligent beings at least. The feelings we have for each other may *seem* to sway easily, but only fickle feelings like anger, joy, gratification, and being comfortable can be greatly manipulated."

Cleve's heart dropped into his stomach. He decided he didn't want to hear anything else about it, but Rek wasn't finished.

"If we truly believe someone to be beautiful, it will take far more than psyche to change that. Pain, however, comes and goes so easily. We can even feel it just by watching someone else being hurt. That unfortunately makes it one of the easier spells to learn." His eyes steadied back on the twisting road ahead. He tucked his loose hair out of sight.

They walked at a lively pace, their footsteps echoing rhythmically up the sides of the mountains. Rek didn't have much to say unless Cleve gave him a question. There was something about him that reminded Cleve of Reela, and it wasn't just the shape of his eyes. There were other things as well: the shine of his hair from the few strands that continued to slip out from his hood, the way he walked with a slight roll of his shoulders.

The silence continued to produce questions. Although they weren't about Reela, Cleve still knew he probably shouldn't ask them. But his curiosity was nagging, getting stronger the longer they remained quiet. He knew it could be the only opportunity he'd get.

Eventually he just blurted it out. "What did King Welson tell you that he meant to keep secret? Was it something about my father?" He tightened his face in hesitation as he waited for Rek to answer.

Rek placed his hand on Cleve's shoulder to stop him. The Elf was about half a head shorter than him, but the way he looked into Cleve's eyes made Cleve feel like a child. Rek tilted his head curiously. His mouth remained flat, indifferent. *He's not trying to figure out how to answer; he's wondering if he should.*

"Some answers are best kept until the right time." Rek's voice was carefully sensitive. "Right now, all you need to know is our plan." Rek removed his hand and picked up the pace. "Keep your mind on getting me in the same room as Welson Kimard and have faith. No man can touch me while I'm conscious. We'll get there."

Cleve felt like he'd just finished a duel. He was breathing heavily, and his lips were dry. He had a gulp from his water pouch. He tried to push his curiosity out of his mind but then a new concern came to him.

"What would you have me do if a guard recognizes you from afar and runs to the castle?"

"Have you ever heard of a warrior running away?" Rek snickered. "Their pride is stronger than common sense." The comment was offensive yet true, Cleve knew, so he didn't argue. "I left Kyrro City nearly twenty years ago," Rek continued. "So it's unlikely I'll be recognized unless my hood comes down."

Cleve was left to dwell on his own thoughts as they walked through the rest of the Fjallejon Pathway in silence. The gravity of what they were about to attempt started to settle into his mind. *Forcing our way past guards to get to the King could be looked at as an attempt to attack him. We could be put to death for that.* A fear fell onto his heart. He tried his best to lift it, but it was too heavy. So he tried to bury that fear somewhere else where he couldn't feel it. He was good at burying feelings he couldn't lift but found no success in this case. It was there to stay.

The evening sun was beginning to set when hunger spoke through Rek's belly with a grumble. "My body is used to eating by now," he said shamefully with a hand on his stomach. "It's not the hunger I'm concerned about but the lack of Bastial Energy that goes along with it."

They'd reached the northern side of the Academy's walls. Food hadn't crossed Cleve's mind as of late, but keeping his psychic fueled was crucial. "They expected me back this evening at the latest. Even without a break we won't be there before dusk, so we may as well rest and eat under the cover of these high walls."

"No, let's go on." Rek's shoulders sank with a sigh. "If Welson sends his guards and they find us before we enter the city, I won't have enough energy to keep them charmed all the way to the castle. The closer we can get before being detected, the better our chances. I can chew and walk." He extended his hand.

Cleve handed him their sack of dried meats.

As they came around the Academy's walls, there was a clear view of the castle sitting in the center of Kyrro City. Suddenly Cleve's fear became twice as heavy. "I may as well eat something now also." *While I still can.* "Let's hope we don't cramp when it matters most."

When they were halfway to Kyrro City, the sky was red with the last light of the low sun. There were no trees along the path, no hills, nothing to hide behind. With little reason to travel between the Academy and the capital, there were no more than two people they'd already passed a mile back. So when a clump of five or six marched toward them with the light of the city on their backs, Cleve thought they might be guards. He and Rek stared ahead in complete silence, squinting for a better look.

As the distance from the King's men closed, what had appeared to be legs morphed into swords hanging from their belts. *Definitely guards,* Cleve said to himself, suddenly feeling naked without his sword or quarterstaff.

Chapter 35: Sweep
CLEVE

"I'll handle this," Rek said with pride. "A simple misdirection to the Academy should suffice."

Cleve nodded but felt his nerves getting the better of him. While the Elf might be confident, Cleve was not. He trusted himself in a battle, but this was nothing near that. This was lying, deceit—something he was never skilled at.

Time slowed during the last mile between them. Cleve had no weapon but his bagged bow and not enough arrows for each of the guards if their plan went awry.

"Remember not to sound nervous," Rek said, "or they'll be more suspicious and harder to manipulate with psyche."

Cleve's throat was as dry as the dirt crunching under each step. He could stand in front of hundreds of people and perform stunts with weapons as long as he didn't have to speak. This was the opposite. He would only be speaking—lying. He took a swig from his leather water pouch, swished, swallowed, and took another.

Night seemed to have come quickly, falling upon them like a shadow. By the time the guards were close, their faces were impossible to see, *which means mine is hidden as well,* Cleve realized with a bit of relief.

"Are you looking for Cleve?" he shouted, keeping his voice low so it wouldn't waver.

There was no response.

Cleve felt a dry swallow move down his throat and continued. "He's hiding at the Academy, told us what happened, so we left to tell the King."

One warrior led the rest of the guards. "Where in the Academy?"

"He probably left by now, but he was in his house," Cleve answered, lowering his face in a way he hoped was inconspicuous.

"Who are you?" the leading man asked, stepping closer. "Put a light on him."

The hands of a robed mage behind the warrior began to glow.

Rek held his hand forward. "That's not necessary. We're no one, just a concerned teacher and student."

The mage's hands lowered as the lead guard spoke. "Thank you for the help." The King's men continued past without another glance.

This may actually work, Cleve thought. Confidence lifted his spirit until he noticed Rek nervously peering back at the guards. "You think they'll come back for us?" Cleve asked.

"Perhaps. If one person becomes suspicious, that's all it takes to sway the group."

Finally, they were nearing the shanty houses along the outer edge of Kyrro City. Rek gave one last look to the King's men, who were now a couple miles back. "It looks as if the group has split. Some are moving back toward us."

Cleve turned to confirm the bad news. He had remarkable eyesight, but with just the light of the moon it was difficult to be certain what he saw. Staring, he strained his eyes until they began to fatigue. "You're wrong," he corrected, his heart sinking. "They're all coming back. We'd better hurry."

Rek sighed, and then they doubled their pace.

Farther into Kyrro City, streets formed between rows of houses. Crooked alleyways were also created from thin gaps between the small homes, connecting the streets and making countless possible routes to the castle. But Cleve soon realized there was a major problem. Unlike the Academy where the roads were straight, each street here was curved like a finger at rest, making it impossible to see if a guard awaited ahead.

Cleve tugged on Rek's shirt to get his attention when they crouched in an alley to catch their breath. "Can you sense where the guards are?"

"No, too many minds around us. I can't tell which belong to Welson Kimard's men."

Cleve missed his blunt quarterstaff. He tried to imagine how he would stop a guard if Rek's psyche failed. The image was messy. With his only weapons being his fists and bow, there would be blood.

The closer to the castle, the more guards patrolled. He and Rek snuck down alleyways to look for unpopulated streets. But the deeper they went, the more footsteps they started hearing behind them.

Dammit! We've gopher-holed in, and the tunnel has collapsed behind us, Cleve thought. The castle was still a mile ahead. He was beginning to have doubts, but it was too late to turn back now.

"If one guard sees us, all he has to do is shout and we'll be swarmed before I can assess the situation," Rek said. "It's time to force our way in so we can maintain control and avoid surprises."

Cleve knew he was right, but it didn't make the idea of being in the open any easier. "You have enough energy to get us inside?"

"We'll see, won't we?" Rek smiled as if excited, then calmly dusted himself off and stepped out from the alley. Cleve followed cautiously, utterly nervous about Rek's strange reaction to the terrible situation.

Cleve had his arms through the straps of his bow bag so he could wear it like a backpack, freeing his hands, which he figured he would need.

A swarm of thoughts buzzed around his mind. *Hurt them only if necessary. I need a blunt weapon. Will the bag work? No. Look for something. A guard could be around this corner, be ready. Check behind. No one there. Need a weapon. No, not the bow, something blunt. What about that? Yes, that.* There was an elderly woman using a broom to sweep the dirt away from her door. It looked nearly as old as her.

"Rek, get me that broom." Cleve pointed.

Rek understood, walking straight to her without a moment of thought. "Madam, can I have that broom?"

"No! Get away!" She swatted at Rek's reaching hand.

Cleve was shocked to see her reaction. *Had Rek forgotten to use psyche?*

"Relax." Rek stepped back, holding out both palms defensively. "Calm yourself."

"Try and take my broom, will you? Get out of here!" The woman swung it wildly as she advanced toward him. "My son bought me this broom!"

"Please lower your voice," Rek said, ducking under a slow swing at his head. "Keep the broom. We're leaving."

"You don't come back!" She threw the broom at Rek and stormed off into her house.

"Well, there's your broom." Rek pointed at it on the ground between them. "I should've known that an old woman sweeping the road in the middle of the night had lost her mind."

Cleve knelt to retrieve it. "You're sure that's the reason you failed? You have to understand I'm far less confident now after seeing you flee from an old woman with a broom." He was completely serious.

Rek frowned at him. "I have no sway over the insane. As long as there's still a mind behind the armor of the guard, we'll be fine."

Cleve felt frustration coming loose within him. Watching Rek fail had caused him to lose all confidence in the Elf. "As long as my hood doesn't come down, as long as the Fjallejons don't send a pigeon," Cleve imitated Rek, letting out his anger. "As long as I remain conscious, as long as the guards aren't crazy...I'm beginning to think this whole thing is insane. One simple surprise and it's all over."

Rek's mouth tightened. His eyes rose to meet Cleve's. "My hood hasn't come down, and it won't. The Fjallejons clearly didn't send a pigeon. Remaining conscious is easier than breathing. And Welson Kimard wouldn't keep someone insane on his staff." Rek let out a slow breath and calmly put his hand on Cleve's shoulder. His face loosened, and Cleve could feel himself relaxing.

"If there was a better option, we would've taken it," Rek continued. "I'm sure neither of us would choose the life of a fugitive, and even worse would be joining Tenred to see to the destruction of our home. This is what we need to do, and it's going to work—there's someone ahead," Rek interrupting himself, quickly readying his hands. But after a breath, they found it was just a man in common clothing. He walked by holding jugs of water against his body, too preoccupied for even a glance.

"I suppose you're right," Cleve said, not sure what else he could do but stay with Rek. Trusting such an important task to someone else had made him uneasy. Too much depended on them getting to the King, and so little control was in his hands.

The street straightened, allowing the sight of maybe fifty houses ahead before they twisted out of view. Cleve saw two people walking their way. From the silhouette of a helmet and sword, the man nearest had to be a guard. His face was difficult but possible to see in the faint light from the windows of the houses, *which means he can see ours as well.*

The guard's walk slowed, and he seemed to strain his neck forward as if to get a better look at them. Cleve quickly turned to see what Rek made of it, his heart going wild with dread.

Rek didn't look calm anymore. He whispered, "If any guard recognizes me, it'll be the one in front of us. Did you see his limp? That's Colin, or Colimp as he came to be known. As a child, I severed two of his toes with a dagger by accident. He wanted nothing more than to scream at me for it every time he saw me during all the years I lived in the castle."

Cleve turned back to the guard and found he was at least still walking toward them. "Has he recognized your face yet?"

"I'll tell you once I'm in range," Rek answered, but then Colimp's neck snapped back into place and he stopped abruptly.

"He knows it's you," Cleve said regretfully, for he knew what was about to happen.

Colimp spun to sprint away from them, shouting something unintelligible. He galloped awkwardly, his sheathed sword banging against his left leg with each hop.

He must be stopped before he can tell anyone. Cleve was off even before his thought was completed. Running with an enormous bag on his back and a broom in hand was restricting, to say the least, but his speed was still far greater than Colimp's. His legs tingled with hot Bastial Energy. He heard Rek's footsteps behind him, but they were too slow to keep up and quickly quieted.

Closer, Colimp's shouts still were impossible to comprehend. The words were mashed together as if the strain of running had disabled his tongue.

Closer still, Cleve might have been able to throw the broom just as the old lady did, and it would do about the same amount of good. Colimp's words finally could be understood: "He's here! Rek is here! Tell the King!" Cleve looked over Colimp's shoulder to see that another guard in the distance was now running to meet them.

Finally in range, Cleve slapped the bristled end of his broom into Colimp's ankle, making his feet collide so that he tripped and fell face first into the rough dirt. Cleve hopped on top of Colimp's back, pulling the broom into his mouth from behind like a gag. Anger was all that came through Colimp's mouth as he screamed into the wood and tried to pry it off.

Cleve checked for Rek and found he was roughly the same distance behind them as the guard approaching from the front.

They each arrived. The guard drew his sword and started at Rek, but Rek stood his ground, raised a hand, and yelled, "Stop, I'm on your side!"

The guard slid to a halt, though he kept the sword aimed at the Elf. "What do you mean?" the guard asked, his face twisted with confusion.

Colimp stopped screaming, and his struggles died down.

Rek's voice was calm. "The King is afraid of me but needs my help. I'm an ally and would never hurt him. Will you both help me get inside the castle so I can explain that to him? He'll be so grateful after he speaks with me." Cleve received a nod from Rek and knew to let the broom out of Colimp's mouth.

"We'll help," Colimp answered, still lying on the dirt. Even with Cleve on top of him, his voice was deep with pride. The other guard nodded in agreement.

Relieved, Cleve helped Colimp to his feet.

"I apologize for that," Cleve said.

Colimp didn't even look at him.

The taste of dirt was in the back of Cleve's throat, but his pity for Colimp was heavier on his mind. Colimp was old for a guard, and he had taken a tumble at full speed at Cleve's doing. Furrows of concern were etched into the old man's forehead, and dirt was caked into them.

The four of them walked toward the castle, with the exception of Colimp who—like Rek said—had a limp. The two guards walked beside each other ahead of Cleve and Rek.

"Colin, what are the King's orders regarding Cleve and me?" Rek asked.

"We are to bring in Cleve and kill the Elf without question." The words sent a jolt through Cleve, but the guards didn't waver.

"The King thinks of me as an enemy when I'm not," Rek answered quickly. "He'll be very pleased with you both after I speak with him."

Cleve waited for them to reply, but neither said anything. They kept their faces forward.

Rek slowed, giving a polite tug on Cleve's wrist. They stopped and Rek whispered, "Don't bring up the limp. Colimp still very much resents me, but he's doing what he thinks is right. That may change if emotions sway his thoughts."

"Understood."

The next person to approach them turned out to be a mage of the King's Guard. It looked like Rek had ahold of him well before he was close enough to act on his own free will.

"These men are helping me get within the castle so I can see the King," Rek told the mage. "Please join us."

They continued on like that, with each guard joining them without so much as a curious squint.

It's frightening how seamless the transition is between a free thinking mind and one that Rek has control over. There were no signs of his psyche, no smell, no feeling, nothing. *Could I be just another body in this equation, used by the Elf to bring him within reach of the King? For all I know, he could have me sever Welson's head and take the throne for himself.* The thought created a sour feeling in Cleve's stomach.

Since meeting Rek, the decisions Cleve had made felt like his own, but now he was wondering how he could be sure. His best option could be finishing his original task. A quick elbow to the Elf's head and he would be unconscious. Then Cleve could be sure his thoughts were only his. He started to consider it, glancing at the Elf and imagining doing it. Some part of him was already telling him to. *Just do it now. Don't think about it anymore.* The voice grew louder.

Rek suddenly glared at him. "Is everything alright with you?"

He must sense my aggression. Cleve's fist tightened. *Do it now, before it's too late—no! If he had control over me I wouldn't even have these thoughts...or would I?* Rek was still glaring, waiting for an answer.

Cleve felt the tension dissolve. He took a long breath.

"It's just...psychics make me nervous," he decided to admit.

Rek's mouth turned in disappointment. "We do that to a lot of people."

Chapter 36: Plan
CLEVE

Their entourage had grown to twelve. Light leaked into the streets from the few houses with lanterns still burning, and the mages within their party produced a yellow glow from their wands that filled in the rest of the black space around them as they passed.

Rek held a sad expression ever since their last conversation. They didn't speak for a while, walking with their group. But eventually, Rek pulled Cleve to the back with a tight grab of his arm.

"You're concerned I have influence over your thoughts." Rek spoke low enough for only Cleve to hear. "But what doesn't?"

Cleve was surprised by the sudden question and didn't quite understand it. "What do you mean?"

"What doesn't have influence over your thoughts? Everything you see and hear can influence you. Think of the people peeking out their window at us, for example." Rek gestured at the houses around them. "The sound of our group pokes at their curiosity, and the sight of guards escorting us fuels new thoughts. I don't need to use psyche to influence them. If I wanted, I could just remove my hood and shout, 'An Elf is here! The King wants my help!' and nearly all would believe it."

Cleve tried to frown at Rek, unsure exactly how it came out. His face was used to holding indifference, not showing disappointment. "But at least then they could choose whether or not to believe you. You wouldn't be controlling their minds."

Rek glanced ahead to check on the guards. He spoke even softer, but more forcefully. "Contrary to the rumors, I can't control minds. I use a person's own doubts to create a thought that's realistic, just like lying. But there's a lot I cannot do."

"Like?"

Rek's eyes squinted as his voice became utterly serious. "I can't change love, for example. It's an urge that we're born with—same with the urge to live. I would never be able to persuade someone who wants to live to think otherwise." He squeezed Cleve's hands. "I couldn't convince you that your hand was cut off or that you don't remember how to use the bow. Such knowledge and urges are buried so deep I have the same chances of changing them with psyche as without. If you're certain about something, I cannot change it." Rek sighed. "But people have many doubts and even more secrets, which is why someone like me is considered to be so dangerous."

It reminded him of Reela and their conversation when they'd first met, but there was conviction in Rek's voice and desperation between his words while Reela had been playfully cheery. *He needs me to believe he's not a danger,* Cleve thought, *but why? Maybe because no one else has?*

Rek released his grip on Cleve's hands and relaxed his shoulders. "I didn't use psyche to get you here, Cleve, only when we first met, when you had intentions of killing me. The rest has been up to you."

Cleve suddenly felt remorse for his accusations. He believed Rek. With a tight mouth, a straight back, and rigid shoulders, Cleve made a decision he was ready to stick by. "I'll help you finish this."

"Good." Rek showed a warm smile. "And a bit of advice: Have more confidence in your strength, not your physical strength, but mental. I know I make you nervous because you're unsure how to fight against psyche. Am I right? Do you know how to stop a psychic?"

Cleve shook his head. He didn't know there was a way without being a psychic himself.

"Strength," Rek answered. "Confidence. Don't doubt your ability to fight back."

Cleve laughed bitterly. "You say it like it's easy."

"True, it takes practice. But if you have a weakness, you improve it. I'm sure you do so here when you train with weapons," Rek said, squeezing Cleve's hands again. "So why not in here?" His fingers rose to tap gently on Cleve's temples.

Cleve took a step back before he even realized he'd done so. "I can't." He'd tried thinking of his parents without pain but it had never worked. The memories would always storm through his entire body like a poison, crippling him from head to toe so that all he could do was lie down and weep.

"It's not going to be easy, much harder than using your hands to learn something new. But the process is the same: practice, patience, progress. I'm sure they still teach you warriors that, don't they?" Rek lifted his eyebrows.

Cleve nodded. “But I don’t see how that applies.”

“Practice is still repetition, even when the issue is purely mental. Put yourself in situations you would normally avoid because of the weakness. If you’re scared of the dark, put yourself somewhere tolerably dark but that you would normally avoid because of the fear. Be patient with yourself because progress is slow but inevitable. Find what works and stick with it.”

Cleve felt himself scowl. The example Rek had used discouraged him. “And if I’m not scared of the dark? How do I practice something I can’t talk about or even think about?”

Rek came to a halt, his hand resting upon his chin for a thought. The yellow glow from the mages danced on his knuckles and around his nose. He drew his knife and held it over Cleve’s forearm. It wasn’t aggressive, somehow gentle even. Cleve knew the Elf wouldn’t harm him.

“If I stuck this blade into your body, how would you address the wound? Would you remove the dagger immediately?” Rek asked.

“No, I’d make sure a clean cloth or rag was ready, as well as plenty of water to make sure the wound didn’t become infected...I don’t see how this is relevant.”

Rek held out his hands. “Just stay with me for now.” He slid the dagger back into its casing on his belt. “You’re referring to stopping the bleeding with hard pressure and then cleaning the wound, which is correct. And how would it feel, after pulling out the dagger, to push on the wound with a cloth?”

“It would hurt, but pulling out the dagger would be far worse.”

“Right.” Rek pointed at Cleve’s forehead. “Right now you have a dagger in there. It’s been there a while, from what I can tell. You’ve probably poked at it, maybe even tried removing it, and that must have been painful. When you finally do manage to pull it out, it’s going to bleed and bleed and bleed, and you’re going to think it would have been better if you’d left it in, but that’s not true. The dagger needs to come out, then the bleeding needs to stop, and then the wound needs to be cleaned. It’s going to be painful, but you need to keep at it. Be patient with yourself and the wound will heal.”

Cleve thought of the monstrous scar that would form from the wound Rek described, even if he were able to stop the bleeding. The image sent a chill through him.

Although some part of him could tell Rek was right, most of him had no intentions of touching the dagger. He'd managed so far with it in.

He put it out of his mind for now, knowing it wouldn't be the last time he thought about it, though.

Colimp shouted from the front of the party, "The King is on a balcony." The old guard pointed high at the castle. "He seems to be yelling something to us, but I cannot understand it."

Sure enough, King Welson was waving his arms about, pointing at them and making frantic gestures.

That can't be good.

Rek pushed his way to the middle. "He's frightened," the Elf announced. Cleve didn't need psyche to see that. "He believes I'm an enemy, but he'll be relieved to find out I'm an ally and will thank you all generously for your assistance."

There were nods within their group. People seemed to believe him.

Cleve found himself believing Rek as well, though something else made him far more nervous. *This is war to King Welson, an enemy storming his castle. What could await us within those walls?* It felt like they were about to enter the cage of a lion.

"Rek, how will we get past the door?" Cleve wondered, suddenly wishing he'd asked earlier what the Elf had planned.

"That's the easy part." Rek's voice trailed off. "It's the heavy pots of boiling water I fear. The King's Guard will drop them upon us continuously as we climb to the sixth floor. That and..." His voice became a whisper. "There's going to be a battle within those walls. Some of our guards may even turn on us."

Cleve examined the decrepit broom. There were teeth marks where it had been shoved into Colimp's mouth. *This old thing looks about ready to shatter upon the first strike.*

Rek took Cleve's shoulder. "Come with me, we need to address our men."

Cleve followed him to the front, where the hooded Elf halted their party with a hand. "Gather close for a moment." The warriors and mages shuffled in, apprehension in their eyes. Cleve could feel terror dwelling in his stomach. He'd always felt prepared for battle if he needed to fight, but he'd never considered he would be storming his own king's castle. He tried to think of the best-case scenario, where no one was killed...

Rek started speaking before he could come up with anything. "Kyrro does have an enemy, but it's not me." Rek spoke loudly, low and proud. "You are members of the King's Guard, loyal to the defense of Kyrro and its ruler, and I'm just as loyal. There has been a terrible mistake that needs to be explained before I can fight for Kyrro, so it's vital that I speak to King Welson. He'll have guards ready to attack us who believe we're the enemy, but once this is over they'll see how wrong they were when I'm fighting beside them."

Many nodded in agreement. Cleve bit his lip, knowing the issue was getting to the King, not convincing him once they were there.

"In case you don't already know, this is Cleve." Rek pointed a hand at him. "In that bag is a longbow, which he may need to use to ensure we're not captured or hurt. So don't be alarmed if he draws it. The King won't be harmed. Regarding his guards, only maim, don't kill. We're all fighting on the same side. They just don't know it yet."

Murmurs of agreement followed.

They returned to marching in silence, their steps falling into unison without an order. Cleve calmed his breathing. Focus would be needed for each shot, and he'd only been given two arrows. "More than enough to kill one Elf," the King had told him the morning before, with a tone like his task was to slay a fly. The memory tightened his fists in frustration.

King Welson had left his balcony to be replaced by a warrior clad in chain mail and a red-robed mage at his side. Another warrior and mage were stationed on the identical balcony to the other side of the entrance.

Rek pointed at them. "They'll use knives and fire when we're near the door," he stated loudly for everyone to hear. "Any mages proficient with Sartious Energy?"

One raised a wand. With her short blonde hair in the dim light, Cleve hadn't noticed she was a woman until now. She was tall with a round and friendly face. She wore a light green robe to represent her skill with the heavy energy. It was embroidered with the gold crown of Kyrro along her chest, outlined with silver.

"Are you familiar with the spell 'wall'?" Rek asked.

She leaned back petulantly. The question must have expected too much of her. "I'm no master mage. I can cast 'shell' for a minute, maybe two, if I drain all my energy, but not 'wall.' "

Shell is only a barrier against magic, not throwing knives, Cleve knew. His eyes met Rek's and his heart jumped. *Is he going to ask me to shoot the warriors who are throwing knives?* Cleve looked up and saw the knife throwers were shielded by the tall stone balconies so only their necks and faces were exposed. Their flesh was outlined by the light flooding from the castle behind them. The image of putting an arrow through them made Cleve cringe. But after a frightening long stare, Rek turned away.

"Other mages, raise your wands," Rek said. Two others did, both men clad in red robes. "When we reach the door, you both cast fireballs at the balconies. Scare them into retreating. If they don't frighten, aim better, give them a better reason to be scared." He pointed back at the Sartious Energy specialist. "If the mages on the balconies do get to cast at us, we'll need 'shell.' Save your energy, though. Only cast it when necessary. We may be out there more than a few minutes."

The three mages nodded. Colimp hobbled forward. "What about us? Are we just bodies to you, expendable protection?"

Rek's losing him, Cleve thought with a sudden panic.

For a breath the Elf's weariness hung on his face, but then his mouth closed and a serious look came into his eyes. "We'll all be in danger, yet I'll be the main target. I need protection, yes, and injuries may occur, but none of you are expendable. I'll fight for you, protect you, and keep you safe all the way to the sixth floor and even after. If you don't trust me or you're scared, then stand aside to watch us fight on our own, but know that I'm asking for your help." He glanced over the top of their mob. "All of your help."

They each stood tall, focused. Cleve felt ready to do whatever was asked of him.

"What's the plan?" Colimp asked.

Rek smiled in relief. "Rodents, lots of them."

Chapter 37: A New Day
EFFIE

No better time to cast than in the quiet morning, Effie thought. The sun had just pushed through the clouds, and the blackened brick walls of the mage's training area—although they were ugly—did well to block any wind that had managed to make it over the Academy's outer wall. She was closed off from the rest of the world, a rare moment of tranquility. Her breaths were clear, without tension.

Her fire spells would start with a loud *whoosh* of hot Bastial Energy gushing from her hands through her black staff that was filled with heavy Sartious Energy. Soon, the crackle of fire forming on the end of her staff would follow, and just for a blink, which is all it took for the swirling yellow and orange fireball to take size, the heat from it hopped down her arm.

That was her cue to shoot, and she'd better have picked the target before then. For in that instant, losing focus could mean a wild spell—the fireball could explode into the ground just before her feet, or more likely it could zoom off anywhere in front of her. She figured this was why the brick wall was blacker than it was red.

Her fireball crashed into the charred metal figure of a man's torso, igniting his chest with the dance of fire for just a breath before it dissipated. With the fire gone, so were the crisp searing sounds it had produced, leaving just the calm after-noise of Effie pulling in air through her nose.

When she'd first learned to cast them, each fireball used to make her feel like she'd just run a mile, but now the physical effects were closer to walking up a small hill.

Ding, ding, ding. The quiet was suddenly interrupted by the startling sound of the Redfield bell. She jumped. Rage consumed her. Luckily, there was no one around to take it out on, and the feeling soon faded. The bell gave a deep ring that somehow seemed shrill, perhaps because it made her ears feel as if she was standing next to a screaming woman.

The Group One mage classroom and training square was near the center of the Academy, just west of Redfield, so she couldn't have been closer to the bell without already being in Redfield, where it hung atop the massive, blood-red pillar.

When the ringing stopped, she could hear her thoughts again. *That's just Liaison Wilfre debunking the rumor of war,* she remembered on the way there.

She'd awoken early even though there were no classes that day. She thought making it into Group One would allow sleep to come easier, but she was wrong. She was more restless last night than she'd been since coming to the Academy. Watching Cleve being taken had put her nerves on edge. He hadn't returned, and she was unsure whether he ever would. Meanwhile, Steffen was hiding something that made him so guilty he couldn't bear to look at her. But the worst of it was still the uncertainty of war. No matter what Liaison Wilfre was about to tell them, she had a strong feeling there was more to it. Effie knew she wouldn't be sleeping well with everything going on. She sighed at the thought.

There were only a few people seated in the wooden stands when she entered Redfield, but more were flooding in so fast through all six entrances that she had no hope of watching for Steffen or Reela. Instead, she let her eyes rest upon Liaison Wilfre and Headmaster Terren conferring in the center of the dirt field. Her mind became numb with drowsiness as she waited for all three thousand students to file into a seat. *All three thousand, except Cleve,* she corrected herself.

Another man joined Wilfre and Terren in the center. He was in the same trench coat as he'd worn last night, Effie noticed, realizing then who it was. *Javy Rayvender, why are you here?*

Someone cleared his throat as he sat next to her. "Hi Gulpy," he said as she turned.

Brady. Her heart leapt into her throat. The sun was on him, giving his skin a polished look. His eyes were brighter than ever, such a blue to them. He had the same smile as when they'd met in the bar. It was wide, so much so it would've looked phony on anyone else, but not on him. She looked around him to see who was seated on his other side, but there was no one.

"Didn't come with your girlfriend?" Effie asked.

"She's around somewhere, I imagine. Any idea why we're here?"

She decided not to pry about why he was alone. "It's just Liaison

Wilfre informing us the rumors of war are false."

"Rumors of war?" That took away his smile.

Wilfre began shouting before Effie could answer. "Welcome to Redfield, home of the Champion Battles. The reason I've called you all here is to make an announcement that's very important."

"So will you give me your true name or am I to call you Gulpy every time I see you?" Brady whispered. He leaned close when he spoke. She could feel the heat of his breath on her ear. She would have said something, but on this cool morning she actually welcomed his warmth.

Effie was still embarrassed about kissing him back in Oakshen. Every time he spoke, the same feeling of shame would swell in her stomach. "You won't have to worry about what to call me because there's no reason for us to talk."

He leaned away without another word. Effie listened to Wilfre continue, now trying to ignore the guilt she felt.

"Before I say any more, you all should know who I am and what I do here."

I'd rather listen to a blacksmith forging a blade with his hammer than to Liaison Wilfre talk about himself again, Effie thought. She turned to Brady. "I never would have..." *Kissed you.* She paused as she waited for Brady to give her an eye. She hoped he might respond before she was forced to finish the sentence, but he only waited in silence with a curious look. "I wouldn't have done what I did in the bar if I'd known you were attending the Academy, especially not if I'd known it would mean you were cheating on your girlfriend."

Half his lip curled. "So, we're speaking now?"

"No, shut up." She folded her arms in embarrassment. She was unused to regretting her words so soon after speaking them. *It's the lack of sleep,* she told herself, *not him.*

Wilfre continued addressing the school with the same speech she'd already heard: "It is up to me to decide who would join such a mission..."

"Why even tell me you have a girlfriend?" Effie asked.

"I wanted to be honest with you."

"Honest?" Effie blurted, completely shocked and unsure she believed him. "Who cares about being honest with someone you'll never see again?"

"I knew I would see you again. You said you would be attending the Academy. I thought you should know the truth." His reply was quick, with a slight hint of anger in his whispered voice.

Oh, that's right. She'd forgotten she'd stupidly revealed that.

He leaned toward her. "Something told me whatever this is between us wouldn't end in that bar. It's something about you I don't quite understand, some sort of connection."

She felt the same way but didn't let it show. She wanted to be disgusted by his brash way of flirting. Instead, she found herself feeling flattered that he would be bold enough to tell her this. He made it seem like he trusted her, though she didn't feel the same way.

"What about being honest to your girlfriend who lives with you? I'm no expert in relationships, but someone living with you sounds pretty serious to me."

He leaned back. "I was honest with her also." Effie could easily hear it in his tone now. He spoke with a determined frustration. "I told her what happened, and she moved out before classes started. She's sharing a room with her friend. I was honest with her just as I was with you. I was honest with everyone." His hands fluttered about. "Everyone says they want to know the truth, but I'm beginning to doubt that they really do."

"I'd rather you lied to me," Effie stated plainly.

"About what?" His eyebrows lifted. The sun caught his blue eyes.

"About everything, about something, anything even." Effie sighed, knowing she was speaking without thinking. She gathered her wits to figure out what she meant. Brady waited patiently, keeping an eye on her and the other on Wilfre in the middle of Redfield. Effie realized her shame mostly came from how she'd practically thrown herself at Brady before knowing anything about him, such as that he was going to the Academy or that he had a girlfriend. She just wanted the shame to go away. When she realized that, her heart sank, for she knew she'd talked herself into a bind—she'd wanted him to lie about having a girlfriend so they could have fun for one night without her feeling guilty. The thought brought even more shame. *I could never tell him that. I shouldn't even be thinking that. That's terrible.*

Effie shook her head and took a moment to hear what Wilfre was saying.

"That brings me to the news I need to share," he announced, glancing at a scroll. "First, it's important we cover a small portion of history between Kyrro and Tenred."

"I guess honesty hasn't done well for you," Effie teased, tuning out the droning voice again.

"I know," Brady replied. "When will I learn?"

"Hopefully never." She felt herself smiling, but then she remembered something. "Since you're so honest, did you also tell your girlfriend about the prostitute?"

What looked like genuine confusion crossed his face. "What prostitute?"

"You see so many prostitutes you can't keep track of them?" Effie asked, now concerned there was far more she didn't want to know about Brady. "The one with you at the bar before you came over to me."

"Oh, her." He shook his head with a light laugh. "I don't see prostitutes. That's just a friend I've known since we were children. The reason I went to the bar that night was to see her before I left. Sometimes we flirt, but nothing would ever happen. My girlfriend has met her many times. She's like a sister."

"A sister that you flirt with?"

"Maybe more like a cousin."

"That's not much better."

"A second cousin then?" He shrugged. "You must know what I mean. Don't you have any platonic relationships with men?"

She thought of Steffen. With one ear to Liaison Wilfre's rambling, she gave a long look around the stadium for him and Reela but couldn't pick them out of the sea of people. The drowsiness was setting in again, tugging on her head. *I need to get more sleep,* she told herself as if it was a simple choice. *I need to figure out how to get more sleep,* she corrected herself.

"Of course," she muttered.

"Why is Liaison Wilfre telling us all this history just to dispel some rumor?" Brady asked. "What do you know that I don't?"

"Nothing," she admitted. "Just my name."

"Would you have me guess it?" he asked playfully.

"I'd rather have you call me Gulpy if you need to call me something."

"What letter does it start with?"

"G," she teased.

"No, your birth name."

Suddenly everyone around them was murmuring to each other. Effie found a frantic expression upon their faces as she glanced around. She asked a girl behind her, "What did he just say?"

"Tenred won't renew the treaty." The girl had a grave tone.

"This does mean there most likely will be battles in the near future," Liaison Wilfre continued regretfully. Then the murmurs burst into a buzz of incomprehensible dialogues.

"I thought you said he would tell us the rumors of war were false?" Brady said.

What is this, some sort of sick joke? Hot anxiety engulfed her. It was the same feeling she'd had when she'd fallen from a cliff in a nightmare the other night. She'd awoken when she'd hit the floor, her heart racing just as it was now. She felt her lungs beginning to tighten. *No, not now, not out here with everyone around me.*

"Headmaster Terren will talk now about how this will affect all of you!" Liaison Wilfre was shouting himself red, but Effie could barely hear him over the students around her.

"Quiet!" Terren had both massive arms up high. His voice was deep, piercing through the noise of everyone else. "We need everyone to remain quiet!"

Effie noticed then that many of the students were standing. Quickly, they each sat back down. Terren waited patiently for the sounds of creaking wood to stop. Everyone began shushing each other for nearly a minute. Then the shushing stopped and there was a burning silence as everyone waited for him to speak.

Effie had to stop herself from grabbing Brady's hand. It was a reflex she was used to with Reela. *I wish she was on my other side.* She interlaced her fingers and squeezed, finding some comfort in that as she tried to calm herself.

She could feel Brady's eyes shift to her hands. He hesitantly extended his hand and rested it on top of hers. It had the opposite effect of what he was probably going for. Her heart only beat faster. For a moment she thought she was going to lose her breath completely, but the moment passed. She realized her breathing was fine. This calmed her, allowing her to enjoy Brady's touch. She freed her fingers so they could hold hands properly. The hot anxiety began to cool. She lowered her head as a chill of sweet relief ran down her neck.

Terren finally was satisfied enough with the silence to begin.

"Thank you. Now...your instructors have been trained well in case such an occasion was to occur. The focus of each class will shift to make sure everyone knows their role in a battle. If you have any questions when I'm finished, your instructor can answer them."

He cleared his throat, and Effie expected him to pull a scroll from his pocket to read. But instead, he calmly glanced around the stadium.

He holds silence so well.

He opened his palms to gesture as he spoke. "Classes—or battle training as they should be addressed from now on—will occur every day to make sure we're prepared for the worst. Both the north and south gates will remain closed now. If you wish to reach someone in a southern city, write a letter and have it addressed and ready to go in your mailbox before nightfall. You're not to leave the Academy without first receiving permission."

Effie noticed annoyed murmurs starting up.

Terren pushed out his palms and quickly continued. "This may seem sudden, but there's no reason to be afraid. While we're the front line to any attack, we're also part of the Kyrro Army. We always have been. At the first sign of any attack, the entire force of the King's Guard will join us to defend our border. We'll also be joined by every able-bodied graduate of the Academy."

Terren had a rallying cadence to each sentence. He was speaking to them the same way Effie would imagine him threatening an enemy on their behalf. He made a fist, and silence followed once again.

"You all have been accepted here because of your ability. Now is the time to put it to use. Our walls are ten feet tall. Kyrro's army is nearly ten thousand strong. And our warriors, mages, chemists, and psychics are far more skilled in their classes than those in Tenred. Until the thick-skulled King of Tenred gets some sense and signs the treaty, we'll ensure that no enemies get through us to harm our friends and families back home."

Effie noticed she was slipping from the bench, being too far on the edge. She plopped herself back an inch and leaned forward once again, matching the position of those around her. Brady squeezed her hand tighter. It sent a tingle down her arm and made her lips curl into a peremptory smile.

"If at any point in the future the Redfield bell is rung twice, then you are all to return here for an important announcement, just like now. But if the bell is rung continuously, then it's time to defend our walls. Keep your spirits high and your heads low and focused. This isn't a time to be petty or pompous. Put all woes aside. This is a time to trust your instructors and your king, but more importantly you need to trust each other."

He stopped for a breath to let his words resonate. Effie felt herself pulled into his speech, eager for more.

"Now, think about the people in our cities, the people who farm our food, cook our meals, make our weapons, sew our clothes, brew our beer. All of *them* take care of us." He pointed south to the rest of Kyrro. "That's how *they* give back to Kyrro."

He took his finger around the stadium to give each of them a chance to figure out what he was about to say. *But how do we give back?* Along with the question, Effie had the answer. *We fight for them!* She wanted to shout it. She could feel the same energy from those around her.

"You may have thought it would be one year, maybe two or even three years before it was your turn to give back," Terren continued. "But that time is now! It's time for you to be proud...proud of what you're part of...of who you are and what you can do. Now stand and meet in your classrooms for your first training as true members of the Kyrro Army!"

There was a boom as everyone rose at once. A wave of cheers and applause roared through the stadium. Effie dropped Brady's hand to clap as loudly as she could. All of her drowsiness had disappeared. She felt ready for anything, never more roused in her life. Brady stood beside her, using his fingers to whistle.

It made Effie realize how silly her anger toward Brady had been. They might now be fighting for their lives and the lives of their families, and she was upset because he'd acted like he didn't have a girlfriend until she'd kissed him? Whatever embarrassment she had before was pointless.

"My name's Effie," she told him.

He extended his hand. "Welcome to the Kyrro Army, Effie."

Chapter 38: Gone
ZOKE

They're all gone, Zoke thought with dismay as he and Vithos overlooked the barren Krepp camp from the high hill to the north. *Vithos was right. Even most of the huts have been moved.* Though he wasn't surprised, it was still a stark and depressing sight that made his heart fall to the base of his stomach.

"They could have Krepps waiting for us," Vithos said as they scurried down the hill. "We should remain close."

Zoke took another look at the empty land ahead of him. The statement seemed absurd. "There's nowhere for them to hide...and I wouldn't think you wanted to stay close. Didn't you say I smelled?" Zoke was still trying to understand why it was the first time he'd heard of it.

"Yes, but no worse than any other Krepp. When it comes to noticing your own odor, all you Krepps are *gurradus*, it seems. None of you can tell how bad the other one smells."

"Maybe you're the only one who thinks we smell," Zoke retorted.

Vithos chuckled. "Probably."

It was clear to Zoke they were both avoiding the inevitable conversation—what were they going to do now? Would they stay together or split up? Zoke still hadn't decided, but he knew Vithos was waiting for an answer.

They'd spent the last week walking back from Merejic. Zoke found it much easier to travel back home than he did away from it, although that might have been because he had hope his home was still there. It would've made Vithos wrong about not only the encampment being moved but possibly everything—including that Zoke was considered a traitor.

Now that he'd returned to the empty camp, it became clear how silly those thoughts really were. He'd never known Vithos to be wrong before. Why expect it to be any different now?

Two days ago, they'd crossed through Lake Lensa, and Vithos had asked Zoke to clean himself in the water. Apparently, the smell he produced had grown to be unpleasant. Krepps tended to bathe only when filth or odor gave them reason to, and from what Zoke understood, Krepps didn't naturally smell bad to each other. It usually took contact with mud or worse filth, and even then, many Krepps only washed the dirty spots on their bodies with a rag. Their skin was naturally dry and hairless except atop their heads, making it easy to clean. After five minutes in the lake, Zoke felt he'd done an adequate job and had left the cold water with no intention of returning in the near future.

Vithos followed Zoke to the hut he'd shared with Zeti, or at least where Zoke thought it used to be. "Where is it?" Zoke asked aloud. There were hardly any huts still there. It was like an enormous wave had run through the camp and the only remains had been scattered, moved from their original spot. "Someone must have taken it."

"Zeti, I would assume. You would want a roof over her head wherever she is now."

"Yes, but how am I supposed to find the sword she buried?" Zoke could feel desperation starting to claw at him.

"Would she take it with her?"

"No, it's too heavy for her. She'd prefer her own, and she knows it's mine." There was a wooden table with a leg an inch shorter than the rest. Zoke climbed on top of it and steadied himself as it wobbled to a stop. He peered out toward the rising sun, shielding his yellow eyes. "She could have left a mark, some way for me to find it." His heart was speeding up. *I'm not leaving until I do.*

"Is it really so important she would risk going against Doe and Haemon to get it to you?"

"It's the sword that saved my life twice." Zoke saw nothing from the table, so he sat on it to get his feet back to the ground. There was a familiar squeak as his weight shifted.

"Could this be...?" He knelt to investigate the legs closer. "This is my table. I built this, but all four legs were equal when I left, and it wasn't chipped and scratched."

"Smart girl." Vithos squatted to inspect the shortened leg. "She made it so no one would want it. Here's your mark."

Zoke put down his bow, quiver, and bag of food, and took the rusted sword from his belt and threw it behind him. With a rush of eagerness, he knelt to the dirt underneath the table and started to dig. He clawed madly, throwing the dirt behind him. Soon he met steel. He took a moment to enjoy the sweet relief he felt, then started pushing the dirt away until he could rip the sword free.

"Satisfied?" Vithos asked.

Zoke ran a claw along the blade. He truly was, though it still beckoned to cut something. "Almost. I'll be perfectly content when I get to use it."

Silence came, and Zoke's grin faded. He knew it was time.

Vithos looked at him with his long, brown eyes, waiting. His mouth remained steady, a flat line. "Will you come with me now that you see I was right?"

Looking back into the Elf's eyes, Zoke knew then what his answer would be, but he still had some questions before he revealed it. "How would I even help?"

Vithos lowered his head, almost shamefully it seemed. "You're the only one I can trust. I thought I've made that clear."

Zoke remained quiet. Though it may be true, that wasn't what he was asking. Vithos seemed reluctant to say more, so Zoke calmly informed him, "That didn't answer my question."

Vithos sighed. "I'm not proud to say it, but I don't know exactly how I'll need you, just that I will. You can speak common tongue—that may be needed. You know more about the Slugari than I do. Let's help each other." Vithos' voice trailed off. It seemed like he was holding something back.

Suddenly, Zoke had a feeling what it was. It felt strange to ask aloud, though. Zoke bit down hard as he waited, hoping Vithos would elaborate, but the Elf said nothing more. He wouldn't even lift his eyes.

He's lonely...or will be without me.

As if he knew Zoke had figured it out, Vithos quickly lifted his head and pointed at him. "You should be asking me why you would want to come instead of how you can help. I have reasons for that."

Zoke already knew that, though. He had his own reason to come. Vithos was right that Zoke knew more about Slugari. Books were not a popular commodity within the tribe, as Krepps hated writing even more than reading. This made books on certain subjects like Slugari, weapon making, and hunting highly valuable. Zoke had traded his way up to a book on Slugari just before his *pra durren* and had read it at least a dozen times in the four years since then. Even with his lack of taste for their green meat, he felt that any knowledge could only be helpful toward his role within the tribe. And in this book was his reason for wanting to find them.

"I've read Slugari keep tabs on movement above ground, making it very difficult for large groups of Krepps to hide where they are," Zoke admitted.

For the first time, it seemed Vithos was confused. His brow furrowed and his mouth twisted. "What are you saying?"

"I'm saying I already know why I would want to come."

Vithos' eyes widened and a grin started to form. "And why is that?"

"Because the Slugari must know where the new camp is. They keep track of Krepp movement."

Vithos showed him an open-mouthed smile. "See what I mean? Your help is valuable...so, you're coming with me?"

Zoke nodded. "What other choice do I really have? I'm not going to get myself killed by walking into the camp alone if I even found it." He pointed his claw at Vithos. "But you'll help me figure out a way to be with Zeti again. That's all I really care about."

Vithos squinted his eyes as if insulted. "Of course I will."

That led Zoke to his other question. "How?"

Vithos wiped some dirt from his arm and spoke calmly. "Once we remove Doe and Haemon's power over the army, Krepps will split into separate tribes as they were before. There's no way a group that large can be led by a Krepp. Their differences will separate them. Then it's just a matter of finding sister to you, which I will help you do."

"And you really think the Slugari will help fight against Doe and Haemon? They're weak creatures—always running from Krepps, never fighting."

"They'll help however they can," Vithos answered with a shrug. "It's in their best interest. And if not, they'll know where the camp is, like you said. Then we can figure something out."

Without a better option, Zoke decided they might as well start walking. "Which direction?"

Vithos grinned. "South." He motioned with his head, and they walked.

"I'm glad you know something about the Slugari," Vithos said. "I know nothing except that it'll be dangerous to meet with them; that is, if we can even find a way."

Zoke felt his heart jump. "What do you mean, find a way? Don't you know exactly where they are?"

"Yes, but I have no idea how to get to their colony besides digging."

"But we can dig just fine."

Vithos gave a laugh. "Yes, but there's something you're not thinking about. They could be fifty yards deep. Even with you and me together, it's going to take a full day of digging or more. Then, once we break through, it will be their roof that we're using as a door. Who knows how high it is or what we'll fall onto? And think of the welcome waiting for us." He laughed once more. "I don't suppose we'll be treated invitingly."

"They must have some way of getting in and out. Slugari have been seen above ground only to disappear minutes later."

Vithos shrugged. "My psyche doesn't have the answers we need."

Neither do books in this case, Zoke thought. But then an idea came to him. "The risk is that our hole will suddenly open underneath our weight, so let's use something else to dig for us. Can you make animals dig?"

"It depends on the creature. I believe we could find one that would."

"We can stay on safe ground so that we don't expose ourselves until the animal digging for us has breached the Slugari colony. Then we can assess what we find below before falling into it."

"Good idea." Vithos raised a finger to point at the rolling land ahead of them. "The Slugari are in northern Satjen. As much as it pains me, we have to cross through Kilmar."

Kilmar. Zoke suddenly felt discouraged. He'd never been in Kilmar but knew of its reputation. The land was riddled with rocky hills. It contained treacherous paths between mountains, and was best known for its sheer lack of even ground, making a twisted ankle become a common injury.

"If the Slugari had chosen their home knowing where Doe and Haemon were, then they were very smart," Vithos said and then explained the annoying route they needed to take to get to the Slugari colony from the abandoned camp.

Directly south was where they were headed, but they had to walk southeast and southwest to avoid the many mountains in their path. But worst of all was the massive desert in the middle of Kilmar, directly between them and their destination. They both agreed it was worth the extra time to avoid it.

With his sword back in its sheath, Zoke had trouble keeping his claws off it. It was all that remained of his childhood with Zeti, and it had always served him well, protecting not only him but his sister many times.

The bow on his back, in contrast, he almost wished he'd never found. The weapon had a shape to it that did not carry well. To make matters worse, the weight of it and its ammo in the quiver around his shoulder had become a distracting pain. *I don't know what Zeti sees in this thing.*

As they went through the dry lands of Kilmar, he asked Vithos to hold the bow, but the Elf wisely convinced him that the one wielding the weapon should know how to use it in case they came under attack. Vithos did offer to carry Zoke's supply bag, which was about as heavy a burden as the dirt caked into the soles of his feet. He spat at the suggestion.

When Zoke caught a glance at Vithos these days, he usually found purpose in his eyes and a grin about his mouth. A month ago, Zoke never had seen him with the same expression, not once.

The hardest part of befriending a psychic, Zoke found, was the inability to determine which of his own emotions were pure and which were manipulated through psyche. He came up with a simple technique. If he couldn't determine the origin of a new feeling, he assumed it to be through psyche and would do everything in his power to rid himself of that feeling. Although no knowledge supported his method, it felt right and was easier than second-guessing everything constantly.

It was rare for him to feel something without knowing why, making him believe Vithos hardly ever used psyche on him. But still, the fear was there as much as he tried to ignore it.

The sun had left the cloudless, dusty-gray sky as they came to the hills surrounding the desert. Besides a few thin paths darting between mountains, they were surrounded by slopes of dirt and rock.

"Tired yet?" Zoke asked.

"Of your stench? Yes."

He wanted to spit, but the dry air had sapped all liquid from his mouth. "I'm sure you smell of rujins," Zoke quipped. He'd heard they had a nice scent.

Vithos sniffed under his arm and released a curious hum. "That I do."

"I may be a *gurradu,* but I can still smell the stench of a lie." He put down his bow and quiver first, his back and shoulders singing with relief. Vithos began letting his bags down as well.

"What do you know of Kilmar?" Zoke asked. "Can we each sleep through the night?"

"Few animals still roam these dry lands. Unless Krepps find us, we'll be safe. Even then, the nights have been fully dark, so they would stumble over us before knowing who we were."

"Good. I'm sick of not sleeping a full night."

Vithos ran his hand along the ground. "You might still have some trouble on this land."

The Elf was right. Finding enough comfort to sleep was an annoying challenge that night—and each night after as well.

The weight of Zoke's weapons strained his body during the day, and his feet ached during the night. The worst, however, were the seemingly infinite rocks digging into his back. It didn't help that Vithos seemed to have no trouble dozing off on any surface, although Zoke did notice him rubbing his back and shoulders every morning.

After each difficult night, Zoke had grown more curious about the idea of psyche helping him rest, but the closer he got to asking, the more frightened he became. The thought of manipulating his mind to knock him unconscious started a wave of fears about what could happen, like nightmares, sleep walking, and even never waking again. He couldn't allow himself to be the first Krepp to test it.

On the third night, Zoke was clearing claw-sized rocks where he wished to lie while Vithos was motionless, breathing rhythmically. *He's already asleep. One night I'd like to get there before him.*

Even with the rocks pulled aside, the ground was still lumpy. Zoke squirmed and rolled until his patience gave out, and he settled where his back and neck were straight but lumps dug into his legs.

Countless times he woke, each time more drowsy and sore than before.

By the time light had spread across the naked sky, he felt like he'd spent the entire night tumbling down the steep hills around them.

He groaned as he sat up. As usual, Vithos was already awake and stretching, but with a worse grimace than the morning before.

"I wish I could say that will be our last night in Kilmar," the Elf said.

"Have you eaten?" Zoke asked with a hand on his neck.

"I was waiting." Vithos undid the string on one of his bags.

The Krepps sent to kill them had bread in their pouches. Most of it had dried by the time it was in the hands of Zoke and Vithos, so it was first to be eaten. There were still hard biscuits left, though. They were made to last and still were edible.

The kupota they'd brought initially had begun to grow stale. They had enough food and water for three days if they rationed well, but Zoke hoped they would join with the Slugari before then. *They may not wish to feed a Krepp, but Vithos should be able to convince them—if they let me come in*. He wondered what their first meeting would be like.

Neither he nor Vithos knew the Slugaren language, but Vithos seemed confident he at least could demonstrate they shared a common enemy even if they didn't share a common language. There was also the bleak hope that one or more Slugari spoke common tongue. Then Zoke could speak for them.

The worst problem was what they would think of a Krepp coming into their home. He couldn't help but feel that the welcome that awaited him would be the same that awaited a wolf that had found a warren of rabbits—utter panic and immediate chaos.

Later, as his thoughts circled back, it seemed his welcome would be more like the way a beehive would welcome any intruder—wild aggression.

The Slugari's claws might be short, but there had to be thousands of them. *Could Vithos really use his psyche to stop that large of a force?* The image Zoke pictured of him and Vithos being swarmed by a sea of shimmering green Slugari made him shudder. *Maybe I'll let him go in first and wait above ground.*

Chapter 39: Listen
ZOKE

Four days and four nights passed before they reached the green hills of Satjen. They agreed never to spend another night in Kilmar if they could avoid it.

All that Zoke knew about Satjen was that its western coast was home to Tenred, and Vithos last felt the presence of Slugari somewhere north of the territory's center. The land seemed mostly untouched by the tribe, as there were trees and tall plants in every direction. The lush grass was a great relief from the dry dirt. It felt moist between the claws on his feet.

"Stomp your foot," Vithos told him while holding a hand toward a cluster of trees. Zoke stomped twice without question then stopped. "Keep at it," Vithos said.

Zoke saw something emerge from behind the base of a tree.

"Stomp harder."

His leg grew tired. His feet were sore even before he'd begun. "Why don't you stomp?"

"I need to concentrate. Tap your sword instead, if you wish."

He did and soon recognized the bushy tail of a fox. It was lifted curiously as it trotted toward him. "Is this to help us dig?"

"No," Vithos answered as he drew his knife. "We won't reach the Slugari location before tomorrow evening." Vithos placed his other hand over the head of the fox, gently pushing down. The shine in its eyes faded as they began to shut. Its head folded down onto its legs. "This is dinner." With startling speed, Vithos slammed his knife into the fox's head.

Zoke's mouth was already beginning to water. "I'll start collecting sticks and rocks." His stomach could handle most meats straight from the carcass, but even a *gurradu* like him could appreciate a hot meal. Vithos, on the other hand, had told him that fish was the only meat he could eat uncooked—another drawback to being an Elf, Zoke assumed.

Vithos assembled the rocks in a circle with sticks and brush inside. "You'll show me how to prepare the fox?"

"Doe never taught you how?" Zoke asked before he realized how stupid the question was.

"When we caught something wild, he would always do it while sending me off for some other task. I'm sure he didn't wish for me to learn how to live on my own."

When Zoke showed him how to separate the good meat from the inedible, they each held a piece over the fire with their daggers.

"It smells wonderful," Vithos commented.

I'm sure it does, Zoke thought. Hearing about the smell of meat was like listening to Krepps laughing over a joke he didn't understand.

With suddenly wide eyes, Vithos seemed to be struck by guilt. "If you were wondering," Vithos added with a touch of regret.

"I don't wonder about smells. It's impossible to wonder about something when you can't imagine it."

Vithos stared into the fire. "So, what do you wonder about then?"

"Most recently about how everything would be different if Krepps had no taste for Slugari meat." He'd spent many nights thinking about that. It was too hard to imagine what he would be like if he could smell and craved the meat like others—impossible even. He could *wonder* about it for hours, staying awake in bed until the sun came up, yet actually imagining it couldn't be done.

But to imagine everyone was a *gurradu* like him? Now, that was easy. He knew what life was like as a *gurradu.*

"You may as well wonder what Ovira would be like without Krepps, then." Vithos paused to give the meat on his dagger a poke from his clawless finger, testing its firmness before returning it over the fire. "From what I understand, the Krepps' goal throughout history has been searching for Slugari. If you took that away, Ovira would be unimaginably different. Doe and Haemon wouldn't have the cause they needed to join the Krepps and merge their tribes, so those two would have to find some other way to get revenge on their kind."

Vithos rested his free hand on his chin again, scrunching his mouth toward his nose like a thought had gotten stuck. "I would still be with my own kind." He shook his head as he tried to speak. A few words started to come out but none completed. Finally he said, "I can't even imagine what that life would be like. I'm trying, but I just can't. I don't know enough about Elves."

"I understand what that's like," Zoke added, knowing Vithos would understand what he meant.

The Elf glanced at the two holes that were Zoke's nose and nodded.

They finished cooking their meat in silence and began to eat. The meat wasn't pork but still delicious, bursting with flavor incomparable to the kupota.

Zoke's thoughts turned to his old leaders as he ripped the meat with his claws and mashed through it with his many sharp teeth. Doe and Haemon's aggression toward their own kind was the only similarity between the real world and the imaginary one Vithos described where Krepps didn't exist.

"Doe and Haemon would still do something to disrupt Ovira, even without Krepps aiding them," Zoke muttered to the fire. "They don't seem capable of living without control over everything."

He realized then that his hatred for them had deepened greatly since he'd left. Not only did their aggression against the Elves infuriate Zoke, he felt completely betrayed that they were ready to kill him just for coming back—for following the orders they'd given him. He tore off a big chunk of meat with a sudden voracious appetite.

"You might be surprised to hear that they used to be in the lowest of ranks among the Slugari colony." Vithos lifted an eyebrow to catch Zoke's attention. "I've heard the story they've created—of them being exiled for a crime they didn't commit. It's false. The truth is that Doe and Haemon were called ground-breakers. At least that was the closest translation they had for it in Kreppen. It was the role given to the weakest Slugari and involved exploring uncharted land underground and above. If they dug wrong, the dirt above them could collapse. If they were seen by a Krepp above ground, obviously they'd be hunted down. If Krepps weren't so dangerous, the Slugari might've had different roles for their weaklings and even might've lived above ground. We can't say what Doe and Haemon would've been doing or what would've become of them in this imaginary world where Krepps didn't hunt them."

"This is the first I've heard of this version of their history." Zoke felt childlike enthusiasm. "What else do you know?"

Vithos had just bitten off a piece of meat and now was hastily chewing it. He lifted a finger and forced a swallow. "Only what I could pry out of them during moments of weakness. Keeping in a secret that big is like holding your breath—the longer you do it, the more your inner voice screams at you to let it out."

He lowered his voice as if someone may overhear him. "They told me they were treated worse than any other Slugari, and that they were small. They *hated* it, couldn't stand being in the lowest of ranks and came together from that shared attitude. Eventually, they discovered the eppil plant somewhere underground, in some cavity they dug into. They claimed they were attacked for their discovery, although I could tell that wasn't quite true, not that I know what happened instead. They said they barely escaped with seeds they would later use to grow more eppils, which led to their size and power." Vithos stopped and took another bite. He showed no signs of continuing.

"That's it?" Zoke longed to hear of something more complete. The Elves were gone. He knew the ending to that story but not the beginning or the dramatic surprise—there was one in every Krepp story.

Now Doe and Haemon were controlling Ovira, and he still didn't know the beginning to that story and especially not how it would end.

"The Slugari should be able to fill the gaps," Vithos said. With that, the Elf finished his meal and lay down.

Zoke did the same. With a full stomach and flat ground, sleeping through the night was easy.

Zoke awoke to the sounds of fire and the cool morning breeze against his now moist face. His leather shorts were damp and clinging to him, but he didn't care. He felt rested and fresh.

After a yawn, he realized Vithos was cooking more of the fox meat.

"You're still hungry?" he asked in disbelief.

"This is so we don't have to cook it later. We may not be able to make another fire before it spoils. I'm almost finished. You ready to leave?"

"Yes," Zoke answered, getting up to stretch his legs. The question, though, made him aware of the dream he'd awakened from. *"Are you ready to say goodbye?"* Someone had asked him that. *Was it Zeti? Yes it was her*, he remembered now. Vithos was being buried. *"Yes, I'm ready,"* Zoke remembered answering. Then Zeti had started to sing. Her tones were strong and confident as she hummed the same background he'd dreamed of during his night in the Elven village. Again, he'd awakened before hearing himself sing the melody.

He thought as hard as he could, but the melody still escaped him.

Then suddenly, and with great satisfaction, he at last remembered the song. *It's the song of the dead! When we buried mother, Zeti and I sang the background and Ruskir sang the melody.*

It was the only burying he'd been to. Ruskir taught him and Zeti what to sing, explaining that the Krepp closest to the deceased would sing the melody while other close friends or family sang the background. Zeti was only two—*pra durren*, and he was six—*pra durren*, so it must've sounded no better than steel against stone.

Why am I dreaming about that? Zoke ran his coarse palm over his scalp and decided not to wonder about it. Dreams about death were always considered an ill omen.

Vithos and Zoke walked eight or nine miles before the urge came to break their fast from the big meal they'd had the night before. They looked for a good place to stop. Walking south had brought them to a ledge too tall to climb down. It overlooked a wide path that was created between the hills they walked on and the edge of the forest.

"South of that forest is where I sensed the Slugari," Vithos said. The trees stood just taller than their ledge, so Zoke could not see over them.

"How far do the trees go?"

"A few miles, if my memory is correct."

They ate the rest of the fox meat under the shade of a tree on the hillside, looking out across Satjen. "This land would serve the tribe well," Zoke said, thinking mostly about the thousands of trees they could use. The thick grass beneath his bare feet was something he could easily get used to as well.

"Slepja used to be more like this," Vithos said. "But after all the years of thousands of Krepps living off it, it has become nearly as barren as Kilmar."

They stared south as they quietly finished their meals.

A sound...and voices? Zoke strained his ears. It was coming from the east. He knew himself to have good hearing, so he figured Vithos hadn't noticed it yet. He walked toward the edge of the hillside to investigate. Vithos stood to follow.

"What is it?" the Elf asked.

"Lower your voice. You can't sense them? Someone's coming."

Vithos whispered, "No, they must be too far for my psyche."

Zoke and Vithos lowered their bodies to the ground by the edge, waiting for someone to emerge from the trees.

"There are four of them," Vithos said, holding out his palm at nothing Zoke could see.

Suddenly three Humans and a familiar-looking Krepp came from the trees, turning onto the wide path just below Zoke and Vithos. Zoke could hear that they were speaking common tongue, but they were too far away to understand their words.

"We should follow them," Vithos whispered.

Zoke knew he was right. They were the first Humans Zoke had seen that weren't a crude drawing, and this was definitely the first time he'd known of Humans sharing company with a Krepp.

It had triggered something. He could feel its importance like a stare from Zeti before she revealed a secret.

"Any idea who the Humans are or what they're doing with a Krepp?"

"No, and they're too far for my psyche to pick up anything besides their presence."

The group continued west, so Vithos and Zoke followed, walking along the northern hills to stay out of view.

When the Humans stopped for food, so did Vithos and Zoke. When one needed to make solid waste, so did Vithos. When another urinated on a tree, so did Zoke. They had no notion of how long they would need to follow before finding out what they were doing, but Zoke was prepared to stay behind them as long as it took. Humans and Krepps together—it had to mean something.

Chapter 40: Chaos
CLEVE

There were two parts to the plan Rek had devised: getting past the thick ironbark door and then making it to the King, who was likely to be deep within the castle and highly protected. When Rek first introduced it, Cleve figured the rodents were a metaphor of some kind, but soon it was clear he meant to *use* rats, literally. Cleve wasn't the only one to express concerns, as no one in their party had any experience with rats being helpful, but Rek won their trust eventually.

Psychics of the King's Guard had taken care of any unwanted creatures within the castle, but the surrounding houses didn't have the same luxury. There were independent psychics who made money from their ability to control pests, but many households weren't aware of their extra inhabitants or didn't care to pay for their removal. Rek was about to do many of them a favor, he explained.

When all were ready, Rek closed his eyes, lowered his head, and lifted both arms.

The sound of the creatures coming toward them was not so much a sound as an incomprehensible feeling. To Cleve, it was the same chilling experience as stepping into a dark room and feeling something move even though no one was there. It was that, but amplified so great that it completely paralyzed him.

Everything seemed to freeze as their group waited in silence.

Some feeling returned to Cleve's legs when they came into view—hundreds of rats scampering into the street all at once. He backed away from Rek and found others doing the same.

More and more and still more kept coming. They swarmed at Rek's feet, a sea of brown and black fur, full of short-lived waves as the rats crawled on top of each other to get closer to Rek.

He was buried up to his knees before he finally let his arms down and opened his eyes.

Rek pushed his hands toward the castle. His minions obeyed, flowing toward the door—a dark wave storming through the streets.

"Is there a word for what I'm seeing?" The blonde mage was next to Cleve, her eyes wide.

"Fearless determination," Cleve answered with an eye on Rek. "It can lead to madness or madness can lead to it."

Cleve and the rest of the party followed Rek and his rodents, jogging to keep up. The ironbark door stood even taller than Cleve remembered.

During Rek's telling of his plan, he mentioned an arrow slit that was roughly twenty yards left of the door. The thin slit in the wall was designed for shooting intruders who couldn't be reached from the balcony directly above it. The castle was symmetrical, so there was an identical arrow slit and balcony twenty yards to the right of the door, but Rek chose the left.

They gathered there, rats jumping and swarming over their feet.

"Get them inside!" Rek screamed. He had assumed correctly that the King would have no one stationed behind the ironbark door to the castle, for it was too much of a risk that Rek would persuade them to open it.

Cleve's bow was slung around his shoulder as he scooped up armfuls of rats. There was only room for one person next to the arrow slit, and Rek had chosen him. "You look like you could pick up the most rats at once with those giant arms. You're not scared of them, I assume?" Rek had said.

Scared of rats, no, but he'd never touched one before. It was hard to tell how he would feel about scooping them five at a time. His worst fear was being bitten and catching something, but Rek had promised they wouldn't bite. Their sole desire was to get inside, so Cleve just needed to provide the elevation.

Sure enough, they seemed to run in on their own, down his arms, wrists, palms, then fingers, and through the arrow slit that was no wider than his hand.

The worst part turned out to be bending down for more. Their jumping enthusiasm to get inside never stopped, so some would land on the back of his head or neck and scamper wildly for balance, only to slip and roll off him. It was truly disgusting. He found himself holding his breath each time his face was close to the ground.

He quickly lost track of both time and rats. Rek was shouting the entire time. "Get those rats in there! Need more rats! Get them in there!"

"I'm trying!" Cleve shouted back.

Soon Cleve realized his strategy of cupping rats and neatly placing them near the arrow slit proved to be too slow. So his method changed to scooping and chucking them into the arrow slit, first by taking a step back from the wall, then closing his arms around five or six of them and jerking them as accurately as he could at the gap.

His new strategy was much faster at gathering rats, as he imagined, but half the rats wouldn't make it in, bouncing off the wall with a high-pitched squeal.

"Bastial hell, Cleve, you're missing the hole!" Rek shouted. The Elf had his palm out, focusing to keep the rats under control.

"I realize that, Rek!"

So then he tried turning and squatting underneath the arrow slit, but this time so that his back was to the wall and his head underneath the opening. He used the same scoop and chuck method, but over his head into the slit directly above him.

It was easier to be more accurate, but there were two problems. Some wouldn't make it into the slit, even with him right below it. They would fall back down onto his shoulders or head, where they would scamper around until they tried to jump into the slit or until another rat fell onto them and pushed them off. The other issue was the rats he threw into his own face out of haste. That was, by far, the worst part of it all.

He threw one against his mouth and had to stop to wipe his lips on his arm, spitting until the tickle of rat fur was gone.

"Don't stop. We need more rats!" Rek continued to shout.

Meanwhile, the King's warriors who Rek had persuaded to help created a protective circle around the party, each wielding a light-blue shield of Kyrro containing the image of a gold crown lined in silver. Not all of them could fit under the balcony above, so one mage shot fireballs at their assailants directly atop them while the other mage aimed at the balcony on the far side of the door.

From what Cleve managed to witness as he hurled rats into the castle, it looked as if the incoming fireballs were of far more concern than the throwing daggers, which were easily defended by the warriors' shields and armor.

He knew a fireball could kill a man through a full plate of armor if it caught him in the head. So each one needed to be dodged, deflected by a shield, or intercepted with the "shell" spell.

Cleve caught sight of a few instances of the spell when the Sartious mage snapped her wand at an incoming fireball, creating a long, rectangular shield of translucent, emerald green color. It was just as tall as the woman casting it and twice her width. Cleve saw how the spell got its name, for it curved slightly around wherever she aimed to give it the shape of a turtle shell.

Cleve had never seen the spell in action before and was too busy with the rats to get a long look at it. But from what he could tell, it appeared to be falling and coming apart immediately after it was cast each time. Though, it was still strong enough to stop fireballs. When they slammed into the Sartious Energy field, the fireballs shattered and dispersed over the green shell, like a ray of sun exploding into an emerald so that the whole thing glistened.

After what felt like a few hundred had made it inside, Rek shouted, "That should be enough rats!"

The sea of fur around them looked no thinner than when they'd started. Rek closed his eyes with his hands against the castle wall as Cleve wiped feces from his hair, face, and neck, spitting a few more times to make sure his mouth was clear.

Rek had told them that once enough rats were inside, he could get them to remove the bolt that held the impenetrable door shut. "A solid steel bar slides up from the ground and into a hole on the underside of the door," he'd told Cleve. "The bar is connected to a lever down the hall from the entrance, hidden inconspicuously on the floor in the corner of an uninhabited room."

Cleve stayed low, behind the wall of warriors. He didn't mind the rats crawling on him as much now, as long as they weren't above his knees.

The mages on the balconies had retreated back into the castle, perhaps needing to regain energy, but the warriors remained. They continued to throw knives, but they weren't capable of piercing armor. A dagger needed to hit bare skin to do damage. *Luckily for us, they haven't any bows yet,* Cleve thought. *Or perhaps they just don't possess the skill.*

There was a deep thud. "I got it," Rek announced. "Open the door!"

Two warriors ran to the door and shoved their shoulders into it. Slowly, it gave under their weight, opening wide enough for them to slip through, but they did not enter. Instead they returned—

following Rek's plan.

Rek's arms pushed outward, and the hundreds of remaining rats ran toward the door. It took a long time for them all to flood in, surprisingly long, like watching a raging river fight its way down a small drain.

Then...an eerie moment of silence.

Their mages needed a few breaths to regain their energy. Cleve used the time to ready his bow and calm his breathing.

When their mages were ready, they provided cover by casting fireballs at the warriors on the balconies while Rek ran toward the door. Cleve and the rest followed.

They had opened the door. The first part of their plan was complete—*the easy part,* Cleve reminded himself.

Chapter 41: Orders
CLEVE

As soon as the Elf was through the doorway, Cleve noticed him glancing straight up.

"Move!" Rek shouted, pushing those who'd gathered in front of him and diving after them. Cleve knew what it must be and went the other way, doing his part to push a few others with his free arm who were slow to react.

Cleve pressed himself to the floor and covered his head as he heard a jug break against the ground behind him. Next came the sound of what had to be boiling water raining around them, but only a few drops found his pants.

He hopped to his feet, anticipating a flood of warriors rushing down the stairway, but no one awaited them on the first floor. It gave Cleve time to check on his group. Most were still rising, checking each other for injuries. Half of them hadn't made it through the door yet when the jug had been pushed over, and they were cautiously entering now.

One of the mages was holding his leg. Under their robes were usually thin garments made of cotton, and Cleve saw this mage was no different. The stone around him was wet, but he reassured everyone he was fine as he gripped his leg.

The screams within the castle took Cleve's focus. He found chaos and panic everywhere from the second floor up. Warriors, mages, and other inhabitants dressed without importance were yelling and running frantically in every direction. Two prostitutes, showing more skin than clothing, hollered their way down the stairs to the first floor as they ran for the door.

A few of Rek's warriors parted to let the women through. The frightened prostitutes were pulling rats from their hair and plunging bodices. One rat fell from between the legs of a poor woman. With incredible speed, it hurried back up the stairs to be lost among the other vermin swarming the second floor.

More people made for the exit. Chefs, servers, chemists...each ran past Cleve without so much as a glance at him or the others. They were all too busy throwing rats from their clothes.

"Are there any other exits?" Cleve asked.

"Not that I'm aware of," Rek answered. "Unless some secret passage was developed, the King has no way out but through us."

Dozens more ran past them to escape the infested castle, each bringing several rats that diligently climbed back up the stairs once their victims had tossed them aside. The second floor was nearly empty by then, so most of the rats had moved farther up. Cleve followed them with his eyes when suddenly a falling water jug intercepted his view. It smashed into the ground where the stairs began, cracking open with a sharp explosion so that boiling water was thrown in all directions. A small cloud of steam quickly rose and dissipated. Luckily, no one was running by as it happened.

Cleve looked for more water jugs waiting to be pushed over. He wasn't sure what caused the others to fall, most likely an accident caused by the rats.

The castle was well lit, so it had taken some time for his eyes to adjust to the brightness. Now he could see there were too many water jugs for his two arrows, but most rested atop banisters on the third and fourth floors, perhaps close enough for the mages. He addressed the two nearby who'd used fire to help defend their party outside. One was the man whose leg was burned.

"Either of you able to knock those water jugs over?" Cleve asked, then pointed.

They each looked with squinted eyes. The victim of boiling water said, "It's a tough shot. No mage is known for accuracy with fireballs over long distances." He shook his leg. "Perhaps from the second floor we may be able to."

They were interrupted by someone shouting, "This is Hem Baom, the commander of the King's Guard!" He stood stoically on the sixth floor, leaning over the railing. He had black hair and wore an ornate steel breastplate "I demand that you stay where you are and call back the rats or you will be attacked!"

Baom...it's Alex's brother. This could get ugly, Cleve realized. *I mean even uglier,* he corrected himself as he watched Hem swat a rat from his shoulder.

Colimp limped forward and held the stair banister, straining his neck to look above him. "Hem, it's Colin." He cupped his other hand around his mouth. "Rek just needs to speak with the King. He's on our side. We need him for this war."

"You know our orders!" Hem pointed aggressively, then shook a rat from his arm. "He must have control over your mind for you to go against the King. Think for yourself!"

Rek put a hand on Colimp's shoulder to draw him back a step. The hooded Elf looked up at the commander. "Hem, you remember me as a child. I would never hurt the King."

"Because of our past you haven't been killed yet, but this is your last chance before the rest of the King's Guard comes at you."

"Come here and detain me. These men will stand down as long as you bring me to the King so I can speak with him. That's all I want."

"I can't allow that. But I'll do everything in my power to set up an audience with him before your trial."

King Welson Kimard would never meet with Rek unless forced, Cleve thought, and figured Rek was thinking the same. In fact, it looked as if that had become obvious to everyone. Members of their party drew their swords and wands while guards from the higher floors ran to rally behind Hem.

"The future of Kyrro depends on the King speaking with me," Rek replied. "These men know it and are willing to fight for Kyrro and its people—but there is no need for bloodshed! Just let me pass, and the King will thank you."

"I'm sorry, Rek," Hem replied.

He must be too far for psyche, Cleve figured. *Or too stubborn.* He readied himself for battle by gathering hot Bastial Energy into his stomach and chest.

Hem stepped away from the banister. In his place appeared a woman with hair as dark as Hem's, but her skin was golden brown, the color of fresh bronze. She stuck out her head as if just curious about what was below, but then she produced a bow and pulled an arrow over her shoulder. To Cleve's surprise, she aimed it at their group. Everyone started to scatter—everyone except Cleve.

He was sizzling with energy. It burst through his arms and danced across his fingertips. Faster than he could think, he drew an arrow of his own, pulled back on his string hard and steady, and aimed at her weapon.

The arrow soared upward, and he saw with relief that his shot was perfect. It smashed her bow in two with a loud snap of what could only be wood shattering.

The young lady gasped so loudly he could hear it six floors below. With half her weapon still in hand, her wide eyes fell on Cleve. She had a silly, open-mouthed grin, and her palms were outstretched with bafflement. She said something, and Cleve thought he heard it as *"Bastial hell!"*

Cleve let down his bow and wagged a finger at her. It came out so naturally, he surprised himself. It was the same feeling as belching after a long drink. The young lady laughed and shook her head.

His showy reaction confirmed a suspicion he had about himself. *I guess I'm one of those kinds of warriors,* he thought, but more self-reflection would have to wait because Hem was rushing down the stairs with dozens of warriors behind him.

Cleve couldn't let poor old Colimp be the first line of defense, but with one arrow left, Cleve needed a different weapon. He'd left the shabby broom outside the castle walls, unable to hold it and his bow.

"Colin, you've been through enough," Cleve said. "Get behind us and lend me your sword."

"If you need a sword, get one from the wall in there. No need to insult me." Colimp pointed to some sort of formal meeting hall.

Looking behind him, Cleve saw the room's walls were adorned with a variety of banners and it hosted a large oval table surrounded by embroidered seats. When he entered, he saw what Colimp was referring to: two swords mounted over a hearth.

Inside, two rats appeared lost. They were running along the walls, stopping to sniff every few feet, giving no sign as to when they would find the door. Cleve couldn't help but wonder if that would be himself and Rek soon, hopelessly looking for the King throughout the massive castle.

Above the swords was an exaggerated portrait of Westin Kimard, the late father of their current king. His arms were folded below a stern expression as if judging Cleve for bringing rats into the castle. *I know,* Cleve agreed, *the rats are a bit much.*

The two rodents followed Cleve out and ran up the stairs toward their attackers, who were now speedily descending to the third floor. The sound of their boots slamming against the wooden steps was a thunderous noise and steadily getting louder.

But Cleve was ready, confident even, and he knew psyche had nothing to do with it. It helped that every guard seemed to have his own battle raging against the rats within his armor, for they all danced and shimmied with wild hands while trying to maintain their speed. But Cleve knew that wasn't the main reason he was unafraid. He trusted his ability. This was battle. This was what he was trained for. This was the opposite of Reela, who made him weak with a mere smile.

Still, he was worried. He felt it low in his stomach, heavy like a brick—not because he was worried about himself but because he didn't want to injure others. Cleve gave the sword a few good swings as he thought about what he should do, but then the longbow around his back slid down his arm.

Realizing he couldn't fight with it equipped, he glanced around for a place to hide his precious bow, soon noticing the room on the other side of the stairway. It was no more than a narrow entranceway to a portcullis that Cleve could only assume separated the rest of the castle from the dungeons below. *That may be where I end up,* he couldn't help but think as he ran toward it.

Outside the locked metal grille that led underground was a jug like those filled with boiling water that were thrown at his party, but this one held quarterstaffs. The tops of the melee weapons rested against the nearby wall. With time to spare, he gladly traded his sword for the blunt weapon and stored his longbow there as well. Rek was saying something to the group, but Cleve was too far away to hear.

Back near the entrance to the castle, Rek's valiant warriors and mages were keeping their feet steady with weapons drawn. All of Hem's men had drawn their weapons as well and now were turning onto the last stairway.

Cleve found a place beside Rek in the front.

"Nice work with the bow earlier," Rek told him. "I'll admit it was impressive, but get ready because I'm about to top it with my own trick."

At that, Cleve decided to take two steps back. Whatever Rek had planned, it felt safer being behind him.

Chapter 42: Heavy Rain
CLEVE

There must have been at least thirty warriors behind Hem descending the last stairway toward them, close enough now that Cleve could count the rats crawling on them if he had the time. It looked to be more than two and less than five per guard, most protruding from the tops of the warriors' chest pieces, poking their little heads out nervously. A few of the more squeamish men were still twitching as they approached, digging rats out of their sleeves and shaking their hips.

Rek was only a few seconds away from the tips of their swords when he finally raised his arm at them and released a deep grunt. All at once the King's men cried out in anguish. Their weapons and bodies fell, rolling over one another in a loud mess. No less than fifty rats exploded from the puddle of steel and flesh, squeaking in terror. Some must have been catapulted, for they flew through the air, flipping at dizzying speeds, their bodies and tails stretched from the force as they soared.

Hem lifted his head to find himself staring down Rek's dagger. "Don't get up," the Elf told him, kicking away the sword nearby. "No one needs to be hurt."

Too late for that, Cleve thought, glancing over the dismayed warriors. He knew what the pain from the psychic spell was like, as well as being covered in rats. The thought of both combined made him empathetic. Still, he readied the quarterstaff, knowing this wasn't over.

Rats were poking their heads from between crevices of steel and pulling themselves out with their tiny front legs. Once atop their carriers, they leapt back to the stairs to find a different host on another floor.

Warriors were gingerly picking themselves up and nursing their wounds. Some cleared the stairs, admitting defeat, while others stayed on the ground grunting. Much of their armor was stained with blood, yet based on the number of crushed rat bodies Cleve spotted, he figured most of it was rodent, not man.

"Rek, I can't disobey an order," Hem said as he strained his neck to look the Elf in the eye. "I can't permit you to see his majesty without his approval. You know that." Hem's tone was dark, and a looming silence followed.

Soon, Rek was nodding his head sadly. "I know," he nearly whispered, switching his hold on the dagger. "But he tried to have me killed. I can't leave until I speak with him or he won't stop until I'm dead."

"That's not going to happen."

"Don't make me do this, old friend." Rek held the dagger close to Hem's scalp.

"Even if you kill me, you won't ever see the King."

"Where is he?"

Hem covered his ears. "You're not going to get that information from me." He got to his feet for a breath before Rek aimed a hand at him for another psychic spell. Hem dropped once more, shivering in pain.

"There is no other end to this. The King and I will speak, and then I will be fighting alongside you, not against you." Rek put the knife back on his belt. "Hem, where is he?" He sounded desperate.

"The safety room, along with many women, children, and others who serve in other ways than fighting. Hundreds of mages and warriors stand in between. Not even all the rats in Kyrro could get you past them. Just surrender now to us." Hem began to stand once again. A few others already on their feet drew their weapons.

Cleve steadied his hands against the smooth wood of his quarterstaff, stepping toward the daring men. His eyes found someone hidden among the pile who was pulling a throwing knife from his belt. As he cocked his arm, Cleve leapt through clusters of chain mail and steel and used the quarterstaff to smack the knife from the man's hand. Before he had time to think, he noticed a sword slicing at him from the side. He ducked under it and swept the legs of his attacker with the hard wood of his weapon.

His heart jumped as he felt his balance slipping. Those nearby who were still on the ground had ahold of his ankles. One drew a dagger, so Cleve slammed the quarterstaff into the man's wrist.

"Discard your weapons and get back down!" Rek shouted. Then Cleve saw that many had risen with their swords drawn, all with a bloodthirsty look in their eyes.

They obeyed, slowly lowering themselves to the ground and letting their weapons fall while their eyes remained hard and steady.

Hem warned Rek, "This is about to get much worse for you and your *helpers*. Let me detain you now before I can't anymore."

"Or you can go back up there and tell the warriors and mages to let me pass," Rek pleaded. "This can all be—"

Hem interrupted by sticking two fingers in his mouth and whistling sharply. "I'm sorry. I can't let you convince me of anything. It's time for this to end."

Cleve heard a storm of boots coming from somewhere above them. The sound of a door being thrown open followed, and the feet carrying each pair of boots were then somewhere within the great room, echoing off every wall.

Hem jumped to his feet. Privy to his plan, the other warriors on the first floor did the same and ran back up the stairs with frantic quickness. They looked to be fleeing from something.

A gust of rats burst through the air on the fifth floor, followed by another burst, then another. Many flew over the banister, raining down on Cleve and his party. They covered their faces with their arms or shields, for there was no chance to dodge all the vermin. Many of the rats died against the stone floor, their heads and bodies cracking open, but some survived to hobble toward a room or a crevice in the wall.

The screech that came from the rats tumbling through the air was that of a hundred rusty reels being wound. Cleve soon deciphered the cause of the flying rats when he saw the shoulders of mages nearing the banister. *Bastial wind. Mages are coming and blowing away any rats in their path with hot Bastial Energy.*

The King's mages each found a spot along the banister that circled almost completely around. The only gap was directly above Rek and his party, as they stood just inside the entrance with the open ironbark door behind them. The mages were mostly women, but all wore red and carried a staff—but no wands—from what Cleve could see. *They care not for mobility, just power,* he realized when he noticed their weapons. He glanced at Rek. The Elf whipped down his hood to get a better look.

"Are they in range?" Cleve asked optimistically.

"No," Rek answered.

"Then we should take cover." Cleve found his tone to be surprisingly calm. Some part of him had grown to believe nothing would stop them, but he was beginning to realize that wasn't the case.

The mages aimed their staffs over the banister.

"Out! Now!" Rek shouted.

Cleve and Rek ran toward the door, shoving their comrades outside as well. Cleve heard the unmistakable sound of burning energy hissing toward him as he fled.

He felt the rough kiss of fire on his back and calves as they re-entered the cool, black night. They darted around the doorway just as a stream of fire shot out after them. The yellow flames curled and spewed from the mouth of the castle with a sizzling belch. Cleve was still too close—the heat was still too much. On reflex, he dove away from it and landed on top of three other people ahead of him.

Expecting hard steel against his chest, he was shocked by the feeling of cloth and soft flesh underneath him.

"Anyone hurt?" Cleve heard Rek asking.

Cleve pulled his head up to find his tongue had latched onto a head of blonde hair. He yanked the hairs from his mouth and stood up quickly. He wasn't a light man and wanted to remove the burden of his weight from whoever was below him. He found the hair he had chewed on belonged to the female mage. She grunted softly.

"I'm sorry," he told her, taking her hand and pulling her to her feet. "Are you hurt?"

"I'll be fine." She dusted off her robe. "I'm not so sure about the person on the bottom, though."

With her pulled from the pile, a warrior in steel was next to rise, but below him was the old guard Colimp. He was supine with his arms and legs sprawled. A creaking moan leaked from his gaping mouth.

Cleve lent him a hand. *I've been on top of him more today than I have any woman,* Cleve thought. Colimp was slow to rise, even with Cleve lifting most of his weight.

"Rek! Rek! Where are you?" someone was calling from the balcony above the Elf. Cleve recognized the gray hair and concerned expression right away. Rek moved farther from the castle wall so he could look at Councilman Kerr. Relief washed over Kerr's face when he saw Rek. "Are any of you injured?"

"No," Rek answered.

"Rek, this is madness. You can't force your way into the castle, and you've made such a mess with all these rats. We've even got some injuries by your doing." His tone was that of a father to a child.

"This is as much your mess as it is mine. How could you allow the King to order my death?"

"I tried to talk him out of it," Kerr said. "When I saw that to be impossible, I helped arrange for Cleve to be the chosen marksman. I knew he could never go through with it and that both of you would be back to work this out with the King like gentlemen."

How could he possibly know that, when I didn't even know if I would go through with it?

"Although, I didn't think you would attack the castle, and with rats!" The councilman looked ready to pull his hair out.

"Well we're here, and no one's been killed yet," Rek said, somewhat mockingly.

"You sure picked a terrible time for this. Do you know who's visiting? Jessend Takary from Goldram! Cleve nearly put an arrow through her. Could you imagine what that would've caused!"

That woman about to shoot at us is a Takary? "I aimed for her weapon, and I hit it," Cleve said defensively.

"Another inch and we would've been looking at war with Goldram as well as Tenred," Kerr said.

"Let's focus on the war at hand!" Rek's anger was startling. "I'm giving King Welson one last chance to let me fight for Kyrro. It shouldn't be this hard when all I want to do is help him."

Kerr nodded, his eyes closed. "Yes I understand. I have convinced his majesty to speak with you to end this savagery." His eyes popped back open, wider than before. "But you must call back the rats. You know how I hate rats."

Rek smiled and let out a long breath. "Of course, Councilman Kerr, if I could've used another creature I would have, but rats are what we've got. You've sent the mages away?"

"I have. You have no plans of hurting your brother, King Welson, right?"

Rek rolled his eyes. "My brother...not unless he hurts me first."

Kerr sighed. "The worst quarrels are always between loved ones."

"Or caused by them," Rek answered with a tight mouth.

"I'll be down to escort you and Cleve in a moment."

Rek thanked those around him with a handshake before calling Cleve over with a wave. Cleve nodded and followed. They met privately some distance from the entrance.

"What's wrong?" Cleve asked.

Rek held his chin. Cleve could almost hear the Elf's mind at work.

"Welson had no need to agree to a meeting. He must know there was no way past his mages without an army. I don't know what he's planning, but it takes weeks, sometimes years for his opinions to change without psyche."

"You think he's still going to have us killed?" Cleve asked.

"No, but even that's more likely than him forgetting about all this." Cleve spotted the councilman waiting in the doorway and motioning for them to follow. "I'm just trying to say, be cautious."

They followed Kerr inside the castle. It smelled of cooked meat. Cleve felt himself salivating and it sickened him, for he knew the aroma was from rat flesh. *I'm hungry is all,* he told himself to relieve the disgust he was beginning to feel.

The urge to eat was completely gone the moment he glimpsed the cesspool of rat bodies. Their insides and outsides were no longer distinguishable. Pieces of rat were spread all over the grand floor with caramel-colored juices holding them there. Some stains had even found their way to the walls.

Kerr stopped to shake his head. "The poor people who have to clean this mess."

There was no way to the stairs without stepping on dead rats, so they all walked with care. Even in rare spots where the stone was still clean enough to be seen, Cleve's shoes were so covered in grime by then there was hardly a difference to the feeling under each step. It was slick enough to make Cleve wonder if he should offer the old councilman a hand for balance.

Soon after the thought, he heard a scream and turned to see one of the mages, who had helped provide cover when they'd first entered, falling to his knees. Colimp was nearby and bent to help him up, only to lose his footing and fall onto his back with a curse and a disgusting splat.

Poor Colimp, Cleve thought.

Life was returning to the castle with the re-appearance of servers, chemists, musicians, and all the others who must have been tucked away during the threat from Rek. The Elf's hood was back on, but he still received many stares. *I wonder what was told to these people,* Cleve thought. Judging by their glares, it seemed as if he and Rek had been described not only as enemies of the King but of Kyrro and all its people as well.

Many needed to get by Rek and Cleve as they progressed to higher floors, and all nervously kept their heads down until they were well past.

"Which throne room will the King be meeting us in?" Rek asked.

"Sixth floor. Fewer rats got up there. When will you be ridding the castle of them?"

"Tomorrow, if I'm still here."

Kerr sighed and removed a small timepiece from his pocket. "I believe you mean later today. The battle went through the night."

Hem Baom was outside the door on the sixth floor. His armor was stained red and brown.

"Rek," he started to apologize.

"I understand," Rek interrupted and offered his hand. Hem grasped it with one steady shake.

Rek wiped rat residue from his hand as Hem turned to Cleve. "That was quite a shot at Jessend Takary. We're all thankful she wasn't hurt. Rumors are already starting that you were actually aiming for her bow. Is it true?"

"I was."

"Impressive. Hopefully, more of us can learn to shoot like you before we come under attack. The King has decided to legalize bows, if you hadn't heard."

Cleve had heard, but he wondered something else. "Is that how Jessend Takary had one?"

"No, hers came with her from Goldram. She and the King await, so I'm afraid we have no more time to talk."

She's in there with him? Cleve didn't feel quite comfortable facing the woman he'd just nearly killed. *I hope she knows I wasn't aiming for her.*

Hem opened the door and walked in after Rek and Cleve. The room was lit by only two gas lamps on the wall. King Welson was seated on his throne. To his right was the lanky, black-eyed psychic who Cleve had somehow managed to forget about, and to the King's left was Jessend Takary.

Hem first took Rek and Cleve's weapons. Then he grabbed a thick rope from a small wooden table, removed the Elf's hood, placed the rope in Rek's mouth, and tied it tightly around his head. He took metal chains from the table and cuffed them around Rek's wrists. There was one other chain on the table for Cleve. Hem closed it around his wrists and left without another look.

"Councilman Kerr, could you please leave us as well?" Welson said, removing a pair of wax earplugs.

Kerr looked at him with confusion before forcing a smile and a nod. "Certainly."

When Kerr was gone and the silence was just beginning to become too heavy to bear, the King began.

"Cleve, where is your bow?"

Cleve glanced at the psychic, who held his head forward in reply to Cleve's silent stare. Cleve's eyes went to the other side of the throne, where Jessend had a curious look for him. From afar, he'd only noticed her black hair over golden-brown skin, but now that he was in the same room as her, there was much more to see. Her face was small yet shapely, full of life. Her skin had a pastel glow. Her hair was parted in the middle. On one side, it hung over her shoulder to be pushed to the side by her full breasts that were impossible not to notice on her petite body. On the other side, her hair fell down her back. By the look of her, she had to be close to Cleve in age. She stood with her broken bow in one hand and the other on the curve of her hip.

She flashed an alluring grin at Cleve, her confidence emanating. Suddenly, all of Cleve's confidence drained out of him.

"On the first floor, outside the portcullis to the dungeon," Cleve answered the King's question about his bow.

The psychic's eyes peeled away from Cleve and he nodded.

"Fine." Welson sat back on his throne. "How did this happen? How did you come to the decision to attack the castle with Rek? I'd really like to know." There was a mixture of curiosity and disgust in his tone.

Cleve looked at Rek. The Elf couldn't speak with the thick rope shoved in his mouth. "Rek convinced me he was no enemy and that he just needed to speak with you."

"What did you tell Rek of what I said, of what your task was?"

"That I was to return with his head or I would be disobeying a direct order and another person would complete the task." He glanced at Jessend Takary, wondering whether she was that person. He still had no idea why a Takary was here—they were the most powerful family he knew of.

"Rek, understand that you were seen shaking hands with the King of Tenred, Tegry Hiller," Welson said. "We have ways of getting information from within their castle walls, and what we found demonstrated that you've become an enemy. We know of the plan to attack Kyrro and that you were to join them. The decision to send Cleve was an impossible one to make, but with the help of my council we decided it was necessary. I'm truly sorry."

The King sounded sincere to Cleve. However, the expression on Rek's face was like he'd just heard a bad joke.

"I realize it's difficult to hear this after all that's happened," Welson continued, "especially when I have you gagged, but allow me to explain. You see, although I feel terrible, I still can't allow you to speak to me. I've been training hard to resist psyche, but I'd rather not risk it. I don't know what you're planning, and your words have too much sway. No matter what Tegry Hiller told you, there is much more to this old rivalry than you could know. I can't risk losing this war, even if it means one man is killed who may be innocent, as much as that pains me. With you on their side, we all would surely die. With the Krepps, they already have more than three times the army as we do."

Rek tried to say something but was muffled by the rope.

"He told me that he wants to fight for Kyrro," Cleve said, hoping that's what Rek wanted to tell Welson. "Also, that he was only meeting with Tegry Hiller to get the help of an army for something that had nothing to do with Kyrro. He had to turn to Tenred, being exiled from Kyrro. Rek agreed to help Tegry Hiller with whatever he wanted, knowing he could convince them otherwise later—"

"I'm sure he's trying to tell me the same thing," the King interrupted, fluttering his hand. Welson sighed, long and exaggerated, the kind of culminating sigh that showed he'd heard enough. "And I bet it would be very convincing, may even be true, but if it's not, then Kyrro is lost. I just can't risk it."

"But with him on our side, the war is won," Cleve tried to argue, as pointless as he knew it was.

"And it may be won without him. But if he fights against Kyrro, we're sure to lose."

"So, what do you intend to do? You're going to kill him?" Cleve had to say it. Asking the question felt like a dagger in his stomach, but holding it in was worse.

"Luckily for me, I don't have to make that decision anymore. Jessend Takary arrived here yesterday, and she has a good use for his ability back in Goldram. With him across the Starving Ocean, he no longer poses a threat to Kyrro."

Taken to Goldram? He can't want that. What else can I say, Rek? Cleve wanted to rip the rope from Rek's mouth but knew it to be impossible with his hands bound behind him. "What about me? Am I to be arrested?" The pace of his heart quickened. *I would rather die fighting on my way to a cell than in one.*

"Cleve, I can't have you running around free. You disobeyed a direct order. Think of how that news would affect all others who are commanded to fight in this war. Surely many of them would throw down their weapons and hide if they believed they could get away with it. Not all who fight wish to do so. And that's not even half of it. You shot at Jessend Takary!" The King shot her a quick glance.

She tilted her head and twisted her mouth. It was a cute expression more than anything else, and Cleve didn't know what to make of it. *Maybe she realizes she was going to shoot at us first. No logical person can hold a grudge after that.*

Welson glared back at Cleve. "I can't begin to wonder what people would think if they saw you free after hearing about that. Then there's the bow you've been using all these years without punishment. You're a walking display of disobedience—the last thing we need right now. Worst of all, I'm not sure I can trust you after seeing you storm in here with Rek. For all I know, he's convinced you to fight against us. We'd love to have you and Rek fighting behind our walls but not enough for the risk it would bring. I'm sorry, Cleve."

He looked around for a weapon, something that would help him escape. He thought of the passageway to the roof behind the throne. *Maybe I could climb down the wall.* The thought was absurd, he knew, but still *something*. Jessend Takary approached him.

"Relax, Cleve. I've made an arrangement with King Welson. You'll be joining us on the journey back to Goldram. I have use for you as well as Rek."

Her voice was deep for a woman, yet not masculine in the slightest. It was thick with a lively accent that made it seem as if this was the first time Cleve had ever heard his language spoken properly. Not that he would ever wish to talk like her, as she had the tone of a queen. It was pleasing to hear—or maybe that was only because she was telling him he wouldn't be killed.

"It's true, the Takary family has saved you," Welson said. "Until Jessend Takary is ready to leave, you and Rek will remain in the dungeons. I'll notify Terren Polken so he can visit before you ship out. I understand he's your only family."

Who is this woman I'm to leave with? Cleve would've traded all his money for a little information about Jessend, not that he had much to trade, just what his parents had left. Most of it had gone to Terren to help take care of him. He wouldn't be able to take it with him anyway, it looked like. *Do they even use the same currency across the Starving Ocean?* It was hard to know what to feel without the faintest clue where he was going or what he would be doing. Having a use for Rek was easy to comprehend, but what did she want with him?

"Can I have a moment with Jessend Takary?" Cleve asked.

"You'll have plenty of time to speak during your voyage," Welson answered. "How many days did it take you to get here?" he asked her.

"Five, and the weather was good."

"Five days, lots of time," the King told him.

Jessend smiled at Cleve and Rek. "I'm sure you're both very curious about this. We'll speak on the boat. You shouldn't worry of anything." She started toward the door but stopped and turned with a sly grin. "Except any giant squid that decides to take the vessel for dinner. It's not called the Starving Ocean for nothing." It seemed like an attempt at a joke, though no one laughed.

Chapter 43: Follow
ZOKE

As Zoke and Vithos crossed through the heart of Satjen, the hills that had done so well to provide cover for the last ten miles finally flattened. This would have been a problem, however the trees were thick with low branches where undisturbed golden-green leaves had swelled into the open air for years. The Krepp and three Humans looked like indistinguishable splotches in the small spaces between plants and trees, and that's only when Zoke and Vithos had found them once again.

Most of the time, Zoke was searching to relocate the party after their backs had been devoured by the forest. They went straight south, though, really the only reason Zoke and Vithos didn't lose them completely.

Eventually, the Humans separated from the Krepp. They went west and the Krepp stayed south.

Zoke and Vithos stopped, unsure who to follow. "The only thing south of here is the Fjallejon Pathway to Kyrro," Vithos whispered hastily. "And the only thing west of here is Tenred."

"I've never heard of Krepps speaking with Humans from Tenred *or* Kyrro," Zoke said, still without an idea of what he wanted to do.

"They don't, unless Doe and Haemon have been sending them there secretly."

Not much had been spoken of the Human territories, at least not to Zoke. The only purpose for leaving the Krepp encampment was for a task, and no task required interaction with a Human.

He tried to remember if anything he'd read about Humans might be helpful. There was plenty about Elves in his books. Zoke had read that the tribes of Krepps living near the Elves in Merejic were often competing for animal meat, but that was before Doe and Haemon came and consolidated all the tribes. The Elves were gone shortly after. The Humans were described as being similar to the Elves in appearance, except their ears were small and round and their skin could vary from light to dark.

Zoke thought as quickly as he could but soon he realized there was nothing he knew about Humans that would help him understand what the Krepp going south had planned. "What could the Krepp possibly want with Kyrro?" Zoke wondered.

"I can't say, but it would be much easier to question one Krepp than three Humans. Let's get closer so I can see what can be gathered from psyche first."

Zoke nodded and it was set. They would follow the Krepp, leaving the Humans, who were going west to Tenred. They scurried behind their quarry, using trees for cover. It didn't take long to reach the Krepp, for his walk was cautiously slow. Vithos pointed out his palm and lowered his head.

"He's nervous," Vithos said in a near whisper. "I'm not picking up on anything else. Unless a thought or emotion is overshadowing the rest, I hardly get a sense, especially from this range."

"What would happen if he crossed into Kyrro?"

"He would be detained or killed, I would guess."

"Unless they were expecting him," Zoke realized.

"I don't see how that would be possible without prior communication between Kyrro and the Krepps," Vithos replied.

"We just found a Krepp walking with Humans from Tenred. That means there's been communication between Tenred and Doe and Haemon. It could be the same with Kyrro."

"Perhaps. But what could Doe and Haemon want with the Humans?" Vithos placed his hand on his chin for two breaths. "All those two care about is finding the Slugari."

One thought came to Zoke. "The Humans could know where the Slugari are."

Vithos slowly shook his head. "Even if that's true, why would Doe and Haemon send a Krepp to Kyrro? Wait, look." Vithos pointed.

The Krepp stopped to pull something from his belt. As he unraveled it, Zoke saw it was a scroll.

"It's probably just a map," he said.

"No," Vithos answered with a palm extended at the Krepp. "He's reading something. It's a note. He has to bring it to wherever he's going. He has to be careful not to damage it. The note is very important." Vithos let down his hand. "It's probably from Doe and Haemon. This Krepp must be delivering a note to the Humans in Kyrro on their behalf."

"A threat, I imagine," Zoke said, still working with his theory that the Humans knew where the Slugari were located. "It's what Doe and Haemon know better than anything else, using fear. If the Humans know where the Slugari are and Doe and Haemon found out, then surely Doe and Haemon would threaten the Humans to get that information."

"That's a possibility," Vithos said, continuing to stare at the scroll.

Zoke spat. "Whatever it is, the answer is in the mind of that Krepp not fifty yards ahead. You can tell when a Krepp is lying, so why not ask him until the truth comes out?" Zoke clenched his teeth. He couldn't shake the feeling that they needed to act fast. It was too easy for the Krepp to turn and see them, but if they hid from view, they were likely to lose track of him.

"Because what will we do after? We can't let him return to the tribe after he sees us."

"Why not?" Zoke asked in a hurry.

"When I sensed the Slugari underground, it was near here. If the Krepp returns to Doe and Haemon with our location, surely they'll come looking for us around here. They could find us before we reach the Slugari. Or worse, we may even inadvertently lead them to the Slugari."

Zoke understood, but they still needed a plan. He was becoming eager to question the Krepp and figure out what to do later. "So what do you suggest? We can't keep following him. Eventually, he'll see us."

"We may have to kill him," Vithos said regretfully.

"Kill him?" Zoke was shocked by the suggestion. It didn't help that the Krepp they were talking about murdering looked familiar.

"I'm just warning you," Vithos said. "I don't want to, either. However, we need to consider it. The opportunity to question this Krepp is too great to pass up. By intercepting this note, it could give us leverage against Doe and Haemon. You know common tongue; you can speak to the Humans. After we figure out how they're involved, we can use that to our advantage. This may end with thousands of Humans on our side, fighting to take power away from Doe and Haemon. Once their leadership crumbles, reuniting you with Zeti will be easy. Krepps have never been able to lead each other. Chaos will separate the army back into different tribes."

"Yes, I know all that. But while questioning the Krepp may result in what you described, it could instead lead to nothing but the death of an innocent Krepp." *We're losing time. The longer we talk about this, the greater the chance we lose him or he sees us.* "Just let me decide if he needs to live or die," Zoke said with a frustration that was sure to erupt if Vithos disagreed. "If he must die, then I'll be the one to do it."

Zoke hadn't decided whether he actually could kill the Krepp, but he knew he wanted control in this instance and that they needed to act now. Vithos stared at the Krepp's back as he took a breath, his hand on his chin. Zoke felt like he was standing on ice. He shifted back and forth. *Hurry, Vithos,* he thought.

"Fine," the Elf finally answered. "He'll run once he sees me, and neither of us is fast. So, we must make sure I'm in range for psyche before we're seen."

"Understood."

They split to increase their chances of catching their target if they were to be seen. Vithos stayed directly behind the Krepp, while Zoke went around.

He slowly closed the distance between them, careful to watch his feet for leaves and sticks. It became clear that this Krepp hadn't been chosen for his awareness, as Zoke never saw the Krepp look anywhere but ahead of him. *He's probably the first one they found who could speak common tongue.*

Zoke, too, could speak the language of Humans and had only met one other Krepp interested in it. They used to practice together. *What was his name?* Zoke tried to remember him, wondering how high the chances were that it was this same Krepp in front of him.

They'd had to be secretive. That part was easy to recall because when they weren't, it brought on aggression from other Krepps for speaking a supposedly stupid language that wasn't Kreppen. Each of them had a book on the funny sounding tongue. It was twice the size of a normal book and thus difficult to hide, so he and his friend wrote down what they wanted to share on folded paper and brought only that to their covert meetings.

But what was his name?

Zoke shuddered as he recalled their last meeting. They were both nearly fluent by then and went to study near the bakers' ovens. They'd never met there before. It was uncomfortably hot, so Zoke figured no one would bother them. When they arrived, they were surprised to find a small table already there. Atop it was something he couldn't remember. Whatever it was, they'd thought it was trash, perhaps scraps of rock-hard bread. They'd wiped it from the table.

There couldn't have been more than two conversations between them before they were interrupted by four older Krepps. One had a deck of cards. They all started yelling at once, so it took a few panicked heartbeats to understand what they were saying. Their bets were gone from the table—that turned out to be the issue. They'd saved their progress of a long game from earlier, only for their chips to be discarded and their table to be taken by a couple of weak-looking Krepps.

The four did not stop after just curses. No, they wanted blood, and they got it. Both Zoke and his friend were beaten until they were unconscious. *I was lucky they didn't kill me or break a bone,* Zoke thought in retrospect. He came back to consciousness first and helped his friend to his feet. They both seemed to be in similar physical condition as they hobbled out of there, but emotionally it did far more damage to his friend than to him. Whenever Zoke mentioned studying again, his friend would twitch with fear and eventually they stopped talking altogether.

As the memories came back to him, so finally did a name. *Nebre, that was it,* Zoke remembered with a breath of satisfaction. The Krepp stopped to glance to his side, giving Zoke a glimpse of his face. A sudden realization squeezed his heart for a beat. *It is Nebre!*

Zoke glimpsed over to see how far Vithos was behind Nebre now. The Elf was skulking behind trees to stay out of view as much as possible, still quite far away.

Zoke checked back on Nebre, who had stopped. His head was turned now, eyes staring wide...right at Zoke.

Panic exploded in Zoke's chest. Before another thought could pass, Nebre burst into a sprint.

"Wait!" Zoke ran after him.

He took a moment to check on Vithos, who was sprinting as well. *He must be too far for psyche,* Zoke thought, for the Krepp wasn't slowing down.

"Nebre!" he shouted. "Stop, it's Zoke. We just need to talk."

Nebre appeared to slow down for two strides. He turned to give Zoke one more look, only to turn back and pick up speed.

"Nebre!" Zoke let his desperation come out in his tone. "*Please!*"

he shouted in common tongue.

It worked. His old friend slowed to a stop with his chest still heaving.

"*It is you,*" Nebre answered in the same language.

The word "please" didn't exist in Kreppen, and it had taken several meetings for Zoke and Nebre to understand its meaning. They had to first learn about manners and polite speech for it to make sense, for that was something that didn't exist for Krepps either. The word felt weak to Zoke, like admitting you needed something that only another person could provide. Nebre, on the other hand, seemed to like it. When they practiced together, Nebre often used the words "please" and "thank you," and Zoke never hid how uncomfortable it made him.

"I thought you might appreciate hearing the word from my mouth, finally," Zoke said. Uttering it had caused a sour taste. He needed to spit, but that gesture would wipe away all sincerity, so he swallowed his saliva and did his best to hide his discomfort.

"*Thank you.*" Nebre smiled. "What are you doing out here?"

Vithos came forward. "We were wondering the same thing."

Nebre's yellow eyes widened as he stepped back from the Elf. "Vithos. They say you're a traitor, and that...and that you're dangerous."

"I'm sure they do," Vithos answered nonchalantly. "But the truth is that Doe and Haemon sent me away and commanded Krepps to come after me to remove my head."

"They said they had to send you away because you were no longer working with the tribe...that you didn't want us to find the Slugari." Nebre was still dragging his feet away from them when he peered back at Zoke. "They say the same of you."

Zoke edged after him. "Don't listen to their lies." He took a breath to think. *Some of it's true, actually*, he realized. Vithos knew where the Slugari were and didn't share it because he didn't want Doe and Haemon to find the creatures. *Many would call him a traitor for that. They might also say I've joined his side, making me one as well.*

"What's untrue?" Nebre asked.

"I never was a traitor," Zoke answered. "I always did my tasks."

"But what about wanting to find the Slugari? You can't smell, and you told me how you didn't care for their meat. Now I see you out here with Vithos."

Zoke had always figured that if he had the chance to explain himself that all would be understood, but now he was beginning to see that might not be true. *Does Zeti think of me as a traitor as well?*

"I've done nothing wrong," he told Nebre. *And nothing right either.* Many Krepps would have removed the Elf's head while he slept and brought it back to the camp, but he'd let Vithos sleep peacefully. Zoke hardly had given a thought to turning on Vithos. *Could I be a traitor?* he wondered for the first time, but he didn't have time to think about it further. "It's true I never cared for Slugari meat," Zoke answered. "But I still did what I could to help us find them."

"But what about Vithos? You *are* out here with him."

Zoke hoped Vithos had an answer, because he sure didn't.

"I am a traitor," Vithos said, "but to Doe and Haemon, not to the tribe."

"How is that? They lead the tribe."

"I have no quarrel with the Krepps, only with Doe and Haemon. They led the attack on my people. They took me from my parents."

Nebre shifted his weight to his heels. "But...but their actions are performed by Krepps."

Vithos leaned forward. "If they commanded you to shoot an arrow at me, I wouldn't seek revenge against you, nor would I against the maker of the bow or arrow that you used. But I would come at them with all my power as soon as the opportunity arose." Vithos turned his head to look from the corner of his eyes. Zoke could almost hear him say the words as he glared at Nebre: *"And you too if you cross me."*

"We're not here to hurt you, Nebre," Zoke said, in an attempt to alleviate some of the fear he found in his old friend's wincing face. "We saw you with Humans. We just need to know what's happening."

Nebre shook his head like he was coming out of a trance. "I'm not supposed to tell you. If I see the Elf I should...I should." He looked down at the knife on his belt.

"There's no need to panic," Vithos said calmly. "They told you to kill yourself before I was close, didn't they?"

Nebre turned shyly and shut his eyes for a breath.

"That's how they are," Vithos continued. "I would never make you do that. It appears that you know Zoke, so you should know he's not like that, either. He would never wish harm upon you, right?"

Nebre asked Zoke in common tongue, *"Can I trust you? Please don't let him hurt me."*

"No harm, I promise," he answered in the same language and knew then that he couldn't kill his old friend, no matter what happened. *"You can trust me,"* he told Nebre, hoping Vithos couldn't sense this peaceful change within him, *otherwise he might take it upon himself to kill Nebre if he thinks it's necessary.*

Zoke glanced at Vithos as subtly as he could. The Elf was looking right back at him, but just like their time at the encampment, his face gave no signs to tell Zoke what he was thinking.

Nebre straightened to his full height. "Those Humans are from Tenred. They were escorted through our camp to meet with Doe and Haemon. Later, the entire tribe gathered for Doe to make an announcement. With the Tenred Humans beside him, Doe told us who they were and what they were doing in our camp. Doe said that the Humans in Kyrro have been in contact with the underground Slugari, that...that they're allied with them, meaning our tribe is now enemies of Kyrro. Tenred and Kyrro are at war. Since we now have a common enemy, Doe and Haemon have agreed to join forces with Tenred."

Could it be true? Zoke shared a glance with Vithos. Opportunity seemed to pull the Elf's eyes open as he held in a smile. *He sees this as gaining an army,* Zoke realized. *The army of Kyrro. I'm not sure I feel the same way.*

"They needed a Krepp who could speak common tongue," Nebre continued. "I...I couldn't think of anything else but the pleasure of using the language for a good purpose, so I volunteered. I was the only Krepp to do so. I'm sure the smarter ones were remaining silent."

"It's not stupid to wish to help your tribe," Zoke told him. "What did they ask of you?"

"To walk into Kyrro and deliver a message. They wrote it in Kreppen because they don't know the language of the Humans and didn't trust anyone else to write it for them."

Nebre pulled the scroll from his belt and handed it to Vithos. It was tied with a thin rope that the Elf undid with an eager twitch of his wrist. "I'm to read it to the King of Kyrro and then return with his answer." Nebre spoke with a tremor in his voice.

Zoke stood beside Vithos to read it over his shoulder: *To the King of Kyrro, Welson Kimard, we will stop at nothing until we have found the underground Slugari. Reveal their location to us or we will burn Kyrro and everyone within the territory. If our intermediary does not return within fifteen days with a map and instructions to find the Slugari, then we will prepare for attack immediately.*

"I still don't understand what Tenred has to do with this," Zoke said when he was finished reading.

"They wish for war," Nebre said.

"That's what I don't understand. Why would Humans in one territory ally with Krepps to fight Humans in another territory?" Zoke asked.

"Krepps kill each other all the time," Vithos retorted. "I'm sure Humans are the same."

"But Krepps would never go to *war* against each other. That's madness. Nebre, did the Humans say why they wanted to start a war?"

"No, but I didn't ask. What they did say was that they didn't even want us to give Kyrro the ultimatum. Instead, they urged us to attack with them without warning, but Doe and Haemon decided otherwise."

"Doe and Haemon care only to find the Slugari," Vithos added. "If there's a way they can do so quicker and easier, they'll always favor that method. It just so happens to be a threat this time, not death. Yet, I imagine there would be no hesitation in attacking if their demands are not met." Vithos handed the note to Zoke, keeping his dark eyes on Nebre. "Zoke and I will accompany you to Kyrro to deliver the note as instructed, but then Zoke and I wish to speak to the King in private before he provides an answer."

Two Krepps and an Elf stroll into Kyrro...could it be the beginning to a joke? "You hope to convince Welson of what?" Zoke asked, accepting the scroll and tucking it into their bag.

"It's better if we discuss that in private," Vithos said. He placed a hand on Nebre's shoulder. Being a head shorter, he needed to lift his arm awkwardly to reach it. Nebre sunk to meet Vithos' eyes. "You should have no worries about your safety, Nebre. I just don't wish for certain information about us to get back to Doe and Haemon. Wait here for a moment while I speak to Zoke."

Nebre nodded subordinately.

Vithos took Zoke aside. "It doesn't matter if we locate the Slugari first if the Humans are going to reveal their location to Doe and

Haemon. There won't be enough time for us to make a difference. We'll simply die with them or worse—join them in slavery. Our only chance to stop this is to ensure the Humans defeat Doe and Haemon. If they can't do it alone, then they can join forces with the Slugari to fight."

"You expect to persuade the King of Kyrro to prepare for war instead of giving up the Slugari?" Zoke asked.

"If needed. I can be very convincing." Vithos lowered his head to look from the top of his eyes. It sent a chill through Zoke. "This is our only chance to gain the help of an army. Before, I assumed we could fight alongside the Slugari, but we can't go to them now unless we know the Humans won't give up their location."

"Zeti would be fighting on the opposing side. I understand your thirst for revenge, but how can we assist in starting a war with sister to me as an enemy? I can't bear the thought of being responsible for her death."

"There's only a small risk of that. This is your opportunity to reunite with Zeti, and if that's not enough, let me tell you what Doe and Haemon plan to do with the Slugari. They'll invade their territory with hungry Krepps who will chase down and bite into them, ripping off chunks of flesh while they're still alive. The Slugari who survive the attack will spend the rest of their lives in cages. They'll be forced to breed. They'll watch their children grow until they're big enough to be killed, cooked, and eaten. This will continue until they're too old to produce offspring, and then they'll be killed for food, but not before realizing that their children who haven't already been killed will take their place to continue the cycle.

"This is certain to happen if Doe and Haemon find the Slugari, but there is no certainty Zeti will die if we convince Welson Kimard to fight. It's our best chance to take out Doe and Haemon, and it's the only way you'll be able to speak to Zeti again."

Zoke jabbed at the dirt with the claws on his feet. It was dry on the surface, cracking open as he prodded. "This feels like the beginning to something I'll regret." He was thankful for the doubts, at least. He took it to mean Vithos hadn't used psyche to persuade him.

"I'll do everything in my power to prevent bloodshed. If Welson Kimard has sufficient bowmen among his army, we should be able to host a surprise attack to take out Doe and Haemon. With them dead, a war may be avoided completely. As I mentioned before, Krepps have never been able to lead themselves. We may even find that there are better options once we speak to the King of Kyrro." Vithos made a fist. "War is not certain, and the death of Zeti certainly isn't either. Going to Kyrro with Nebre is our best option."

"I have a terrible feeling about this, like someone will surely die, someone other than Doe or Haemon." Zoke picked up a slab of dirt to crush in his palm. "But you're right, doing nothing would be worse."

Nebre approached. "The sun is setting. If you still wish to come, we should prepare for night."

"We do," Zoke said, letting the dirt fall from his claw.

"I hope you have food and water with you," Nebre said. "I didn't bring enough for three."

"We have enough," Vithos answered. "We should walk for another two or three hours, otherwise it will still be dark when we rise."

At that, Nebre twitched nervously. *He still has that same habit*, Zoke thought. "Rest will come easier then," he said, trying to console.

"You lead," Nebre said. "Without the sun, my sense of direction is lost."

Vithos pointed south. "It's this way. Go on ahead. There's just one more thing Zoke and I need to discuss."

Nebre gave a twitchy nod and went.

"What else?" Zoke asked.

"It's Nebre," Vithos answered with a grave tone. "He's grown far more anxious and untrusting. I don't believe that he'll come so willingly. He might try something during the night. We should sleep in shifts, but don't let him know. I want to see how he behaves when he believes we're both asleep."

Zoke spat at the idea. "I know him. He always has avoided confrontation. He scares easily, and I'm very tired."

"It's been many years. He may not be the same Krepp you remember. I'll stay awake as long as I can, but I'm going to wake you when I can't keep my eyes open any longer. If all goes well this night, we won't have to do it again."

Zoke slumped his head and gave it a slow shake. "Another half night of sleep—I'd hoped we were done with that. Wake me when you need to, but he won't try anything."

"Let's hope so," Vithos muttered.

Chapter 44: Awake
ZOKE

There were trees in every direction but with enough room between for the three of them to walk beside each other. The dirt was mostly bare except for animal tracks and droppings. Rarely, Zoke glimpsed the stub of a tree that had been chopped down. With the castle of Tenred nearby, he wondered why more trees weren't cut. "Don't they use wood in Tenred?" He hoped Vithos might know.

"They do, but the castle sits upon a great source of iron. It was lucky for them to settle there. Do you know the story?"

"Of what?" Zoke asked.

Nebre answered for Vithos, "Of Tenred. I read about it in a book." His eagerness to share was palpable.

"I don't," Zoke said. "I'm in the mood for a story." *Anything to get my mind off another pointlessly vigilant night.*

"I know only what was told to me," Vithos said. "Tell me if any of this doesn't match what you read, Nebre."

Nebre's bright yellow eyes faded to the dirt when he realized he wouldn't get to start. Stories of the Humans were rare, and Nebre seemed to hold more appreciation for them than anyone else Zoke had met.

Vithos cleared his throat. "Tenred was established recently, sometime in the last one hundred years. The Humans who founded it were from Kyrro. They were part of the King's army there, and they plotted to overthrow his power, but their plan was discovered and many were captured."

Nebre added, "Some were even council to the King. They were planning to replace the King with a different leader after he was dead, but one of them snitched to reveal the takeover before it could happen." He spat.

"As the rebels started getting captured, the rest tried to escape," Vithos continued. "Only ten made it out of Kyrro. They were chased north, running until they couldn't run any farther. They climbed the hills of southwestern Satjen where only one path could reach them.

That's where they prepared for battle. Five hundred of the King's men came after them but couldn't win the battle. The ten men atop the hill were all skilled archers and held off each attack thanks to their position."

"I read that it was two hundred men who chased them," Nebre added with a tone like he was ready to argue.

"If Humans are anything like Krepps, then it is likely even two hundred is an exaggeration of the truth," Zoke said, trying to alleviate the discord he could feel growing between Nebre and Vithos.

"Whatever it was," Vithos said, "the King's men weren't prepared for such a standoff and retreated back to Kyrro for the appropriate supplies. More battles ensued, but the numbers in Tenred grew because more and more from Kyrro kept coming to join them. Although they were considered traitors at first, eventually there were so many switching sides that the King of Kyrro had no choice but to agree to a treaty."

"They weren't traitors," Nebre tried to correct Vithos in an obvious attempt to defend Tenred's honor—the honor of the Krepps' new allies. "The King of Kyrro was not a deserving leader like Doe and Haemon."

"They didn't agree with their leader and planned to overthrow him," Vithos said with a slow, careful shrug. It was the most sinister shrug Zoke had ever seen. "Those sound like the actions of a traitor to me." Vithos turned to raise an eyebrow at Nebre. "If they aren't traitors, then I shouldn't be thought of as one, either."

Nebre wouldn't return a look, staring instead at the dirt. An unnerving silence fell over them. Zoke asked a question to disrupt it. "Kyrro and Tenred have been at peace this whole time until now?"

"No other battles since then," Nebre answered softly.

"I wonder what reason they suddenly have to fight," Zoke said.

"There have been several generations of kings on both sides," Vithos said. "So it seems unlikely for it to be something that happened many years ago, unless Humans are even better than us at holding on to the grudges of their dead."

The three of them grew quiet again. It was the first time Zoke had heard Vithos refer to himself and Krepps as *us*. Zoke wondered if it was just to convince Nebre that he and Zoke weren't a threat. *Or could Vithos really consider himself just as much a part of the tribe as Nebre?* Zoke shook his head. *No, that can't be.*

When Zoke thought of the tribe, he thought of a tight sphere pushing all the Krepps together, more so than they wished at times. He used to believe that Doe, Haemon, and Vithos shared their own smaller bubble within the sphere of the tribe. But since learning more about Vithos, Zoke realized the Elf was really within his own bubble, separate from everyone else in the tribe, including Doe and Haemon, whether he wanted to be or not.

Vithos was never part of the tribe in the way that Zoke and Nebre were, and now he'd pulled Zoke into that bubble. Together, they'd drifted further and further from the sphere, but with war starting to boil, the heat from it was likely to reach them no matter where they went. He felt that it was only a matter of time before their bubble burst.

It almost had already during their first week together. Zoke was close to leaving Vithos. He blamed Vithos for taking him away from the tribe. He'd thought that his anger would never subside, but to his surprise it did. It helped that the days with Vithos were far easier to endure than his days in the tribe. Vithos didn't call him *gurradu* or force him to perform tasks he didn't wish to do. The constant voice that told him to watch his back had quieted. He felt secure with the Elf, trusting his judgment.

Although he worried for Zeti, he knew her to be strong. *She doesn't need me to protect her anymore,* Zoke thought. *She's a woman now and has acted as such for years already.* It wasn't so much the time away from her that disturbed him, but the thought that he might never see her again. He could endure months, even years, as long as he had hope—be it a small chance—that they would see each other again.

The night had blackened in the last hour with stars taking shape in the sky. The air was warm and fresh. Zoke let out a yawn that had been sneaking up on him in the last few steps. "Let's find a place to rest," he suggested.

They found an agreeable spot nearby where the dirt opened into a wide area between two thick trees. Nebre made no motion to lie down until Zoke and Vithos were completely settled. Zoke was half asleep already when he heard Nebre trying to get comfortable somewhere in the distance.

Zoke wasn't sure how long he slept. He woke with Vithos pushing on his shoulder. "I cannot stay awake." Vithos whispered so softly it took Zoke until his yawn had finished before understanding what he'd said.

Zoke gave a grunt to acknowledge he'd heard and looked around to find Nebre. He saw him lying at the base of a tree ten yards away. *This is pointless*, he told himself, but he held his eyes open as long as he could.

Eventually, he let his body rest against the dirt again. He drifted in and out of sleep. Every so often, he gave a glance to Nebre, who was always still.

He must've been asleep when it happened because he never heard Nebre coming until he was already above them.

At the sound of something shifting in the dirt next to Zoke's ear, he shot to his feet. Nebre had both hands awkwardly around his knife. He must've been startled by Zoke, for he gave Zoke a quick look, but that didn't stop him for more than a heartbeat. He went to his knees over Vithos with the knife raised high.

"Stop!" Zoke shouted. He dove and pushed Nebre away from Vithos.

"Get off me!" Nebre yelled.

Before Zoke knew it, they had begun to wrestle. Wild limbs were being thrown, and weight was shifting back and forth faster than insults between two Krepps before a fight. They rolled farther from Vithos, and Zoke noticed a change in Nebre. He was no longer trying to get away from Zoke. Instead, he was trying to find a way to push the knife into him.

"Coward!" Nebre yelled as he forced the knife a little closer to Zoke's stomach. "Coward, coward, coward!" Zoke had Nebre's wrist, pushing it away from him.

Zoke drove his knee into Nebre's side and flipped, managing to roll himself on top. He had Nebre pinned, though Nebre was still forcing the knife toward him. Vithos came over them and aimed his palm at Nebre. His struggles ceased and he went limp, letting the knife out of his grip. Zoke took it, rolling off Nebre.

Nebre scampered to his feet. "Why did you stop me, Zoke?" Nebre shouted, hopping away. "You must be a traitor to let Vithos live all this time!"

Zoke felt a deep sadness to hear the accusation from his old friend, especially with such conviction. "Nebre, there's a lot you don't understand."

"I always thought I was a coward and you were brave. But you're the coward, not me. I'm the one who fought." Nebre thumped his chest. "I'm the one who tried to kill the Elf. You would rather be a traitor than risk your life for the tribe." He spat, and his saliva found Zoke's feet. "Coward!" Nebre searched his belt in a panic. "You still have the scroll. Give it back. Throw it to me."

"We'll deliver it," Zoke answered, wiping his foot on the dirt. "The Humans need to know of the threat, so we'll tell them. Get out of here. Go back to the camp." He was surprised to hear how calm he sounded. He wasn't mad, though, so he didn't know how else he should sound.

Nebre ran. He was out of sight in a blink, although the sound of leaves and sticks being crushed under his weight continued for another two breaths.

"We shouldn't have let him go." Vithos spoke with the same calmness as Zoke. "He knows where the new camp is. We should have at least gotten that information."

"Perhaps," Zoke said. "But it's too late for that now."

"You were protecting him, weren't you? If we didn't let him go, you knew what we would have to do." The Elf's voice became loud and forced. "What *you* would have to do."

"He doesn't need to die."

"No one needs to die. But many will." Vithos lifted a thumb to his face. "I didn't start this war, but I'm part of it, just like you." He jabbed a finger at Zoke. "We're going to have to make tough decisions that will determine who lives and who dies. So, you should figure out what you're willing to do now while you still have time to think about it. What would it take for you to kill another Krepp? What would it take for you to kill Zeti? What would you trade your life for? No one wants to think about these things, but we need to. If we don't, we risk making a mistake when it's time to take action. And mistakes can lead to even more death."

Zoke spat but made sure to avoid Vithos' feet. He was frustrated but knew most of it wasn't directed at the Elf. "If it's so easy, what would you trade your life for, then?"

"Revenge, exposing the truth, stopping Doe and Haemon, saving someone I care about." Vithos replied so quickly, it did seem as if he had the answer prepared. "You don't need to know your answers now, but you'd better come up with them soon."

Zoke waved his claws dismissively. "I already know I would never kill Zeti. Never. And she would never kill me."

"You're sure of this?"

"As sure as I am of the sun rising tomorrow," Zoke said, remembering she used the same line the last time he'd spoken to her.

Vithos leaned in close, staring for a breath. Then he nodded and the anger melted from his face. "It must be nice to know that about someone."

Zoke's frustration turned to pity. "It is."

Vithos knelt to roll up his blanket. "You're not a coward, you know. He's wrong about that. It takes more courage to make decisions for yourself than to blindly follow orders."

"So, you're not afraid I'll attack you as you sleep?"

"Should I be?"

Zoke shook his head. "No."

Vithos smiled, slung his bag over his shoulder and started south.

"Where are you going?"

"Toward Kyrro. We're not going to get any sleep tonight after what's happened, so we might as well walk and rest later. Come, and I'll tell you the story of when I asked Haemon where Krepps come from."

"Does it have a surprise?" He was disappointed when the story of Tenred and Kyrro had no surprise. Usually the twist in Kreppen stories was fun, pleasing to discover—the exact opposite of what had just happened with Nebre. Zoke wanted a robust surprise more than anything at that moment. He craved it.

"Yes, he brought two Krepps in to demonstrate. I couldn't have been older than eight or nine when I was forced to watch that disturbing act."

Zoke hissed and wanted to spit. "Why would you give away the surprise?"

"No, that's just the beginning. The surprise is still to come." Vithos started south, waving Zoke forward.

Zoke laughed heartily from his stomach. He buckled his belt, threw the quiver over his back, and hoisted the bow onto his shoulder.

Soon they were walking toward Kyrro abreast, sharing stories.

Chapter 45: Uncaged
STEFFEN

"Come on, Steffen," Reela said, tapping on his door. "It's 9:30. I know you're aching, but if you don't hurry you'll miss breakfast."

Steffen jerked upright in bed. His heavy blanket slipped from his shoulders, and cold air gripped his skin. "Don't come in!" he hollered back. "I'll be right out."

He slipped into clean underwear that he'd laid out the night before.

"You should consider wearing some clothes to bed," Reela said from behind the door. "The days are getting colder."

"I'll consider it." He took a folded, long-sleeve shirt from his drawer and threw it over his head.

"No, you won't," Reela said.

"I might." Pants were the last thing he needed. "How did you know I'm aching?"

"You were thinking it so loud during the night, it nearly kept me up."

Steffen pulled open the door. Reela had her arms folded but dropped them when she saw Steffen. She wore a light blue dress. It had a gold-colored stripe around the waist, outlined in silver.

"The colors of Kyrro," Steffen commented. His curtain was shut, so the light flooding into his room came from behind her, giving a literal glow to her presence. It was a slight surprise to see her wear something so extravagant, but a pleasant surprise nonetheless. The dress looked beautiful on her, tightly fitting around the curves of her body.

She grabbed the sides of it and twisted playfully. "I thought it would be appropriate to show my dedication to Kyrro." Her voice grew grave, "given the threat of battle. Are you ready to go to the dining hall?"

"I still have all my body parts, right? I feel like something may have fallen off during the night." He spun his head left, then right, checking each arm facetiously.

Reela rolled her eyes but held a smile. "They can't be working you chemists that hard."

"It's awful, Reela. Oh, just a moment. Let me feed Leonard."

"Leonard?" Her mouth straightened. "He's either dead or not here."

"What?" Steffen pushed back the curtain covering his closet. Leonard's cage was there, but the rat wasn't in it. Two bars had been snapped, creating a big enough hole for Steffen's fist. "He must've squeezed through this. Quick, close all the doors and windows!"

"He's not here, Steffen. I sense no other presence. He's not in the house, unless he died in here."

Steffen went around the room in a panic, looking for some sort of clue to tell him where Leonard went. It was the only thing he could think to do. However, after just a few quick breaths, he knew that, unless the rat had learned how to write a note, there was no hope in finding anything useful.

"Well, this is bad."

Reela ran her finger along the broken bars of the cage. "This is steel. If he can bite through this, he can bite through bone."

"Yes. That's why I said, this is bad."

"We'd better tell Headmaster Terren so they can do whatever it is they do when a monstrous rat is on the loose. But first, breakfast. We can listen for screams of terror as we go. That should tell us where he is."

"He's probably the one terrified."

"I doubt that."

The walk to the dining hall was about a mile. As they made their way out of the student housing area, they passed by countless empty houses. The quiet was a discomforting change from every other morning. It was like walking along a beach that was silent because the ocean's waves had stopped.

"You didn't leave with Effie?" Steffen asked to disrupt the silence. His two female friends had always been inseparable, their need for proximity only increasing throughout the years.

Reela shook her head. "Eff's been rising early to train before breakfast, hasn't been sleeping well. As worried as I am for her, I like to wait until the sun wakes up before I do."

They walked along the edge of Warrior's Field. There was a group of ten warriors stretching in a circle around two men sparring.

Farther down, three warriors were standing beside a fourth with a bow. He had an arrow at the ready, but as he pulled back, one of the others said something and pushed the bow down. A few of them laughed. Steffen saw that Reela had noticed it as well.

"I see at least one bow has been made already," she commented. "Not that anyone knows how to use it besides Cleve." Her eyes were locked on the man with the bow, her tone filled with remorse.

"I'm worried about him as well, Reela. Who knows what they've done to him. He could be in a cell, and we might never see him again. He might even be dead, executed."

Reela grunted with disgust. "You sure know how to cheer me up," she said sarcastically.

Steffen realized his mistake. "Sorry. I meant to say we'll see him again, probably."

"Help me take my mind off him and tell me this: What have you been keeping from Effie that's caused you to act so strange? Is something the matter?"

His heart flipped in his chest. "Nothing! Everything's fine with Effie and with her sister."

"Her sister?" Reela held his shoulder to turn him toward her.

"And her father, and mother, and you." Steffen pointed at Reela in an attempt to cover his nervous reply, but his straightened finger only made him feel more awkward. His arm sagged back to his side. "Everything's fine with everyone."

"Steffen, you're the worst person I know at hiding something. What happened with you and Gabby? Are you two...romantically involved somehow?"

Now his heart felt as if it had spun in a circle. "How can you say that so calmly? Wouldn't it upset you to find out if that was true?"

"It wouldn't surprise me, very little does, and I'm only upset by surprises that I don't like. So what happened?"

He sighed, knowing there was no point in trying to cover it up. "We kissed, and I think I like her."

"And?"

"What do you mean? I think I have feelings for her. And we kissed, more than once!" *Doesn't she understand what I'm saying?*

"That's all?" Reela's palms opened as she shrugged. "How can you think that compares to finding out we're at war? Just tell Eff. Better to get it out than to hold it in."

"She'll be upset."

"However she reacts, it'll be better than you trying to keep it from her."

Steffen sighed again. He knew there was no point in going against Reela, especially when it came to Effie. "I hope you're right."

"I always am."

They came up to the dining hall, where three meals a day were served. Like most other students, Steffen hadn't missed one yet. Even if what they made was rarely delectable, being able to put food preparation and cleanup out of his mind was a welcome change, as his mother always had made him help.

The building was a massive brick structure. Inside were maybe two hundred tables, each long enough to seat twenty people. There were more people on staff as cooks, maintenance workers, and farmers at the Academy than there were as teachers. He'd heard that from a farmer he'd met when he'd visited the farm in the southeast corner of the Academy. It was because an entire third of the campus space was dedicated to the animals and crops that fed everyone each day.

They were late enough to avoid the queue for food. Steffen took a recently washed, but still wet, plate from the pile and put it on the counter for the woman behind it to fill. She ripped a loaf of bread in half, tossing one end on his plate, and poked a square of butter into it.

"The bread's gone cold," she told him. She threw three pieces of bacon on next. "So has the bacon."

Reela got the other half of his bread as well as the same lines from the woman behind the counter.

They sat at the nearest table. Reela shook her bread until the butter came out. She used a finger to dab at it and then spread her finger over the bread before nibbling it. She did this before every bite.

"Doesn't that get annoying?" Steffen asked.

"No. And if you had to learn from the psychic instructor I have, you'd be craving the extra activity. We do nothing useful."

"At least you don't have to run laps. Laps, Reela! They brought us to Warrior's Field for endurance exercises. Imagine a group of chemists sprinting, then panting, then sprinting, then panting, over and over again. And we're all terribly slow, only to get slower as the day goes on."

He used his teeth to rip a chunk from his bread. It was twice the size he'd meant to get, but he fit his lips around it anyway. "It was so embarrassing." The words barely made it out of his mouth without the bread going with them. "The warriors got more than a laugh from it. Then, the instructor gave us all what they call chemist shields, which are these silly little wooden barriers that we're supposed to use to stop the *steel* of a sword when we're attacked. We latch them onto our arms, and they're our only protection while we're expected to run across the battlefield to help wounded fighters."

He rolled back a sleeve to show the deep bruise on his forearm. "This is what I got when I used it to block an overhead swing from our instructor's dull blade."

Reela reached out to graze her fingers over it. Immediately, Steffen felt the dull pain subside. But it returned the moment she took her hand away. "Did you mean to relieve my pain right then?" Steffen asked, running his own finger along the bruise.

Reela shrugged. "Yes, but I didn't put much energy into it. I mostly wanted to see how strong the pain was."

Steffen hated not knowing anything about psyche. He'd read books on it, but all they did was confuse him with their abstract images and deeply layered hypotheticals. Reela had told him he was wasting his time with books, explaining they were only helpful after getting a base knowledge about psyche from a good teacher. Eagerly, Steffen then asked Reela to show him the basics, but she just touched his cheek with her palm and told him it would be like teaching poetry to a dog.

It was a bit insulting.

He felt somewhat frustrated from the memory. "Reela, why won't you tell me more about psyche?"

She finished a sip of water and rolled her lips together. "I thought that was just a phase. You're really still curious?"

"Yes!" Steffen could already feel excitement bubbling up.

Reela tilted her head curiously. "Then, why didn't you bring it up again?"

"Because of what you said last time." Steffen let his voice trail off.

Reela furrowed her brow. "Which was what?"

Steffen grumbled for needing to repeat it. "That it would be like teaching poetry to a dog."

A laugh erupted from Reela before she covered her mouth to

contain it. "I'm sorry. It's not exactly like that, but it is extremely difficult to describe. It's more like..." Reela's eyes fell to the table, then lifted to search around the room. "See this is the problem." She looked back at Steffen and sighed. "It's not comparable to anything. All psychics perform psyche differently. I wouldn't know how to help you understand it. So, I usually just avoid trying."

Steffen's excitement was ready to burst. "No." He shook his head vigorously. "You can't leave it at that. Just give me something, some idea to get a better sense."

The corner of Reela's mouth twisted. "I can try."

"Please do."

Reela set down her bread, placed her hands on the table, and took the slowest breath Steffen had ever seen. Her eyes seemed to stare deep within him.

Somewhat startled, Steffen leaned away from her. "You're just going to describe it with words, right?"

"Words alone won't be enough." Her face relaxed. "But we can start with them."

Steffen had a small breath of relief, though he still felt some tension about what Reela had planned.

"You need to start with a strong emotion, something you've felt recently so it's still fresh." She snapped her fingers. "Quickly, what's the first thing that comes to mind?"

"Gabby," Steffen muttered without thinking, "when she came into my room during the night." He was worried Reela would be shocked by his choice, but she kept her face serious, seemingly unaffected.

"And what was the feeling you're thinking of?"

"When I first realized why she was there. I don't know how to describe it. Worry, excitement, but guilt because of the excitement that seemed wrong to have, something like that."

"You don't need to know how to describe it, but can you feel it again right now when you think about it?"

Steffen felt the familiar flutter of his heart and the tingle on the back of his neck. "Very much so."

"Good. Now, close your eyes. What do you see?"

He closed his eyes. "Nothing. Just black with some white dots." The feeling had faded.

"That's fine. Don't try to imagine anything. Let the image develop on its own. Focus instead on the feeling—this guilty, nervous excitement you felt. Relive it. Use the memory of her to do so."

He kept his eyes shut, and Gabby's voice came back to him. *"I was thinking we should lie together."* That was all Steffen needed. Suddenly his heart was swelling, his stomach was dancing, and chills were running down his body.

An X shape floated to the surface of the sea of black. It was the darkest of reds, close to the black surrounding it, immediately reminding him of blackberry pie—the smell of her that night.

"I see an X."

"You do?" Reela sounded surprised, which startled Steffen, causing him to quickly lose focus and open his eyes.

"Is that bad?" Steffen asked.

"No, the opposite." Reela smiled wide. "Either I'm a good teacher or you have some natural ability with psyche. You just created your first association."

"Association?"

"That's what psychics call it. That shape is now associated with that feeling of nervous, guilty excitement, unless you force yourself to change the shape, which isn't easy and I wouldn't recommend."

Steffen shifted on the bench, desperately eager for more. "Now what? What can I do with that?"

Reela reached out to pat his wrist, holding a friendly smile. "Nothing. This is just a way to demonstrate how psyche is performed. That's what you wanted to know, right?"

Steffen slumped, feeling his excitement begin to dwindle. "Yes." For a brief moment he thought he might have stumbled onto something spectacular, but it was a silly hope, a childish fantasy.

"Close your eyes again but focus on nothing this time," Reela said.

Steffen nodded and closed his eyes, letting the sea of black take shape once again.

"I'm going to reproduce this feeling that I felt from you, this nervous excitement. It might take me a moment because I have to imagine a situation with someone that will evoke this emotion, but be patient."

Someone? Does she have feelings for someone the same way I have feelings for Gabby? Steffen chose to ignore this curiosity, pushing it from his mind to be revisited later.

"Get ready for the X to come back," Reela said. "When you see it, grab hold as tightly as you can. Don't let go."

“How do I do that?”

“However you can. Don’t think about it. Just do it.”

Silence followed. Then Steffen could hear Reela breathing loudly. He waited, staring deeply into the black, hoping to find the X slowly rising to the surface as it had before.

He saw its outline beginning to push through, making the black bulge around it. The black fell away from the X shape like water, allowing its red color to be seen, brighter than last time, blood red now. With all his might he tried to hold onto it. All his muscles clenched, and he heard himself grunting loudly, an embarrassing sound, but he didn’t let that stop him. It was fading back into the black sea. He tried harder to pull it out, to keep hold, but he was losing it. His grunt grew louder and rougher, scratching his throat, but he didn’t want to give up.

But then it was gone, completely covered by black.

Reela burst into laughter. Steffen opened his eyes to find everyone nearby staring at him with perplexed expressions. Reela was covering her face, trying to hold in her giggles.

“Do you have to check your pants?” Reela managed to get out.

Though Steffen didn’t know what she meant, he already felt hot shame spreading to his face. “Why?”

“Because it sounded like you just shat yourself!” Reela gasped for air between laughs and tried to calm herself.

Steffen felt as if he could die from embarrassment. “No,” he muttered. “I didn’t do that.”

Reela squeezed his hand, finally in control of her laughter now. “I’m sorry. You actually did pretty well. That was my emotion of nervous excitement you were holding onto, causing it to last longer than it would have usually. What did you see happening when you tried to grab it?”

“There were curved white lines on either side of the X. I was trying to crunch them together to take hold of it.”

Reela nodded with a surprised smile. “That’s another association you’ve made—your way of manipulating emotions. These white lines are your tool.”

Steffen grinned. All the shame was gone. This was real progress. “Now what?” he asked eagerly.

But then Reela frowned. “That’s it,” she said gravely. “That’s the basics of psyche. Associations, manipulation, and then years of training."

"So, you have an association for every emotion?"

"Yes, and strong thoughts and urges, like needing to use the bathroom, hunger, even when someone considers an object to be extremely important."

It was discouraging to hear. Steffen was always eager to learn something new, but that eagerness was now completely gone for psyche. "I don't see how you can keep track of them all."

Reela had a sly grin. "The associations get easier. I can now feel emotions and strong thoughts the same way you can sympathize with someone being sad. But manipulating them is infinitely harder. You felt how difficult it was just to hold on to one. Can you imagine trying to change its shape into something else?"

Steffen shook his head. His stomach was still tight from being clenched too hard.

"It's physically exhausting as well as mentally, just like every other class that manipulates Bastial Energy. Psychics also have to learn how to sense emotions in others. That's a whole new challenge."

Steffen was done. He knew then that he couldn't be a psychic. It wasn't that he was ever serious about being one, more that he was always curious if he could. "Well, thank you for explaining it."

Reela squeezed his hand with a warm smile. Her eyes fell to his bruise again, and she pointed to it. "Will you and the other chemists be training with the warriors from now on?"

"No, thankfully. Some days are field training, like yesterday. Other days are for learning potions that'll be used in battle and for medical purposes. Today, we'll be back in the classroom."

"That doesn't sound so bad. First-year psychics have no role in battle. They assume we aren't strong enough for any spells that would help. They're wrong, though, and I intend to prove that. I'm not going to sit on my hands while everyone else fights." Reela dabbed her butter with two fingers, fiercely rubbing it on the bread and ripping off a chunk with her teeth.

"Do I even want to ask what you intend to do?"

Reela showed him a sneaky smile. "I don't think so."

Alex flipped his legs over the bench to sit beside Reela. "I was just leaving when I noticed you two. I saw that Cleve made Group One, but he hasn't been on the field with me and the others. Is he ill?"

"Hi, Alex," Steffen replied, relieved he must have not heard his embarrassing grunting earlier. "I don't know if he's ill, but he's not here. Reela and Effie told me that someone from the King's Council came to pick him up, and he hasn't been back since."

Alex leaned toward Reela. "What?" His voice was just louder than a whisper. "Reela, when was this?"

"Two days ago, when the evaluations were posted." Her voice was weak, as if the words were painful. "It was Javy Rayvender and three guards. It must've been because of the bow."

"Why would the King wait?" From the way Alex stared at the table, he looked to be asking the question to himself. "I could be next." His eyes went up to Reela. "He hasn't returned...not once?"

"No. Any idea what they would be doing with him?" Reela asked, a glimmer of hope in her bright green eyes.

Alex scrunched his mouth for a breath. He opened his palms to gesture. "If it were any other time, they'd put him in the dungeons under the castle. But a man who's skilled with the bow is useful while we have enemies, and our King isn't as proud as his father was. He wouldn't use spite at his law being broken to alter his judgment."

Alex drummed his fingers on the table in silence as he thought. "The best case I can think of is that Cleve was asked to do something, to use his skill to shoot something or someone. Worse case, he would be in the dungeons. But given that they took his bow and waited nearly a week before detaining him, the former seems to be more logical. I see no reason why they would wait just to put him in a cell. They probably made him do something with the bow."

Reela threw her arms around Alex and squeezed. "Thank you. That's good news. See, Steffen, this is how you cheer someone up."

Alex's smile showed off a mouth full of white teeth. "If I knew being positive was all it took to get a girl's hands on me, I would try that more often." But then his mouth straightened as he noticed the grease on his sleeve from her buttered fingers. "Maybe next time I'll make sure her hands are clean first."

Someone let out a whistle that pierced through the room, stopping all chatter at once. Steffen turned and found the whistler at the door, now cupping his hands around his mouth to shout, "There's an Elf and a Krepp being taken through the school by two guards!"

A Krepp and an Elf? Did I hear that right?

"Come on!" Alex exclaimed, jumping from his seat.

"What about our plates?" Steffen said.

"Leave them," Reela answered. "Don't you want to see a Krepp?"

"Yes, and an Elf for that matter," Steffen agreed.

Reela turned as if to say something but closed her mouth and turned back before any words came out.

Chapter 46: Common Tongue
STEFFEN

Steffen followed the swarm of people outside. Hundreds were rushing south, and he ran along with them. The stomping of everyone's feet was so strong, he felt as if the ground was shaking. He saw they were all headed toward hundreds more, who already were gathered along the south side of Warrior's Field where the Krepp and Elf must be.

Steffen was still beside Reela when they arrived, but Alex had been lost in the crowd. He and Reela joined hands and walked along the backside of the mass, looking for an opening.

"Here," Reela said, twisting sideways to push through toward the front. People leaned away from Reela as she passed them, thanks to some psychic spell, Steffen figured.

He gasped when they made it to the front and he saw them. *Bastial stars, it's true! A Krepp and an Elf!*

The Krepp was just like he'd seen in drawings. His reptilian skin was gray, like the dark mist Steffen had seen after the sun set in Raywhite Forest. But his eyes were so very yellow, two goldbellows with black pupils. There was a dark tuft of hair on his head but nowhere else. His legs were covered by worn leather pants. His chest was bare. There were sharp claws at the ends of his humanlike fingers and toes. Five claws, Steffen counted, on each hand and foot. His limbs had a strong bend at the elbows and knees, and his whole body was covered in bulging muscles.

He seems about my height, Steffen thought. *His strength matches what has been written, but his height is far shorter. That's good.* The thought of an army of creatures both taller and stronger than Cleve had been worrisome.

"Make room!" a guard shouted. "They're to be brought to the King unharmed."

The Elf whispered something to the Krepp that Steffen couldn't overhear. The Elf was too similar to a Human to cause the same marvel. His skin was light, although it was covered in dirt. The hair close to his scalp had a glow to it, the same shine often found in Reela's hair as the sun hit it. But the ends of the Elf's hair, which came down to his shoulders, were dark with dirt and sweat. His eyes were long, tired but fierce, and deeply brown. The pointed tips of his ears poked out from his hair.

To everyone's shock, the Krepp spoke to them in common tongue. "We're on your side." His voice was low and throaty. It was followed by gasps and confused murmurs from the crowd, and Steffen felt a flurry of excitement.

Suddenly, a girl somewhere among the hundreds of watchers gave a short squeal. "A rat bit me!" She was almost in tears.

A man followed with a loud curse. Then, "It bit me also!"

Steffen's excitement turned to dread. "It's Leonard! Reela, can you connect with him?"

There was another scream, and with it the crowd grew restless.

"I can't unless I can see him." Reela's tone was heavy with worry. "Too many minds clustered together."

Curses and screams were spreading. People began shoving. Someone fell into Steffen, pushing him hard into Reela. The Krepp was yelling something now, but no longer in common tongue. Steffen felt panic taking control. He started looking for a way out of the crowd.

Then a calm slowed Steffen's breathing. He was no longer panicked, and the chaos in the crowd had died as well. The transition seemed oddly quick, but Steffen was so relaxed he didn't even care to wonder about it.

He helped the young lady up who'd fallen into him. Nearly all was quiet. A few people were asking each other if they were hurt. Steffen noticed the Elf was facing them.

He had a palm extended. From the midst of the crowd, Leonard appeared, his fat body wobbling along toward the Elf.

The Elf knelt down to pick up Leonard, muttering something in another language. Steffen would have guessed it was Elvish, but he knew a little of the language and the words were far too harsh to be it. *Could that be Kreppen?* he wondered with disbelief.

"You have large rats," the Krepp said to the crowd. "Do you wish for us to kill it?" The Elf had his hands cupped around Leonard.

Steffen stepped forward. "No, the rat is mine. Sorry."

The Krepp seemed puzzled. Steffen figured it was because he

didn't understand the idea of a pet. But instead, the Krepp surprised him by saying, "Why are you sorry?"

"Sorry for the trouble," Steffen answered, somewhat confused himself now.

"There's no trouble," the Krepp replied with what seemed to be a disgusted tone. He said something to the Elf in his language, and the Elf offered Leonard back to Steffen with a smile.

The giant rat was still, something Steffen had never seen unless Leonard was sleeping. Leonard looked comfortable, resting his head in front of his paws. He remained that way even when Steffen cupped his hands under him to lift him away.

His heart raced when he turned and suddenly noticed Reela beside him. She was reaching out a hand tentatively toward the Elf's. *Reela what are you doing?*

"Rek?" she asked in a whisper. "Is that you?"

What is this? Steffen almost grabbed her to move her away but decided against it. He trusted Reela's judgment, as strange as it seemed.

The Elf was first concerned, taking back his hand. But a breath later his face loosened. He accepted Reela's hand, giving her a curious look. Reela looked to be on the verge of tears but with a crooked smile.

The Elf said something to the Krepp, who appeared to translate for him. "He wonders who you are," the Krepp said to Reela. "He thinks he knows you."

"He doesn't know me." She was still whispering. "But I think I know him."

As the Krepp translated for the Elf, a guard startled them with an announcement. "That's enough, everyone. It's time we move." He waved the Krepp forward. "Follow us. The King is expecting you both."

Reela and the Elf dropped each other's hands, but their gazes held until the Krepp put his palm on the Elf's back to escort him forward. The Elf finally straightened his head, walking a few steps before giving one last look back at Reela.

What just happened? Steffen wondered. He waited for some sort of sign from Reela to reveal what he'd just witnessed. But she didn't move. Her hand was still out, her face pale like she'd just seen someone rise from the dead. She didn't even seem to notice everyone in the crowd murmuring and staring at her. Her eyes were locked on the Elf.

"Reela? How could you know him?" Steffen asked hesitantly.

"I..." She gave no answer, finally letting her hand drop.

Alex burst from the crowd. "What was that, Reela? What did you say to him?"

"I have to go speak to my mother," Reela muttered. Then she broke into a run.

A long "*uhhhh*," leaked out of Alex. He gave a confused glance to Steffen.

"I haven't the faintest idea," Steffen answered. Then he remembered Leonard was in his hands. He almost dropped the rat after the realization that the Elf's powerful spell should be over by now. But Leonard was still. He had been this whole time. Steffen lifted his pet to his eyes. The rat sniffed...and then nothing else. He didn't bite, or growl, or look for something to chew on.

"What did the Elf do to you?" Steffen asked.

"What did he do to all of us?" Alex added. "Did you feel that blissful relaxation in the middle of everyone nearly killing each other?"

"Yes, what was that?"

And what in Bastial hell happened with Reela?

Chapter 47: Traitors
ZETI

Jumping over the fence was the worst part about returning to camp. After Zeti had walked a hundred and fifty miles in a week, with little sleep and less conversation, the wooden wall that bordered the Krepps' territory looked daunting. It was built without doors. The only way through it was over it, which normally wasn't difficult. A simple run and hop would get Zeti's belly on it so she could swing her legs over, but even a task as easy as that was monumental in her exhausted state.

The fence was designed more so to slow anyone leaving than to prevent intruders from coming in. It gave the post guards a chance to chase after any Krepp who wasn't permitted to go.

Ever since the move to this new encampment, their giant Slugari leaders had been unreasonably strict about Krepps leaving the camp. She heard a Krepp had an arrow shot into his leg when he tried to climb over when all he'd done was forget to notify the post guard first.

During her team's searches for the underground Slugari colony, most of her physical fatigue came from the poor company she had to endure, not from the miles they walked. It's not that they didn't speak, for they did—too much. It's that they had nothing to say worth hearing. When they spoke, it was either to boast or belittle each other. When they spoke to her, it was always one of the same three things. The men without a *seshar* would try to convince her that they should be hers. The men with a *seshar* would ask why she hadn't chosen one. And all would ask what it felt like to know her brother was a traitor.

Zeti found herself considering taking one of them as a *seshar* just so she wouldn't have to deal with it anymore.

Their nonstop annoyance made her welcome the nights. While the bumps on the ground sometimes kept her awake, at least they were silent in doing so.

Paramar, the chief of the search group, was the only one she could tolerate. Since their fight, she'd taken a small liking to him. He didn't have much to say, but he was always willing to help. When they needed to hunt for food, he would always go. When they decided to make a fire, he would gather tinder and start it. And he was always the one to carry the chamoline—what could be the most important flower to the Krepps—acting as the replacement for Vithos' ability to sense the Slugari, which they lost when he was labeled a traitor.

The chamoline flower had a friendly green color, five long petals, and a small tongue coming from the middle where the petals met. Paramar had told her of its power: It mimics the colors of some plants when there's a high enough concentration of them around.

"It's very susceptible to rujins, turning red if enough of them are nearby," Paramar said when he showed it to her.

"Why does that matter?" she asked, not knowing what use the rujin flowers had.

"You don't know about the Dajrik, do you? It's something Doe and Haemon taught us."

She'd never heard the word before. "Dajrik? No."

"A giant with skin twice as tough as mine." Paramar showed her his arm and clawed at it to demonstrate his point. "Dajriks might as well be made from rock, and sure look to be from how Doe and Haemon have described them. The Slugari have one. It wears an amulet with pure rujin fused as a gem. It needs to. Otherwise, it has terrible nightmares for whatever reason. Doe and Haemon think it's because of its age. The older Dajriks get, the worse their nightmares, and this one is thousands of years old."

It sounded like a fanciful tale to Zeti. But the way Paramar was describing it made it clear these were facts. It was hard for her to believe, especially when she'd never seen a giant or any creature with skin tougher than a Krepp's.

"Why is it with the Slugari? I don't understand."

"The Slugari have the ability to create the gem it needs from rujins and of course the rujins to make it. The rujin gem doesn't last more than a hundred years. Its concentration fades. The Dajrik doesn't have the ability to make it himself. He needs the Slugari, so he protects them."

Paramar twisted the chamoline carefully between his claws. "Now that we have this, we can find them just by standing over their hidden colony. It'll become red because of the rujin gem the Dajrik wears." He grinned in a way that would've sent Zeti's heart jumping if she had any fear he might want to harm her. "The cowards can't hide for long, even if the Humans don't give them up."

"Why don't the Slugari stop making it if they know we can use the chamoline to track them?"

"They might not know. Anyway, Doe and Haemon say the Slugari would never let the Dajrik suffer through the nightmares. The Dajrik saved them from the destruction of their race—from two other Dajriks hundreds of years ago. It's a long story, and I don't remember all the details even if I wished to tell it. Just make sure you don't harm the chamoline."

"I wouldn't dare." *So much difference one plant can make.* She went to her toes to get a good look at it, holding Paramar's arm in place. His skin was so tough it seemed as if it would chip rather than scrape.

"Once torn from the ground, these chamolines only last a week before they can no longer change color. We have many seeds planted, but they don't grow well. There are only a few old enough to work right now." He spat.

"We've just recently discovered the chamoline, I figure?" It was an answer as to why they chose now to send off Vithos—because he was no longer needed.

"Yes, our scouts did well."

Maybe he wasn't a traitor after all. But why did Zoke get dragged into this?

They'd searched the eastern side of Satjen with the chamoline but it hadn't changed color. Now that they were back, they would have one night of rest, giving Paramar time to meet with Doe while Zeti looked forward to her quiet hut and bed.

Right after she jumped off the wall, she felt a sting to her lower back. The nick was just below her short leather shirt where her stomach was exposed. She spun to see what got her. Paramar was sitting on the wall. He must have sliced her with a claw on his foot.

"Your skin is still very soft," he said, hopping down so close his chin would have hit her head if she were a neck taller. He reached his hand around her, pressing his palm into the fresh wound for a heartbeat. He brought his hand back to show her the small amount of her blood he took from her. "Even the short claw of a Slugari would open you up. I have to make sure your skin is tough enough for battle before we strike, otherwise you'll be staying behind."

"It doesn't matter how soft my skin is if I don't get touched. That's what this is for." She lifted her bow. "I can fight."

"Paramar," someone called. It was a voice she didn't recognize. When she turned to see Keenu, the chief of the scouts, she took it as her cue to leave. She found it to be common for other chiefs to meet with Paramar and even saw him speaking with Doe and Haemon a few times around camp.

But Keenu stopped her with a hand to her shoulder as she tried to walk by him. "Zeti, right? Sister to Zoke?"

"Yes, what of it?" Whenever someone led with her connection to Zoke, the conversation never went well.

"Doe needs you and Paramar to come with me. Nebre has returned. Follow, and I'll explain as we walk."

Nebre...the one who was sent to Kyrro because he could speak their language? He couldn't have made it there and back already. What happened?

Zeti checked the thin cut on her back for blood as she started after Keenu. Her gray finger came back just a bit redder. She stuck it in her mouth to suck off the stain. *And what could Doe want with me?*

Keenu spoke while they walked. "Doe and Haemon didn't trust the Humans from Tenred because the Humans didn't like our idea of threatening Kyrro to reveal the location of the Slugari. Instead, Tenred wanted us to attack Kyrro with them, take their cities, and use force to get the Slugari location out of them once Kyrro's hope was lost." Keenu spat. "But it would be thousands of Krepps in the frontline, risking their blood. Wisely, Doe and Haemon decided to give Kyrro a chance to avoid war. The three Tenred Humans were very displeased by that decision, so Doe and Haemon thought they might kill Nebre and dispose of his body to make it seem as if Kyrro had killed or captured him, forcing us to war because of the threat we issued. So they had me trail a day behind Nebre and the Humans from Tenred."

This information wouldn't usually be shared with Zeti, and that made her nervous. *Something must have happened when he followed them, but how does it involve me?* She knew she would find out soon but was in no way eager.

"So I tracked them," Keenu continued, "following the footprints of a Krepp and the shoes of three Humans all the way to the center of Satjen to make sure the plan was followed, and it was. They didn't kill

Nebre. The Humans continued west to Tenred, Nebre went south. Then I found something strange. Remember, I was a day behind to ensure I wasn't seen, so I can only tell you about the footprints and not what created them."

"More footprints of shoes?" Paramar asked. "Humans coming back to kill Nebre?"

"There was one shoe print, but it was different than the other three. A cruder form of leather, like from the shoes Vithos wore. Next to his footprints were that of a Krepp, someone walking close to him. They trailed Nebre together..." Keenu gave Zeti a long look. His yellow eyes said it all.

"You think it was Vithos and Zoke," she said for him, holding back spit. "You think Zoke is a traitor."

"I know it was Vithos and Zoke," Keenu answered flatly. "Nebre confirmed it."

Their next few yards passed in silence.

"I'll let Nebre tell the rest."

Zeti felt her heart speeding up. *Even if it was Zoke and Vithos, what am I supposed to do about it?* "Where are we meeting Doe?" she asked.

"The judgment chambers," he answered with a soft voice, clearly aware what he was implying.

The judgment chambers, she repeated in her mind, *should be called the burning chambers*.

Since their move to the new camp without Vithos, she'd heard the judgment chambers had been taken over by Haemon, with Doe making an appearance every so often. Judgment was no longer part of the process. There was only punishment. If you didn't complete your task, you received a burning, simple as that. The more you missed your quota, the worse the burning. If you broke a rule, you got a burning. Any dispute between Krepps needed to be resolved by those involved, otherwise each received a burning. From what she'd heard, no one left the chambers without a burning.

While the new judgment chambers kept the same name as the old, everything else had changed. There weren't even four walls, just one crude stone wall and a few chiseled rocks to sit on. The Krepp to be burned would stand in front of the only wall. Its sole purpose was to block the fire from reaching anywhere else but the accused's skin. After the burning, the Krepp would leave, and the next awaiting judgment would file into place.

She heard there was no sitting for deliberation anymore. Doe and Haemon couldn't sit anyway, Zeti figured, as they didn't have legs. Or maybe that meant they couldn't stand. She didn't care to think about it.

But when she entered, Doe surprised her by pointing to a rock with his gnarled Slugari claw and telling her, "Sit." His fat face was contorted with a grimace, his beady eyes nearly devoured by the lumps of flesh around them. His two small antennae hung limply atop his head, as they had the last time she'd spoken to him. Somehow, he seemed even longer and wider than before, his bulbous tail rounder and fatter, barely thinner than the rest of his body now. It slowly swished back and forth as he glared, waiting for her to sit.

She sat, and Paramar sat on the rock beside her. She noticed then that Keenu hadn't gone in with them.

Then she saw Nebre. He no longer had the nervous squint in his eyes, the one he'd had when he was the only Krepp to raise his hand after Doe shouted to the tribe asking who spoke the language of the Humans. *No, now he looks like a different Krepp, one with resolve.* And he was staring at Zeti, but not in the same way other Krepps stared at her. He looked ready to jump from his rock with a knife.

Then she noticed the waxy white line across his wrist. It looked fresh. *He's just been burned*, she realized.

"Tell them what happened," Doe said to Nebre, slithering close to the Krepp. With Nebre sitting, Doe was well over twice his height. Nebre kept his eyes on Zeti but did seem to wince when Doe looked down at him.

"It was brother to you," he pointed at her. "Him and the Elf. They're both traitors."

She felt a twitch in her legs. It nearly stood her upright, but she ignored it and sat forward with her arms crossed. She remained silent, waiting what felt like days for him to continue.

"I had the note, the one for the King of Kyrro," Nebre said. "Not long after I split from the Tenred Humans, I was chased down by Zoke and Vithos. They insisted on knowing my business but wouldn't say why. The Elf was so close, I had no chance to lie without him knowing. I thought they were going to kill me." He took a quick look at Doe.

Zoke would never hurt you unless you deserved it. But Zeti held her tongue.

"When I told them where I was going, what I was doing, they insisted on coming with me. I decided to go along with it. I...I knew Zoke when he was younger. I used to trust him, and some part of me still did. I figured his mind might be twisted from a psychic spell. If I just waited until the Elf was asleep and killed him, Zoke would be thankful. So I waited hours into the night to make sure both were asleep. I took my dagger and just as I knelt over Vithos, Zoke pushed me off him. Even while the Elf was unconscious, Zoke still saved him!"

Nebre stood and made two fists. "He couldn't have been under any spell. He's a true traitor and a coward for not doing the job himself."

The fury within Zeti made her dig her claws into her palm hard enough to draw blood. Her sharp teeth were pushed together so fiercely under her lips a surge of pain went through her jaw.

"I wanted you to hear that," Doe told her. "I know what you stubborn Krepps are like."

She couldn't handle it anymore. She stood and pointed at Nebre. "He's a liar." She noticed then that she wasn't using a claw to point, but her dagger. Somehow, she'd drawn it from her belt without realizing it. "Zoke would never protect the Elf over his own kind!"

"It's the truth!" Nebre yelled back.

"It is," Doe said. "Haemon already made sure of that before he left the judgment chambers. Tell her what happened next, after she sits back down." He waved his black claw at her.

Zeti sat on the edge of the rock, barely stopping herself from spitting in the judgment chambers.

"I tried to wrestle Zoke off me, but I couldn't." Nebre spoke softly, ashamed. "Vithos awoke and pained me with psyche until I let go of the dagger. Zoke then screamed at me to leave, saying they would deliver the note to Kyrro. He'd taken it earlier. With no other option besides death, I ran. I came back here. He's a traitor, Zeti. I didn't want to believe it at first, either."

What are you doing, Zoke? It felt as if she was hearing a story about someone else's brother, not hers, not the brother who'd always done the right thing no matter how difficult. *Why protect the Elf? It must be some psychic spell that has kept you with him...no, Vithos was asleep and you protected him, so it couldn't be. You've been with him through many nights even, and he still lives. Could you be that much of a coward? Too scared to kill the Elf, so you've joined him?*

No. No, there must be more to it than that...I wish I could just speak to you. What are you doing out there?

"Why did he say he would deliver the note?" Zeti asked.

"I cannot say, but I truly believe they will," Nebre answered. "When they found out about the note, they spoke in private before deciding to come with me. I can only guess they wish to join with the Humans. With a war to fight, the Humans are likely to accept any ally. They are traitors, after all. It makes sense for them to wish to join our enemy."

"Nebre is right," Doe added. "Haemon and I have known Vithos his whole life, and something changed in recent years. He is no longer interested in helping. I am even sure that he knows where the Slugari are, but he pretends not to. We have covered nearly all the places they could be. I know he's sensed them, but he refuses to admit it. Paramar, that is why you're here."

Paramar stood with his chest out. He was especially tall, matching Doe's height, though the Slugari was longer than he was tall, weighing three times as much as any Krepp.

"I believe Vithos may be trying to make contact with the Slugari," Doe said. "Being the traitor that he is, he would wish to bring harm to our tribe by helping the Slugari stay out of our reach, perhaps even convincing them to attack us if he's that stupid. I don't think he was there by chance but instead because that's where the Slugari are hiding. Take the chamoline and follow the route that Nebre took. It was mostly along northern Satjen."

"Understood," Paramar replied dutifully.

"Vithos is probably on his way to the Humans in Kyrro to convince them not to reveal the Slugari location," Doe continued. "But before we fight Kyrro for this information, we should keep looking for my cowardly race of Slugari. Taking the cities of Kyrro would be easy wins, but not without many deaths to our tribe. I'd like to avoid that. Have your group set out tomorrow morning, Paramar, and move quickly. But keep an eye on her." Doe pointed at Zeti. "She has traitorous blood flowing through her."

She stood ready to scream but knew all that would accomplish was a burning. So she took a long breath, gulped down her pride, and said, "I'll do everything in my power to find the Slugari. Brother to me may be a traitor." Her words felt like a dagger slicing through her heart, but she held steady with her chest out and head up. "But I would never go against the tribe."

"Good," Doe answered. "Because when we see Zoke again, you're going to prove that by being the one to kill him."

Chapter 48: Stone
CLEVE

"Rek?" Cleve asked, standing with his back against the cold stone wall of his cell.

Behind it came the muffled answer from the next cell. "What?"

With the only light coming from a few torches along the walls, it was difficult to know when one day ended and the next began. Rek could convince the jailer of many things, but King Welson had given the jailer no means of getting to other areas of the dungeons. This made him stuck in their section just like a prisoner, but at least he had long hallways to walk about when he pleased. Cleve could already feel his legs stiffening, calling to be used.

"When the jailer brings us food, will you ask him how long we've been in here?" Cleve asked.

This time, the response came from the cell on Cleve's other side before Rek answered. "Ya only been here for four meals, boy. That's one day and one meal. Ol' Captain Mmzaza has been here eighty-four meals for spittin' a guard in his face. I get out at ninety, and I can barely keep me pants on about it." Captain Mmzaza had a way of talking that Cleve had never heard. Not only was his accent strong and rhythmic, but he spoke as if he'd learned common tongue from a child. "When will ya be out, boy?"

"I told you, CM, I don't want to answer any more of your questions."

Captain Mmzaza let out a shaky *hohoho* sound, then said, "Again, with the CM. And I tell ya, the name is Captain Mmzaza. That's *mmm-zah-zah*," he pronounced slowly. "The Starving Ocean may have devoured me sanity, but I haven't lost me name. I'll be a captain when I return to the Gendocks, and if you were on me ship—"

"I'd call you Captain Mmzaza," Cleve finished the sentence for him. "I know. You've said that many times already. Luckily, I'm not on your ship, CM, and I never will be."

Rek had been in no mood to talk. Cleve had tried to speak to him several times, only to be answered by Captain Mmzaza when Rek would not respond. When Cleve had asked if Rek wanted him to say anything else to the King before they were sent to the dungeons, Rek simply replied, "You did all you could."

When Cleve gathered enough courage to ask Rek what he knew of his mother or father, the Elf replied, "It's best to save that conversation for when we're not filled with despair. Despair makes us weak. You should be content and confident before pulling out that dagger."

When he asked Rek what he knew of Goldram and Jessend Takary, Rek answered with only two words: "Not much."

It wasn't much better than speaking to the wall that separated them. Though, he didn't blame the Elf. Rek was depressed and understandably so. The only reason Cleve didn't feel the same was because he was trying to stay strong, ignoring the deep sadness swelling within.

Cleve heard voices bouncing down the hall. Usually this meant the jailer had just received their meals from the other section of the dungeons. The jailer sometimes stayed and chatted after delivering their food, putting up with Captain Mmzaza's nonsense far longer than Cleve would.

There was just enough space for Cleve to fit his head through the bars, so he stuck it out for a look. He saw that, for the first time, the jailer hadn't come alone. The silhouette of someone behind the jailer came around the turn and into their hallway. It was a woman, one with thick, long hair. *Has Jessend Takary finally come to take me from Kyrro?* Cleve thought.

"Cleve, you have a visitor," the jailer announced.

Then he heard what sounded like Rek's bars being kicked. Cleve flipped his head to find that the Elf was also leaning out from his cell—his shoulders must have crashed into the bars in his eagerness to see who it was. When Cleve turned back to see for himself, she was still hidden behind the jailer. Yet somehow, Rek knew who it was, for he was already calling her name.

"Reela, Reela! What are you doing here?"

"Rek! They didn't tell me you were here, too." She ran to him and they held onto each other's hands. "Why do they have you both in the dungeons?"

Cleve could feel his blood flowing faster, heating his body with nervous wonder. "How do you know Rek?" he blurted out.

Reela took a shaky breath as she opened her mouth to answer, but she turned and touched the shoulder of the jailer instead. “I’ll be fine here—if we could have some privacy?” The jailer nodded and was off.

Reela had on a blue dress with some other color around her waist, maybe gold. It was too dark to be sure. Though, it was clear the dress was tightly wrapped around her body, accentuating the curve of her hips and bosom. Even in the dim light, he could see the burning green of her eyes, along with the pink of her soft, pouty lips.

“Cleve, it’s so good to see you. I was very worried.”

Cleve felt his throat tighten and his stomach crunch. “You as well.”

Captain Mmzaza gave a whistle. “Me o’ me, what a spicy girl.” His head was leaning out as far as his neck could push it. A scruffy beard of red and gray covered his chin. A pronounced mustache of the same colors curved over his mouth and stuck out from his face. His eyes were two slits in long eyelids. His skin that wasn’t covered by hair was windburned, especially along his forehead. On the top of his head were thin strands of gray that fell to his ears. “And she wants privacy. Got a nice show for ol’ Captain Mmzaza? Come over here, pretty. Let me get a closer look before ya get started.”

She walked over and held out the back of her hand like she was allowing the old seaman to kiss it. He reached out, but just before they could touch, Reela flipped her palm up and let out a soft grunt.

He recoiled with a quick scream.

“What didja do? Even me horn gotta sting from that.”

“Rek, you mind putting him to sleep?” Reela asked politely.

“I would be happy to,” he answered with cheer Cleve hadn’t heard since they’d entered the dungeons. “Captain Mmzaza, lie down so you don’t fall on something.”

“Aww, a bunch of psychics, they are. Fine. The captain will take a nap. Was just trying to send a compliment, was all.”

“On your side,” Rek said. “I don’t want to listen to your snoring.”

“Fine. But I’m pointing my ass toward ya. It may snore just as well, if ya catch my drift.” He started a laugh, but it was cut off. All that remained was the quiet breathing sound of him sleeping.

“Can you keep a secret, Cleve?” Reela asked.

“Yes,” he answered. “Not that it matters, as Rek and I are being sent to Goldram as soon as Jessend Takary is ready to take us.”

“To Goldram?” Her voice grew shrill. “For what purpose? When will you return?”

"We're not," Rek answered. "King Welson is convinced I'm a threat to Kyrro. He has similar thoughts about Cleve. Letting him stay would do more harm than good, the King believes."

"That's completely absurd. How can he think that?"

"They saw me meet with Tegry Hiller," Rek answered. "They think I side with the enemy. They sent Cleve to kill me with his bow. As you can see, he didn't."

"I don't understand. Why send you over the Starving Ocean if he thinks you fight for the enemy?"

"He believes it to be his most humane option. I'm sure he's getting a trade out of it as well. The Takary family has much to offer, and Jessend Takary says she has use for us, whatever that may be."

"If I could just speak to the King, I could convince him to let you both stay." Reela had a desperation in her voice Cleve hadn't heard from her before. "I'm sure of it. He's speaking to my mother right now. I came here with her. He doesn't know I'm a psychic."

"Nor will he!" Rek was so stern it gave Cleve a startle. "He mustn't know who you are or you could be in here just like us...or exiled...or worse!"

What am I missing here? "The King welcomes psychics within Kyrro. Why can't he know that she's one?"

Reela sighed. "That's the secret. I'm not just any psychic. You wondered how I knew Rek...well." She came to his cell and grabbed the bars, leaning close. Her eyes were tense, burning with a secret that made Cleve's heart start to jump.

"Rek is my half-brother." Reela reached her hand to an ear hidden beneath her hair and looked to unhook something. Then she pulled back the many thick, wavy strands to show her ear. It wasn't rounded at the top but came to more of a point. This made it longer than a Human's ear but still shorter than Rek's. If Cleve was to guess what it would look like to mix an Elf ear with a Human's, he was looking at it.

He could see it in the rest of her now, her creamy skin, her big almond eyes, her soft features, even the shine in her hair. *That's why Rek looked so familiar.*

It was the kind of revelation that sent a chill down his back and arms, that gave answers to questions he hadn't thought of until now.

A silence followed that tried to tug words out of him. *"They're beautiful,"* he kept wanting to say. *"Your ears are beautiful."* He could think of nothing else but managed to refrain from speaking it. Finally, she pinned her ear back and let her hair return to rest over it.

"He likes them," Rek said with a happy laugh.

"I can tell," Reela said and smiled, her head bowed as if she was flattered.

He felt a dry gulp down his choking throat and didn't know what to say.

Luckily, Reela wasn't waiting for him to come up with something. "After what happened to Rek, there's too much of a risk in letting people know what I am. But Rek..." She moved back to his cell. "I don't think the King would find out if I just talked to him once. I could convince him with psyche to keep you both here."

"No, he's been training against it," Rek replied with a peremptory tone. "And King Welson is smart. Even if you did, he'll figure out later that you used psyche. Then he'll change his mind back and have you investigated to see why you're so interested in helping. He'll find the connection through Airy—you did say she was upstairs with him right now. It's sure to put you at risk. You're not going to do it."

"What am I supposed to do, then?" Reela said, desperation thick in her voice again. "You expect me to let you go without a fight? We need you both here." Her hand struck the top of her chest. "I need you both here."

"You'll fight, but not for us," Cleve answered. "Fight for Kyrro and all the people in it. The first chance I get, I'll come back. I don't care what it takes. If I have to steal a ship, sail it across the ocean myself, and sneak back into the Academy to fight, I'll do it."

"What he says," Rek agreed, with a spirit behind his words that Cleve hadn't heard in far too long. "You do what you can, Reela. So will we."

"I understand," she spoke regretfully. "There's something else, Rek, before the jailer returns. Vithos is here." She pointed toward the ceiling. "He and a Krepp came through the Academy and I met him. I touched him. I know it's him. Even though we've never met before, I can tell we share blood. He could feel it too. I could tell."

"He's here now?" Rek whispered incredulously. Cleve had never heard Rek sound surprised before. He would've guessed the Elf was incapable of it.

"Yes, which is why I brought Airy. She'll tell me what they said when she's done translating."

"Make sure you speak to her in private, not in the castle." Rek added. "There are ears everywhere in here."

Reela nodded. "The Krepp he was with spoke common tongue. He said they're on our side."

"Can someone help me understand if I got this?" Cleve couldn't hold his tongue any longer. There was too much he didn't know, and he was barely keeping up. "Another relative of yours came into Kyrro, with a Krepp who speaks our language?"

"Yes, his name is Vithos," Rek answered hastily. "He's an Elf, my full brother, Reela's half-brother through our father."

"So Vithos and the Krepp are speaking with the King right now but through a translator? Didn't you say the Krepp can speak our language?" Cleve had never heard of Krepps speaking common tongue, so he wanted to make sure he'd understood Reela correctly.

"Yes, but the King would want to speak to the Krepp and Vithos directly with his own trusted translator," Rek answered. "Airy is that. She knows Elvish and Kreppen. She was the castle's translator for many years, but she was never needed except to transcribe Elvish and Kreppen books."

"Vithos and the Krepp also had some sort of Kreppen scroll with them," Reela added. "I'm sure the King wanted his own translator to read it. Airy is my biological mother but also stepmother to Rek. He lived with her for many years. She'll tell us what she learns from the translation. She retired from the castle a while ago, but the only other person who knows both Elvish and Kreppen is in Trentyre. So I was certain the King would gladly accept her help rather than wait to retrieve the translator from Trentyre."

"I see," Cleve answered. "Airy is full Human. It's your father who's the Elf?"

"Yes," Reela answered. "He was also the father of Rek and Vithos, who are twins. He died before he even knew that Airy was pregnant with me."

"I'm sorry," Cleve responded. He wasn't sure what else to say. He was still in too much shock to really feel anything else. *Reela is half-Elf. Rek has a twin brother and shares a father with Reela. A Krepp speaks common tongue and traveled here with Rek's brother, Vithos, and they're all here in this castle right now.* It was a bit much all at once.

"Our father died by the fire from Doe and Haemon's magic while trying to get Vithos out of their camp." Rek's tone had turned sour. "Doe and Haemon are two giant Slugari, tall as Krepps and long like, well, slugs. But that's a story for another time. Reela, make sure you don't speak about Doe and Haemon. Let Kyrro's scouts find out about them. Otherwise, Welson might discover I told you and connect you back to me."

The sound of voices down the hall interrupted them.

"Don't speak of any of this to anyone, Cleve," Rek whispered quickly.

The jailer approached. At the sight of Reela, he stopped a moment. "Oh, you're still here!" His voice was unusually loud, though he didn't sound upset. "Somehow, I'd forgotten, which is strange as we don't see many women down here! Rek, the King wishes to speak to you soon! I'm to bring you to him! I do apologize, but I'll need to put the gag in!" He held out two thick ropes. "And bind your hands as well! Go ahead and put them behind you and stick them through the food hole! And don't bother trying to say anything; my ears have been plugged!" He pointed to the side of his head where long plugs were sticking from his ears.

"Reela, if I don't see you again, know that I'll always love you. Tell Airy the same." Rek put his hands behind him and pushed them through the wide slot in the middle of the door to his cell.

"I love you, too," she replied. "I'll tell her."

When Rek's hands were tied and his mouth gagged, the jailer removed his earplugs and turned to Reela. "I'm sorry, young lady, but I'll need you out of here before I transport Rek. I'm sure you wouldn't try anything funny, but procedure needs to be followed. I'll walk you out."

"Give me one minute, if you wouldn't mind?" She set a hand on his shoulder and smiled sweetly.

"Sure," he smiled back. "I'll be waiting by the door. You have one minute to meet me there." He walked away, putting in his earplugs as he went.

Reela would get away with so little if people knew what she was capable of, Cleve thought.

Reela went back to Rek's cell. Cleve watched as she pushed her face and arms through the gaps in the bars for what looked like a one-way hug. "Until next time, brother," she said.

Then she came over to Cleve. Her eyes were glistening. "Cleve, I want to tell you something before I must go."

Chapter 49: Coming Loose
CLEVE

His stomach tightened. He realized what he wanted to hear, and it scared him. *Don't say it,* he thought. A shiver went through him. He backed a step away from the bars. *Don't tell me you have feelings for me. I don't have the strength for it.*

She grabbed on to two of his cell bars, leaning her brilliant green eyes closer. "I'm frightened, Cleve."

Relieved, he took a calming breath. But then she leaned even closer, and the serious look on her face let him know it was too early to relax. "I know you are, too." Her tone was sweet, matching her fragrance. Her light-brown hair was close enough to touch. The thought of her ears beneath it caused a chill to course through him. "But I don't know if it's for the same reason as me. Will you tell me what you're scared of?"

He took another step back as fright started growing within him. "I'm scared of losing myself, losing who I am. You make me weak, Reela." He hated admitting it. It made him feel like his heart was being pried open, but he wanted her to know. He always did, and if not now, then it might be never. "I'm supposed to be strong. If I'm not strong, I'm nothing. I don't expect you to understand." Reela was the strongest person he'd ever met, besides his father. He couldn't imagine her ever feeling weak.

"I wouldn't have understood weeks ago, but I do now. I'm the same way, Cleve. You're the source of my fear."

He was so shocked that he spoke before a single thought crossed his mind. "How could I frighten you?"

"I'm not scared of you. I'm scared of losing you. I want you here with me. From the moment we met, I could feel something between us. Couldn't you?"

He understood now. Every look, every touch she'd given him he'd taken to mean nothing, but some part of him always argued back. Cleve found himself nodding, but then stopping as soon as he noticed it.

"I did feel something, but it was mostly fear." *Mostly*, he repeated to himself, remembering the lust.

"What if you took away all the fear, what would be left? Think about how you would feel about me without it."

He didn't wish to think about that. "I can't disconnect you from the fear." He tapped his temple. "You are fear. You are weakness. If the fear was gone, I don't know...you would just be another beautiful woman," he lied.

"That's not true, Cleve, and you know it. I'm not just another woman, and you're not just another man. There's a connection between us, one you don't need psyche to feel. You're not letting go of the fear. Let it go. Truly see what's behind it. Come here, take my hand." She reached into his cell.

Effie had told Cleve that Reela never dated, that she was far too straightforward with men, usually about their lies or poor qualities. However, that didn't seem true. In all his time with Reela she didn't seem that way. It was always as if there was something behind her eyes she wouldn't say, a secret too powerful to divulge.

But as he looked at her now, her eyes were wide open with everything behind them ready to come out. Her hand stretched to him, and she was ready to show him what it was. But he stayed back, unsure he wanted to see. *What psyche does she have planned?*

As with many of their conversations, she answered his pause as if his thoughts had been spoken. "No psyche, just my hand." She gave it a small shake and he could feel the terror deepening into his bones. "Hold it and look at me. Let the fear go. Embrace the feeling that I know is in you somewhere. My touch will help it come loose."

No. Nothing's coming loose. No good ever came from anything coming loose. At just the thought of touching her, he could already feel the hairs on his arms beginning to stand. He never wished to think about Reela without the fear, for it was the fear that had kept him strong. Without the fear, he'd think about her every second of every minute. He'd do anything to see her, to be with her. Without the fear, he was obsessed with her. What kind of warrior would that make him? *A weak warrior. A woman-chasing warrior who has no dedication to his class.* The kind of warrior he'd seen every day growing up in Trentyre. A warrior he'd promised himself he wouldn't be.

But her eyes were so beautiful it hurt him to see sadness forming there as she waited. His glance went down to her mouth. Never had he seen such inviting lips that called so loudly to be kissed.

"Cleve," she whispered. "What could I possibly do to you?" She kept her hand steady, waiting for him to touch it.

Everything, he thought. *Everything and anything you wanted.* He kept himself away from her hand but decided to let out the truth. Half of him was relieved, the other half screamed for him not to speak.

"You make my heart jump into my throat whenever I think of you. You keep me up at night when I try to sleep. You make me think you're more important than anything else. You make me into someone I'm not, someone weak again, like I was after my parents died. And that makes me hate myself. I've worked so hard to get control of myself after my parents died. But in a blink, all that becomes undone when I see you."

Cleve could feel the pain in her burning eyes. "Don't you see it?" she said imploringly. "That's what love is. That multiplied by a thousand."

"No, love is something else." He shook his head but couldn't take his eyes off her. "It's when you care about someone so much they become more important than anything else." That's what he'd heard, at least.

"Didn't you just say you felt that way about me?"

"That's different. That's not genuine."

"How is it not genuine?"

"Because I don't know *why* I feel that way. I can't understand how you have this effect on me. It feels like a psychic spell. When someone is in love, don't they know why?" He hoped she had a rebuttal he could believe. *I want her to convince me I'm wrong*, he realized, and found himself taking a step closer.

"That's not always true," Reela answered. "Sometimes your body knows what your mind doesn't. Let your body guide you, Cleve. Isn't that what you're good at? Isn't that why you're such a skilled warrior? Why trust your body with a deadly weapon without trusting your own heart? Let go of the barrier you put up. Let it down, even if it's just for right now."

"I can't."

"You're stronger than you think. You can. Just let the fear go."

He took another step to her. The blood pumping from his heart was burning. His head felt clouded, unable to think of anything besides her lips. He fought so hard to stop himself from going toward her.

Just breathe, he told himself. *Think about this. You can stop yourself.* But he'd been trying to stop himself since he'd met her, and he was exhausted.

When his legs did not stop moving toward her, he knew he'd lost, so he embraced the heat boiling within.

He came up to her hand but ignored it, instead wrapping his arms around the bars to place his hands through her hair and onto the back of her head. The last thing he saw before closing his eyes was her lips opening ever so slightly, welcoming him. They locked with his.

He kissed her so hard she gave a soft moan of surprise, but then she pushed just as hard right back. Her hands came up to latch onto his arms, squeezing tighter as they kissed.

His entire world became her mouth. There were no thoughts, nothing but the rhythmic smacking that they created as they frantically closed their lips around each other's. His breathing became heavy, sucking in and out violently through his nose. He noticed the same about her, but she was breathing out through her mouth.

The sweet taste of her breath was mixed with the honey smell of her intoxicating hair, creating an insatiable desire for more of her. The heat in his body was building. Her lips gave him a surge of pleasure that ran down his neck. But it was still not enough. Cleve lost control of himself through a mixture of frustration, excitement, and pleasure, bundled together and spinning wildly somewhere in his chest.

He wanted to break down the bars, throw her onto his small prison bed, and rip off her dress. She bit down on his lip for a quick nibble, then put her tongue in his mouth. He pushed his tongue deep into her mouth, forcing her tongue back playfully. Reela moaned softly and opened her mouth wide to accept him. Soon she pushed back, and their tongues danced together for a few wild breaths before he and Reela returned to locking lips.

They were pushing so hard against each other that it hurt. Or maybe that was just him knowing this was likely to be the last time he'd ever be with her.

Someone was tapping on his shoulder with a stick of some sort. He realized it had been tapping at him for a while now. Then he heard the jailer's voice, again suddenly realizing it had been speaking for some time. "I must take the lady away. We have to escort Rek, and her visiting time is up. Procedures need to be followed."

Reela pulled away, only for a blink, returning immediately for more. He grabbed her face and kissed her hard.

The jailer shook his shoulder. "She needs to go."

Again she leaned away. Her eyes were longing, and Cleve was certain he had the same look for her.

Cleve peeled his body from the metal bars. His heart ached. It could've been from the force he'd used to push himself into the bars, but it didn't seem to fade like the pain in his collar did. It was a deeper ache, a pinch in the back of his heart. It grew worse when he took his eyes off Reela for a moment, so he stared back at her.

Then he noticed muffled hollers from Rek's cell. It sounded like Rek might've been trying to shout at Cleve through the gag. However, later when he was escorted past Cleve's cell and gave a wink, Cleve realized it must've been cheering.

Before Reela left, she grabbed his hands tightly with both of hers and pressed them together so that his palms were flat against each other. He felt weak in her grasp, but he didn't mind it.

"Reela, I—" he started.

"Me, too," she ended. "Whatever it is, me, too."

The last he saw of her was a sad smile.

A few minutes after they were both gone, Cleve heard Captain Mmzaza wake with a snort and walk to the bars. "Ah, the pretty is gone. Did I miss anything?"

A smile came to Cleve that was so wide, he wondered if his cheeks had ever been pushed so far out before. It felt like stretching a muscle that had never been used. He crashed onto the bed. His chest was still heaving in and out.

Perhaps he didn't want to give his mind a chance to take over again, or maybe he just wanted to break the silence. For whatever reason, he asked a strange question to a strange man. It was a question he never would have asked to a person whose answer he never would have cared to hear, but so many *never would haves* had just been broken, so he found no reason to hold on to those that remained.

"What do you think love is, CM?"

"Love, ah, Captain Mmzaza knows about that. Love makes a frail man tough, and a tough man frail. I've known boys who would sail with me into the heaviest storm. They were never scared until they met a woman, had themselves a family. Then what they thought was bravery before, they suddenly thought to be stupidity. The thought of being away from their woman was worse than any storm. So they took different work, safe work."

Captain Mmzaza sat back down on his bed, letting out a long groan. "I've also known the other side of it, boys who were cowards until they had love. One of them was me brother. He hated the water, nothing scared him more. But then his wife became sick with the wet cough, and he didn't have the money they needed for the doctor and his potions. Me brother took a crabbing sail, good money in that. They were to fish for crabs around the Ice Isle. And even though the weather was bad, they went."

Captain Mmzaza stopped to let out a soft burp, then chose to grumble something instead of continuing the story.

"Did something happen to him?" Cleve asked.

"Sure did, he died, but not from that trip. They caught many crabs, made lots of money. He paid for the doctor, wife got better. He was killed in a bar fight, one he started. Love doesn't make ya immune to your own foolishness." He had a bitter grunt of a laugh. "Are ya in love, boy?"

Cleve could feel his mind taking control again. It was feeding him regrets, burying his feelings for Reela. "I hope not," he muttered.

She makes you weak. Don't long for something you can't have. You'll probably never see her again. You shouldn't lose control like that. Imagine if that happened during thoughts of your parents?

He felt a sudden rage storm into him. He balled his fist and sat up. He was ready to fight, but what was his enemy? Then he realized it was these thoughts. *"What are you scared of? Don't be such a coward!"* He wanted to shout it.

It felt like a war was going on within him, his heart against his mind, and if he didn't pick a side it would tear him in half.

So without another thought, he did. *I don't care about logic. I want her.*

A sweet satisfaction started down his neck, moving toward his heart. But before he could truly enjoy his victory, more voices came down the stone hallway. It was two men this time—the jailer and someone else.

When he saw the silhouette of the man, he knew it had to be his uncle. Terren's hair was blonde, although it had begun to turn brown in some spots. Terren combed it to the side, leaving it to hang loosely as long as it was out of his face. After a good bout, it would be spread across his forehead before he pushed it back to the side. His chin was round and small, his nose nothing threatening, but toughness could always be found in his eyes. They were deep into his skull, dark, long, and thin. The jailer walked in front of him, but Cleve still could see most of Terren's face behind the jailer because of his height, which almost matched his own.

"Another visitor for you, Cleve. I've never seen such a popular prisoner."

Captain Mmzaza's face came out for a glance. "Ah, just a man. I was hoping the pretty had returned."

Cleve had hoped for the same. He was unsure how his uncle would react to his reason for being imprisoned. When he'd imagined this moment, he was there because the bow was discovered, not because he'd tried—and failed—to kill Terren's only friend.

"I'll leave you to it." The jailer left.

"What have you heard?" Cleve reluctantly asked his uncle.

"The King told me all of it. I have to say, the rats were the best part." Terren forced a smile. "Rek really is something special, isn't he?"

"Why don't you sound upset?" Cleve asked, beginning to feel confused frustration.

Terren sighed loudly. "I was trying to lighten the mood. You never let yourself feel better when something bad happens, even when others try to cheer you up. Of course I'm upset. But I'm still proud of you."

Cleve figured Terren was talking about not shooting Rek. There was nothing else to be proud about. "Don't be. I would've taken the shot if I'd had one to take. I fell asleep, and Rek found me before I woke. I would've done it. Not that I wanted to."

"You can't be sure of that. It's not like shooting a tree, Cleve. Once you're aiming at a man, it's likely to trigger something deep. Do you remember how many deer you missed before finally hitting one? We both knew you were capable of making the shot, but it took weeks before you finally did. Deep down, you knew you couldn't take the animal's life, so you missed. It wasn't even a conscious decision. Now you think you could shoot a man who you've never met? Do you really think that?"

"If I knew for certain that he was an enemy."

"But you didn't know that about Rek. You couldn't have."

"No, I didn't."

"And I'm proud of you for that, even if the King isn't."

The old seaman poked his head out. "Want to know what Captain Mmzaza thinks?"

"No, we don't care," Cleve answered quickly.

Terren peered around curiously at the other cells. There were four in their hall, two of which were empty now with Rek gone.

The captain continued anyway. "Captain Mmzaza has taken the lives of thousands of fish, but never a man. But if the King said to shoot a man, then Captain Mmzaza would do it."

Again Terren checked the other cells for someone else. "Who is Captain Mmzaza?" Terren finally asked. "And why do we care?"

"Captain Mmzaza is I, the greatest captain of our day. I can guide a ship through any water, any storm."

"Ignore him," Cleve said.

"Right, already decided that as soon as I found out he was talking in third person," Terren replied.

Captain Mmzaza continued, "If the King wants me to drive a ship, I would do it. I would expect some payment, though..."

Terren was now pushing his head through the bars of Cleve's cell. He spoke softly as Captain Mmzaza rambled in the background about something. "Cleve, I wish there was more I could do, but I can't. I never should've let you take that bow."

"They knew I had it even before I moved from your house. They would've found it anyway. Don't blame yourself. It was my choice to keep it all these years, and I don't regret it."

Terren's mouth twisted, and for a breath Cleve couldn't tell if he would yell or whisper. Then Terren gave one quick nod and let out a sad smile. "I'm going to get you back here as soon as possible. It's going to be difficult with the war going on, but I'll find a way to convince the King to bring you back."

He doesn't know King Welson as well as he thinks he does, Cleve realized. "I know." He felt too bad for his uncle to tell him how impossible that would be. "I know you will."

"There's something else I need to speak to you about. King Welson has a mission for first-year students. He just told me about it right before I saw you."

"You were just with him now? Who else was up there?" Cleve wondered if the King would be stupid enough to put Rek in the same room as his Elven brother.

"An Elf and a Krepp. They're coming along on the mission with the first-years and me. The King was too busy to spend any time discussing the Elf and the Krepp with me, though. Says we'll get to know each other soon enough."

Yes, he's going to be too busy for you from now on, especially when you start asking about bringing me back to Kyrro. "You didn't see Rek?"

"I saw him after I spoke to the King. He was gagged, waiting to be brought in. We didn't get to speak. Unfortunately, I don't have a lot of time, so I must get to business. We're supposed to be leaving now. The King wants me to select first-year students for the mission, and I can use your opinion about some of them."

"Why first-years and not more experienced students?"

"Because we need as many for battle as we can, and the first-years aren't ready yet, but some still possess the skill this mission requires. You know the people I'm thinking about bringing because two of them are your roommates. What do you know of Effie Elegin? Her ranks are very good, and we need a mage. Marie Fyremore spoke highly of her."

That's an easy answer. "She's strong and confident, a good mage for any task."

"Good. We also need a chemist who may be familiar with rare plants and Slugari. Jack Rose told me about Steffen Duroby, said he's exceptionally knowledgeable. I met him briefly as you already know, but I didn't learn much about him. What can you tell me now that you know him?"

Cleve gave a sigh as he thought about how he should answer this one. "I don't know about Slugari, but if you're looking for someone knowledgeable, then I doubt you'll find any other first-year who knows as much as he does. Whatever rare plant it is, he'll probably know. I'm not sure how well his decisions are under pressure, however." Cleve thought about the first time they'd met and the rocks Steffen stupidly had thrown at the bear. Cleve was furious at the time, but now he found himself smiling at the absurdity of it. "He might be a bit unorthodox."

"I see," Terren replied. "You probably don't know the first-year warrior I want to take. I don't know anything about him, just that—except for you—he had the highest ranks after evaluation week, and he's brothers with the commander of the King's Guard."

"Alarex," Cleve said when he realized who it was. "I would like to think I know him. You can trust him with any mission. He goes by Alex."

"Great." Terren had one of his rare smiles he would get sometimes when Cleve surprised him during a bout. "I'm happy you've finally made some friends."

Captain Mmzaza whistled. "The boy has trouble with the social life? Don't worry, I'll teach ya some songs and riddles. Captain Mmzaza will show ya how to make friends."

"I can't wait for that," Cleve replied sarcastically. "What is this mission for anyway?"

"We may have an unexpected ally in this war," Terren said. He began explaining the mission to Cleve, ignoring Captain Mmzaza's panicked questions about Kyrro being at war. However, before Terren could finish, the jailer had returned.

When Cleve saw the woman behind the jailer, his heart started beating wildly. It was in that moment he saw Reela's face under the thick, long hair. But as she came closer, he noticed her hair was dark, not light, and she was a whole head shorter than Reela, thinner as well. It couldn't be her.

"Sorry this has taken so long," Jessend Takary said. She wore an enthralling smile.

Captain Mmzaza whistled. "Another pretty! What a day it's been."

Jessend took a quick, indifferent glance at him before turning back to Cleve and continuing. "My captain has been ill and doesn't look to be recovering for a few days more. But I must be going back to Goldram now so my father doesn't worry. Welson Kimard has offered a captain for me to use so mine can rest during the voyage. They say he's a prisoner but not dangerous and a very good captain."

"This is him right here." The jailer pointed at Captain Mmzaza.

No, this can't be happening, Cleve thought. *Anyone else.* But before he could say anything, Captain Mmzaza gave a laugh and a stinging whistle. "No, not dangerous, and very happy to get out early, especially with you, lovely."

"Oh." Jessend Takary was startled but then forced a friendly grin. "How fortunate, two out of three right here. And where is Rek?"

"He's waiting outside the castle, gagged and restrained," the jailer said.

"Wonderful," Jessend said. "If you would please restrain these men and escort them out, we can leave. I'll be outside."

"Certainly," the jailer replied with his eyes falling on Terren. "As soon as I escort this visitor out, the rest will be brought to you. Procedures must be followed."

"Thank you," Jessend said. She made a point to show Cleve a comforting smile before leaving.

Terren's usually hard eyes were now soft with sadness. "This is it, then. I *will* see you again."

They hugged as tightly as the bars allowed. "Yes you will," Cleve promised.

Terren whispered as they still embraced each other, "Behave yourself. The Takary family is a very proud one. Whatever they want you to do, do it. I'll come for you as soon as I can convince the King to let me."

"Just focus on the war. I can handle whatever it is they want me to do in Goldram," Cleve whispered back, knowing any conversation about him with King Welson would be a waste of time. He would find a way back himself and didn't want to worry his uncle with it.

Cleve poked his head out to watch the jailer and Terren walk down the hall.

Then Captain Mmzaza's head snuck out from his cell to block the view. He had a showy grin. "Looks like you're going to be calling me captain after all."

Chapter 50: Confidence
EFFIE

Effie wearily pushed through the door to her campus house. *I don't see how sleep can elude me tonight.*

Marie Fyremore had been working the Group One mages until exhaustion overcame them each day. Effie had never seen so much life out of someone so old.

Her grandmother was a mage, but Effie never saw a spell from her. She liked to knit instead and talk about how she used to impress boys with magic. Marie Fyremore was definitely not like her grandmother.

Marie had a tough voice, and it rang through Effie's mind all the way back from the classroom. *"You can't let an old woman outcast you!"* That was her favorite saying, and she did outcast them, even made it look easy. Her fireballs were impressive, nearly as large as the five-foot-tall metal training dummy. When students were keeled over and searching for breath, she would shoot a gust of hot Bastial wind at them, yelling, "Don't breathe, meditate. Your breath will come back while you regain energy. Do it standing tall. You're an easy target staring at the ground."

Sometimes, Marie would cast "shell" in front of students who were just about to shoot a fireball at their dummies. "If you can't get through this shell, your fire will have no effect on the tough skin of a Krepp!" Then she'd snap her wand and hold the shell there as easily as if it were a simple spell of light.

"Shell" was an emerald green rectangle, always slightly curved toward the student caster Marie chose to block. Its Sartious Energy was translucent and held steady until Marie let her wand rest. Then it would shatter apart like glass, dissolving into the air. Effie hoped her master mage instructor was exaggerating about Krepp skin being tougher than her spell of "shell," because no one could shoot through it, not even Effie. She nearly passed out trying.

Marie Fyremore seemed to push Effie harder than anyone else, perhaps because she'd said she wished to specialize in Sartious Energy, and no other student had said the same.

"Green mages are extremely useful, especially in a time of war," Marie told Effie after their first class. "But to get anywhere with the heavy energy, you have to be completely dedicated. Manipulating the stuff is dangerous. Too much SE flowing through you can stop your heart. I never advise students to take on its study unless they have expert self-control. So I always recommend men stay with Bastial." She laughed and leaned in close. "SE brings its caster an orgasmic feeling when it runs through the body. Have you felt it, dear?"

Effie nodded. She thought she had, at least. She was never sure exactly what it was, and the tingling pleasure had only happened a few times.

"It'll be stronger as you get more powerful. Men have no self-control. Once the pleasure is discovered, it takes over, and their focus is usually lost. They're not used to multiple orgasms, like us," Marie said with a wink.

Effie laughed politely, but truthfully the discussion of orgasms with the old woman was too strange, even for her.

Effie found Steffen reading at the kitchen table when she entered their home. He looked up and closed the book at the sound of her.

"Eff, there's something I need to tell you."

Finally, here it comes. "What is it?" *What have you been hiding from me?*

Steffen sucked in a long breath. "Gabby and I kissed. I think I like her."

Effie let her arms fold over her training gown. "So?"

"So, you're fine with it?"

"Yeah, why not?" She'd kissed many men she thought she liked—Brady being one of them, and she barely knew him. It was actually a shock that Steffen and her sister hadn't kissed before.

Steffen let the air out of his chest. His shoulders slumped in relief as he smiled. "I always thought if your sister and I were together, it would be a major issue."

"It would be," Effie answered. "Wait, you're telling me you're going to start *dating* my sister?"

Steffen's face tightened as if ready for pain. "When you say it like that, it sounds so wrong."

"It sounds so wrong because it is wrong! That's my sister!"

For a breath, all was silent. Steffen kept his eyes on Effie, giving no sign as to what he was going to say next. It seemed as if his fear had morphed into confusion. "But you just said you were fine with it."

"If you think you like her and kissed a few times, sure, fine with me. But actually dating? No." She noticed she was pointing at Steffen like he was a dog that had pooped in the house. Effie knew sometimes it was necessary to be completely straightforward with Steffen, especially in conversations about the opposite sex. Still, she never felt good about it. She took a breath to let out some frustration. "You shouldn't touch her at all until you're sure about the way you feel."

Steffen leaned away from her finger as if it was about to cast a fireball. "What do you mean, until I'm sure about the way I feel?"

"Because you're not even sure if you like her. You're going to mess with her mind and end up really hurting her. You've known her nearly her whole life, and you're still not certain about the way you feel?" *Compared to Reela, who was in here the other day practically writing poetry on the spot as she described what Cleve does to her. Men are the worst.* Effie could feel her eyes rolling, but she tried to stop them, knowing it wouldn't help.

Steffen seemed to be chewing his cheek, avoiding Effie's face.

She decided to take another breath. Feeling calmer, she took Steffen's hand and gave it a gentle squeeze. "Gabby's impressionable to a fault, and for some reason you have a bigger impact on her than anyone else. If you started doing stuff together..." Effie dropped Steffen's hand so she could gesture descriptively as she cringed. "She's already in love with you. It will tear her to pieces if you don't feel the same way. She's technically an adult, but that doesn't mean she really is one. There's a lot she can't handle."

A smile was forming at the corners of Steffen's mouth. It wasn't quite there yet, but Effie knew she'd see it soon. "I think I get it. However, my interpersonal skills have always been below average, so correct me if I'm wrong. Gabby is like a sponge, and we're all like water to her, soaking us up?"

"Yes," Effie nodded at him.

"But I make her wetter than anyone else."

"Yes. Wait...no." *Does he realize what he's saying?*

"No? But she *is* like a sponge?"

"Forget the sponge analogy." Effie held her head for a moment to think. His perplexed expression was starting to frustrate her again. "Just make sure you're completely certain you really like her before you do anything. Otherwise, you'll hurt her."

His hands came up to show that was the last thing he wanted. "Definitely." Guilt seemed to strike his face. "But how do I know if I really like her or not? I think I like her already."

You're asking me, and I don't even know how I feel about Brady with any certainty.

It may have been from the tightness she felt forming in her stomach, or just the pity she had for Steffen, but she suddenly had the urge to share an embrace. She nestled against Steffen's chest, wrapping her arms around his lower back. He returned the hug, and Effie felt warmth spread through her stomach, immediately relieving the tension.

"Reela will know that," Effie said, parting from Steffen. Reela had always been the answer to emotional dilemmas. *And now she's got one of her own,* Effie said to herself, thinking about Cleve.

"Thank you, Effie."

Effie smiled but took his shoulder in a firm grip to let him know how serious she was. "Don't touch Gabby. Don't go to see her. Don't even write to her until you know how you feel. You don't want to give her the idea you feel one way when you actually feel another."

"I understand."

A culminating silence followed.

"Where is Reela? The sun has almost set," Effie asked.

Just as Steffen opened his mouth to speak, they heard the front door unlatch. Reela came through wearing a dress with the colors of Kyrro. It was showier than Effie was used to seeing on her, but the surprise was nothing but pleasant. Effie always wanted her friend to show off her body more. It seemed like a waste not to.

Reela had a tired smile. "Pack your bags, both of you. Headmaster Terren will be here soon." She walked by them toward her room.

"What?" Effie blurted, still thinking about Reela's dress. "Pack our bags?" She turned to check Steffen's expression to see if he understood what Reela was talking about, but his face was squished together just like hers. Effie started after Reela. "Why pack our bags?"

"Because we're leaving for a mission." Reela entered her room, grabbed a backpack, and flipped it over her bed to make sure it was empty. "Pack light," she said without a look back. "We're walking about eighty miles there and eighty miles back. We may be gone a fortnight or more."

Effie stood next to Steffen in Reela's doorway. They watched in confused silence as Reela went to her wardrobe and started palming through it. She stopped suddenly and looked over her shoulder at them. "Get started, will you?"

"Reela." Effie held up her hands in an attempt to stop her. "How do you know any of this?"

Reela halted for a breath and then spoke a burst of rapid sentences without the slightest pause. "I went to Oakshen to get my mother and took her to the castle in Kyrro City to translate for the Elf and Krepp. While she was translating, I found out they had Cleve in the dungeons, so I went down to visit him. Then I met with my mother outside the castle to find out what she knew, and then I started back to the Academy and saw Terren on the way there." She took one quick breath. "We started talking about Cleve and then everything else. I got Terren to tell me about this mission and convinced him that I would be helpful to bring along. He's at Alex's house right now, then he's coming here."

When they didn't move, Reela put her hands on her hips. "Get started."

Again Effie was lost. She looked over and found Steffen to be the same.

"Cleve's in prison?" they both asked at once.

"Yes, I'll explain everything later." Reela fluttered her hand, turning her attention to her backpack. "I told Terren we would be ready to leave when he gets here, so pack while I talk about the mission."

Effie gave in and went to her room. There were clothes everywhere, so finding her backpack wasn't as easy as it was for Reela. She rummaged around for it as Reela started talking again.

"The reason the Krepps joined with Tenred is because the Krepps believe we know where the underground Slugari are. The Krepps have been searching for the underground colony to take it over, enslave the Slugari, and feed upon them. They sent someone to deliver a threat to King Welson that stated if we don't give up the underground colony's location, they'll attack us."

Steffen shouted from his room, "That was the Krepp and Elf we saw going through the Academy?"

Effie had heard the news of this Krepp and Elf but nothing more than that. She listened carefully, eager for more.

"No," Reela answered as Effie heard her door close, likely to change out of her dress. "The Krepp and the Elf are allies with us," Reela shouted from behind the door. "They intercepted the messenger the Krepps had sent, but they didn't know what he was doing until they questioned him. The messenger tried to kill one of them, for they're both enemies of the Krepps. Luckily, the messenger failed and ran, leaving the scroll with them. They brought it through the Fjallejon Pathway, and the Fjallejons sent a pigeon to the castle because the pair looked suspicious. Guards came to pick them up, heard their story, and escorted them to the castle to meet with the King."

"The Krepp spoke our language, Effie!" Steffen added from his room. "And the Elf is a psychic, a very strong one. Leonard is still calm after whatever the Elf did to him."

Effie finished stuffing all the socks, undergarments, and other clothes she could fit in her bag. She went down their short hallway and stood in Steffen's doorway. He was holding his pet rat in his cupped hands.

"I need to bring Leonard to a friend's house so she can keep him fed while we're gone," he announced.

"She?" Effie teased. "You have a friend who's a girl?"

"Yeah, Marratrice. She's in my class, hates running, loves potions, and likes Leonard, even though he did try to bite her nose once. I'll do it as we're leaving."

Effie heard Reela's door open.

"Once Reela tells us where we're going," Effie said, turning to find her friend standing behind her and buttoning the last few buttons of her black shirt.

"We're going to the underground Slugari colony," Reela answered.

Steffen put Leonard back in his cage. "I thought we didn't know where it was?"

"We don't," Reela answered, raising her eyebrows. "But the Elf does. He and the Krepp were on the way there when they saw the messenger. He hasn't ever met the Slugari, only sensed their presence below ground with psyche." Reela put a hand on Steffen's shoulder. "Terren was instructed to bring a chemist who's familiar with the caregelow plant that's rumored to be with the Slugari, so I told him while we walked that you're definitely that chemist. You're supposed to bring scrolls and pens to document what you find and get samples if they allow it."

Steffen's mouth dropped open and his eyes widened. "They trust such a task to a first-year chemist?"

It didn't seem nearly as special to Effie, and it must not have to Reela, either, because she shrugged. "Terren says they're only taking first-years because we're capable but also less useful in a battle. The Academy may be attacked while we're gone. Marie Fyremore will be the temporary head while Terren is away. He says she's more than capable."

"She is," Effie agreed. "So it's obvious why the encyclopedia is going. What about me? What's my role in this?"

"Extra protection, light when we need it, fire for camp." Reela took Effie's hands in hers. Only then did Effie realize how excited she was starting to feel. It was making her heart race, spreading quickly over her body. "There are no other mages coming, just you. Terren isn't all that familiar with first-years, but he spoke to Cleve, who recommended you both."

The mention of Cleve made them quiet. Her excitement dulled. Effie gave a look to his empty bedroom across from Steffen's. *Reela will explain what's happening with him,* she reminded herself.

Effie was glad Cleve felt that he knew her well enough to recommend her. He'd never seen her use any advanced spells, just Bastial light here and there around the dark house at night. However, she'd never seen him use a weapon, either, and that didn't matter. She knew how strong he was just by being around him. It was the way he carried himself, the words he chose. She could feel his passion to improve in everything he did. *He must have figured the same about me,* Effie liked to think. *It's funny how you can know certain things about someone without ever witnessing them.*

"He'll be back, Reela?" Steffen asked.

Effie could hear Reela gulp before letting out the soft cough of her throat clearing. "He will. I'll tell you more as we walk," she answered quietly.

I've never heard Reela answer a question with so little confidence. It made Effie's nerves bundle and twist.

"I'm glad," Steffen answered happily, seemingly unaware of Reela's tone. "But before Terren gets here, will you let us know ultimately what the King wants with the Slugari? Don't tell me he's verifying their location so we can give it away to the Krepps. That will lead to the destruction of their race. The Krepps have already driven the Elves away, but the Slugari don't have the same ability to run. They'll be wiped out. Killed, cooked, and eaten, all of them. We can't let that—"

"Calm yourself." Reela patted his shoulder. "We don't even know where the Krepps are even if we wanted to tell them the location of the Slugari. The Elf and Krepp who've come here have convinced the King that the Slugari have ways to help us with this war. It's just as important to the Slugari as it is to us for the Krepps and Tenred to be defeated. We're going to bring them to our side and find a way to stop this war together—he's here." Reela started toward the door. Effie and Steffen followed.

Just as Terren began to knock, Reela opened the door.

"The Elf and Krepp are waiting outside the northern walls," Terren said without preamble. By the rough look in his eyes, Effie figured he was probably not one for formalities. "Did you explain everything?" he asked Reela.

"Yes, we're ready. Steffen just needs to leave his rat at someone's house."

Terren's mouth straightened. "Make it fast. We have ten miles to walk if we wish to spend our first night in a friend's cabin in Corin Forest. Otherwise, we're sleeping in the middle of the Fjallejon Pathway."

"Ten miles!" Steffen blurted. "It will be night in a few hours."

"Are you telling me you can't walk ten miles?" Terren said with an edge to his voice.

"I can walk ten miles, but—"

"Good," Terren interrupted. "We'll meet you at the north gate. Go."

Steffen hustled out the door with his cloth bag bouncing around his back and his rat's cage swinging in his hand.

So this is what a warrior instructor is like, Effie thought. *This explains a lot about Cleve.*

But just then, Terren surprised Effie with a warm smile. "Ready?" he asked nicely. It was like she was seeing a different person.

"Yes, Headmaster Terren," Effie answered.

"Terren is fine," he said, turning to start toward the north gate.

Effie and Reela followed him for a step, but Effie stopped to lock the door behind her. When she turned back, she met Reela's eyes.

They spoke to Effie, but she couldn't tell what they were saying. Then Reela pushed out her hand from her waist, fingers extended, and Effie knew what it was: *We'll be safe with each other.* Effie took it with her own hand. A warm comfort came through her, setting the corners of her mouth up in a wide smile.

Chapter 51: Strangers and Handshakes
ZOKE

Five Humans, there they were, close enough to spit at—three men and two women. Two of the men were taller than him and Vithos, but the one with sandy hair seemed to be in charge. He had an extra bag tied on to the bottom of his backpack. When he came through the gate, he knelt to untie it, and the other Humans watched and waited.

Zoke and Vithos stood in silence, waiting for the Humans to approach. The one in charge pulled open his second bag and took out bread and dried meat, distributing it among the others. Then he walked to them, his eyes hard and set. If he was half as uncomfortable as Zoke, then he hid it well.

He led with a loaf of bread. "You speak common tongue?" he asked Zoke.

"Yes," Zoke answered, accepting the gift. "But the Elf doesn't."

"Will you translate for me?" the Human asked.

"Yes," Zoke said again, ripping the bread and handing half to Vithos.

The man held out his hand vertically, like he was pointing at Zoke's stomach with all five clawless fingers. "My name is Terren. What are your names?"

"Mine is Zoke, his is Vithos." He then translated for Vithos.

"Why is his hand out like that?" Vithos asked Zoke in Kreppen, the only language he knew.

Zoke asked Terren about it. The Human's mouth tightened into a grin, and his hand fell back to his side. By then, the rest of the Humans had circled around. Of the three men, one had black hair and a light brown beard that was almost red. Zoke noticed him first because he was carrying a cage with a bird in it that struck Zoke as strange.

"When we meet someone, we usually shake hands," Terren said.

Zoke translated.

"Then we should shake our hands," Vithos said. "We are in

Human company. We shouldn't insult them." Vithos extended his fingers and waggled both his hands. Zoke couldn't understand why the Humans would want to do that, but he joined Vithos in moving his hands back and forth through the air.

A few of the Humans started to laugh. Then Zoke recognized the taller of the two girls. She had fair skin like Vithos. Her hair had the same brightness as his as well, except it was lighter in color and far thicker and wavier. *She was the one who touched Vithos,* Zoke realized. *She said she knew him.*

She was the first to open her hands and wiggle them like Zoke and Vithos before the rest of the Humans joined in. It brought no pleasure to Zoke, but all the Humans seemed to find it funny. Their smiles were like that of a Krepp, but their mouths were half the size and with white, dull teeth. They looked more like Vithos than any Krepp, except for their ears, which were small and round, at least the ears that weren't covered by hair.

As each stopped shaking, Terren started introducing the others. He pointed to one Human at a time, saying a name and giving Zoke and Vithos a chance to repeat it. The oddest name was the first one, which Zoke heard as *"Owl-licks."* But when he asked the man with the birdcage how his name was spelled, he replied with the letters "A, l, e, x." That made it easier to realize his mistake. Alex had a sword on his belt, as did Terren.

The others were easy to pronounce: *Reela, Effie, and Steffen.* While all the Humans had a bag on their backs, the shorter trio introduced last had no weapons, except Reela, who had just a small dagger on her belt. It was confusing why the two taller male Humans had swords while the other three Humans didn't. Every Krepp carried a sword or a bow when traveling.

The smallest was Effie, who had dark hair, and was short and very thin. There was something about her that reminded Zoke of Zeti, a confidence in the way she carried herself, perhaps. She had something latched onto her belt, but it wasn't a dagger. It was like a stick in the shape of a thin rod but unlike any wood he'd ever seen. It was black and sleek with a sturdy look about it. He pointed at it and asked.

She drew it gracefully with three fingers as if it was as light as a feather. "This is a wand," she said.

A wand, of course. Zoke had read about them but hadn't

recognized it right away. "You're a mage?"

"Yes," she answered, putting her wand back in its place.

"I was told we can find the Slugari in northern Satjen?" Terren asked.

"Yes," Zoke answered and then translated for Vithos.

"Tell them we want to get there as soon as we can," Vithos said. Zoke translated.

"We do as well," Terren replied. "You lead and we'll follow."

And so their introductions had ended. Zoke was pleased that the Humans didn't ask many questions. He had a feeling he would need to explain what had led him and Vithos here, but he was glad that didn't have to happen yet. Although familiar with the language, Zoke was reluctant to reveal so much before he understood more about the Humans. He needed some sort of clue as to what kind of reputation his story would give him among this race.

He and Vithos walked in front while the Humans trailed a few yards behind, talking amongst themselves. They seemed to be having a conversation about someone with the name "Cleve." Zoke didn't give it any thought.

Soon, they reentered the Fjallejon Pathway that he and Vithos had crossed through that morning. It was where they met the small brown men who made them wait for guards to come escort them the rest of the way to the King of Kyrro.

"I think it's time I learn some common tongue," Vithos said.

Zoke agreed, but he was barely still on his feet after everything that had happened that day. Not only had they walked more than twenty miles already, translating all day hadn't been easy. He wasn't used to talking and listening at the same time, which seemed to be expected of him by the Humans, who wouldn't wait for him to finish translating to Kreppen before they continued talking.

"Yes, I wish we'd known to start your training weeks ago," Zoke told Vithos. "I'll give you a few words to practice for tonight, but I'm too tired for any more than that."

He thought back to the first book he'd ever had on the language. It was obviously written by a Human who'd learned Kreppen because its style was unlike any other book Zoke had seen. Its first twenty pages were dedicated to charts of grammar, tenses, key words, and notes about pronunciation. The rest of it was divided into sections labeled as chapters. There were sometimes little numbers next to a word, and at the bottom of the page the number would show up again with some note next to it. It was overwhelming at first, but as he started to learn phrases, it became addicting.

In the market a few years later, someone was trading a book about common tongue that was different from his. Other Krepps didn't have an interest in it, so he was able to get it for just a wooden spoon. He quickly realized this one had been written by a Krepp because there were no charts, no notes, and no chapters. It was basically a list of translations that started with words and eventually led to phrases. It was the kind of writing he'd expected upon opening the first book, but now that he had seen both, he discovered the one written by the Human was superior in teaching him the language. It gave him more respect for the race that all Krepps thought of as weaker.

One of the Humans approached, and Zoke tried to remember his name. He was the shortest of the three men, the one of equal height to Zoke.

"Mind if I ask you a question?" he asked. Each of the Humans had a soft tone compared to Krepps. It sounded like their voices were coming from the tops of their throats instead of their stomachs, making them higher pitched and feeble.

The name came back to him. "Steffen," Zoke said to practice it. Saying words aloud had always been his method of learning common tongue. "You can ask."

Steffen seemed to hold an excited smile. "I read a lot of history, but there is none written about Krepps and Humans interacting. Obviously, some Humans and Krepps must have met before because there are some books about the Kreppen language, and we use the same measurement system. Did you learn our language from a book as well, or from a Human?"

He wasn't sure why the Human was interested, but he found no reason not to answer his question. "I learned from books. Most Krepps never meet Humans, this is true."

"I see. I was wondering something else, also." Steffen's voice was even softer now, somewhat fearful even, as if he could be hurt easily by Zoke's answer. "What do Krepps think about Humans?"

His tone made Zoke think twice about what words to use. "Humans have soft skin, easily cut, easily hurt, but you're good builders." He would have said Humans were weak, frail, that they stood little chance against Krepps in battle, but something held him back. He thought Steffen might not be able to endure those words, as true as they were.

The answer seemed to satisfy Steffen, whose head was lowered and nodding subtly. "Do you wonder what Humans think of Krepps?" he asked with a look from the side of his eye. It seemed as if Steffen was barely holding back a stare.

"I haven't wondered about that," Zoke answered honestly. Humans were interesting, the way they could build monumental castles even though they themselves were frail. But he'd never once wondered what they thought of Krepps. It had never seemed like something that mattered, and it still didn't. War would be fought no matter if the Humans hated the Krepps or loved them. "Why are you curious about what Krepps think of Humans?"

Steffen scratched his head with a finger. "I'm not sure." He started to say something else, only to close his mouth and rest his hand on his forehead. "I don't know. I guess right now it wouldn't make a difference no matter what Krepps thought of us. But I'm still curious."

"Is it normal for Humans to be curious and unable to explain why?" Zoke asked. There was nothing in his book about that. It seemed like a major flaw with their race. Krepps were born with curiosity, but it faded as they got older. It was never looked at as a valuable trait. Hunting, leatherworking, learning a weapon, these were seen as important, and curiosity had nothing to do with any of them. Curiosity usually just led to injury. Their children were taught not to act upon it.

Steffen let out a soft humming sound. "It might be," he said. "Curiosity is a strange thing. Often I can't explain it, but then again I'm not good at understanding my feelings, at least that's what I've been told." His tone changed like he'd just lost a fight. He let out air loudly and slowed down to walk with the other Humans.

Humans seem to be confused easily, Zoke thought.

While he never had issues understanding his own feelings, there *was* something else he'd had much difficulty with, and he was just reminded of it again—the question of whether he was a traitor. He couldn't seem to get it out of his mind.

When Nebre had called him a coward, he knew that to be untrue. It was the word "traitor" that he couldn't let go of as easily. *"You must be a traitor to let Vithos live all this time."* Zoke could still hear him screaming it every time thoughts of his old friend came to him. *"I'm the one who fought. I'm the one who tried to kill the Elf. You would rather be a traitor than risk your life for the tribe."* Zoke wished he could go back to that moment after he'd wrestled Nebre off Vithos. He had an easy answer for the accusations, now that he'd had time to think about it.

"Vithos doesn't deserve to die." It was as simple as that. He felt stupid for needing four days since the incident to realize it.

It made him a traitor. He couldn't deny it any longer. He fit the definition.

Every Krepp is taught that traitors deserve to die, so he never would have thought he'd be one.

It's not like being a traitor happened by accident. You had to do something malicious to the tribe as a whole, like attack Doe or Haemon, assault a chief, sabotage the farms, or prevent the Slugari from being found. Siding with someone who was a traitor was just as bad. *And traitors deserve to die*—Zoke even had believed it himself until recently. *But Vithos doesn't deserve to die, and neither do I, although we're both traitors.*

But Doe and Haemon...he had different thoughts about them.

Chapter 52: We
ZOKE

After half a mile into the Fjallejon Pathway, Zoke heard voices somewhere within the mountain. It sounded like an unseen Human was shouting at another. Then there was the distinct sound of steel clanking. Both sounds together created an image of a blacksmith screaming at someone while hammering on a hot sword.

Some thoughts later, he realized there were actually more than two voices. He heard distant screams, some of anger, others of anguish. The sound of steel became clearer, and he realized he heard swords clashing.

The Human leader halted. "Stop, listen."

Zoke gave a small tug on Vithos' arm to stop him.

"We're under attack," the leader said with urgency in his voice.

Terren, that's his name, Zoke remembered. Utterly confused, he looked around and saw no one. "If we're under attack, where are our enemies?"

"On the mountaintop!" Terren's voice was loud and low. "Alex, take out the pigeon." Terren pulled a small scroll and pen from a pouch on his belt. "Hopefully, they already sent one from up there, but in case they couldn't, we're telling the castle about the attack."

Alex set down the cage, unlatched its door, and grabbed the bird with both hands. Terren wrapped the scroll around one of the pigeon's legs, and then Alex threw the bird into the air. It flew back the way they'd come, rising higher as it went until it disappeared over the mountains.

"Leave the empty cage. Everyone follow me and hurry. There's a way up in a tunnel ahead." Terren sprinted past Zoke.

Steffen and the others were running after him. "I thought the only way to the mountaintop was going miles around to the east?" Steffen's tone had a mixture of panic and confusion.

Zoke kept close to them, translating for Vithos as best he could. He still didn't know what Terren meant when he said they were under attack because he found no one in sight. He started to believe that by the word *"we,"* Terren was referring to Humans somewhere atop the mountain and not specifically to their group.

"There's a reason you thought that," Terren told Steffen while they followed the mountain path along a tight twist, their bags shaking violently as they ran. "The passage up the mountain is supposed to be kept from Tenred. Best way to make sure of that is for as few people as possible to know about it. It was designed so that we could quickly offer support to the Fjallejons if they were attacked."

After another turn, a tunnel came into view. It was created by both sides of the mountains coming together ten feet from the ground. The tunnel had been dark when Zoke and Vithos were escorted through it that morning. By now, with night upon them, it was pitch black.

"Effie!" Terren shouted over the sounds of battle echoing in circles around them. "Get us some light, bright as you can."

A burst of yellow exploded from her wand. It was too much to look at, so Zoke turned away.

"Find a crevice between rocks," Terren told them, sweeping his hands along a wall.

Within the tunnel, there were countless crevices along the walls. Zoke frantically felt each one nearby, but they were all too small to stick more than a hand through.

"It's a low gap we need to find," Terren added. "About half the height of a Fjallejon."

Zoke explained it to Vithos. They each stomped down the tunnel, swinging their heads left and right to search for a big enough opening. The Humans were doing the same.

Zoke soon realized that if he was more than a few steps from the mage, there was no point in looking. Only around her was there enough light to see a claw's distance into the black crevices littered throughout the walls.

"Tenred is attacking the Fjallejons?" Steffen asked.

"No, the Fjallejons should be hiding within the mountain," Terren said. "They'll be safe as long as our men still stand. The King sent warriors and mages to guard this pathway. He figured Tenred would want to take control, as it's the only way through the mountains, looks like he was right. They could be dying up there. Find that crevice! Effie, more light over here."

The mage ran to him, leaving Zoke and Vithos in sudden

darkness.

"Wait!" Vithos shouted in common tongue. It was one of the few words Zoke had taught him. Effie slid to a stop and came back with the rest of the Humans following.

Vithos was pointing at the wall. But from where Zoke was, it just looked like he was pointing at rock. Then Vithos squatted as low as possible and edged into the wall, disappearing from view.

"Good work, Vithos," Terren said, following on his hands and knees because he was too big to fit otherwise. "Effie behind me, we need light in here! Alex behind her. Reela and Steffen, stay here in the tunnel."

"I can fight," Reela said as she squatted to follow Effie. Steffen stood motionless with unblinking eyes.

"Fine," Terren replied. "Just stay with me."

Zoke was last in, leaving Steffen by himself. Zoke was wider than the Humans, barely able to squeeze through, and not at all with the bow around his shoulder. He had to push it through first, then his quiver, and squeeze himself through last.

The crevice opened into a stairway that had been carved out of the mountain. Inside, the walls and ceiling were only a foot wider than the opening he'd barely managed to fit through. Zoke had to keep his back bent while he climbed the stairs, but he saw it was the same for Reela in front of him.

The walkway was so dark it seemed to devour light. From the mage's glow, he could see the steps well enough when they were four ahead. But by the time he stepped on them, they'd disappeared into the blackness.

They climbed hundreds of steps. At one point, Reela slipped and fell out of the light, and Zoke heard the sound of her flesh slapping against stone. The noise itself was quiet, but it still gave him a start, perhaps because it had been the only disruption to the muffled interminable battle cries that had been growing louder as they progressed.

Zoke almost stepped on her but managed to shoot his foot to the side instead. Once over her, he looked down, but she'd disappeared into the black. He reached his hands into it to find her and scooped her up. He threw one hand on her back as she rose to make sure she didn't go too high.

"Roof is low," he said.

"Thank you," she replied.

The woman's flesh was so soft that if he'd used his claws at all they would have melted right into her. It made him sigh. *These Humans don't stand a chance in a battle against Krepps, and here I am fighting beside them.*

"Zoke!" Vithos was shouting from the front, but Zoke couldn't see past Reela.

"What?" he shouted back in Kreppen.

"Ask them what the enemies look like compared to allies. I need to know in order to help."

So he asked. Terren shouted back to him, "Humans of Kyrro will be in light blue. Can't say what the enemies are wearing until I see them. Colors of Tenred are black and red, though. It will most likely be that."

Zoke translated for Vithos.

The unmistakable sounds of killing and dying grew to a roar.

"No more light, Effie," Terren said after the final turn that brought them to the top of the enclosed stairway. "Keep your voices down."

After her light went out, there was still just enough illumination to see the stone beneath Zoke's feet. Looking for the source of the light, he found a wall ahead that was shrouded in darkness except at its bottom, where light was seeping into their cave.

From outside, one Human's voice came through louder than the sound of steel and screams. "Fall back to the tunnel. Fall back, Kyrro!" Then boots stampeded from Zoke's left to his right.

Vithos bravely started toward the small opening until Terren tugged on his shirt. "Wait," Terren said loudly enough for them all to hear through the sound of the boots outside. Zoke didn't need to translate. Vithos stopped on his own.

"Effie, Reela." Terren turned to them, crouching to let down his bag and check on a knife strapped to his ankle. "You're not trained for battle. Inside our own walls is one thing, but I don't know what's out there. I can't force you into such an unpredictable situation when you have no experience fighting." His eyes lifted to Zoke. "Zoke and Vithos, I don't know what kind of training you have, but you're not forced to come. If I don't return, keep going to the Slugari."

Effie and Reela spoke at once: "I'm coming with you."

Zoke finished translating and asked Vithos what he wanted to do.

"We're with Kyrro now," the Elf told him. "We can no longer

choose our battles, just change their result."

He was somewhat surprised to find his friend so dedicated to Kyrro. It almost seemed as if Vithos wanted to prove that he was no traitor—that just because he'd switched sides once didn't mean he was likely to turn again. *He never got to choose his side in the first place,* Zoke realized. *He was forced into the tribe through false information. Now, he must've chosen a side, and he isn't one to change his mind. Never has been.*

Zoke didn't feel the same. Yes, being with the Humans for now was his best option, but that could change. He even saw himself back with Zeti and the other Krepps in the future. *Does that make me more of a traitor than Vithos? I cannot let that be.*

"We're fighting as well," Zoke told the Humans.

A light broke in behind them. Zoke spun with his sword ready only to find Steffen making the last turn into their cave with some sort of glowing object in his hand. "So am I," he said.

"Put out that light!" Terren whispered loudly. "What is that?"

Steffen turned his hand upside down. The liquid became a glowing waterfall, going out as soon as it hit the ground. "Just a potion. The stairs were too dark without it."

"You don't even have a weapon!" Terren's whisper had become angry. "Stay here. Everyone else, follow me and stay together."

Without waiting for a response, Terren drew his sword and crept past Vithos. As Zoke followed, he could hear Steffen behind him fumbling through his bag.

To squeeze under the opening, the Humans needed to lie down and crawl through. A dismal realization popped into Zoke's thoughts when he was lowering himself to the ground to follow: *How will Kyrro know I'm on their side? The moment they see a Krepp, they'll attack.*

The opening put them into a small cove. Tall edges of the mountain came up on all sides except in front of them, where there was a thin crevice—the only way out.

Terren was leaning into the crevice for a glimpse. Then he snapped back, pushing everyone behind him until they were all clustered around Zoke in the opposite corner.

"Do you hear all the men rushing this way?" Terren gestured toward the crevice. His voice was a loud whisper. "They're from Tenred, possibly a hundred or more. They're running past us, chasing our allies into a tunnel."

Zoke did hear them going past, but the sounds of their shoes against the stone had begun to quiet. The noise of battle moved with them, stopping somewhere past the opening to their cove.

"You see this tall mountaintop?" Terren pointed to a triangular peak jetting into the sky a hundred feet ahead of them. "The mountain flats up here stretch for miles, but many natural gaps in the stone make it so only one route is available between two points. There's a tunnel through that tall mountaintop. It's the only way from our current side to the other side of that peak. Kyrro has been pushed back through the tunnel, and Tenred is following through from our side. That means we're behind the enemy."

Steffen crawled through the crevice they were huddled around. He and Terren exchanged some words in a stern tone, but Zoke was too busy translating for Vithos to catch it.

"Tell them I'll stun the enemies," Vithos said. "We'll all run in and finish them off before I'm drained of energy."

"And how long can you manage to stun them all? There are over a hundred men," Zoke asked.

"Not long for that many, I admit. Maybe enough to cut down twenty. If I had more time to rest it could be more."

"But there's no time."

"What are you talking about with Vithos?" Terren asked.

"He wants to run in first," Zoke said in common tongue, "and stun them all with psyche," Zoke quickly continued before Terren could consider it. "But he won't be able hold the spell for long. The moment it wears off, they'll turn and swarm us."

"Unless they can't find us," Steffen added. He held a glass bottle in each hand. "Mix these together and it'll create enough smoke to make the whole mountain look ablaze."

A quick silence followed with everyone's eyes on Terren.

"How certain are you the potion will work?" Terren asked, reaching for the bottles.

"Absolutely certain," Steffen replied.

"Fine. Vithos and I will go in first," Terren said, pointing to the crevice that led out of their cove. "Alex close behind, watching our rear for anyone coming for us. Effie and Zoke, we need you both looking for archers off to the sides. Take them out. Otherwise, we'll be shot down as soon as the smoke clears. Reela with Effie, Steffen with Zoke."

Terren had transitioned into a plan so quickly Zoke didn't understand how his mind could work that fast. Then, he remembered Terren had mentioned training for situations like this.

A chill ran down his back. *Humans may be more prepared for battle than I thought.*

Zoke gave the dagger from his belt to Steffen and readied his bow.

"Steffen," Terren said. "How long does the smoke take to work?"

"It'll start smoking the moment you pour one bottle into the other."

"Fine. Listen, everyone." Terren leaned toward them and moved a glance through each of their eyes. "If we don't kill the attackers from Tenred, it could be us and the rest of our allies behind that mountaintop who die. You can't hesitate when you get an opportunity to take out an enemy. Some of them will be women, but the moment you give them a chance, they'll burn your nipples off with a fireball. Tenred isn't going to think twice about driving a knife through Effie or Reela's stomach, so don't do the same for them."

"What's he saying?" Vithos whispered.

"Kill or be killed," Zoke replied.

"It takes so many words for that?" Vithos was surprised.

"And don't let your nipples get burned off," Zoke added to give some credit to Terren's inspiring speech, but Vithos just glanced down at his chest curiously.

"On my lead," Terren said, walking toward the opening.

Terren mixed the bottles, peeked out, and heaved the mixture. He spun back behind cover to wait, readying his sword.

Zoke noticed everyone tensing their muscles. They were still, waiting for the order from their leader. Zoke looked to Vithos and received a nod from the Elf.

"Endure," Vithos whispered.

"Endure," Zoke replied, feeling a rush of strength that set his eyes hard and ready.

Chapter 53: Smoke
ZOKE

Zoke never heard the sound of the smoke potion breaking. The clatter of steel was too loud for that. But then, like the dying swell of thunder, the clatter faded into nothing.

A wave of panic replaced it, growing louder with each breath Zoke took. The Humans were shouting unintelligibly, and many of them began coughing.

Terren held three fingers...two...one. Upon dropping the last finger, he darted out with Vithos and Alex behind him.

Zoke ran out next with Steffen trailing him, adrenaline erasing all fear. He was hungry for blood.

Zoke quickly realized the smoke did look like that from fire but far thicker. There was an enormous cloud of it in front of the tunnel. It was spreading in every direction, leaving only a few Humans outside of its reach—archers and mages, from what Zoke could see. *My targets*, he said to himself. Time was against them. He knew he had to be merciless. Otherwise, the smoke would clear and Vithos would be slain along with the rest of them.

The Elf and the two tall male Humans already had disappeared into the smoke. He could hear screams of death but saw nothing of it. Zoke darted left out of the cove, putting him on the opposite side of the smoke as Effie and Reela.

He lost sight of the archers and mages he'd found earlier. The smoke had engulfed them. He pulled Steffen farther toward the outskirts of the smoke and found an archer moving in the same direction to escape it.

Zoke readied his bow and shot. The arrow whizzed by his target's shoulder. Zeti had always been better with the bow. He was tempted to throw it down and run at them with his sword, but his target—along with two others coming out of the smoke—turned and found him. They scrambled to load arrows.

"Go to the smoke!" he shouted to Steffen. They dashed toward it, getting inside just as he heard an arrow fly by. He gave the bow to

Steffen and the quiver as well. "Watch behind us," Zoke said, drawing his sword.

"I don't know how to use this!" Steffen replied.

"Pointy end of arrow goes out, pull back string, and aim."

Zoke moved toward where he'd seen the archers last. He'd never been in smoke so thick. He couldn't see farther than he could spit, so he tried to listen instead, but coughing and dying were in every direction. There was no way to hear anything else.

He came behind a male Human wearing a black leather tunic with red stars. *Tenred,* Zoke knew, remembering what Terren had said about their colors. The Human was frantically looking in every direction, eventually turning to see Zoke and Steffen.

"A Krepp?" he spoke barely loud enough to hear. After the initial shock, his eyes tightened, and he scrambled to load an arrow. But Zoke ran to him before he could shoot, slicing his sharp sword across the Human's chest. The blade severed the man's bow and cut open his tunic as well. Without a thought, Zoke took another swing at his neck, taking his head clean off.

"Behind!" Steffen shouted as he fumbled with an arrow.

Zoke spun around to find a man with a black robe pointing a wand at them. It started to glow just as Haemon's claws would before he burned a Krepp. Zoke saw he was too far from the mage to stop him, and Steffen's arrow had fallen in his attempt to load it. Without thinking, he turned his back and jumped in front of Steffen to protect him from the fireball.

It felt like a giant had ripped a tree from the ground, lit it on fire, and slammed it into Zoke's back. The force of it picked him up off his feet for a blink, knocking him into Steffen and sending them both to the ground for a roll.

Dazed, Zoke slipped getting to his feet. He managed it the second time and looked back, but the mage was out of view for the moment.

Just after turning back to give Steffen a glance, Zoke saw him driving his knife into the stomach of someone. It was a man in Tenred garb holding a sword over his head. Another heartbeat and that sword would have been stuck down across Zoke's chest.

The attacker fell to his knees, letting the sword drop. Steffen took a step away, leaving the dagger within his enemy. Zoke grabbed the man's sword with his free hand and held it toward Steffen. He wouldn't accept it. He might not even have seen it. Steffen's eyes were locked on the man he'd just stabbed. Without any time to spare, Zoke checked again on the mage but found no one. His back was raw, stinging with pain.

"Take it," Zoke said, forcing Steffen's hands around the sword hilt.

By then the smoke was no longer thickening but starting to clear instead.

No, not yet. Zoke dashed toward where the mage had shot him, only to find a burned corpse on the ground.

With the smoke thinning, Zoke could see farther now and spotted Effie and Reela ahead of him. They were backing up toward him, looking somewhere else.

Rushing forward, Zoke soon saw what they did—three men with swords trudging their way. Zoke leapt in front of them with his sword pointed. The three enemies stopped and whipped back their heads.

"What are you doing here, Krepp?" one of them asked.

"He's the short one with the Elf. The traitors," another answered. "We're to watch for them after taking the pathway."

"Good," the first replied. "That makes our job easier." He came at Zoke.

The Human may have been taller, but his strength was half what Zoke was used to. The man screamed and swung his sword in an overhead arc. Zoke blocked the blow with his sword and kicked his attacker back with a hard heel to his stomach.

The other two came from either side, raising their swords to attack at once. A fireball flew past Zoke's shoulder into one of them, and the other dropped his weapon and fell to his knees, groaning with pain.

Zoke drove his sword through the chest of the one who'd fallen and then looked over toward the one hit by the fireball. He was dead.

The last one was the first man to attack them. He ran toward them valiantly with his sword high, but he too stopped, crying out in pain and dropping his weapon. His scream was cut short when an arrow zoomed past Zoke and into the enemy's chest.

Zoke turned around to check on the three Humans behind him. Effie had her wand out, Reela's hand was propelled forward, and Steffen had two shaking hands on the bow as if letting go could kill him.

"I didn't take the sword," Steffen said with a quiet, startled tone.

"Keep the bow. It's yours," Zoke answered. He'd always wanted a good reason to get rid of it. "The smoke is clearing. We must hurry to find the other archers and mages."

With the others following him, Zoke ran toward the outer reaches of the smoke, figuring those with long-range weapons would try to stay out of it.

He was right. He found five enemies—four archers and a mage. They were clustered together fifty feet from Zoke and had searching eyes. Steffen and the others emerged from the smoke to join him. That's when they were spotted. One of the archers pointed, and they all aimed their weapons.

"Effie!" Reela shouted.

"On it," Effie replied. She snapped her wand and a burst of light came from it even brighter than it had been in the tunnel below. "Take cover behind this rock," Effie instructed as she ran.

Zoke saw the pillar of stone she meant to hide behind. It was five steps from them. He grabbed Steffen's wrist—for he hadn't moved yet—and nearly tossed him behind the pillar as he ran there himself. Zoke felt the hot wind of a fireball sailing over his head just before he was behind the pillar with the rest of them.

Effie grabbed Reela's hand. "Too far for psyche?"

"Yes. I couldn't give them more than a tickle from all the way over here."

"We have to kill them now," Zoke said. "Once smoke clears, friends die."

"If they're still alive," Steffen said.

Zoke spat in disgust at the comment, but Reela spoke before he could say anything of it. "Vithos is. I can feel him. So the rest probably are, too."

"Not for long if we stay here," Zoke said and whipped his head around the pillar. The archers were staring back at him with arrows at the ready. They fired as he brought his head back again. Four arrows zipped by. "Any other smoke potion with you?"

"That was the only one I had. It takes too many ingredients. Taviray flower and bat feces in one, sugar and—"

"Steffen, we get it," Reela said to stop him. "Effie, got enough juice for one more spell?"

Zoke didn't hear a response, so he glanced at Effie. The mage was sitting with her back against the stone pillar. Her mouth hung open, sucking in air. Her eyes were closed.

"She's meditating," Steffen said.

Reela knelt down in front of her. She put her palm on Effie's cheek and whispered, "Eff, we need you."

The mage opened her eyes, shut her mouth, and climbed to her feet gingerly. "I have something we can use, but after this I'm spent. Let me focus while I cast. One mistake and this explodes in my hands."

Zoke kept his eyes on the smoke. It was dissipating as he watched. For each breath he took, he could see a foot farther. The ground was littered with corpses dressed in red and black. He checked back on the mage's progress. Effie had her wand pointed into a cupped hand. A yellow glow came from it with green laces of dancing smoke. With squinted eyes, her head followed her wand around.

Finishing, she let her shoulders slouch. She passed whatever it was to Reela.

"Throw it at their feet." Effie pushed out her words through breaths of exhaustion. "Run in after it's thrown. Careful not to squeeze it too tightly." She let her body melt to the ground, allowing her back to rest against the wall once again. "Better do it quick. The Sartious barrier is already mixing with the Bastial Energy inside. It's about to explode."

"I can't throw well," Reela said, giving it to Zoke. "Here, hurry."

He grabbed it as gently as he could with his palm, careful to keep his claws away. It was already hot in his hand, and burning hotter with each passing moment. He jumped out from the pillar and hurled it at the four archers and enemy mage as he ran horizontally to avoid being shot. Only one archer released his arrow, missing behind Zoke. The rest held their strings, their eyes shifting to the green ball sailing toward them. The mage must've recognized it, for she was the only one to face the other way and drop her body flat. Zoke had circled around to face them just as it hit the ground at their feet.

Dancing claws of fire four feet high erupted from the ball of energy. Zoke couldn't say exactly how long the fire wavered there because as soon as the blast happened, a gust of burning air slammed into him like the shoulder of a Krepp running past, spinning him sideways. When he turned back, the fire was out and his enemies were on the ground. Not one of them was visibly burned. In fact, they were all rising quickly. The spell wasn't for damage, he realized then with dismay, but to give him and the others time to attack. He sprinted at his enemies as quickly as he could. Reela had caught up to him by then.

The five enemies ahead had recovered too fast. They already were loading their arrows, and the mage was aiming her wand. Zoke was too far to stop them.

Reela threw out both hands as if pushing an invisible man in front of her. With it, she gave a raspy shout and their foes grunted, grimacing in pain. Two of them dropped their bows, but it only stopped the others for a breath.

Zoke had pulled ahead of Reela. Her psychic spell had gotten them closer, but he still couldn't make it in time—that gravely became clear, yet he did not let himself slow.

Strangely without fear, he prepared his body for the arrows, hoping to at least drive his sword through one of them before being felled.

The female mage was able to let off a fireball before any arrows were shot. All he saw was a flash of light, then what felt like a burning rock slammed into his arm and half of his chest. The force of it not only stopped his advance but toppled him.

He tried to lift himself with his arms, but the one that had been hit was numb. With just one arm pushing him up while he was expecting two, he fell over.

He flipped onto the side of him that wasn't numb, preparing for death. *I at least want to look them in the eye before they do it. Give them something to remember.* He wanted to spit as well, but it felt as if all saliva had been burned from his mouth.

At first, he thought he must've hit his head during the tumble because it looked like the Humans had drawn swords and turned to fight one another. Zoke sat up, too dizzy to lift himself from the ground. There were two blurry images swirling around each other. As he blinked and focused, they merged into one clear image.

His heart swelled with relief when he saw that Vithos, Alex, and Terren had arrived. Vithos paralyzed their enemies with pain as Alex and Terren drove their blades through each of them.

It was over before he even knew what was happening.

Then Terren's eyes shifted around and stopped at Zoke. Concern flooded Terren's face. "Stop!" he shouted.

Zoke thought to look behind him and saw a man in light blue rushing at him, sword first. Zoke tried to hop to his feet to scamper away, but dizziness overtook him as soon as he rose, sending him tumbling to the ground. He crawled away from the man as fast as he could, but his arm was still numb. Again he fell. He felt a boot on his hip. It twisted him onto his back, holding him against the ground.

Zoke could hear Steffen and Terren shouting, "He's with Kyrro! Stop!"

The man stood over Zoke with his blade aimed at Zoke's heart. "How do you know that?" the man grunted.

"Because he saved my life," Steffen answered.

Vithos rushed over and put his hand on the man's wrist. A blank look came across the man's face. Slowly, the weapon was lowered, and Vithos cautiously took the sword from the loose grip of the man's hands.

The first thing Zoke saw was that the smoke had cleared completely by then. Taking more time to look around, Zoke noticed only Humans of Kyrro were left. Many of them were approaching, circling around him.

We've won?

"Sorry about that," the man said, extending his hand with fingers out, just as Terren had done when they'd first met.

Zoke sat up. He extended his hands, straightened his fingers, and shook his hands side to side, figuring this was what the Human wanted. Vithos noticed it and quickly did the same.

"What's this?" the man asked, seemingly confused.

"We're shaking hands," Zoke replied, confused as well now. "Don't Humans do that?"

A woman behind him burst out laughing. He turned and found that it was Reela. She was shaking her hands again. Steffen joined in, laughing heartily as well. Zoke couldn't understand what the Humans enjoyed so much about it.

Soon the dancing hands spread quicker than fire, and nearly all of the Humans from Kyrro were shaking their hands and laughing.

"I don't understand," Vithos whispered, continuing to shake his hands. "They genuinely find this to be funny."

The laughter slowly morphed into cheers, then hands became fists thrown into the air. They hollered together. The noise was high and deep, loud and uplifting. Zoke could hear the feeling in each voice as their pitches stormed together to create one sound. There was no purpose behind it. That became clear. It wasn't to announce their location or prove anything. They yelled because they wanted to.

Zoke had never seen someone shout for no other reason than to do it. It seemed so pure—an urge acted upon and nothing else. It was unlike any Krepp behavior. It was so new, so fresh.

It's so Human, he realized.

Chapter 54: Quick Heal
ZOKE

The few mages of Kyrro still standing dragged themselves around and burned the bodies of each deceased Human after they'd been looted.

Soon the whole mountain was lit with the burning of the dead. The many small fires made a soft crackle. Normally the sound was soothing, but in that moment it reminded Zoke too much of the threat from Doe and Haemon: *"Reveal their location to us or we will burn Kyrro and everyone within the territory."*

The way their soft flesh melted under the heat made Zoke fearful when he thought of the Humans trying to stand against his old leaders.

"At least we have twenty new bows from Tenred," a man was telling Terren. Zoke found out he was the chief of the one hundred men sent from Kyrro to protect the Fjallejon Pathway, although the Humans used the word "commander" for him instead. "Not that I would ever trade fifty-one men for any number of bows."

"That's the death count for Kyrro?" Terren asked.

"For now. Many of the injured aren't going to make it through the night."

Some of the party Zoke was travelling with had gone inside the mountain already. Effie had lost consciousness after the battle ended but looked uninjured. Reela assured them that the young mage was just exhausted. Alex had carried her inside the mountain with Steffen at his side, trying and mostly succeeding in transporting all three of their bags along with the bow Zoke had given him.

Vithos was on his back next to Zoke, dead asleep. Reela was on Vithos' other side. Her knees were crunched to her stomach with her arms folded around them while she appeared to be listening to Terren and the commander.

The only thing keeping Zoke awake was the pain from the fireballs he'd endured. Full feeling had come back, and the agony from it made him wish his body was still numb. His back, one arm, and half his chest were dark and tender like charred yet undercooked meat. They ached, but at least that was bearable. When he tried to lie down, on the other hand, the stinging pain felt like his shedding all over again.

"How many enemies were there?" Terren asked.

"Only two hundred," the commander answered. "Though, if there were more, we would've seen them long before it was too late. We had two scouts watching, but it turned out they were spies. They snuck in a psychic first to find and kill our two pigeons so we couldn't send a distress message to the castle. Then they took out two of our mages who were on backup watch duty. The poor women didn't stand a chance, cut down from behind by people they'd thought to be with Kyrro."

Zoke expected at least one of them to spit at that, but none did.

"It looked like about a hundred enemies were left when we got here," Terren said.

"Sounds about right," the commander said. "The battle went half the day. They had archers shooting four times farther than our mages could reach. We got pushed back, trapped behind rocks. It was a series of advances and retreats." He shook his head bitterly as his eyes drifted to somewhere distant. "They had too many archers set up on the cliffs that hang high above this mountaintop. We managed to take out their warriors who were brave enough to engage us without archers behind them, but that was it. We couldn't touch their archers. We were going to have our final stand at the tunnel, but I'm sure glad you all showed up. Spirits were low. That could have been it for us."

"You didn't have any archers?" Zoke asked. He expected to have misunderstood what the commander was saying.

"The bow has been illegal until just recently," the commander replied. "We're making them and training now, but it'll take some time."

"Ill-eagle," Zoke repeated. "I don't know this word."

"Outlawed," Reela answered. "Not allowed."

"Against the laws," Terren added.

The word *law* was familiar to him, but he couldn't remember what it was. His face must have shown it.

"Krepps don't have laws?" Reela asked.

"I don't know," he replied. "What is it?"

"Basically rules. If you break them, you're punished," she said.

"Yes, rules and punishments we have." *Or we did when Vithos was still there. I can't say what's happening now.* "You break a rule, you get burned here." He pointed a claw at his wrist. "Why would they burn you for being an archer?" No one appeared to have mentioned the bow around Zoke's shoulder as they'd brought him through Kyrro. *No, they were too busy staring at my face and body to notice the weapon.* The Humans' eyes had lingered. He could feel their gazes, but when he looked back at them most feigned disinterest. Not the little ones, though. They pointed with excitement as if they were the ones to discover him, some even exclaiming, "He looked at me!"

"They don't burn us. We have different punishments," Reela said.

"The King's father was killed by a bow," Terren said. "Our king was young and scared when it happened, and there was no threat of war. So he considered the weapon more dangerous than good. After the decision was made, he would have looked weak if he'd reversed it, and there was generally no reason to. People took up throwing daggers, got good with them. With psychics, mages, and skilled throwers, hunting was just as easy as it was before, and we have plenty of farms as well. The law was recently changed when it became clear we'll have to fight Tenred and..." he swallowed the next words before deciding to let them out, "and the Krepps."

Zoke had no response to that. It seemed like the Humans were waiting for him to speak, but he didn't know what they wanted to hear. Their eyes lingered, making him feel he was being escorted through Kyrro City again. But this look was different. *They want an explanation,* he realized. He wanted to spit but held back and dealt with the sour taste. *But they're not going to get it from me. I'm not the one fighting them.*

He decided he was tired enough to sleep through the pain at that point, but he wanted some space from the curious glances that were falling upon him.

"I understand now," he said, referring to the bow while he tried to ignore their eyes. "I'm going to find a place to rest." Zoke got to his feet gingerly. Even with slow movements, pain surged through his body like a river of daggers running over him.

Feeling responsible for Vithos, he pushed on the Elf's arm to wake him. "I'm going into the mountain for rest," Zoke told him in Kreppen.

Vithos had drooping eyelids and a slack mouth. After a slow breath, he pushed himself up, and soon they were walking together.

Neither spoke. Vithos was clearly too tired, and Zoke was exhausted and in too much pain. All was quiet except for the fires of burning cloth and flesh in every direction.

Reela came after them. “Zoke, I was hoping to speak to Vithos with your help.”

Zoke gave her a glance with worn-out eyes.

“There’s a lot he’ll want to hear,” she said, just before he could tell her he was too tired.

He translated for Vithos.

“Whatever she thinks she knows, I’d like to hear it,” Vithos replied, looking at her inquisitively as he spoke. Some of the tiredness in his face already had faded.

Zoke sighed. “I will help.”

The only reason Zoke agreed was because he was interested himself, as this was the Human who’d said she knew Vithos but had never explained how.

“Thank you,” she replied with a smile. It looked as if she was reaching out to touch his arm, but she stopped herself and slowly retracted.

They came to one of the supposed many entrances to the mountain’s carved-out interior. Terren had explained that the Fjallejons lived in these mountains. When the Humans came from across the sea and started expanding, the Fjallejons made an agreement to watch over the pathway leading into Kyrro from the north, notifying the King of any strange incomers. In exchange, the Humans wouldn’t use any resources from the mountains, including the vast water supply flowing underneath it.

The entrance that led them below the surface was a small cave excavated out of a jagged mountainside that reached high into the sky. The air was heavier. Zoke could feel it on his burns.

They had to crouch to keep their heads from scraping against the top of the cave. There were stairs twisting down, maybe thirty of them before the enclosed walkway opened to a cavern so wide and deep it must have been at least the size of his tribe’s old encampment. In the middle was a gaping hole half a mile in diameter. There appeared to be no bottom, just thicker darkness as it went on.

Reela gasped as she entered behind Zoke. "It's enormous. The time it must've taken to carve out so much space, and with such small hands."

They were met by a Fjallejon. "Any injured?" He had the same deep voice and choppy dialect as the few who had stopped Zoke and Vithos that morning.

"No," Zoke answered.

"Yes," Reela argued. "I can feel your pain." She pointed at Zoke. "He's been struck by two fireballs. Any Human would've been killed."

"We fix it," the Fjallejon replied. "Follow this tunnel." He pointed to the second tunnel from the entrance. "Walking injured go there. Dying injured go first tunnel."

Zoke looked out over the rest of the cavern. There must have been fifty tunnels that he could see, and that was just on their floor. There were layers upon layers of stone wrapped around the gaping hole in the middle that made up countless more floors. Most of the Fjallejons he saw were carrying something as they walked: a bowl, a metal pick, a spear, sticks.

Again, the tunnel they needed to pass through was low, requiring them to hunch their backs. It was the only time Zoke felt tall, and he already was sick of it. The tunnel opened into a square room with unfamiliar letters and etchings on the walls. Some images were diagrams of body parts and plants. The rest he didn't recognize.

A Human woman was leaving just as they got there. She held one of her arms, her face full of pain. "Don't take the quick heal if they ask," she whispered to them.

"Which one hurt?" the Fjallejon shouted from the middle of the room before Zoke had a moment to consider what the Human had told him. When his eyes shifted to the Fjallejon, he realized it was the first female Fjallejon he'd seen. She had long dark hair and a ragged cloth dress that covered her from shoulders to shins.

"He is." Reela pointed at Zoke.

"Come sit. Show me injury," the Fjallejon replied. She patted her hand on a child-size stool that looked ready to break.

Zoke squatted beside the stool, reaching a claw over his back. "I've been burned with fireballs here and here." His hand traveled around the tender areas.

"You must use stool, Krepp," the Fjallejon said.

"I'm much heavier than these Humans. It'll break."

"No, it strong." She gave it a hard slap. "Never break. Come."

He sat upon it. It sang with squeaks but seemed to hold.

"See? Now I fix you."

She fiddled behind him with something that sounded like leaves. He shifted his eyes to Reela. "I'll translate whatever you wish to share with Vithos."

Reela started with a breath instead of words. She, Vithos, and Zoke made a triangle. The two of them stood while he sat. When she spoke, Zoke translated, but she and Vithos remained facing each other. It was clear this would be a conversation between them, and Zoke was relieved. All day he'd been translating, but this was the first he didn't need to worry about answering any questions himself.

"Do you know about your past?" she asked Vithos.

"My true past?" Vithos replied after Zoke had translated. "Before I was taken by the enormous Slugari?"

"Yes, when you were still with the Elves," Reela said.

"I know nothing of that. How much of it could you know?"

Reela's eyes darted back and forth between Zoke and Vithos. "Everything."

Chapter 55: Words of Death and Birth
ZOKE

Vithos leaned closer to Reela, peering through the tops of his eyes in the same way he used to in the judgment chambers. *He's looking past her words, into the intent behind them. It feels like that was years ago,* Zoke pondered.

"How do you know about my past?" Vithos asked warily.

"Because your father survived the attack. Do you know anything about him?" Reela spoke in a rush, like she was expecting something to stop her at any moment.

"Just that he's gone, along with the rest of the Elves." Although it wasn't a question, there was a lift in pitch as if Vithos was hoping for it to be answered like one. He leaned even closer toward Reela.

Her eyes were heavy with worry. "When the Krepps attacked the Elves with Doe and Haemon, your mother tied you and your brother to wolves that had been befriended over years of psyche. She had them run south in hopes of reaching the Humans in Kyrro. She was killed by Krepps soon after."

Reela stopped so Zoke could translate. She watched Vithos patiently, waiting for any questions. But he said nothing when Zoke had finished. Instead, he nodded to himself with a tight mouth as if he already knew.

"Your father ran with the wolves," Reela said, "doing everything he could to distract the Krepps away from them so they could escape. He was King of the Elves and the strongest psychic of them. But he got held up when Krepps tackled him. He managed to break free, but he lost sight of the wolves. He found a dead wolf later without any signs of you nearby. By the tracks, he could tell you'd been taken, while the other wolf made it out with no signs of your brother falling off."

Vithos clung to every word as Zoke translated, but his eyes rarely darted away from Reela. "Neither father nor brother to me died in the battle?" Vithos asked.

"No," she answered, but her face was not as happy as it should have been by her answer. When Vithos heard it from Zoke, his mouth twitched as if starting to grin, but it never made it there. "Your father followed the Krepp tracks and found you," Reela continued, "but there was nothing he could do against so many Krepps that Doe and Haemon had guarding you. So he went to Kyrro first, hoping to find his other son and get help from the Humans to retrieve you. Your brother, Rek—his name is Rek. His name was the only thing they could get out of him when King Westin Kimard took him in. They spoke different languages, and Rek was very young. Do you recognize the name?"

Vithos made a face like the shapes of memories were taking over his vision. "Yes, I do!" he answered in shock. "Rek..." he whispered the name to himself.

Zoke had been so caught up in translating he hadn't even noticed the Fjallejon wiping his back with leaves. That is, until she started rubbing something on him that made his scaly skin feel like it had caught on fire.

He jumped from the stool in reflex. "That burns!"

"Sit, still much to do," the Fjallejon said sternly. "Sit."

He wiped a claw along his back, bringing it around to have a look at the substance she was putting on him. It was a thick cream, colored bright orange. Reela waved her hand in front of her nose. "Quite a smell to it," she said.

"You want quick heal, do you?" the Fjallejon asked as Zoke reluctantly sat back on the tiny stool. It gave a loud squeak.

"Yes," he replied. He didn't care about the Human's warning from earlier. If it would get him out sooner, that's what he preferred.

"Good. I make cups."

Having no idea what that meant, he went back to translating Vithos' last words for Reela.

Her smile doubled in length when she heard. "I had a feeling you said that you remembered," she said with eyes locked on Vithos. "Even though we don't speak the same language, I can still feel much of what you feel."

Vithos was nodding his head in agreement as Zoke translated what Reela had said. "Keep going," Vithos said when Zoke was finished. "What happened next?"

Zoke couldn't remember the last time he'd seen Vithos this eager for anything. The Elf stood with one foot forward, leaning most of his weight on it. Zoke imagined he'd feel the same way if he was about to find out whether or not Zeti was still alive.

"Once your father was in Kyrro, he looked for your brother, Rek, but there were three large cities, and no one spoke Elvish. When he finally came to Kyrro City, which has the King's castle in its center, everyone was gathering there for an announcement from Westin Kimard. The King had a child with him—a small Elf, the only Elf in the entire city. Your father knew it was Rek but not what was being said."

Reela waited for Zoke to finish translating. Vithos' eyes went even wider when he heard, but he said nothing.

"What your father didn't know," Reela continued, "was that the King was announcing that the 'mistreated' Elf boy had come into the city tied to a wolf, and that the boy was to be looked after like a son by the King and his staff. While everyone applauded and cheered the King's generosity, your father tried to push through the guards to get to Rek. They took it as a threat to the King and threw him to the ground. He used psyche to fight back, but he couldn't get through, and he was eventually beaten unconscious."

The Fjallejon returned and said something to Zoke while he was finishing translating. He didn't catch it but could feel something round being pushed against his back. There was a sudden sharp pain like a knife piercing his skin. He jumped up and flipped around to see what it was.

He caught sight of a wooden bowl falling to the ground. Out of it came some sort of insect he hadn't seen before. It was the size of two fingers side by side with a stinger on its rear that was just longer than a claw. Its head was just an extension of its rod-like body, with small eyes and a strange puckering mouth that looked out of place.

"I said get ready for puckersting," the Fjallejon said with a hint of annoyance. Quicker than Zoke could pull his dagger, she scooped up the creature, tossed it back into the bowl, and pointed at the stool. "Sit. Puckersting make you better. Bring blood to wound. Ancient remedy. Krepp should know. You been in Ovira long as Fjallejon."

"Krepp don't know," Zoke replied with frustration from the painful surprise. "Krepp never seen that before." He touched his back where he'd been stung. It sent a flash of excruciating pain through his heart and to his chest on the other side. He winced through his teeth.

"Be calm and sit. It hurt now but better later," she said, pushing down on his shoulder with tiny hands as light as a gentle breeze.

"Zoke." Vithos put a hand on his other shoulder. Immediately he felt soothed, and the pain became a mere distraction. "I need to hear the rest of the story from Reela." With raised eyebrows, his face was pleading. In all the years Zoke had seen Vithos pass judgment, never did he have this expression. Zoke nodded forgivingly and asked Reela to go on.

She smiled as her eyes stayed on Vithos. It was a tranquil grin behind a sad face. "Your father was taken to prison." She gave a quick glance to Zoke. "Do you know what prison is?"

"No," he answered.

"A small room with locked doors," she said. "No way out." She waited for him to translate as best he could.

"How do you know all this?" Vithos asked with nothing in his tone to show he had any doubt that Reela spoke the truth. Zoke realized it was a question based on curiosity, not accusation. He tried to demonstrate this when he translated.

"The King questioned your father with the help of my mother. Her name is Airy. She was a translator for the King. Through Airy's translation, your father explained everything that I'm telling you now—everything that Doe and Haemon and the Krepps did to the Elves that lead your father and Rek to Kyrro City."

The moment Zoke finished translating, Reela continued without waiting for Vithos to respond. "Unfortunately, the King at the time was a greedy man. He was very power-hungry and nervous, for he'd just stolen leadership through force, and he was worried the same might happen to him. He wanted to use Rek for his psychic ability. There were hardly any psychics then, and they couldn't do more than cause a pinch of pain. But your father was different, giving his Elven son great potential. The King wanted Rek to himself. So he banished your father, told him to leave the city and never come back."

"The King banished my father?" Vithos grew angry. "The current king, Welson Kimard?"

Reela nervously shook her head as she heard Vithos say the name. "No," she answered, not needing Zoke to finish translating. "It was the *father* to our current King. He was killed nineteen years ago by a long-range arrow. The shooter was never discovered."

"I understand," Vithos answered, although his face was still tense. "I want to know what happened to father and brother to me."

"Your father couldn't give up when Rek was so close," Reela said. "But when he tried returning to the castle, he was attacked by the King's Guard. They broke many of his bones and left him for dead. That's when my mother found him. She took your father into her home and nursed him back to health. She wanted to help him get his sons back."

Zoke felt the Fjallejon tapping around his back with the bowl as he translated. He was still calm from when Vithos had touched him but couldn't ignore that he was being stung. The sharp pain made him grit his teeth and grunt whenever it happened, but he found focusing on the translations was helping to ignore it.

"Together, they tried to get Rek back," Reela continued. "Also, your father travelled once a year to the camp of the Krepps to check on you. That went on for five years until Westin Kimard was killed. His son Welson Kimard—our current king—took over. He was never comfortable with his *older brother,* Rek," she said with a disdain that Zoke tried to translate into words as best he could. "So, Welson happily released Rek from the confinement of the castle. With the help of Airy's friend, Councilman Kerr, Rek was moved to Airy's house in Oakshen to live with your father and her."

"They're all still alive?" Vithos asked. Zoke could tell Vithos had been holding in the question as long as possible. Given the first positive turn in the story, it made sense the Elf chose then to finally let it out, but Reela's face was tight with grief.

"Your father died, Vithos," she said. "I'm so sorry."

Zoke had no way of translating the word "sorry." "Reela feels bad" was the closest he could do, he figured, but her face said it louder than any words, so he didn't even try.

Again, Vithos was nodding to himself like he knew all along, but this time he couldn't hide the sadness in his eyes as well as he had the last time.

Meanwhile, the Fjallejon brought the wooden bowl around to Zoke's arm and then his chest. She tapped it with two small fingers as she slid it around, stopping to put her ear against it every few taps. The momentary distraction made Zoke realize how attached to the story he was. He found himself fearful about the ending, for Reela's face was full of regret. *Vithos' family lives and dies in between her breaths. She's already killed off mother and father to him. The only one left is brother to him.*

"With Rek safe, your father focused entirely on getting you away from the Krepps and Doe and Haemon," Reela continued. "There was no way to get the army he needed to take you by force, but Airy did have enough money for them to hire a skilled assassin for a stealth mission." Zoke didn't know the words "assassin," "stealth," or "mission," so it took some time for Reela to explain.

The Fjallejon returned the bowl to wherever she'd gotten it and started chanting a soft song heavy in rhythm while wiping petals of an orange flower over his body. Sometimes, she swayed back and forth, grabbing his shoulders to move him with her as best she could. The stool creaked so loudly that Zoke nearly had to shout to be heard.

When Zoke finished describing the stealth mission to Vithos, Reela continued. "Your father and the assassin never got to you, Vithos. They were stopped by Doe and Haemon and thousands of Krepps. It was impossible to sneak in. The assassin said so when she made it back. She and your father got closed in from behind. They tried to fight their way out, but Doe and Haemon saw them and cast fireballs the size of boulders. Your father was hit, killed instantly. The assassin barely made it out, coming back to tell my mother what happened."

The Fjallejon had stopped chanting by the time Zoke finished translating. Reela didn't continue right away, in case Vithos had something to say.

For a while, Vithos just looked at her with empty eyes. The Fjallejon went to the corner of the room to get something. The only sound was her tiny feet shuffling around the stone floor.

"I remember that," Vithos said eventually. "They announced that we were attacked. I saw the charred body. I was happy to see him dead, to hear that Doe and Haemon killed him. I had no idea he was my father. I can't say how old I was, as I never knew my birthday, but I was still a child." A tear fell from his cheek. "I was happy for his death. I thought he was an enemy. I was so stupid. I saw my father's dead body, and I was happy." Vithos looked as if he wanted to leave the room, like he wanted to curl into a ball and cry where no one could see him. His eyes avoided everyone, staring nowhere specific.

Even without any translation from Zoke, Reela moved close to Vithos and threw her arms around him. He seemed to embrace it with affection, wrapping his arms around her as well. It was a hug. He knew Humans did this with each other—he'd read about it—but seeing it for the first time was interesting. Though he would never want one of them to grab him like that.

"You couldn't have known," Zoke told Vithos in Kreppen before translating for Reela. "Don't be mad at yourself for this." Then he gave Reela the short version of what Vithos had said, knowing she already could see the Elf's sadness.

"At least I can help you know your age," Reela told Vithos with reserved excitement. "You're nine years older than me, the same age as your brother, Rek. I'm seventeen. You and Rek are twenty-six. Your brother still lives, Vithos." She raised her arms as if to warn him. "But he's being sent hundreds of miles away, across the ocean. He's going to Goldram. It's north of Meritar, where the Elves came from and sailed back to when they were attacked here in Ovira. Rek wants to stay here and fight, but he was forced to leave. He knows about you. He's been trying to find a way to come and get you."

She took Vithos' hand as Zoke translated. She leaned in and spoke with a soft, yet stern tone. "I know you want revenge against Doe and Haemon. I can feel it. Rek does, too. And so do I." With those last words, her eyes were hard with resolve.

When Zoke finished translating, Vithos didn't move. His eyebrows made no motion of rising, and his mouth remained a gentle frown. However, there was a palpable change in the way he looked at Reela. He knew something about her now. Even Zoke could feel it. But Zoke didn't know what it was until Vithos spoke.

"You're his blood. That's what it is, why I know you. You're half him. You're half sister to me."

Reela nodded before Zoke even began translating. "Your father didn't know Airy was pregnant with me when he left," she said when Zoke was ready.

"Sister to me..." His eyes were wide in shock. "Can I see them?" he asked, reaching a hand toward the side of her head. "A sister and a brother," he said incredulously.

Reela understood without Zoke's help. She started to reach into her hair, but she stopped suddenly, holding a hand up. "Someone's coming," she whispered. "This has to remain a secret for now. I'll explain later."

Realizing no one coming would know Kreppen, Zoke translated her whispers to Vithos as he saw Steffen speed into the room with a smile, completely oblivious to the solemn mood of everyone else. He was holding Zoke's bow and wore the quiver around his back.

"I wanted to return this," he said, holding out the bow to Zoke. "And thank you for saving my life."

A flood of saliva came to Zoke's mouth. The insult of offering back the weapon, along with the weak gratitude of *thanking him,* was too much for him to swallow. He spat toward a corner of the room. "The bow was a gift, and there's no need to thank me when you saved mine as well."

"No spit," the Fjallejon told him. "This clean room. Very bad luck."

"I don't believe in luck," he replied, readying his feet to stand. Just then, the stool gave one last squeak before one of its legs snapped in half. It sent him into the ground face first. He lay sprawled on his stomach for two breaths as he gathered the strength to get up. When he lifted his head, the Fjallejon was there in front of him with her arms folded.

"Now you believe? You have bad luck. You must kiss someone you like for it to go away. This is known. Do Krepps kiss?"

"Not this Krepp." Krepps did kiss, but rarely. He'd read that Humans kiss for many reasons, even on each other's mouth. It was a strange concept, as Krepps would only kiss another's cheek or forehead when welcoming another family member or when saying goodbye to them. The last time he'd been kissed was by his mother the morning before she died.

"Then you keep bad luck," the Fjallejon replied. "You bring danger to friends."

He lifted himself to his knees. Steffen walked around in front of him, holding an expression of embarrassment. "You can kiss me if you want, not that it would mean anything, just to repay you for your gift."

"Gifts are not meant to be repaid, and don't mention kissing again without expecting spit on your feet." Zoke spat again, though he made sure to avoid Steffen.

The Fjallejon shook her head and let out a quick ticking sound. "Bad luck. Very bad luck for big-mouth Krepp."

Chapter 56: Blanketed
EFFIE

When Effie's eyes peeled open, she didn't know where she was or how long she'd been unconscious. There was a soft roar. It sounded like a waterfall was somewhere in the distance. Her vision was blurred as if she was wearing someone else's glasses. She tried to raise her hands to rub her eyes but couldn't find the strength. It looked like people were still fighting, but the image of them was slowly turning away from her. Every time she blinked, they jumped back to standing upright, yet the slow spin wouldn't stop.

The battle is still happening. Get up and fight. Again she tried to rub her eyes so she could see her enemies, but her arm never moved.

Someone started calling her name from beneath her. The voice was asking if Effie could hear it.

I can hear you, she wanted to say but couldn't speak. Her voice was too heavy. She couldn't get it out of her throat. *Are you in the mountain?* she wanted to ask.

The roar of the waterfall sharpened, transforming into men shouting at each other. *Battle cries*, she realized her earlier mistake. *Get up and help.*

Her name was being called in front of her now. "Effie, Effie." It was the same voice but crisp, no longer muffled by the mountain.

How did you get here so quickly? Was she asking aloud? Effie couldn't tell if her words came out. Then she heard a voice she recognized.

"Let me try." It was Reela. Effie could make out her light hair turning away from her like everything else. "Effie, we've won. You passed out."

No, they're fighting behind you, watch out. Effie still couldn't tell if her words were coming out.

"That's cheering you hear," Reela said. "Drink this."

She heard the waterfall again, but this time it was pouring into her mouth. She let it run down her throat, surprised she couldn't feel it crash against the base of her stomach.

"I'm going to use psyche to help you rest," Reela said. "Alex will carry you inside the mountain."

Someone put his hands under her knees and around her back, then lifted her.

Effie sat up suddenly, her chest heaving with heavy breaths. Her hand was caught on something. She looked down to find it cupped between both of Reela's and felt some relief. But then her heart started up again with a frightful thought. *Did we lose? Was Reela killed?* She put two fingers under Reela's nose and held her breath. Feeling Reela's warm air against her knuckles, Effie let out an exhausted sigh.

She noticed then that she wasn't on the mountaintop anymore. Somehow, she was in a room made of stone. As she shifted her weight to look around, she noticed a crunch coming from beneath her. She felt the rough sheet that shaped her bed and realized that straw was beneath it, supporting her.

Looking past Reela, she found Steffen sleeping on his back with one arm clutching a bow to his bare chest. He was sleeping next to the gray wall of the cave that was covered with bumps. She turned to her other side and saw Alex asleep on his stomach. The sight of him made her remember the last moments on the mountaintop, Reela's words coming back to her. *"I'm going to use psyche to help you rest. Alex will carry you inside the mountain."*

We're in the Fjallejons' home within the mountain, Effie realized. *And we've won.* Though she did not smile with her lips, it felt as if her heart was grinning, sending a warm tingle down to her stomach.

There was a hearth carved out of the wall in front of her. The fire within it was nearly dead. Effie turned to check behind her and found a small tunnel lit by one sconce on the wall. She started to remove her hand from Reela's grasp in order to get up and investigate, but Reela's eyes popped open.

"You're safe," Reela whispered. "We all are, but you need to rest. We have many miles to walk tomorrow and the days after." Reela sat up, yawned, and then turned toward the fire.

She let go of Effie, pushed herself to her feet, grabbed three cuts of wood, and placed them on top of the dying fire. "Could you light this first?"

Effie found her wand beside her bed as Reela came back to sit next to her and watch. Reela had on a black nightgown that would've reached her ankles if she'd been standing, but it fell and bunched around her waist when Reela pulled her knees to her chest. Her skin looked even smoother than usual as the low light danced along her long shins. Reela pulled a blanket up over her bare legs for warmth. A faint glow from the tunnel wrapped around her back, bringing light to the side of her breast. The top of it was bursting out from her nightgown by the light press of her knees.

"Look at you, so pretty. How is it you look like you were never in a battle?" Effie didn't need a mirror to know she didn't look the same. She could feel the dirt and oil packed into her hair and face. "How long have I been asleep?"

"A few hours." Reela smiled. "I had a bath. They have naturally warm water in some areas of the mountain, but the rest of the mountain is very cold without fire." She pointed at the wood. "I know you haven't been sleeping well. I'll make sure you do after you light it."

Effie brushed the hair from her face, making sure it all fell behind her back so as not to catch on fire. She pushed the coarse blanket off her lap to find Reela had removed her pants while she was sleeping, leaving just her short underwear. She would have made an effort to cover herself if others were awake, but there was nothing about her that Reela hadn't seen already.

She lit a fire by sticking her wand under the wood and pushing Bastial Energy through it. She was almost skilled enough with Sartious Energy to create fire without the pellets of it that filled her wand, but spells that required both forms of energy, like all fire spells, would always be easier with the support of her wand, and safer as well. Producing fire from her bare hand was just as dangerous as it sounded.

When the fire spread to the first cut of wood, she returned to the straw bed.

She and Reela lay on their sides, facing each other. Reela reached out a hand, then Effie gave her one of her own to hold. The moment Reela's touch came around her, Effie's whole body was blanketed in a heavy comfort, and sleep took her a breath later.

Chapter 57: Safe as Skin
EFFIE

The quiet four days that followed were a welcome change from the recent chaos.

Terren pushed them to walk as far as they could each day, but Effie was used to being on her feet all day, so she didn't mind. Steffen, on the other hand, was having far more trouble. He suffered in silence as best he could, saying nothing of it, but his body spoke volumes. The bow Zoke gave him was constantly slipping off his shoulder. By the time the sun had begun to set each day, Steffen was huffing loudly. For reasons Effie couldn't understand, the bag on his back just looked heavier as the day went on. It had to do with the way he carried it, she figured.

The first day, after the battle atop the mountain, he wore his bag around one shoulder with the bow over it and his quiver around the other shoulder. He couldn't walk one mile without something coming loose. As they prepared a fire that first night, Zoke removed the quiver from its strap and fashioned it to Steffen's belt instead.

Zoke and Vithos were both experienced travelers. That became clear quickly. Zoke reminded her of Cleve sometimes, specifically the way he distanced himself from them like Cleve did when they first met. However, Cleve seemed to do it as a choice, while it was more inherent to Zoke. It made Effie think that was just the nature of Krepps.

Another similarity between them was their power. Cleve exuded strength, so it hadn't surprised Effie when Reela had told her of his inner strength as well. But even Cleve, with all his inner and outer strength, couldn't survive two fireballs like Zoke had. When Steffen and Reela told her about it, Effie was thankful he'd lived but even more frightened of what it meant. The Krepps had size, numbers, and strength, yet Kyrro had magic. But if their fireballs couldn't even kill the Krepps, what was the point?

They did have Vithos, though. That helped to relieve Effie whenever distressing thoughts tightened her chest. Alex told Effie that he, Terren, and Vithos had killed more than fifty men in a minute. No one stood a chance against them. Not one of them had come even close to being injured. Vithos subdued any enemies nearby with psyche. Then, it was just a matter of running a sword through them.

Reela had a similar effect with her psyche, stunning enemies long enough to give Effie time to shoot them with a fireball. But from what Alex had told her of Vithos, Reela still had far to go to match his power. Having Vithos with them gave Effie the same hope as if ten thousand warriors had come from Goldram to help them fight—a fantasy she often went to when thoughts of the war kept her awake. Ever since Reela had told her about Cleve being sent to Goldram, she liked to imagine him coming back with ships overcrowded by men and women ready to fight for Kyrro.

"Cleve will come back," Reela had led with before explaining everything that she and Cleve had shared during her visit to the castle, including their kisses.

"What was it like?" Effie had asked.

"Strong." Reela had the same coy smile as the last time they'd spoken about Cleve. "Fierce," Reela added, then sighed. "Wonderful," she whispered, half to herself.

Effie found herself wishing Cleve was still in Kyrro. She'd never met someone she could tell was reliable even without yet needing to rely on him. It reminded her of a poem she'd memorized long ago.

I knew a warrior. He smelled of shit.
Skilled with sword but had no wit.
He never let me be alone.
Said I couldn't be on my own.
You are too beautiful, he would say
Trouble will come to you one day.
I'll take my chances, go away.
You are the source of my dismay.
With that he left, and all was good,
Until a man came masked in hood.
He stole my money and broke my bones.
No one was there to heed my groans.
I realized then what I know today
Which to you I will convey

A warrior's kiss is never missed,
Eventually he'll get the clue.
But in his fist that you dismissed,
Was a sword protecting you.

Every so often in bars, Effie would hear the last four lines chanted by a group of warriors who'd been drinking too much.

Cleve was little like the warrior she imagined in the poem, though. While his massive stature wasn't her type, he was still pleasing to the eye and certainly didn't smell like shit. In fact, if anyone had an unpleasant odor, it was Zoke. There was a musky smell he seemed to produce that had similarity to stale beer and sweat. The way it seemed to always be there, even after they washed themselves with the water of the Satjen River, made her believe it must be a natural odor of all Krepps.

It had taken some convincing before Terren agreed to let them stop at the river for a quick bath. It was Reela who eventually persuaded him with the argument that they wouldn't lose an extra day by taking the time.

The men stripped down to their underwear like they were undressing in the privacy of their own rooms. They were sitting in the shallow river and rubbing water over their backs and onto their faces before Effie and Reela had any clothes removed.

Reela grabbed Effie's hand and ran about a hundred feet down the river before she stopped and started unbuttoning. "I'm going naked, and so are you," she said.

"Am I?" Effie replied with a shocked grin.

"I don't want to walk hours with wet cotton against my lady parts, and you don't either."

"You just don't want to be the only one," Effie said, removing her pants. She looked behind them at the rest of the party. She caught Alex's eyes darting away. She knew he liked her but figured it was just a physical attraction. His eyes often were on her already when she'd give him a glance. "They can see us, you know."

"Let them look. They've killed people in close combat. Our bodies can't be worse than the sight of that."

When they were both in their underwear, Reela counted down from three. They slipped off their tops and drew down their bottoms, then locked hands and ran into the cold water with a giddy scream.

They threw water onto their own faces and each other's, laughing and screaming hysterically. Effie forgot all about the men up the river.

The moment Reela started splashing Effie, it reminded her of the last time she'd had the same innocent fun. It must have been at least three years ago, when she and Reela were still swimming in Lake Kayvol. They always went at night and stripped down to nothing. The bite of cold water mixed with the thrill of being exposed created an excitement that couldn't be achieved through anything else nearly as simple as jumping into water.

But as they got older, the urge seemed to burn out. For Effie, it was replaced with boys. She'd never known what replaced it for Reela. The young psychic would often leave with her mother and her journal for days at a time, never saying where they were going. Effie always figured that, whatever it was they were doing, it was Reela's way of finding the same innocent fun. Reela always had more of a sister-like relationship with her mother than Effie did with hers.

"Let's make camp here," Terren said, swinging his bag off his shoulder. "Rise early and we'll reach the Slugari in northern Satjen by midday tomorrow."

"Zoke, shoot a few arrows with me?" Steffen asked.

The Krepp nodded and walked to him without a word. They set off to find a good target. Effie noticed that Steffen was using the bow any chance he got, which was usually only when waiting for someone in the party to relieve him or herself, in the mornings if he rose early enough, or at night as others gathered sticks and leaves for a fire.

When Zoke wasn't answering questions about the Krepps, or explaining why he and Vithos had left the tribe, or showing Steffen how to shoot, Effie could hear him teaching Vithos words in common tongue. The Elf had learned quickly. Like Steffen, his ability to memorize was uncanny. Along with hundreds of words, he even knew many short phrases now.

"What's the plan for the Slugari?" Alex asked Terren while they cleared small rocks to create a smooth surface for sleeping.

"Zoke says Vithos can demonstrate to the Slugari that we're there to help," Terren answered. "Steffen knows some Slugaren, so he'll translate."

"But how are we going to get to them once Vithos senses their colony below us?" Alex wondered. "We can't just dig and hope to fall somewhere safe when we break through their roof."

"Zoke and Vithos have thought about that," Terren replied. "Vithos will charm an animal to dig for us, test the water, so to speak. Once it digs through to them, we'll call from above so the Slugari can come up and show us how to get down there. Then we'll bury the hole and follow them through whatever secret passage it is they use to go between the surface and underground. It's the best plan we've got." He spoke the last words as if they tasted sour.

Alex hummed discouragingly. "No one knows how they go from above ground to below?"

"No one in Kyrro." The pitch of Terren's voice rose, as if to demonstrate he was open to suggestions.

"How do we even know the Slugari ever come up?" Effie butted in.

"There have been sightings," Terren replied. "Not that I've seen one myself."

Vithos came over and dumped a pile of sticks in the middle of them. "I find rocks," he said with his Kreppen accent. It gave his words a rough sound, like he was forcing them out with his stomach.

"I'll help," Reela said, placing her hand on his arm and walking off with him.

Supine, Effie lost herself among the stars in the pure black sky. Thoughts of her family in Oakshen came to her. She nearly had their letter memorized by then but decided to pull it from her pocket anyway for another read. She unfolded it and held it in front of the stars. With her other hand she produced a white glow of Bastial Energy.

We're so happy you wrote to us. We have heard the announcement about the treaty being declined. Everything's fine here except we miss you, especially Gabby! She also wants you to say hi to Steffen for her.

Even though you didn't seem scared in your letter, we are. If the Academy is attacked, will you have to fight? We wish we'd known that war was even a possibility before we let you sign that contract. As soon as you're allowed to leave, come home and we (your mother) will make you whatever you want to eat.

Love you. Keep yourself safe.

—Mother, Father, and Gabby

She'd been wondering how she would answer the only question

they asked. She *was* required to fight, even had killed people already, but would they really want to know that?

I don't think they would.

Chapter 58: Hidden
EFFIE

Effie remained awake long after everyone else. As had happened so many nights before, the moment her mind began to transition into sleep, the realization she was finally drifting off would wake her again with a quick jab of excitement to her heart. The only way to make the transition complete was to distract herself with pleasant thoughts. She tried to think of some, but none would come. All just caused more despair.

Turning to her back, she noticed her heart's sporadic beats changing from rapid to normal to rapid again, every few breaths. It would not relax. She pushed both hands onto her chest to suppress it.

Why does this happen to me? And why now? Could I be worried about the Slugari tomorrow? With that thought began the familiar feeling of someone sitting on her collarbone. Her right hand moved from her heart to the base of her throat. With a gentle touch, she pressed her fingers there. The inability to breathe properly was always slightly relieved as she rubbed around the top of her chest, but the moment she stopped, it would return.

Just sleep, just sleep, Effie repeated in desperation. She hated this inability to find a breath of relief no matter how deeply she breathed. She wanted to fight it but didn't know how.

As if to torment her, when her mind finally succumbed to sleep, the dream it produced was a nightmare.

She was back on the mountaintop. A man was stomping on something, his head low and focused. The sudden urge to stop him came over her. She saw why a breath later. With the soles of his thick black boots, he was flattening slugs as they slowly tried to crawl away to safety.

"Stop, those are Slugari!" she yelled.

He splattered two more. "I know," he uttered back through clenched teeth.

She cast a fireball. It exploded into his stomach, ripping his black and red Tenred tunic into a hundred pieces that were blasted away into the sky. All that remained was a charred skeleton. But his boots stayed on and his head stayed low, unfazed. He slammed his boots down onto another Slugari and then let out a sinister cackle.

She tried another fireball, but this one just passed through his rib cage like wind. His laugh grew louder until his head snapped up to look right at her. Loose flesh still hung around the gaping holes that were his eyes. "Your fire does nothing to someone already burned."

She realized it was someone she'd killed—the man with a bow who'd seen her just long enough for a puzzled glare before she'd engulfed his body in flames. He was back for a second chance.

"After the Slugari, you're next." He lifted his bony finger to point.

Overwhelmed with panic, she fled. She tripped on the stairs leading into the mountain, rolling deeper into the darkness. She rolled, and rolled, and finally bounced against Reela, who was already lying there waiting.

"Everything's fine," Reela said, pulling Effie in close and shushing her.

But the panic remained, for all was still dark. She couldn't see which way to go, and the stairs had flattened to dirt.

She realized then that she was now awake and had Reela's arms around her. "Everything's fine, you were dreaming." It was not Reela's voice, however. The arms were not Reela's, either. They were a man's arms, hairy, coarse, strong warrior's arms. At first she thought she felt Reela's full breasts against her back, but as the man's arms came to light, Reela's breasts were replaced by hard flesh. Effie was engulfed by him. His arms pressed her tight stomach and collar. Her back squeezed against the bulging muscles of his chest.

"Everything's fine, Effie," he whispered once again.

As she realized who it was, the tightness melted out from her. "Alex," she whispered, looking around her. "Where's my blanket?"

He took a hand from her stomach to point. "All the way over there." He pressed his hand back down. She liked the feeling of his hold on her, so she didn't move. "You rolled into me terror-stricken by some dream. Are you anxious about tomorrow? I get bad dreams when that happens to me."

Anxious. The word shook her with fright as she realized that's what it was. "I must be, but I don't know why."

"That's simple," he whispered and pulled his blanket around her. "Because we don't know what will happen. Uncertainty can produce playfully malicious thoughts."

"That can't be it. I thrive on not knowing what dangers await."

Effie realized that tumbling into his arms while they slept probably wasn't far from a fantasy of his. She didn't want to lead Alex on by cuddling against him, but crawling away from his warmth was the last thing she wanted. So she pressed herself against him, making herself comfortable in his embrace.

"Back in Oakshen, I always went out to bars and flirted with the uncertainty of the night. I never knew what would happen, and *that's* what brought me comfort."

The sound of a soft laugh came in three gusts of air from his nose. "I think I've caught you lying to yourself, Effie. I bet I can guess what happens when you visit bars. I know so just by knowing you. There's nothing uncertain about it, in fact. Let me describe it for you to prove how predictable the nights go."

Effie let out a slightly contemptuous giggle. "You can try."

Alex cleared his throat and lowered his voice to a whisper. "I'm sure that men are drawn to you because you're gorgeous."

Suddenly her heart started up, thumping hard against her chest. It was one thing to catch him staring but another to hear him admit it.

He continued before allowing her to respond. "Whatever they say, you'll have some quick retort because of that sharp tongue of yours. Sure, it can be dangerous being out by yourself, but not for you. No matter what happens, you can find a way out of it with your magic, which you almost never need. I don't think you find comfort in the uncertainty of those nights. No, it's actually the opposite. You know what to expect, and you know that you can handle it. You can be any version of yourself in those predictable situations and come away safe. It was the first thought I had when I met you at the party I hosted: *Whoever this girl is, she's ready for anything.* There's no uncertainty in a night out for Effie Elegin, and that's what comforts you."

She didn't even need to consider it for more than a heartbeat. He was right. She *did* know what to expect on a night out. *How could I have never seen that? I can't believe I've been lying to myself for so long.* She opened her mouth to speak, but no words came to mind to demonstrate the profound feeling she had. So Alex continued.

"This war, classes, everything since coming to the Academy, no one can know what will happen during this time or even after. That's what it is to become an adult—not knowing and being confused. Whether we're facing war, figuring out what we want to do with our lives, or simply talking to a girl we're infatuated with, there are scary and confusing moments we all must go through, and it's tough as boiled leather. It's in our nature to be uncomfortable in our own skin. It comes with the age. It means changes are coming, and life will never be the same as it was. That's the best and worst part about growing out of childhood."

"And here I thought sex and liquor were the best and worst parts of growing out of childhood," she replied before she could even consider his words.

He gave his throat an awkward clearing sound like something had obstructed it for a brief moment. Effie figured it must have been from the mention of sex.

"Yes, well, each of these things can be both terrible and wonderful; this at least is true." As he spoke, she felt him pull his waist away from her rear, his grip around her stomach loosening. "I've thought about this many nights. What helps me is to keep in mind that we all have expectations of the future, but it's up to each of us whether or not we grow into our expectations, change our expectations, or stay confused."

A silence followed that she knew to mean he was done. Alex had given her much to think about, too much for her even to respond. She'd known there was a deeper layer to him, and she was happy to find it had answers about herself.

As they lay there in silence, Effie thought about flipping over, wrapping her nearly bare legs around him, and kissing him. She knew it would be more than welcomed, might even start them on a frenzy, like the night she'd lost her virginity. Her mood pushed for it, especially after his embrace had done so well to relieve her, but logic fought against the idea. They were surrounded by others, and possibly the most important day of her life began at sunrise. The last thing she needed was more excitement.

She took his blanket off her, turned, and gave him a sweet kiss on the cheek. His short beard tickled her as he smiled and leaned into it. She liked pressing her lips against him but decided to stop at one.

"I gather you're feeling better?" he asked.

"For now," she answered and tiptoed off to slip her legs under her lonely blanket. *If I'm going to be rolling around while I sleep, I should probably wear more,* she joked to herself.

On her other side, Reela had also seemed to roll away from her original spot but in the opposite direction, toward Vithos. They were lying quite close, and her hand looked to be on his stomach.

Reela had been spending much of her time with the Elf. At first, Effie figured it was because they both were psychics, but as of late she'd started wondering whether there was more to it. She shuddered as the image came of Reela's naked body on his lap, holding on to his neck as she leaned back and bounced. It made her feel sick, but she didn't know why.

Effie had just gotten used to the idea of Reela and Cleve kissing passionately between jail bars, even had begun to think they were cute. Now had Reela fallen for the Elf? Would Effie need to get comfortable with Reela and Vithos being intimate? *Why is it such a disgusting thought?* She wanted to spit to clear the sour taste in her mouth but refrained.

The thought of Reela and Vithos together made Effie wonder if she was too hard on Steffen for his interest in Gabby. Steffen and her sister would be good for each other, always had been. On the other hand, the two psychics enjoying the pleasures of their bodies seemed truly wrong, immeasurably worse than Steffen and Gabby. With Reela and Vithos, it felt like she was imagining a brother and sister.

She wondered if other girls thought about sex in the same way she did, with vivid images of friends' naked bodies intertwined when they started to become close. *Probably not,* she figured.

Eventually, pleasant thoughts of Alex holding her distracted her easily enough for sleep to come.

When Effie woke the next morning, there was a taut eagerness bubbling up from the pit of her stomach. It felt like her whole life was about to reach a climax, and not in a good way.

If their plan worked, they would join forces with the elusive Slugari and return to Kyrro with a massive swing of hope. It was the first morning that she didn't awaken with drowsiness. It was like her body knew this day would be important, whether they failed or succeeded.

After a few miles through the sparse Satjen forest, Vithos stopped them, announcing, "We close. Need animal dig."

A long while they wandered, before Zoke finally spotted a badger to the east. Its face was striped by black and white, its back a dark gray color like Zoke's reptilian skin. He said something in Kreppen as he pointed. After Vithos replied in the same throaty language, Zoke translated for them.

"Badger digs well. It's too far for psyche, and they run fast. We have to not be seen. Stealth, yes?" He turned to Reela.

"Stealth," Reela replied with a nod.

By that, Effie figured Reela had been teaching Zoke some words he didn't know. Reela had been spending a lot of time with him and Vithos, after all.

They crept closer, using the thick trees as cover. The badger's nose wiggled like it was sniffing something. Then its head poked forward. When it decided to move, it got so low to the ground that Effie lost sight of it. Luckily, the animal stopped every few seconds to pop its body up and sniff the air again.

Soon, it seemed to catch the scent of something because it kept to one direction and increased its pace, stopping less to sniff the air as it went.

As they followed it through a cluster of shrubbery, they found the source of the scent the badger had been tracking. It was some creature Effie had never seen before, twice the size of the badger in length and height. But its color was something Effie had only seen in emeralds or thick smoke strands of Sartious Energy—it was a radiant, shimmering green that let through some light while reflecting the rest, brighter even than Reela's eyes.

"What is that?" Terren asked. They all stopped to keep the cover of the thick bushes.

Steffen let out a gasp when he leaned out for a glimpse. "A Slugari, it's a Slugari." He pointed with a jabbing finger. "That's a Slugari."

"Slugari?" Vithos repeated, glancing curiously at Zoke.

"It must be," Zoke replied. "Looks like the drawings."

The Slugari was a chubby little animal. Effie understood the name better now that she was looking at one. It had a shape that was similar to a slug, but there was nothing disgusting about it.

Reela let out one quiet giggle. "It's cute."

The Slugari had two short arms with talon-like hands. It pulled a flower from the ground, leaned its head back, and held the flower to its face. There was something atop its head that bent forward toward the flower. It looked like a plant stem, but it was hooked at the end.

"She's smelling the flower," Steffen whispered. "That long thing is her nose."

There were two antennae on either side of her hooked stem nose atop her head. They hung forward loosely as if not in use. The fat of her plump body lessened gradually from her front to her back, forming a thin tail that slowly slithered back and forth.

Effie figured the Slugari's stomach was the light gray coloration on her front. Small arms came around from her sides. Her face was no more than a rounded apex to her body, connecting to the top of her stomach without a neck, and she had two beady eyes and a thin mouth with cute, rabbit-like teeth.

The badger had become excited by the Slugari's scent, darting around it with curious pokes of its nose. The Slugari must have noticed the badger but chose to ignore it, seemingly too busy brushing something from the flower into a small pouch around her arm.

But then the badger stuck its nose a little too close, and the Slugari waved a claw in its direction. At the motion, the badger jumped away and hissed.

The badger didn't stay away for long, though. It darted around again, edging closer with more sniffs. The Slugari finished with the flower and let it drop so she could aim both three-fingered claws at the badger as if casting some sort of spell. Whatever it was, the badger ran off whimpering.

"Close enough for psyche?" Zoke asked in common tongue.

"Yes," Vithos replied. "I make calm. Krepp hide." Vithos transitioned into Kreppen to finish whatever he was telling Zoke. Then he held out his hand and walked toward the Slugari from the cover of the bushes.

"Steffen," Terren whispered. "Follow Vithos and tell the Slugari we're here to help."

Steffen stumbled out behind Vithos. At the sight of them, the Slugari tilted her head curiously. When she spoke, her mouth became animated but the words were light, dying the moment they were produced. There was an "S" or "H" sound in nearly every word Effie could hear clearly enough.

"Sodu harena sigh go dusa?" Effie thought it said.

Steffen said something back in what had to be the same language. He repeated the same word three times at the end: *hytu, hytu, hytu.*

The Slugari and Steffen went back and forth for five long minutes before Steffen turned around and called to them in common tongue. "You can come out. She smelled us already, anyway. Her name is Shudu." They each filtered out from the trees as Steffen continued. "Their crop of janjin has been dying. Shudu was sent to gather seeds. She says my Slugaren is very bad. She also says it's been fifty years since the last time they had contact with a Human—"

"You can tell us that later," Terren interrupted. "Will she lead us to their colony?"

"Yes." Steffen nodded enthusiastically. "As soon as we're ready."

"We're ready! We should get out of sight as soon as possible." Terren's tone was as if he was playing a game with a child and had just gotten fed up with their naivety.

Steffen spoke to Shudu in Slugaren again, and then the green creature started to slither away. "Follow her," Steffen told them.

Shudu moved a lot but didn't cover much ground for her efforts. Her tail folded and slithered like a snake while rippling waves cascaded down the rest of her unbending body.

When Effie noticed that Terren and Vithos were looking around in every direction, it made her feel exposed, and not in the same fun way as jumping into the river naked with Reela. It felt more like something was about to jump out at her, though she didn't know what or when. She checked around as well. There were hills to the north and trees in every direction. Someone could be watching them and easily remain hidden.

"How far is it from here?" Terren asked.

"It's right up ahead," Steffen replied.

Shudu stopped at an old tree. It was nearly twice as wide as most others and with bark that had faded to gray over the years. The Slugari went around the tree's funnel-shaped base, pointing at part of it. Like many trees in Satjen, clusters of long green leaves came from every crevice within the tree's base.

"No, couldn't be," Steffen whispered incredulously, kneeling in front of the biggest patch of leaves. He used both hands to pull them aside. They slid out like a piece of pie, leaving a hole easily big enough to crawl through. "Unbelievable."

The Slugari said something to Steffen, which he translated. "Shudu will go last to put the plant back properly, but it's a maze down there. So once we go down, wait for Shudu before going any farther. I think that's what she said." Steffen scratched his head. "She used a few words I don't know."

"Effie, go first, will you?" Terren was telling her more than asking her. "You can give us light from below."

She squatted in front of the hole to shine her wand down. The tunnel was steeper than she would have liked and went on farther than she could see. She got to her elbows and knees, grasping her wand tightly.

As she crawled in and tried to remain calm, her shoulders pushed against the edges of the tree and her backpack scraped against the top. *This is where Slugari could move five times the speed of Humans,* Effie thought, trying to manage her body through the tight space. *It's a good thing I don't mind close spaces that much.*

The dirt was damp, sticking to her hands and wrists. Her lower back quickly began to ache, and soon her neck became sore from being held up to see where she was going.

"Effie, anything to report?" She could tell Terren was shouting, but his voice was muffled like he was talking with a cupped hand over his mouth. From his tone, Effie figured this was the second or third time he'd tried asking before she'd finally heard.

Because it was impossible to turn around, she bent the top of her head to the ground to shout between her legs. "May as well start following. I have no idea when this ends."

When she flipped her head back up, all her hair had come down over her face and become heavy with dirt. She took a moment to shake some out before flipping her hair behind her neck so she could see in front of her. Dirt trickled down her back. She sighed, dragging on.

Not a moment too soon, the tunnel widened drastically. Not only could she now stand, so could a giant. *How could the Slugari have made this hole so big, and more importantly, why?* She was still on a slope, but there was no longer only one direction to descend. She could continue forward, but there were two new pathways, one to either side of her.

The start of the maze, she realized. She turned to aim light from her wand back into the tunnel, waiting as patiently as she could for the rest of them. With excitement pumping through her, each breath was clear, drawn without trouble.

Nothing is going to stop us from getting to the Slugari. She felt all the tension drain out of her as a wide smile formed.

Chapter 59: The Moment
ZETI

Zeti watched from the hills in horror as her brother and Vithos followed the Humans underneath the tree.

"They're ours now," Paramar muttered under his breath, pushing himself from his stomach to his feet.

The rest of their Slugari search group was waiting behind them for their report of what they saw, but that was only twelve Krepps. They needed many more before invading the Slugari colony.

Six days ago, their search group was too overjoyed for words when the chamoline flower finally turned a deep red while they passed over the heart of northern Satjen. Even though they all knew what it meant, no one could say it aloud. The Slugari colony had been found. Already being unbelievable, it seemed as if speaking the words would push it over the edge to untrue.

Instead, they all gawked silently at the red flower in Paramar's claws until he shouted for two of the Krepps to run back to camp to gather their army. It was a four-day walk, so Paramar demanded they make it there in three. The rest of their group stayed behind to be vigilant, watching for signs of Slugari, Humans, or the traitors Zoke and Vithos.

When they found all three, the feeling it gave Zeti was beyond her comprehension. It was unlike Krepps to feel ambivalent, but ambivalence couldn't be more of an understatement when she saw Zoke going underground with the Slugari—going where the Krepps would be attacking as soon as their army got there.

"When will our army arrive?" she asked Paramar, trying to mask her feeling of dread with an indifferent tone.

"Doe and the rest of them should be here by tomorrow morning," Paramar answered.

"Doe is coming for this?" Zeti couldn't forget what he'd told her: "*When we see Zoke again, you're going to be the one to kill him.*"

"Certainly, yes." Paramar gave one hard laugh. "He's never wanted anything more than storming the underground colony and taking revenge on his own kind. Imagine his delight when we tell him that Zoke and Vithos are down there as well."

Zeti thought about what Suba—the task coordinator for all Krepps and the closest thing to a mother—had told her when they'd last spoken: "*Certainty is important, remember that. When you're put in a confusing spot, find something you're sure about.*"

Zeti fished around her thoughts for something she could be sure about. Usually it was easy—the taste of Slugari meat. But now that taste had gone sour because mixed with it was the blood of her brother.

Next, she tried focusing on her feelings for Zoke. It did no good. She felt as if she hardly knew him anymore now that he was a traitor. She wondered how it came to be that the two things she was most certain of a month ago now gave her ambivalence, even apprehension.

A question popped into Zeti's mind. Thankful for the distraction, she asked it. "What of the Humans? Our treaty with Tenred—they want us to take arms against Kyrro. Are we to abandon that alliance now that we have the Slugari?"

"That's up to our leaders, but if it were my decision we'd tear Kyrro to the ground. You saw it." Paramar pointed to the tree they'd just watched the Humans crawl under. "Kyrro is with the Slugari, and the traitors are with Kyrro. That means Kyrro must be against us. If we leave them, we give them the chance to attack our underground colony after we take it over. Doe would never allow that." He ripped grass from the dirt with a quick yank. "Doe said it before, he'll say it again: Kyrro will burn. Right after we tear through the Slugari colony, we'll turn their cities to ash." He let the green grass blades fall between his fingers and sprinkle back to the forest floor.

With a deep pain in her heart, Zeti finally knew exactly what she was feeling. This was the moment she'd feared. This was the moment when her last bit of hope was gone. It had been dwindling, slowly disappearing like drops of water under the sun. But now there was none. The last of it left her as quickly and quietly as her next breath. A gust of wind came from behind to carry the air from her lungs down to the trees below. She could almost see her hope going with it, never to return.

Chapter 60: Size and Strength
STEFFEN

"We must have passed by twenty different tunnels by now," Steffen commented to Shudu in her language. The slow-moving Slugari had been leading them through the massive tunnels for nearly an hour already. Every time they came to a fork, Shudu chose a direction and slithered on without a moment of consideration.

When the Slugari replied, Steffen couldn't quite understand the exact numbers she told him. He was nowhere near fluent in the language and hadn't practiced numbers in Slugaren for many years. He realized she was listing the amount of times the maze led to a wall, how many wrong ways the maze had, and how many times two paths circled to meet each other later. Of the numbers he did recognize, it sounded like she said five hundred-something when she was describing the number of incorrect paths, but he figured he'd misheard. That many seemed impossible.

"How is the roof so high?" Steffen asked.

"The tunnel was made by a Dajrik," Shudu replied.

"They really exist?" Steffen blurted out in common tongue without thinking. He took a breath to compose himself and then asked the same question in Slugaren. Implication was not enough in this case. He wanted Shudu to answer definitively.

"Yes, you will meet ours soon. We are almost there."

"There's one here?" Steffen shouted this time, again in common tongue.

"Why are you suddenly so excited?" Reela asked. "What's here?"

"A Dajrik! What a day! I get to meet a Slugari, travel into their underground colony, and even see a Dajrik."

Reela said something, but Steffen was too busy trying to ask Shudu a question to listen. "Is the Dajrik really..." He stopped himself. He wanted to ask if it was twenty feet tall, but he couldn't remember the number for twenty and didn't even know if the Slugari used the same measurement system. "Is it really as tall as the roof of these tunnels?" He pointed above them.

"Yes," Shudu answered calmly.

"Does it truly have skin as tough as bone?"

"Yes."

Exhilaration was bursting through his body. An involuntary squeak escaped from behind closed lips. *It's true. All of it's true!* Everything he'd read of Slugari, their language, their history, their Dajrik, it was all accurate. He was so thankful he didn't listen to his mother when she'd told him not to fill his brilliant mind with books of silly fantasies.

He was ten when he spoke Slugaren to her for the first time. Her eyebrows bent as she tried to understand his words.

"What are you saying?" she finally asked after he repeated it three times.

"It's Slugaren. It means you're my mother. It's so fun to speak!"

"Slugaren, where could you have read about that?" Her tone was bitter.

Immediately, Steffen knew he shouldn't have brought it up. "The last book we bought. It's about the language of the Slugari," he admitted.

"That's what you had me buy for you, a book about a made-up language? I don't want you wasting time with that. I thought you loved history."

It would take him four more years before he'd start convincing his mother of anything about which she disagreed. He couldn't remember how that conversation ended. He probably had agreed with whatever she'd said, only to change his mind later, back to what it was before. It was the usual result to a disagreement between them until he got older and she started listening to logic.

"It is just past this bend," Shudu said after what felt like a mile through a maze so long and elaborate that Steffen had no chance of remembering the way out without careful attention to their route, and it was too late to start now.

The only light to guide them thus far was a faint glow emanating from Shudu's body as well as Effie's wand. But as they came around the last turn, the tunnel became lit with what looked to be natural sunlight.

Ahead was a sight Steffen only thought he'd see in his imagination—a great underground chasm with hundreds, no thousands, of glistening Slugari. The pillars that connected the ground to the ceiling had a melting-candle look that made it appear as if the pillars were dripping. But upon closer investigation, Steffen saw they were sturdy, composed of hard clay.

As he came closer to the end of the tunnel and the beginning of the colony, Steffen could start to see around the many pillars. He found the sources of the light that looked just like that of the sun. There were balls of burning white that were just bright enough to bring a tear to his eye, but not so bright that it pained him to look.

"Are those caregelows?" he asked Shudu, pointing at the flowers. He already knew the answer but wanted her to say it.

"Yes."

"So beautiful," he whispered back. Something deep in his stomach began to ache, not painful, but warm and gripping. It swelled slowly up to his chest, and the moment it touched his heart, he felt raw and exposed, ready to laugh and cry at the same time.

The caregelows were everywhere, some of them brighter than others. Each was surrounded by bursts of unreal mixtures of blue, red, green, and everything in between. It took finding a dim caregelow to realize the source of these hallucinatory bubbles of colored light: All around the caregelow were plants so pure and bright it felt like Steffen was finally seeing true color for the first time.

While he was watching the dim caregelow, a Slugari wiggled its fat body through the mass of fantastic flowers and held its claws over the caregelow in the center. The caregelow grew brighter until its white light overtook the Slugari nearby, completely hiding him from view until he slithered back out of the cluster.

"Wait here," Shudu told Steffen as they were just about out of the tunnel. "I need to get the leader before you come in."

Steffen translated for Terren and the rest of them but couldn't even be sure he was heard. Their heads were stretched forward, eyes wide open. Even Zoke, who claimed the Fjallejon Mountains didn't amaze him, had a look of sheer astonishment.

"How can such a place exist?" Reela was first to speak.

"Because it's their only way of surviving," Steffen answered. "Above ground, they would be destroyed by the Krepps. They needed to live underground, so they found a way."

"What is that?" Zoke asked with a claw extended. Steffen didn't need to see where he was pointing. He already knew what Zoke saw, for it had just come around a pillar and was impossible not to notice.

"That's a Dajrik," Steffen replied, letting out a knowing grin.

Everyone's awe was palpable.

The twenty-foot-tall creature was even more marvelous than Steffen had seen in drawings. From afar, its skin looked just like rock but molded around the figure of a man like a suit of armor. Its face was like that of a Human but with horns of rock protruding upward from the sides of its head instead of ears. Steffen had seen helmets of war with the same design.

There was no color to the black and gray Dajrik except for a radiant red jewel that hung on a necklace it carried around its thick neck. *The ruby of a hundred rujins,* Steffen realized. Of all that was written in his books about Slugari and Dajriks, the story of the rujin ruby necklace to cure the Dajrik's terrorizing nightmares was the least believable to him. He'd never been happier to be wrong.

There was a crash like a boulder falling from a small peak with every step the Dajrik took toward them. An entourage of Slugari followed behind. If Shudu was among them, Steffen couldn't pick her out.

Terren stepped ahead with a hand on the hilt of his sword. Vithos and Reela took to his sides.

"Steffen," Terren said. "What's happening?"

"The Dajrik and a bunch of Slugari are coming to meet us."

"I can see that. What are they going to do with us?" Terren asked, his voice growing heavy with urgency. "What did Shudu say exactly?"

"Just to wait here for her to get their leader."

"There was nothing she said to give you the impression we wouldn't be harmed?" Terren asked, now clearly troubled.

"No..." A rush of fear pulled at Steffen's heart. He'd never even considered they might be attacked.

The Dajrik was close enough now for his eyes to be seen, black as shadows. The group of Slugari behind had come around to the Dajrik's sides. Their beady eyes didn't look curious but aggressive. Steffen took two steps back and reached over his shoulder to make sure his bow was there and ready.

"Tell them to stop. That's close enough," Terren told Steffen. Another two steps and the Dajrik's next would be on top of one of them.

Before Steffen could remember the word for stop, the Dajrik and

Slugari did so on their own.

Steffen felt a burst of relief and let out a loud breath.

A Slugari came to them from between the Dajrik's massive feet. "Who is your leader?" she asked in common tongue.

"You speak our language," Terren replied with amazement, taking a step toward her. "I'm leading this small party."

"You have a Krepp with you, I am told. Where is he?"

Zoke stepped around them to show himself. "I don't wish to hurt any Slugari," he said.

"Come out here," the Slugari replied in a tone that made it seem like Zoke's words had never reached her. Her speech was deep and soft at the same time, like a young woman with a low voice.

Zoke followed her order but turned to share a look with Vithos as he puttered forward. It seemed as if the Elf was nodding his head.

"Turn around with hands behind you." The Slugari spoke before Zoke was close enough to touch her.

He stopped and obeyed.

"You may not want to hurt us, but there is no such thing as a Krepp uninterested in the taste of us."

The Dajrik closed a massive hand around Zoke's torso so that the Krepp's arms were stuck behind him.

Vithos blurted out some Kreppen words before composing himself and speaking in common tongue. "Don't hurt."

"He's with us," Terren added. "We're friends with your race. We want to help."

"So I have heard," the Slugari replied. "But we are not taking risks." Another Slugari came forward with some sort of vine, wrapping it around Zoke's wrists. The Dajrik took another hand to Zoke's legs and lifted him as if pulling out a weed.

It walked away, holding Zoke like a pigeon ready to take flight.

"Where are you taking him?" Terren asked.

"He will be safe for now," the Slugari who had spoken first answered. "We do not want him too tempted by our smell."

"He..." Vithos had a hand on his chin, his face twisting. "He no..." Vithos pointed to his nose desperately. "He no..."

"He can't smell?" Reela asked.

Vithos nodded enthusiastically. "Yes. He can't smell. *Gurradu.* He no like Slugari."

"Whether or not that is true, we will feel safer with him not around. Now, I heard it from Shudu, but I want your leader to tell me. What are you doing here, and how did you convince Shudu to show you our secret passage?"

"We were sent here by our king, Welson Kimard of Kyrro," Terren answered proudly. "A war has started above ground. The Krepps have joined with Tenred to fight against us. Are you aware that the Krepps have been searching for your colony for many years?"

"Yes," the Slugari answered. "We are aware of the search but not of this war. Before you tell me more, answer how you convinced Shudu to let you down here. Any Slugari in her position would let herself die over compromising the colony."

Terren bit his lip.

If we tell them about the psychics, they won't trust anything else we say, Steffen realized.

Reela came toward the Slugari. "May I speak?" she asked politely.

"Yes," the Slugari answered.

She knelt down so that her face was level with the Slugari. "We explained the situation between the Humans and Krepps to Shudu. This war involves your race as well. You're in great danger. Please allow us to explain, and you'll understand why Shudu felt it was worth the risk to bring us down here. We wish to work with you to help each other."

Steffen didn't doubt she was using all the psyche she could to alleviate the Slugari's worry.

"I understand," the Slugari replied with a crooked twist to her mouth that looked closer to a smile than anything else. "Explain and we will listen, but I do not promise anything else."

Terren started at the beginning, when Tenred didn't renew the treaty. For a warrior, Steffen thought, Terren was an excellent storyteller. As he described the journey that had led them here, all nearby Slugari slithered over to join the mass of listeners. While Steffen couldn't tell if even half of them could understand Terren's language, they still seemed enthralled by his voice and gestures.

"What would you have us do?" the Slugari replied when Terren had finished.

"Fight with us," he answered. "Help us defeat the Krepps and worry no more about hiding."

"How would we go about doing that? We stand no taller than your waist. Our magic is not strong enough to burn through the skin of a

Krepp. Our movement is slow, and our claws can pierce through the ground but not through an enemy."

"What of your Dajrik?" Terren asked.

"Our Dajrik is older than he can remember. He has forgotten all battles but one, and in that he was forced to run. He does not wish to fight any more than we do."

"No one wishes to fight, but you can't hide forever. You'll be found eventually." Terren spoke bluntly.

"We realize that, which is why there are escape routes to another hideout. You say we cannot hide forever. To that, we say you cannot fight the Krepps." The Slugari squeezed her claws together as if it pained her to say it. "They are far too strong. Especially when led by Doe and Haemon. Their magic ability has grown to be unparalleled. You think it is silly to run and hide, I can hear it in your tone, but in truth, fighting is far more insane. I am sorry you came all this way to hear that." The Slugari started to turn.

"We were offered a way out of this war!" Terren called after her, but she didn't stop. "If we gave up your location to the Krepps. It's you they want, not us!"

At that the Slugari turned back. Her eyes looked to burrow deeper into her head. She said nothing.

Terren continued. "But we're not ready to see to the destruction of your race, and we'll probably be next." He gestured to Reela. "As Reela said earlier, we came here to help each other. Now you wish for us to lay down our swords and let the Krepps tear down our cities and kill our people?"

"I never said these words." The Slugari's voice had softened to a murmur.

"You might as well have when you said our enemy is too strong to fight." Terren pulled his blade from its sheath, the metal singing as he spoke. The cluster of Slugari rustled, the front line of them slithering backward. "You don't know our strength. A single Krepp knows to fight, but Krepps know nothing of war. Kyrro has war in its blood. We were born from war. We know how to battle. We know when to fight and when to flee, and this is no time to flee."

He drove his blade into the ground so that it sliced deep into the hard dirt. Murmurs echoed through the crowd at the sight of his strength. "Stand with us, even though it be only up to our waists. Share resources, give us information of the Krepp leaders, and lend us your Dajrik so we can save your asses before you're all torn apart by Krepps!" He slammed his fist into his other hand.

The Slugari's eyes had grown so dim that Steffen wondered if she could still see from them. The crowd of Slugari watching was dead quiet, still as stone. Terren's heavy breath was all that could be heard.

Finally, the Slugari's eyes came back to size and she spoke in a calm voice. "Let me take a day to scout some things and ponder this. You and your party can stay here for the night. I will give you an answer tomorrow." She waved her claw at the group of Slugari that had gathered behind her. From it slithered another. "This is Hejel. He knows common tongue as well. He will lead you to your sleeping quarters."

Before leaving them, she slithered back to Terren. "Please do try and refrain from drawing your weapon in here." Her voice was stern, but her crooked smile served to make her words sound less serious.

Terren pulled the weapon from the dirt and put it away. "We never got your name," he called after her.

"Refer to me as Queen," she replied without as much as a look back, disappearing into the crowd nearby.

Hejel was male. Steffen could tell by his tail, as it was shorter and rounder than female Slugari. Other than that he looked nearly the same as Queen. Like Shudu, there was a small pouch around his arm.

Steffen pointed at it. "Do you go above ground like Shudu?" he asked.

"Because of this?" Hejel lifted his arm. "Many of us carry these seed pouches, but very few of us go above ground. I have not been in years. It is far too dangerous. In case we need to flee our home in a hurry, we carry fertile seeds at all times." Hejel gave the strap of his pouch a testing tug. "Let me show you where you will be staying. It has been so long since we have had visitors. I must admit I am excited to see you try our flower beds. Follow me."

Flower beds? Steffen had never heard of such a thing. He reached for his bag over his shoulder, retrieving his pen and scroll. The moment his hand grasped the pen, words poured out of him without thought. "*Caregelows are their source of light, stationed within clumps of plants so as to feed the plants with energy. The Slugari seem to use their own Bastial Energy to keep the caregelows lit and healthy...*"

Steffen had to pause to watch where he was going. The group of Slugari that had gathered at the entrance was in the hundreds by now. Hejel slithered right through them, expecting to be followed. Steffen found himself in the back, behind Effie and Reela, who were holding hands as they filtered through the sea of shimmering green. Many of the waist-high creatures lifted their claws to be grazed by Steffen's forearms as he passed them. They squeaked and murmured excitedly with each touch, which was surprisingly warm.

After just a few steps, Effie gasped loudly. "I've never felt so much Bastial Energy. I feel as if I could fly if I tried," she said.

"Make sure you don't," Reela replied. "When you fall, I'm going to lose you among all these Slugari."

"The Slugari naturally have far more Bastial Energy than Humans. They must be transferring some to us as some sort of greeting," Steffen guessed.

Up ahead, Terren was shouting. "Hejel! Why are they clawing at me? Hejel, I've lost you."

"I am waiting up here," their guide called out. Hejel already was through the mass of animated Slugari, and Steffen had just entered. "As I said, we do not get visitors down here. Many are thrilled to meet Humans and an Elf."

"My body is absorbing the Bastial Energy," Effie said, her voice strained. "I can't hold it in." A faint white glow started pulsing from her arms. With each pulse, Steffen felt a gust of heat.

Reela dropped Effie's hand and tried to get some distance. "I'll clear them," she said.

With Steffen's next breath, a terror clutched his heart. *Need to get away from Effie, now!* He pushed away from her and found all the Slugari doing the same.

The moment he was no longer touched by her heat, he felt like himself again.

Effie was on her knees. From her skin pulsed a white glow that made the sand dance beneath her feet with each rhythmic throb of light. Then a burst of pure white exploded from her hands. It was straight, like a sunbeam piercing into a pitch-black cave through a small opening. She aimed it overhead, and immediately the thin ray of light began expanding into the surrounding space. In the duration of a blink, it exploded like a flash of lightning, finding every wall and pillar around them. A blaze of heat lived and died with it.

Effie warily picked herself up. "I apologize for that. I've never had so much Bastial Energy within me. I didn't know how to handle it."

The Slugari clattered together in groups while many others rushed to check on nearby plants.

"I had no idea some Humans had the potential to absorb so much Bastial Energy," Hejel said with bright eyes. "Perhaps we may be of use to you in times of battle. I will report this to Queen later."

Chapter 61: Touch
STEFFEN

With the rest of the Slugari now keeping their distance, it became far easier to stay with Hejel. Steffen stayed toward the back and tried to take notes as best he could. For each plant he recognized, he made a note of it. For each plant he didn't, he described it as best he could. Most of them he knew, although they were far brighter in color than he'd ever seen. The copper red of queensblood, the ink and indigo streaks of riverdilly, the glow of golden yellow in the goldbellows—he'd only seen such mixtures of colors in paintings. Even the white found on the taviray flowers was so fresh and bright that it seemed as if a single speck of dirt would ruin it.

He made notes that some Slugari were watering the plants, but he didn't know where they were getting the water.

The cavern seemed to twist on forever. With each turn, he kept expecting to see the end of it. But after what must have been a mile of plants, pillars, and caregelows lighting their way, he started to wonder if they'd just gone in a big circle. That is, until they came to the lake.

"This is clean water," Hejel told them. "Make sure not to fall in."

The Slugari had surrounded the massive body of water with blocks of hardened clay. The room containing it was the largest yet, stretching well past one hundred yards, and the lake touched two sides of its walls. Upon closer investigation, it even looked to be moving, as if the entire body of water was seeping in through one side of the room and flowing out the other.

"How have you brought so much water down here?" Alex asked.

"Brought?" Hejel questioned. "This is groundwater. It was here long before us. There are many places under Ovira where water exists. We can sense the Bastial Energy within it to make it easier to locate. That is what these are for." Hejel leaned forward. His two short antennae wiggled. "There is Bastial Energy in everything natural. There is more in water than there is in the dirt, although the deeper we dig, the more in the dirt we find. There is more in plants than in water, especially some plants."

He squirmed toward Terren, his antennae stretching out at Terren's hand. "And there is much in Humans as well, some more than others. Like her." He lifted a claw to Effie. "I can feel a lot of Bastial Energy in her, although she is still nowhere near what Slugari have."

Steffen hurried to write it all down. He'd read some of what Hejel was saying but never with as much specificity. With one eye he noticed Hejel coming over to him.

"What is that you are doing?"

"Taking notes to report back to the King," Steffen replied, continuing to scribble.

"I understand...and is this all the notes you have taken right there in your hand?" Hejel pointed.

"These scrolls, yes."

"Good," Hejel said. He snatched them from Steffen's grasp. A flicker came from Hejel's claws, catching the edge of the scrolls aflame. He dropped them to the dirt as fire washed over them. "We cannot have you keeping records of our hidden colony until we are absolutely sure they will remain in safe hands."

A defeated whimper squeaked out of Steffen as he watched hours of notes melt into the dirt. Reela gave a comforting squeeze to his shoulder.

The boom of the Dajrik's footsteps came around a pillar. Walking next to him was a chagrined Zoke, his bright yellow eyes avoiding them.

"It appears Queen has decided your Krepp is not a threat," Hejel said. "It must be true that he cannot smell, otherwise he surely would have succumbed to his urges to eat by now."

Reela and Effie were whispering loudly to each other. A laugh erupted from Effie that she tried unsuccessfully to stifle with her hand.

When the silence and gazes of the others stopped them, Reela showed Hejel wide eyes above a troubled smile. "Can we pet the Dajrik?" she asked.

What? Pet that thing? Steffen had known his childhood friends to be adventurous, but their request still came as a shock. He could've spent years in the Slugari colony without once thinking of touching the bone-hard skin of the creature more than three times his size.

"Pet?" Hejel asked. "I do not know this word."

For all I know, there might not even be a word for it in Slugaren, Steffen thought. "They want to touch the Dajrik," he explained.

"Touch him?" Hejel was even more confused. "Why?"

Steffen shrugged.

Effie quickly tried to explain. "There's a connection when we touch another living creature. It's like sharing a conversation without words."

Everyone turned to Hejel. His beady eyes were shifting slowly between Effie and Reela. "I will ask him," Hejel finally replied. His tone was as if he was sure the Dajrik would disagree.

As Hejel began speaking to the Dajrik in Slugaren, Alex leaned over to whisper to Steffen. "You don't want to pet the Dajrik?"

"Now that I think about it, I would. Not that I know why. His skin surely won't be soft."

"It's not the pleasure of the touch but what it means," Alex said.

"It doesn't really matter," Steffen retorted without giving Alex's words any thought. "It's not going to want to be petted anyway."

"The Dajrik says you can touch him," Hejel announced to Steffen's surprise. At that, the giant took a step toward them. His foot displaced the hard dirt in front of them the same way Steffen's might on a sandy beach.

Zoke and Terren were the only ones uninterested. Steffen overheard them speaking quietly about Queen while he gathered the courage to make contact with the Dajrik's leg in front of him.

The skin of the Dajrik, if it could even be called skin, was iron gray. It looked as if someone had taken slabs of mountain and shaped them around his limbs. Steffen was surprised when he pushed his palm against it, for it bent slightly, giving way to thick muscle. The texture of the skin was like the coarse mountain walls within the Fjallejon Pathway, but it was far softer, even stretchy.

"This isn't as hard as bone," Steffen said with sheer disappointment.

"He is very old," Hejel answered. "Over two thousand years. I am sure it used to be far tougher."

"When was the last time he was touched?" Effie asked. She and Reela were at the other leg, running their hands down to his feet intimately.

Before Hejel could ask, the Dajrik stepped back to take his feet away. At first he looked as if he'd grown tired of the attention, but then he let down a knee so that he could rest two open hands on the dirt. He waited patiently, but Steffen didn't know what he wanted.

Reela seemed to, though. She had an open-mouthed smile and squeaked with glee. "Come on," she said, grabbing Effie's hand and guiding her into one of the Dajrik's open palms. Then Reela hurried over to the other.

The Dajrik closed his palms around them and brought them to his shoulders, where they sat and held on to his horn-like ears. They each gave a squeal of approval as the Dajrik gingerly rose to both feet.

He proceeded to parade them around, and their squeals became giddy screams.

Alex had a long belly laugh. Steffen, meanwhile, was at a loss for words. Not only did he not know what to say, he was too shocked to even know what to think. So he stared in silence, knowing full well it would be a sight he'd never forget.

Their sleeping quarters was an alcove that was attached to that same vast room with the lake. It was easily big enough for their entire party, but all it contained were a few hundred flowers Steffen didn't recognize. They had long stems that were thick, about as wide as Steffen's wrist. Atop the stems were milky brown petals with their edges curling inward like a hand at rest. They were packed so tightly together, just navigating through them would be tough.

"We think you will be very pleased with this flower bed." Hejel had a knowing tone as if he was telling a joke. "It is our understanding that all the begardeens above ground died off before the Humans came to Ovira. Have any of you seen this plant before?"

It seemed as if they all looked at Steffen for the answer. *Begardeens?* "No," he spoke for them. "We've never heard of it."

"Humans like surprises, do they not?" Hejel asked.

"It depends," Terren answered before anyone else could, holding his hand near his hilt.

"Go lie on them," Hejel said. "They are quite strong in numbers."

Again, they each turned to Steffen and waited.

"Go ahead, Steffen," Terren pointed. "You're the chemist. You should try it out first."

Unsure what to expect, he nodded and started toward the begardeens. When he got close, their fingers curled outward and they leaned toward him, stretching out surprisingly far. Some even came up to his chest. As he tried to push his way through them, they softly pressed back. When he tried to guide his hands between some so that he could make a path, they rushed in front to meet his touch.

"How am I supposed to lie on them?" he asked.

"You have to jump. They will catch you," Hejel replied. "They want to touch you. They are a very needy plant, highly attracted to warmth and Bastial Energy. It makes it quite difficult to feed the begardeens in the middle of this large cluster. Honestly, if there is any use to the plant for Slugari, we have not discovered it yet. We just cannot possibly let it become extinct like so many other amazing plants have already."

By how hard the begardeens were pressing against him, Steffen knew they could support his weight. With nervous excitement, he removed his backpack and tightened his belt. He hurried to the wall behind him to give himself more room. Then he took a quick breath and broke into a run to get the speed he needed to leap over the front row of begardeens.

When he jumped, they reached out to hold him as he soared above. His momentum carried him across their tops, giving him the feeling that he was flying for a heartbeat. Now *he* was the one letting out a giddy squeal, Steffen realized.

He was a good ten feet into the cluster when he finally slowed to a halt. He wiggled and tried to get his feet on the ground, but couldn't. Soon, his mind came around to the notion that they weren't going to let him down. So he flipped on his back to get more comfortable. Then he bent his neck to lift his head, and to his surprise, begardeens stretched higher to support him.

When he sat up, they pushed on his back to keep him upright. When he pushed hard against them to lie back down, they gave until he pushed no more. Though he had no idea how he would get out, he didn't mind. It was quite relaxing. He stretched out his arms and legs and yawned.

One by one, the others set down their bags and leapt onto the flower bed. Everyone screamed with excitement as they soared toward the middle of the begardeens. Even Terren had a hearty laugh.

Zoke and Vithos were the only ones left who hadn't. They seemed busy talking to each other in Kreppen until Vithos set down his bag and ran to join the rest of them atop the begardeens with a deep giggle.

"Come, Zoke," Vithos called to him.

Zoke formed a smile with his long mouth and then broke into a sprint. He was quicker than anyone else had been, speeding to the begardeens and leaping impressively high into the air—only they didn't reach out to hold him as they did for everyone else. Instead, they shrank and twisted away from his falling body. He screamed, but it was a yelp of sudden fear, not of excitement like everyone else.

Steffen heard a deep thud as Zoke slammed into the dirt with a loud grunt. In a breath, the Krepp was back on his feet with a dumbfounded look. He reached out to the begardeens nearby, and they only leaned farther away.

"Interesting," Hejel said. "They must not like the stink of Krepps."

Zoke let out a long sigh before dragging his feet out of the cluster of begardeens. Each plant leaned away from him as he went. "I'm used to sleeping on the dirt by now anyway," he muttered.

"It from bad luck," Vithos said in his thick Kreppen accent. "Fjallejon said. You need kiss." The Elf made a loud kissing sound three times.

Steffen felt a laugh burst out of him and then he noticed the others laughing as well.

Zoke spat at that, though Steffen thought he could see a hint of a smile at the corner of his long mouth.

Chapter 62: We Think We Know
EFFIE

After an hour of phasing in and out of sleep, Effie was wide awake again. She sighed and pushed herself to sit upright. The begardeens rose with her back and held her there. She felt a tickle along her inner thigh. Glancing down curiously, she saw one of the begardeens had come through her legs to kiss the hand resting on her lap. She twitched her fingers to play with it, and it twitched right back.

The only light within their nook was a faint glow from the dimly lit caregelows outside. It was just enough for her to see the shadowy outline of Alex and Steffen next to her. They were each deeply asleep, breathing in a rhythmic flow. As her eyes found a resting place upon Alex, some of the shadow peeled away so that she could see his features. She let out a soft giggle when she realized he was sleeping on his stomach, for the begardeens had latched onto his face, squishing his cheeks to cause his features to mush together. She couldn't believe he found it to be comfortable, but he was asleep and she wasn't.

Startled by sudden footsteps of someone entering, she aimed white light from her hand in their direction. It was just Zoke. He held up a claw to cover his eyes before continuing to the corner, where he rested with his back against the wall.

Effie swam her way out of the begardeens and cautiously went over to join him.

"Can't sleep?" she asked, sitting down beside him.

"Just needed to urinate," he answered. He closed his eyes as if disinterested in her company.

For a while they sat together in silence while Effie listened to his breathing. He let out air so slowly that he took one breath for every two of hers. The tranquil sound made her feel like she was floating on the body of water just outside. She might even have been asleep when Zoke finally asked her, "You don't like the plants?"

"They're fun, but nothing compares to my bed at home."

Zoke seemed to be nodding. His golden eyes were open now,

staring absently at the sharp claws on his long feet stretched out before them. "I have no home," he whispered.

Zoke told his tale of exile after the battle on the Fjallejon Mountains. The way he told it made it seem like he was marked as a traitor and then had no options other than to really become one. It made her wonder how many Humans had been forced down a certain path simply because of how they were labeled.

"You ever feel lost?" she asked.

"Vithos knows Ovira well. We never get lost."

Sometimes Effie forgot common tongue was the Krepp's second language. He spoke it very well. "By lost, I mean do you ever get confused when you think about who you were before compared to now? Like you feel as if you've lost who you are?"

Zoke didn't respond. At first Effie thought she had confused him or given him a question he didn't want to answer. But after a few breaths, he muttered, "More recently, yes." His head turned slightly to glance at her from the side. "This happens to Humans?"

"At least to me it does," Effie whispered. "Just last year I thought I knew everything about myself, about my future, and the type of person I would be in it. I thought I would go to the Academy, excel in my classes, become a recognized mage in three years, and find a job I love. It was all so simple. But the older I get, the more I realize there's nothing simple about it. I'm not even the same person I was a month ago."

"A month ago." Zoke paused to grind his tongue against his teeth. "I was different as well. My fears and troubles back then seem trivial now." He spat away from her. "Now everything matters."

"It certainly feels that way, doesn't it—that the smallest choice can change our lives. Sometimes I wish I could go back to childhood, when the only decisions I needed to make were what to do with my free time." She laughed as she remembered something. "Every night as I fell asleep back then, I hoped to wake up ten years into the future, when I would be grown and ready for my life to begin. I was so eager to get older, but only because I thought most things would stay the same."

She'd thought much about what Alex had told her that night she'd rolled into his arms, realizing he was right about everything. And now, she had enough knowledge to admit something she never would have believed earlier.

"I still can't help but think of the future as I fall asleep these nights, but now it makes me so anxious I can barely breathe."

Zoke turned his indifferent glance to her bare, outstretched legs beside his. Effie wondered how much he cared to hear of her issues, if at all. When Zoke had described the tribe of Krepps, he'd made it seem like they lived to endure life, not to enjoy it. *They're far too different,* she thought. *He probably just thinks I'm weak.*

But she was pleasantly surprised when Zoke lifted an eye to her and said something she would have guessed only a Human would say.

"We think we know our future as children," Zoke said. "We think we know everything about ourselves, but we don't. We change." He lowered his gaze back to his feet, and then he curled his toes.

"That's right," Effie said. "It seems that the older I get, the more I realize I don't know, not only about myself but about my future."

Zoke's hand rested on the dirt between them. She wanted to run a finger down his claws, just to see what they felt like. As she stared and thought about how he might react, he squeezed his hand together so that his claws dug into the ground.

"So follow what you believe," Zoke said, letting his head relax against the wall and closing his eyes. "Stay with what feels right. That's what I'm doing."

Effie found herself nodding. She felt as if she'd learned something about herself but was too tired to figure out what it was. "All I know is that I'll be tired tomorrow if I don't sleep."

"That's all you need to know this moment. Tomorrow, we'll know something new."

With that, her anxious thoughts finally quieted, and the soothing sound of Zoke's slow breath in and out was all she heard until she fell asleep.

Chapter 63: Collapse
EFFIE

The next day, Queen greeted them on the edge of the lake. Bright, white light had returned to each of the caregelows, giving the vast cavern a robust glow that made it seem like the sun should be found in the sky. However, there was no sky to find. Whenever Effie looked above her, all she saw was the hard ceiling and the tops of clay pillars that held it in place.

"I thought about your proposal for many hours, Terren," Queen began. "I have decided that we do have a number of resources you may find useful. I have prepared many fertile seeds for each of you to carry back to Kyrro. Please come collect them."

She waved a claw at a number of pouches beside her. Terren stood motionless.

"What am I to tell our king?" he asked. "Will you be fighting with us?"

"While we do wish to help, we are not safe above ground. You overestimate our ability to assist you. Yes, Hejel told me of your little mage and her ability to cast from the Bastial Energy we transferred, but that would require we stand next to your mages during battle, huddled around them like scared children clinging to their parents. We are more likely to be in your way than do any good. Our place is not there but here where we are safe."

Terren's mouth was flat, his eyes hard. "What of your Dajrik? If you're safe down here, have him fight for you by sending him with us."

"We are safe down here because of him, and not for his ability to fight. Just like the maze leading into our home, there is a maze leading out of it. If we ever come under attack, we will all hurry to the exit maze, and the Dajrik will remove the wood that holds many rocks. They will fall and block the path so that we cannot be followed. Once we are out of sight, the Dajrik will cave in the correct path, leaving only hundreds of false routes. We need him to make our escape if the day ever comes."

Terren's face was pinched now. Effie could feel the same tension in her chest.

"Surely if you're attacked, you can't expect all Slugari to make it into the exit maze before the Dajrik needs to block the path," Terren said.

"Unfortunately, that is correct. Many are likely to die, but that is still far better than all of us."

Silence came over them.

Steffen walked toward her to collect a pouch. Zoke and Vithos followed.

Effie was waiting for Terren to do something before she moved. *This can't be it,* she thought. *Say something, Terren. Convince her she's wrong.*

His arms were crossed, one hand touching the hilt of his sheathed sword. He opened his mouth to talk but closed it before any words were spoken. His eyes were slits deep in his skull.

If Effie knew what to say, she wouldn't hesitate, but nothing came to mind. *We were supposed to convince the Slugari to fight with us. We can't have come all this way just to be sent home with seeds.*

"I can see you are not pleased." Queen spoke with quiet empathy. "But you must consider our position. We have taken extreme measures for the Krepps not to find us. Going to battle would be undoing generations of work."

Hejel came shouting from behind them. "Queen! There's heavy movement above us. Krepp foot patterns, and our *halendan* have just reported the sounds of digging."

Both of Queen's eyes shrank like a pupil burned by the sun. "How could they have found us?" Suddenly her eyes not only came back to size but doubled what they were before. She raised a claw at Terren. "You brought them here!"

Krepps, here? Terror seized Effie's heart.

"We did no such thing!" Terren pointed back with two fingers, as if one wasn't enough. "We're your allies."

Vithos raised his hand as well. "Allies. Here help."

"*Seshala!*" Queen yelled. Effie could tell it was some sort of curse by her tone. "Then prove it and help as many of us escape as we can. We do not have time to discuss this. Hejel, give the order to flee. You all, come."

With hot panic overwhelming her body, Effie and the others

hurried after Queen to the tunnel of the exit maze in the next room. There were two Slugari already there who slithered to Queen quickly when they saw her. She said something in Slugaren, and they hurried off. Panicked Slugari were already flooding past them and disappearing into the turns of the maze.

"You say you can fight Krepps, then do so," Queen told them. "Stand ahead of the exit and kill any that try to chase us into it. They must not follow us."

"Where is your Dajrik to seal the exit?" Terren asked, not giving any sign as to whether or not he would help.

Queen's eyes dimmed. "I am about to find out."

A Slugari stopped beside Queen, wheezing for breath. When he spoke, Effie realized it was Hejel again.

"I have an update. They have broken through our ceiling. They pushed a tall mound of dirt down the opening to break their fall. There are hundreds. They dropped near the center of the colony."

"Tell me our Dajrik is on our side of the breach!" There was such desperation in Queen's voice it seemed as if the wrong answer was the same as death.

"Yes, he will be here soon, but as you can expect, all those on the other side of the Krepps surely will not make it."

Queen's claws and mouth tightened. "I hope their end is swift and painless," she uttered.

"Doe is with them," Hejel said, "and even greater in size than we last saw."

"*Seshala!* We must be long gone before he arrives. His magic is strong enough to blast away the rocks."

"One more dreadful thing." Hejel glanced at Terren with sunken eyes, his mouth straight with terror. He turned back to Queen. "We know how they found us. It was not the Humans."

Queen was silent as she waited for Hejel to gather his strength for the words. He wheezed and struggled for breath.

"They have chamolines."

Queen was petrified. Only her eyes moved, shrinking back to nothing again. "I was told we had found all the chamolines."

"We must have missed some..."

For a moment it looked like Queen had given in to defeat. Her flesh sagged around her body. Her head lowered. Her tail stopped. Suddenly, she shot a glance at Terren as if she'd just remembered he was there.

"You wish to ally?"

"That's why we came."

"Then we will fight with you. We can no longer hide if they have chamolines." Queen shook her head slightly as she spoke. "It has come to war. But our battle will not be here. There are too many Krepps and too few Humans. Will you help us flee?"

The shaking ground suddenly grabbed Effie's attention. She was thankful to find it was just the Dajrik coming around the turn.

There were so many fleeing Slugari, hundreds of them must already have passed into the exit maze by then. The Dajrik found his place just beneath its entrance. It was a thin tunnel, just wider than the giant's shoulders. The fleeing Slugari filed in between his legs. Queen's eyes remained on Terren, who watched the Dajrik with folded arms.

"Allies always help," he finally answered. "We'll defend you as long as we can. But the moment we become overwhelmed we'll retreat to the maze so that the Dajrik can cave in the rocks."

"I will tell the Dajrik to wait. We are allies, now and forever." Queen touched her claw to Terren's arm. "We have more to discuss on the other side, but for now, thank you." Queen lowered her head for a breath, Terren lowering his as well. Then Hejel escorted her to the exit.

The moment they were out of sight, Effie realized how alone she felt. *Not one Slugari will stay with us?*

"Listen, everyone." Terren huddled them together with his long arms.

This all felt too fast to Effie. Must they fight again so soon after the last battle? When she thought of war, she thought of knowing days in advance that an army was marching to meet them, not unexpected battles one after the next. She thought of hundreds standing shoulder to shoulder, not seven.

More expectations I'm going to have to change, she thought, remembering what Alex had told her: *"It's up to each of us whether or not we grow into our expectations, change our expectations, or stay confused."* She looked at him to find his eyes were already on her. She smiled and he returned it.

Terren took a breath and shared a quick look with each of them. It seemed as if he already knew what he wished to say but wanted to give the rest of them a chance to prepare for it. Effie squeezed Reela's hand and took a calming breath to ready herself as best she could for whatever would happen.

"We're going to form a wall at that bend." Terren pointed ahead where the wide tunnel narrowed into a turn. "That's the only way in here. Shoot, burn, cut, stab, use psyche, do whatever it takes to make sure they don't get through. They won't expect us to be waiting for them as they come around. Use that to our advantage. When there are no more Slugari coming through, it means we're about to be overwhelmed and it's time to move to the exit. I'll give that command. Now, ready your weapon and yourself. Protect each other. Trust each other. Keep each other safe. We can't save every Slugari, but no Human, Elf, or Krepp will be left behind."

Effie felt the same rush of adrenaline as when she was at Redfield and Terren had finished making the announcement of war. She drew her wand with the burning eagerness of a child about to play with a new toy.

"Well said," Alex echoed.

Zoke finished translating for Vithos, and then the Elf put his hand on Terren's shoulder with a light but firm grin. The motion reminded Effie so much of Reela it sent a chill down her spine. She didn't know what she was witnessing, but it felt strangely profound.

"We fight," Vithos said.

Terren formed them into a half circle twenty feet before the turn that led to their tunnel-like room—the last room before the exit tunnel where the Dajrik stood. Terren, Alex, and Zoke would be seen first by Krepps coming through because the three of them were directly in front of the turn. To Zoke's side was Vithos, and next to Alex was Reela. Then Terren put Effie and Steffen even farther out to the sides so that they faced each other, becoming the diameter of the half circle. She and Steffen were out wide enough that no Krepps coming through the turn would notice them unless they stopped to look over their shoulders.

For what felt like too long, no Krepps came, and Effie's boiling adrenaline had begun to cool. A thousand Slugari must have run by before someone finally spoke. Effie was surprised to find that it was herself.

"Steffen," she called to him.

His nervous eyes seemed to relax as they shifted to her.

"If you think you like Gabby, then you should be with her."

"Where's this coming from?" he asked. The arrow latched to his string came loose and fell. He hurried to pick it up.

Ignoring his question, she continued. "If it doesn't work out, she'll get over it. I was silly to think one failed attempt at a relationship could destroy anyone, especially her. We all need to go through trials, and some we will surely fail—that's part of becoming an adult, and she's one now. The sooner she realizes that, the better."

Steffen tilted his head. "Are you saying our relationship would surely fail?"

Effie didn't mean to imply that, but given the question, she took the opportunity to think about it before answering. It was only during that brief, quiet moment when Slugari finally stopped passing through. The rate of them storming around the turn had slowed in the last few minutes, but this was the first that there were none. She noticed it but didn't consider what it meant.

"No," she began to answer, "that's not—"

Terren held up his hand to quiet her. His head shifted sideways as if to listen. Effie strained her ears as well. She heard what sounded like shouts in the distance. They were distinctly not that of a Human and couldn't be the feeble voice of a Slugari, either. It sounded like nothing she'd heard before—a cross between Terren's low voice and the aggressive roar of a tiger.

Krepps, she realized with sudden tension in her stomach. *They're close.*

Another Slugari slithered around the turn in a panic. Right behind it was a Krepp who looked to be at least a whole head taller than Zoke. His massive size froze Effie. He grabbed the Slugari by the tail. Out from his mouth swirled a long tongue that was there and gone in a blink while the Slugari squealed like a baby pig about to be slaughtered.

When Effie finally composed herself and started gathering the energy for a fireball, the Krepp dropped the Slugari to clutch his chest, falling to the ground and writhing in pain. Effie kept the energy static within her stomach when she saw Terren and Alex run to the incapacitated Krepp and stab him with their swords.

The dropped Slugari looked around with small gray eyes before it squeaked out something in Slugaren and slithered past them.

Two more Krepps came around the turn next. Effie cast a torso-sized fireball into the broad chest of one of them. It disappeared into his flesh, sending his smoking body sliding across the dirt toward Steffen, who released an arrow into his heart. The other Krepp was taken by psyche, his weapon falling to the ground before his claws had even closed around its handle. This time Zoke was the first to drive his weapon into the enemy's chest.

They saw a dozen more Slugari before another Krepp. Like the Krepps before, his eyes grew wide in surprise when he saw them, and he was dead before he could draw his sword.

This continued long enough for Effie to grow confident that nothing could get by them. That is, until a group of five Krepps came through while Effie and the others were still finishing off two others. Some of these new Krepps had bows, and one of them had his yellow eyes set on Effie.

She hurried to cast before he could pull back his string. Without enough time, she fired only a small fireball that hit him in the stomach. It curled him over and took him back a step, but he regained his posture and quickly readied the arrow before she could cast another.

She saw that Terren, Alex, and Zoke were engaged with the Krepps behind him. Her heart stopped as the realization set in that there was nothing more she could do before he shot. She caught sight of Alex's sword slicing across one of the Krepps, and in one motion, his sword came around to take the head off the Krepp about to shoot her.

There was only one left, and suddenly she felt a strong urge not to see him die. She lowered her wand and found others were lowering their weapons as well. Vithos had his palm pressed against the Krepp's forehead, saying something in Kreppen.

They spoke back and forth twice before Vithos thrust his dagger into the Krepp's chest.

Zoke translated for them. "There are only a few Slugari still alive out there, too far to make it here," he said. "And Vithos wanted to know how far Doe is from here. The Krepp didn't know. I'm not sure why Vithos even asked."

Zoke transitioned into Kreppen to say something, but Vithos didn't respond.

"Then it's time we exit," Terren said, wiping the blood from his sword on the leather pants of a nearby dead Krepp.

They ran to the Dajrik. Effie figured he must have seen them fighting from where he stood. She found herself wondering what his thoughts were. She hoped observing from the side wasn't good enough for the Dajrik, that it made him eager to fight, but his relaxed body language told none of that.

"Hurry," Steffen said, being the last one past the Dajrik. "They're coming behind us."

As Steffen started transitioning to Slugaren, Effie looked for herself. He was right. There were maybe ten Krepps running toward them. Their speed was frightening. Their strides were long but also quick, inhumanly quick.

The Dajrik had its massive fingers into the crevice of a plank of wood over the entrance to the thin tunnel. The rocks must have been stacked above it. The Dajrik wailed and grunted as he pulled, but it wouldn't move.

"Reela," Effie called, growing more nervous with each beat of her thumping heart. "Anything you can do?"

"They're too far." Reela's voice held the same panic that Effie felt. "Vithos?"

"Too far," he agreed.

So Effie readied as much energy as she could, though she knew it would never be enough.

The Krepps stopped and yelled at each other in Kreppen. Three of them had bows and began drawing their arrows.

Steffen already had his arrow ready and released. It pierced the chest of one of their archers, who fell with a squeal. Effie cast a fireball right after. The Krepps were so far she had to arc the shot. She was inexperienced with distance casting, so the fireball landed in front of them. It caused an explosion of dirt to splash in their faces, stopping them for the moment but not long enough...for the Dajrik still hadn't moved the wood.

The Dajrik was roaring now. It sounded like a mix between a man and a bear. The plank of wood moved slightly, causing some dust and dirt to sprinkle down, but the Krepp archers were ready to shoot now.

They released their arrows at once. Effie fell on reflex to get low. She felt Alex come down on top of her, either by coincidence or to cover her, she couldn't tell. The roar of the Dajrik changed into a growl of pain as he staggered back a step. Both arrows had found their way to his body. The archers readied for another shot before the Dajrik could get his hands on the wood again.

Vithos stormed out, his long hair thrashing back and forth. He was sprinting as if he was running away from certain death, not toward it. Vithos threw his hands out before the archers could release the next set of arrows. All of the Krepps fell to the ground, their bodies curled in pain.

"Vithos!" Reela desperately cried out to him. "Steffen, tell the Dajrik to wait."

"No!" Vithos shouted back. "Leave!"

Krepps were streaming through the turn by then, too many to count. They flooded into the skinny room like a river bursting through a dam.

Reela started out from between the legs of the Dajrik, but Vithos raised one hand to her with the other still aimed at the Krepps. "Stop! Go back!" he yelled.

Reela screamed and fell into a crawl, forcing herself forward against Vithos' psychic spell. Vithos was visibly shaking by then.

Terren sped out to grab Reela. He hoisted her up with an arm around her stomach and dragged her back toward the thin tunnel while she shouted for Vithos to run to them. But the Elf remained, holding his arms toward the Krepps to debilitate them with pain.

The moment Terren and Reela returned, there was a loud crack from the wood above, and the rocks started coming down hard like a waterfall. The Dajrik pushed everyone back as he too moved away from the hundreds of rocks slamming down in front of them.

When the sound of stone crashing against itself stopped, it had ended so quick Effie still hadn't comprehended what had happened. *But Vithos is on the other side? How's he going to get through?*

There was a dust so thick Effie thought it had caused everything to go black. But then she realized the tunnel had just become too dark to see because their only source of light was on the other side...the side with all the Krepps—all the Krepps and Vithos. That's when she started to realize that Vithos wasn't coming through, not now, not ever.

She pushed energy through her wand to create her own light so they could see. The Dajrik walked past them and said something in Slugaren as he pulled the arrows from his stomach and chest.

"He says to follow him." Steffen's voice was a murmur.

Reela had collapsed to her knees. Effie knelt and slipped her knees in between Reela's to hug her tightly. Reela rested her chin on Effie's shoulder and squeezed her as well.

"We have to go." Terren spoke as if he didn't wish to follow his own order. "There's still another tunnel to collapse so they can never find the correct route through the maze."

Reela lifted her sniffling nose off Effie's shoulder. "I know," she said softly and let Effie help her up. When they rose, Effie found Zoke staring absently at the rocks.

"Vithos...goodbye," he whispered. "And thank you." His tone was utterly morose, full of pain.

It was the first time Effie had heard him say "thank you." There had been many times she'd expected to hear it from him—after passing him his share of their dinner, after giving him a compliment—but he never said it. She'd figured Krepps just didn't.

But now that he had, and for reasons she couldn't understand, it made her weep uncontrollably.

Chapter 64: Mazed
ZETI

"Paramar!" Zeti called to stop him.

He ignored her, tramping forward without pause. "The Slugari are nearby. I can smell them."

They came to another fork in the maze, maybe the tenth since they'd entered. Zeti had lost track. Paramar sniffed in each direction. "This way, hurry." He pointed with the light-giving plant he'd picked. It was the only source of light they had, and it was quickly dimming.

"We've gone too far," she desperately tried to tell him as she held her feet in place. But the moment he was five steps away, darkness fell upon her so thick it gave her a panic like jumping into freezing water. She scurried after him. "Paramar, stop. We're lost."

"Doe sent us after the Slugari that went this way, and we're going to find them."

They came to another fork, this one with three options. Paramar squatted, holding the light-giving plant to the ground. "Do these look like Slugari tracks to you?"

She squatted next to him, squinting. "I don't know. This dirt is so tough even our tracks can barely be seen. When that light goes out, which looks to be happening soon, we'll be stuck in here. We need to leave now, while we can still see our tracks."

"I'm not willing to give up on all the Slugari that made it this far." Paramar's tone was strict. Anger seemed to have boiled past reason. He let out a loud curse, then said, "They think a maze can hide them? We've dug through nearly fifty yards of dirt, and they think we can't figure out a maze?" He spat.

"We've got them, Paramar, thousands of them. We can let some get away. We need to go back while we still have enough light. Don't you want to see what happened with the Slugari that went the other way? Surely the Krepps chasing them couldn't have made the same mistake that we did."

They hadn't searched for the exit; that was their mistake. They were too busy chasing after the nearest Slugari to worry about the ones near the perimeter. Zeti and Paramar were among the first to drop into the cavern, just after Doe. And just like Zeti and Paramar, the next five hundred Krepps to follow were too overwhelmed with excitement to listen to Doe's orders.

He'd told them to ignore the Slugari nearby, seek out the ones farthest first, and then come back to intercept the rest. Doe put Paramar in charge of all the Slugari on one side of the breach while he took the other side. The five hundred Krepps split, half following Paramar, the other half following Doe.

But Doe didn't realize how impossible it was for the Krepps to simply pass by thousands of fleeing Slugari. The amount of saliva Zeti's mouth was producing as she tried to ignore their overwhelming scent was enough for a lifetime. As other Krepps around her began succumbing to their urge, so did she and Paramar. They shot, stabbed, and clawed, killing any way they knew how. The Slugari didn't even fight back, just squealed in terror.

Before she even was aware what she'd done, her belly was so full of Slugari meat she could barely run. She even vomited but didn't mind. The Slugari were endless, so she could fill her stomach once again. At least that's what she'd thought.

But each time they came to a turn in the cavern, there were fewer Slugari than in the last room. The more they killed and ate, the farther the rest of the Slugari were ahead. Catching up soon became impossible.

They killed many more before finally reaching the maze and knew hundreds had to have escaped. They had failed Doe, directly disobeyed his order. Now, Paramar seemed as if he would rather die in a pitch black maze than face Doe, but Zeti wouldn't let that happen, not if she could help it.

The quiet darkness, the uncertainty of whether she was going deeper into the maze or working her way out, the shame of dying because she was too stubborn to admit she'd made a mistake—she would rather face Doe, albeit only slightly.

Paramar ignored her, though, running his fingertips along the dirt instead. He was searching for a trail that might not even exist.

A sound caught her attention. She listened closer and realized it was footsteps, definitely not a Slugari. They had to be of another Krepp. Without pride stopping her, she shouted, "We're lost in here! Zeti and Para—"

Paramar slapped a hand over her mouth, and complete silence followed. Whoever the footsteps belonged to moved no farther.

The light from the plant Paramar had picked outside the maze was dying even faster now. It must have been a fourth of what it was when they'd entered. The light it gave off wasn't enough even to see whether someone was in the same hallway as them.

A voice surprised her. "Zeti?" he asked. "Did you say Zeti?"

A terrorizing chill stopped her from thinking, for she realized to whom the voice belonged. Paramar slowly lifted his hand from her mouth. Quietly, he pulled his sword from the sheath on his belt.

"Zeti, who else is with you? Is it Paramar?"

Zeti was too shocked to speak.

"Yes, I'm here," Paramar said with angry disbelief. "How did you get by everyone?"

"A few hundred overstuffed, vomiting Krepps. It wasn't impossible. Quite difficult, yes, but not impossible."

"What about Doe?" Paramar asked. "Did you see him?"

"No, unfortunately, he wasn't along the path I took from the other side of the cavern. He and I have a lot to discuss, but that'll have to be the next time we meet..."

Silence.

Zeti took a step away from the direction of the voice, putting herself behind Paramar.

"Now, if I cross paths with you and Zeti in this maze, what will happen?" The footsteps picked up again. Neither Zeti nor Paramar gave an answer, just listened in silence. *He's coming closer to us,* she realized by the sound of his feet.

Light flooded into their hall from the left side of a fork ahead. The light brightened as the footsteps grew louder. His clawless, pale hand was the first to follow the light around the turn. It held another light-giving plant, much brighter than Paramar's.

By the look of it, he couldn't have been in the maze nearly as long as they had. When he brought the rest of his body into view, she was intrigued to find a smile on his face. She couldn't remember the last time he'd smiled, if ever.

"So here we are," Vithos said.

Zeti reached a hand toward her bow, but Paramar grabbed her by the wrist. "That won't help," he said. "Psyche would stop you before you drew an arrow." He slid his sword back into its sheath.

As the three of them stared in silence, Zeti's wits started returning. *I have questions for him,* she realized, *questions I never thought I'd get to ask.* Her heart beat harder against her chest as a nervous feeling swelled in her stomach. Paramar had let go of her wrist, and she replaced his grasp with her own hand. It brought some comfort to hold herself as she thought of what to say first. The most obvious question came to mind then.

"Where's Zoke?"

"I don't know. We had to separate, but he's alive."

A hurricane of questions swirled around her mind next, but as she thought of them, she realized they each had an answer she already knew. *Why didn't he come back? Because he would have been killed as a traitor. How did he know that? He's smart, must have figured it out. Does he miss me as much as I miss him? Paramar can't hear me ask that.*

"Has he said anything about me?"

"I have a very good memory." Vithos paused for a slow breath but held his smile. "Not only do I remember the way out of this maze, I remember everything Zoke said about you. I remember everything he felt whenever he spoke of you. He would die before harming you, Zeti."

Vithos confidently walked toward her as he spoke, reaching out his pale hand. "Come with me, and I'll tell you everything. Even better, I'll bring you to him. I may not know where he is at this moment, but I'll find him again."

The Elf was so close now that Paramar could've touched him with the end of his sword if it had still been drawn.

"He wants to see you, Zeti. I'm sure you want to see him as well. I know the feeling of being separated from your family for reasons outside of your control. I've known nothing to be worse, but I've also never known anything to make me stronger than the determination to be with them once again."

Vithos was so steadfast it frightened her just to stand before him. If he needed to get by them, he would, and just being in his way could be dangerous.

Her hands dropped to her sides as she began to consider the thought. It was pleasant to think of seeing Zoke again. She could feel hope—the same hope she thought would never return. But then she realized they would only have a few months together before the army of Krepps destroyed the Humans, and she and Zoke along with them.

Vithos turned to Paramar as Zeti pondered. "What about you, old friend? Will you join us?"

Paramar spat. "As much as I miss our jokes, I'm the most important Krepp of this tribe, and no joke can be better than Slugari meat." He squeezed Zeti's shoulder. "We're staying. Tell us the way back. We'll let you by."

"*You'll* let *me* by?" Vithos dramatically raised a thumb to point to his own face. "I thought *I* was letting *you* by."

"No." Paramar smiled. "And it's just this once, friend. When I see you on the battlefield, I won't be so nice."

"I understand. We've picked our sides, haven't we?" The Elf's smile finally faded. "Although there's something you should know about the Humans on your side, the ones in Tenred. They lied to you. Kyrro never knew where the Slugari are located. Only I knew that. You shouldn't be so quick to join their side in battle. If they were desperate enough for war to deliver such a risky lie, can you imagine what else they might do? That kind of desperation is dangerous. Trust me on that."

"How do we know you're not lying?" Paramar asked.

Vithos held his chin. "I suppose you don't." He took a breath as he thought about it further. "Interesting, isn't it? I can tell when others lie, but I have no way of proving my honesty. So the burden of truth falls on you. Trust me or not, I can't force you into either decision. But it would be unwise to completely disregard what I've told you."

Is it like Vithos to lie? Zeti wondered. *Paramar would know.* She turned for a glimpse, but his face said nothing of his thoughts. It was still as usual, ready to smile or furrow in anger.

Vithos turned and reached out to her with an open palm. "Zeti? I don't have any more time for this conversation. I'll ask just once more. Are you certain you wish to stay with them?"

His eyes were longing, as if channeling Zoke. Vithos did it so well she almost could see her brother's face within his. She even felt as if she was answering Zoke.

It made it infinitely harder for her to nod her head, but she did. While Zoke might not have had a choice, she did, and she wasn't a traitor. It wasn't time for her and Zoke, not yet. *Vithos will keep him safe, just as he did today. He'll survive this war. Then we'll be together. I can't prove Father to be right about both of us. I have to see this through.*

She knew then that her hope was there to stay.

Stronger than it all, though, was the thought of the Slugari meat waiting for her back in the cavern and Paramar's hand squeezing down on her shoulder, holding her in place. Both of these things were more powerful than she was, she realized with bitter frustration.

Her side had been chosen, and she did not have the strength to change it, not then.

Chapter 65: Perception
CLEVE

Jessend Takary had taken Cleve and Rek straight to Gendock, nearly a ten-mile walk from their jail cells in Kyrro City. Cleve's hands and feet were chained, but at least he had no reason to worry about being uncomfortably gagged like Rek, not that he had anything to say to Jessend or her guards.

He'd already asked her his only question of what the purpose was behind bringing him to Goldram, to which she'd simply replied, "I'll tell you later" with her accent that made Cleve imagine her nibbling off dainty bites of crackers while holding a table napkin underneath to catch the crumbs. When he began to wonder why that image came to mind, he figured he'd always imagined that's what queens and princesses did, and her accent made her sound like one.

And that's precisely what she was—a princess. "Daughter to the King of Goldram," she'd told him as they traveled.

It was one of many things she said about herself, always pausing to give Cleve a chance to reply, but he never did. Whenever she asked him a question that he didn't answer, which was every question, she followed up with a playful smile. Sometimes she even guessed how he would answer if he'd spoken, adding at the end, "I'll have you talking before we get on the boat."

But they were at the boat now. Captain Mmzaza and the rest of her seamen, servants, and guards were close behind. It was Jessend's choice to bring Cleve and Rek to the front to walk with her, and Cleve was thankful for the distance from Captain Mmzaza. Spending more than a day in the cell next to him had been enough for a lifetime, and now he was about to be stuck with him on a boat, taking orders.

"Did you know that Gendock was originally called Gen Takary's Dock, for Gen Takary was the first of my family to come here from Goldram? He helped build this dock that we still use today over one hundred and fifty years later," Jessend rambled.

Rek was nodding, half like he knew, half like he was about to fall asleep from boredom.

"I'll answer any of your questions if you answer just one of mine," Cleve replied.

Her head sank with a dramatic sigh. "Fine, you wore me out with your silence. I'll tell you why you're coming, although you should be thankful. If it wasn't for me, you'd still be in that prison cell. You're one lucky man, Cleve Polken, for I've chosen you to marry me."

"What?" He gagged for a breath, choking on nothing. She took his hand, and his heart leapt into his strangled throat.

She giggled. "Don't fret, that's not the only reason you're coming." She used an overly cute tone. "There's far more in store for you than frolicking about our palace with Takary at the end of your name. We have many uses for a warrior like you."

"I find it hard to believe there isn't a man more suited for you in all of Goldram," Cleve said.

She giggled again. "You're funny. I like that."

"No, I'm not," he grumbled. Never before had anyone called him funny. It only deepened the thought that she must see some side of him that didn't exist. "You don't want to marry me. I wouldn't be a good husband." Just using the words "I" and "husband" in the same sentence made him feel like he was speaking for someone else.

"I see no ring. You're not already married, right?" she asked with some of her glee dropping from her voice.

Not once had he thought of marriage. Not once, not ever. It was too strange to be asked if he was married already. Some part of him wondered if she could be asking Rek, but Cleve knew better. She stood close to him, staring. Being a foot shorter, her eyes looked up with steady confidence.

"No," he finally answered, his thoughts turning to Reela.

"Good. I was almost married, two times in fact." She started to say another word but let a slow breath of air end her sentence instead. It seemed as if she was hinting at something sinister.

"What happened?" Cleve asked, feeling the answer might be helpful to know.

"I loved the first one very much. My father arranged the marriage when I was twelve. We were to marry when I reached the legal age at fourteen. He was a shotmarl bowman, big like you and just as quick with the bow."

"Shotmarl?" Cleve had never heard the word.

"Yes, he was very good at the sport. You would be, too." She studied his face for a breath, then ran her eyes down to his stomach and back up again. "You remind me so much of him."

A strange feeling was coming on, like he really was someone else in her eyes. There was an eerie stubbornness about the way she'd been speaking to him, as if they'd known each other for many years. Now she was looking at him in that same way.

Something happened to this man she loved, Cleve realized. *Do I even want to know? Will the same happen to me?* His curiosity was too strong to resist.

"What happened with the marriage?"

Her eyes fell off him, down to her feet. "He died before we were wed. His team was sent to battle the desmarls." Jessend spoke as if the words were painful to utter.

It appeared that Cleve finally had found a subject she didn't wish to discuss. He felt conflicted about what to say. *In that barrel of worms are answers about what she expects to happen between us. Then, there's even another failed marriage pact to investigate. Terren always says there's more to learn about someone by how they take defeat, not success. It seems best to wait for a more prudent time, though. I'm not sure I'm even prepared for the answers if she were to give them.*

There was something else she'd mentioned that made him curious, so he went with that. "What are desmarls?" Cleve asked.

"Desmarls are a terrible, man-eating creature and why Gen Takary sailed across the starving ocean to look for new land. They are the reason behind the sport of shotmarl." Her eyes fluttered up from the ground to meet his face. "We have a lot to discuss. I'm sure you want to know more about our marriage. I wanted to wait until after you saw our magnificent palace to deliver the news. You'll be far more excited when you see where you'll be living. You're going to love it, Cleve Polken, just as I'm sure you're going to love Goldram." She sounded cheerful, but Cleve thought he heard some doubt underneath her tone.

He could feel himself starting to care less and less about the words coming from this delirious princess' mouth. *Whatever she expects to happen in Goldram doesn't matter,* he told himself. *I'll be leaving as soon as I can anyway.* He thought of Reela fighting without him.

As if she could see it on his face, she told him, "I realize you want to stay here because you're worried about the war, but you can do a lot for Kyrro in Goldram. You can help me convince my father to send help back here after we arrive in your new home. We have a whole army ready to fight. And you should see the swords! Made with pure Bastial steel, more valuable than gold. Can you relax knowing your friends and family will be safe?"

"I can relax when I'm fighting alongside them."

She tried to close her hands around his, just as Reela had in the dungeons, but they were far too small to do more than awkwardly hold the edges of his palms together.

"You need to let it go," she begged. "The sooner you realize that you will not return to Kyrro, the better off you'll be. If you continue with these thoughts, they'll just lead to wretched misery. You will not be coming back."

Cleve and Rek shared an extended look. He didn't need psyche to tell they were thinking the same thing.

We'll see about that.

End of Book 1

Author Information

B.T. Narro would love to hear from you. All feedback is welcome.
Please email him at btnarro@gmail.com

For information on the series, and to sign up to receive an email when a new book is released, please visit the author's website:

www.btnarro.com

Made in the USA
Middletown, DE
08 April 2018